HARD BROKE SERIES, BOOK ONE

ENGLISH MICHAELS

Visit the author's website at www.englishmichaels.com

First Edition

ISBN: 978-1-7321229-1-8

Cover design by Sarah Hansen, Okay Creations *okaycreations.com*
Editing by Aquila Editing *aquilaediting.com*
Proofreading by Twin Tweaks Editing *twintweaksediting.com*
Formatting by Champagne Book Design *champagnebookdesign.com*

Rash daredevils with a score to settle. Swaggering jet jocks with no regard for rules or safety. Unchecked egos battling for superiority. This is the picture Hollywood paints of the military fighter pilot—but what *really* happens behind the closed doors of an Air Force fighter squadron?

English Michaels knows.

When the 82nd Tactical Fighter Squadron pays the ultimate price for reckless leadership, Lieutenant Colonel Nathan Morgan is tasked with the responsibility of instilling discipline in the talented, untamed fighter pilots.

The Scorpions like to play hard, but Nathan's trademark is hard work. There's been no room for anything but career and accomplishment since his hopes for love and family were felled in one devastating instant, and Nate's never given another thought to the possibility of opening his heart or his life to another woman.

Not until Camille. She's funny, successful, whip-smart, and utterly broken. Nathan has no indication she's branded by heartbreak and loss to rival what's shaped him, but when circumstances intertwine their lives, the blazing attraction is impossible to ignore. And the chemistry is off the charts.

Both lives are crowded with careers where life and death hang in the balance daily. Seconds count and a momentary loss of focus can result in tragedy. And their longing for deeper connection is hampered by the scars of old heartbreak. Can Nathan persuade Camille to give love another chance even as he hesitates to trust his own heart?

Dedication

To Mister English: my one and only, my bueno taco technical advisor, and The Best Pilot I Ever Saw.
More than anything else it is, this book is a love letter to you.
The best moments in life truly *are* the ones you can't tell anyone about.

and

To the two squadrons that inspired me: the Mafia from Possum Town and the Boneheads from the Rendlesham Forest: both full to the brim with some of the most interesting people in the world—hilarious, wise, fearless, inspired, patient, generous— and so attractive, both inside and out, that I've been forever drawn to know them better and spend time in their company. Those who served and the people they love are those I gratefully count among my nearest and dearest to this day. "Lord, Guard and Guide"

A NOTE TO THE READER

The concept of flight is a romantic one; the military pilot, in particular, holds strong appeal for many women, especially romance enthusiasts. I am only one example of a young woman who was secretly taken with the raw magnetism and power of a handsome man in a flight suit striding toward his jet, helmet in hand, ready to casually stare death in the eye.

Reality invaded my youthful, dramatic fantasy life when I fell in love and married a kind-hearted, ridiculously sexy, utterly flawed, devastatingly handsome Air Force pilot. While our love match has enjoyed the qualities of many long-lived marriages—the marvelous and the mundane—his military career over the first decade of our lives together also afforded me a front row seat to the fascinating world of the fighter pilot.

In July of 1984, a little over a year before we married, I took a seat in a stiflingly hot Air Force base auditorium, dressed in a black taffeta cocktail dress and fidgeting like the twenty-year-old I was. That afternoon, I watched my boyfriend stride across the stage to receive his Air Force wings, signifying his successful completion of Undergraduate Pilot Training. It was a defining moment in his life, as it is for every military pilot. Printed on the last page of the cheap paper program was a poem I'd never seen but would come to know by heart.

John Gillespie Magee was a young pilot in the Royal Canadian Air Force who died in the service of his country in 1941. Mere months before his passing, at the tender age of nineteen, he penned this sonnet and beautifully captured the allure and romance of flight.

"High Flight"

By

John Gillespie Magee

"Oh! I have slipped the surly bonds of earth

And danced the skies on laughter-silvered wings;

Sunward I've climbed, and joined the tumbling mirth

Of sun-split clouds—and done a hundred things

You have not dreamed of—wheeled and soared and swung

High in the sunlit silence. Hov'ring there,

I've chased the shouting wind along, and flung

My eager craft through footless halls of air.

Up, up the long, delirious, burning blue

I've topped the wind-swept heights with easy grace

Where never lark, or even eagle flew—

And, while with silent lifting mind I've trod

The high untrespassed sanctity of space

Put out my hand and touched the face of God."

GLOSSARY

The world of the military pilot has a language all its own, as confusing as a foreign tongue to the uninitiated. This glossary is offered to assist those unfamiliar in navigating the technicalities, jargon, and buffoonery. A few medical terms are included for additional clarification. The first occurrence of each term within the text of the book is bolded.

A-10 Warthog—The Fairchild Republic A-10 Thunderbolt II. More commonly, "the Warthog" or just "the Hawg." The only USAF aircraft designed specifically for the Close Air Support mission: supporting troops on the ground in contact with the enemy. Designed around the lessons of Vietnam and the threat of massed Soviet tanks in Europe. Maneuverable, survivable, and lethal. Pilots refer to themselves as "Hawg drivers."

Beer call—Official but informal meeting of squadron pilots held in the squadron lounge or bar , usually on Friday, after all flying for the day is complete.

Below the zone—Selected for promotion earlier than one's primary promotion zone. A rare distinction and often an indicator of an officer whose career is on the fast track. A "fast burner."

BFM—Basic Fighter Maneuvers. The essential building blocks of air combat maneuvering. When a single aircraft is engaged in aerial combat with another single aircraft, BFM is the set of maneuvers and techniques used to move from a neutral to an attacking position relative to one's opponent. Developed in World War I and formalized by German ace Oswald Boelcke.

Blues—A common reference to the Air Force's daily uniform. Flight suits or ABU's (Airman's Battle Uniform—camos) are considered utility uniforms and inappropriate for many venues. Pilots generally view being compelled to squeeze into their often ill-fitting blues as a particularly loathsome form of punishment.

BOQ—Bachelor Officer Quarters. A holdover from a bygone era. The "Q" would be a small efficiency apartment in a dormitory-style building on base, often with a shared kitchen. Unless required to live there, most single officers elect to live off base in apartments or rentals.

Butterbar—A second lieutenant. Newly commissioned officer recognized by his single gold bar rank insignia.

Call sign/Tactical—A fighter pilot's semi-official nickname. Generally bestowed by other members of the squadron based on some egregious or hilarious buffoonery. Glorified in the movies with names like Viper and Maverick, but, most often, far less flattering. Pilots generally address one another exclusively by their tactical, and it goes with one to the grave.

Code Brown—Hospital-speak for an epic cleanup of actual feces. Often requires stacks of linens, more than one set of hands, and a mop bucket.

Cord accident—Disruption of the umbilical cord blood flow supplying a fetus with oxygen and nutrients before birth; ordinarily a knot in the cord or a prolapse. A prolapse occurs when the cord becomes pinched between the baby and the mother, commonly when the water breaks and "washes" the cord into the birth canal in front of the baby. Cord accidents are a relatively rare complication of pregnancy.

<u>Crosscheck</u>—The piloting skill of referencing all available instrumentation and visual cues to determine proper control inputs required to achieve desired parameters. The more complex and challenging the maneuver, the faster the required crosscheck.

<u>Deployment</u>—Moving some or all of a military unit away from its home base for a specific purpose and length of time.

<u>FAIP</u>—First Assignment Instructor Pilot (aka how the Air Force eats its young). Typically, the top ten percent of pilot training class graduates get one of their top three choices of aircraft assignments. The next ten percent are returned to their pilot training base as instructors which is almost universally regarded as a bad deal.

<u>Field grade</u>—A traditional term for officers of a rank to command troops "upon the field of battle." In modern parlance, a major (an O-4) or lieutenant colonel (an O-5) in the Air Force.

<u>FNG</u>—Fucking New Guy. A term of endearment.

<u>Fornicating the canine</u>—Screwing the pooch, fucking the dog—a major screwup.

<u>GAU-8</u>—The General Electric GAU-8/A Avenger is the weapon mounted on the USAF's A-10 Thunderbolt II. Its unique 30 mm Gatling autocannon can deliver up to 4200 rounds per minute and was designed specifically for the anti-tank role against Soviet armor. The heart and soul of the Warthog.

<u>G-forces</u>—Also "G's" or "pulling G's." One G is the force gravity exerts on the body. Acceleration away from the earth increases the G-forces; the sensation of being forced down into the seat

at the bottom of a big hill on a roller coaster is approximately 3-4 G's of short duration. Fighter pilots routinely sustain 4-6 G's; sustained G's of 7-9 are not unusual.

G-LOC (G-induced loss of consciousness)—As the body accelerates away from the earth, blood supply intended for the head pools in the lower extremities. Manifestations of decreased blood supply range from a loss of peripheral vision to a complete loss of vision, followed shortly by G-induced loss of consciousness. Several tools are used to combat these effects: excellent anaerobic fitness and muscle tone, the anti-G straining maneuver, and the G-suit worn by every fighter pilot. G-LOC is—obviously—potentially fatal in a single seat fighter.

Gunsmoke—Formerly, a biannual USAF gunnery competition between teams in various fighter aircraft from across the Air Force. No longer held due to budget constraints.

Hard broke—An aircraft with a maintenance issue is referred to as "broke," provided it's expected to be repaired in time to launch with only minor delays. With a longer, or even indeterminate, delay of return to status by maintenance, the aircraft is said to be "hard broke."

LPA—Lieutenants Protection Association. A mythical association of young officers in a squadron having one another's back, protecting themselves from the OFA—Old Farts Association, aka everyone else. In reality, the LPA usually represents the lieutenants as a group when they are assigned unsavory non-flying tasks: snack bar maintenance, party planning, going-away skits, etc. A long-standing tradition in fighter squadrons.

Manual reversion—In the A-10, a rudimentary system

connecting some of the flight controls to the stick via cables. This gives the pilot basic control of the airplane during flight in the absence of hydraulics. A key survivability feature designed into the A-10 to get the pilot back over friendly territory before an ejection may be required.

Missing man—Formation flown for a lost comrade at a funeral or memorial service. A flight of four aircraft in close formation approach; number three pulls aggressively up and out of the formation, symbolizing the lost pilot.

NICU—Neonatal Intensive Care Unit. Nursery specializing in the care of ill or prematurely born newborns.

O-5—Fifth level of the U.S. Military officer's pay scale. In the USAF, a Lieutenant Colonel. This officer will typically have 15-20 years of service.

Officers' Club—Also O'Club, The Club; in the past, the Officers' Open Mess. A members-only restaurant and lounge on base that is restricted to officers, their families, and accompanied guests. While membership is theoretically optional, not joining is an instant career killer. Site of most formal military functions. At a flying base, it usually includes a casual bar where the standards of decorum are somewhat more "relaxed."

Operations officer—Second in command to the squadron commander. Focus is strictly on day-to-day operations like scheduling and training. Flight commanders report to the operations officer. "The OpsO."

PACU—Post Anesthesia Care Unit. The "recovery room" where patients are moved immediately following surgery for stabilization after the administration of anesthesia and before transfer to a critical care or regular hospital bed.

PCS—Permanent Change of Station. Military-speak for a reassignment and move.

PDP—Pre-departure Piss.

Perch—In this context, a position for beginning a BFM exercise. The attacker is positioned above and behind the defender, figuratively "on a perch" with both an energy and positional advantage.

Piano burning—A Royal Air Force (RAF) tradition. When an exceptionally boisterous party at the Officers' Club is drawing to a close, pilots will sometimes end the evening by hauling the club piano outdoors and, inexplicably, setting it on fire.

PROJO—Project Officer. An officer tasked with supervising a specific project, an additional duty.

Remote—A tour of duty, usually one year, unaccompanied by dependents (family).

ROK—Republic of Korea. The most common remote assignment for A-10 pilots.

SAREX—Search and Rescue Exercise. Leading and directing combat search and rescue of downed airmen in enemy territory is one of the primary roles of the A-10. During the exercise, various elements are able to train together in real time to recover the "survivor."

Schoolhouse—Generic term for the organizations that qualify

new or returning pilots in a specific aircraft type. For the A-10, the Schoolhouse is at Davis-Monthan Air Force Base in Tucson.

SNAP—Sensitive New Age Pilot. Mildly derogatory term for Gen Y and Millennial pilots who might get a case of butt hurt in the old-school fighter pilot Land of No Slack.

Socks check—Uniform regulations require the wearing of black or blue socks with any uniform. If one pilot suspects another's socks may be in noncompliance, he may call for a socks check. The most expeditious way to perform this ritual in a flight suit (one-piece coverall) is to unzip and drop the entire garment around one's ankles. Loser of this challenge buys a round.

SOF—Supervisor of Flying. A qualified pilot and supervisor on duty (usually in the control tower) as a resource to airborne aircraft. Makes decisions regarding weather, coordinates with outside agencies, and assists with checklists and technical support in the event of an aircraft emergency.

Squid—A member of the U.S. Navy, generally. In context here, a Navy pilot, though they prefer the term "Naval Aviator."

Squadron tee shirt—Tee shirt in the squadron's color emblazoned with the squadron patch (logo). Mandatory wear on Fridays under the flight suit. Failure to wear it costs the offender a round.

Stick—The control stick in an aircraft as differentiated from a traditional control yoke or wheel. In a fighter aircraft, the pilot flies with right hand on the stick and left hand on the throttles. Both stick and throttles are festooned with multi-function buttons and switches to control aircraft and weapon systems. Also, in context, a naturally gifted pilot.

<u>TDY</u>—Temporary Duty. Personnel temporarily performing duty away from their home base.

<u>UCMJ</u>—Uniform Code of Military Justice. An additional set of laws applicable to all military members in addition to local and national laws.

<u>UPT</u>—Undergraduate Pilot Training. Air Force flight school. A rigorous course, approximately one year long, culminating in students being awarded Air Force Pilot Wings.

<u>Weapons Officer</u>—An officer in each squadron who has attended an intensive, aircraft-specific course at Nellis Air Force Base, literally a doctorate in flying fighters. The singular expert in the squadron on all weapons, tactics, and employment. Often referred to as "Patch Wearers" or "Target Arms" owing to the distinctive bullseye patch they wear.

<u>Wing King</u>—The Wing Commander. Typically an O-6 (Colonel) but often an O-7 (one-star Brigadier General), depending on the size and complexity of the base. Commander of all functions on a base.

<u>Zap</u>—A custom adhesive sticker of the squadron patch (logo). To place a zap where it doesn't belong or isn't wanted is a point of squadron pride as in, "I zapped that Russian MiG at the airshow in Geneva." Typically, zaps are seen in Officers' Club casual bars, placed there by visiting crews.

Surly

BONDS

Chapter
ONE

"I Won't Back Down"

Nathan "Happy" Morgan

"**E**verybody say hello to the new guy."

"Hello, asshole!" The whole room sang out the traditional greeting as Coach swung open the door to the squadron bar. Not my first time, by any means, to greet a new group of pilots, but this one was popping my cherry all the same. I was the shiny new squadron commander, almost as young as several under my command. The discomfort was as acute as that nightmare you have about showing up at work without your pants.

The light was flagging this hot Friday afternoon as **beer call** in the squadron bar was well underway; apparently, the pilots had awaited my arrival like one dog on another. The place was ripe with the gritty smell of a long day of flying under the Tucson sun. Zippers were pulled down to mid-chest to reveal Scorpion **squadron tee shirts**, worn each Friday under flight suits without fail. No one wanted to be the guy buying the first round tonight at the **O'Club**.

But all that had to wait as the men and women of the 82nd Tactical Fighter Squadron, the "Scorpions," anticipated meeting the new boss—me. First, though, a little strategic socializing. Lieutenant Colonel Chuck "Coach" Ditka, my **operations officer** and second in command, met me beforehand. He was a fireplug of a guy with a steely grip and a wrestler's build, all of it tempered by a relaxed, friendly demeanor. He steered me skillfully through the crowded room toward the long, polished bar where a smiling lieutenant offered me a draft beer he'd pulled from the keg. Pulling up a stool, I parked my boots on the polished footrest made of the **GAU-8** mounted near the bottom of the bar. "Pretty shit-hot bar, gentlemen. Anybody want to tell me who you had to have carnal knowledge of to get the Hawg footrest?"

Cautious smiles all around, but it was Coach who answered: "We could tell you, Happy. But then we'd have to kill you." The response was delivered with a friendly smirk, so I guessed we were off on a decent foot.

"Let me handle some introductions before things get started," Coach offered, gesturing toward those perched around our immediate area of the large room. "Meet Jake 'Bashful' Travis, recently arrived from a **remote** in the **ROK**; Hayes 'Rock' Hudson, our freshly minted **butterbar**; Charlotte 'Miles' Christman; Walker 'Hung' Jackson, your B flight commander."

At my singular raised eyebrow and half-smile, Walker groaned and shook his head with a grin. "Don't even ask, sir."

"And this hillbilly is Davis 'Deliverance' Foster, your **weapons officer**." Coach finished introductions by indicating the giant human seated at the far end of the bar.

"The pleasure's mine, folks. I'm looking forward to my time as a Scorpion." I raised my full mug in salute.

Not as painful as I anticipated; I just need to stay upbeat.

My throat worked, and the Blue Moon slid down easy; a

little social lubricant was just what the doctor ordered in situations like this. Not everyone was thrilled to hear the news of a fast-burning, **below-the-zone 0-5** getting his very own squadron command at the tender age of thirty-six. Especially not a bachelor. Sure, the Air Force had come a long way, but they still chafed at the idea of putting a single man in charge of a flying squadron—or any other one for that matter. I wasn't even a bachelor, but it's for damned sure that no one wanted to talk about putting a widower in charge. Definitely not sexy enough for a flying squadron.

But these were problems I'd address later with Coach. Good thing he was happily married to a woman reportedly quite adept at wrangling the spouse madness that inevitably arose within active duty squadrons. That shit was well above my pay grade.

Coach sidled up. "Game time, Happy. Shoot straight with them; they might not like all you have to say, but you'll earn their respect a nickel at a time."

He topped off my mug, and I raised my glass once again. "From your lips to God's ears. I'm gonna need all the help I can get with this room."

Coach cleared his throat and raised his voice. "Give me your attention, Stingers." He called the informal meeting to order. "Grab some pine; hey—Miles, Hung? Shut the fuck up." He grinned, and the bar settled. "I'll get right to it, everyone. The 82nd is glad to welcome our new boss, Lieutenant Colonel Nathan 'Happy' Morgan. He hails from **squid** central, San Francisco, but try not to hold that against him." There was a ripple of laughter, and he grinned engagingly. "He is a fighter pilot's fighter pilot, with enough bombing and shooting hardware to make even Deliverance green with envy. But he also comes to us with a leadership pedigree that is just what the Scorpions need to become the premier **A-10** squadron we once were. Everybody join me in welcoming 'Happy' Morgan."

I swallowed hard, letting a relaxed smile play over my lips, and lifted my mug to toast my new squadron. They whooped and stomped and grunted in response, not unlike fifth grade boys seeing naked boobs for the first time.

Ah, some things don't ever change.

I swallowed again and raised my voice. "I'd be remiss if I didn't say this is a day I've dreamed about. Thank you for your welcome; I do look forward to taking command and working alongside each of you. To fly in the finest air force the world has ever known is a dream in itself; to do so in the best damned aircraft in the inventory, now that's more fun than anyone should be allowed to have.

"The Warthog is a machine that's performed more than admirably in a variety of circumstances, destroying the enemy and the aircraft's many detractors time and again. It's as ugly as a mud fence, slow as shit, and more lethal and survivable than fighters costing five times as much. Of course, I use that number just as an example." I smiled slowly as the guys and gals murmured their approval at my F-35 jab.

"That said," I continued, "you'll see changes here as I take over. You'll be unsurprised to learn that your reputation precedes you." My face hardened a little, and the smile disappeared. I'd been brought in to get the Stinger house in order, and it was no secret. "If we have the talent to be the best but don't take advantage and hone that talent with discipline and hard work, we're leaving on the table who we could be. Without credibility and integrity, we're nothing. If you don't buy what I'm selling, I can convince you; but I'd rather we were on the same side to begin this road together."

The lazy grins had been mostly replaced with tightened brows and an occasional scowl. I sighed, but I didn't expect differently. I needed to lighten the fuck up, so I made a Herculean effort and relaxed my face. "I can't think of a better start than an evening at the O'Club. There's a keg each of Stella and Guinness with Scorpion **zaps** on them over there—and they won't drink themselves. I'm looking forward to flying and shooting and bombing with each of you. Let's adjourn, Stingers."

Coach extended his hand as the barstools scraped on the worn wooden floor of the squadron bar, and the crowd began to thin. "You didn't pull any punches, and that's a good thing, Nate. They'll get there." I could relax a little with his pronouncement. We walked together toward his pickup in the parking lot.

"Got a kitchen pass tonight, Coach?" I taunted him mildly since we'd only now begun getting to know each other.

"Kitchen pass? Hell, boss, Bibi's already got her fine ass parked on a barstool over at the Club, if I don't miss my bet. I'd watch her if I were you. She'll bat her lashes and smile while she drinks your sorry ass under the table. Look what happened to me." He roared with laughter, threw the truck in drive, and we made for the Club.

Chapter TWO

"Work to Do"

Nathan

Moving day. Nothing worse.

The movers weren't notified about the mild hangover and pounding headache I'd be sporting courtesy of a late night at the Club—bullshitting, exaggerating, and drinking plenty of the beer I'd bought for my new squadron. Accordingly, they hadn't cut me any slack on the projected early morning delivery of my "household goods." That's military speak for the hand-me-downs and IKEA furnishings that populated my pathetic, beige surroundings. They say it takes a woman to make a house a home, but the woman who once filled my heart never had the chance to fill my house. She was part of me for such a short time, it sometimes seemed I'd dreamed it.

As a Lieutenant Colonel, I was assigned a three-bedroom, two-story house in the "Soaring Heights" neighborhood. Holy shit, who named these places? I'd be lucky to fill the living area and one bedroom; an apartment in the **BOQ** would have been more appropriate to the shell of existence I'd been carrying on since Eliott died. The assumption was that a squadron commander had a wife, a family, and social obligations to attend to—not the least of which was fifty or so active duty members assigned to him, as well as their families. There were monthly social occasions, squadron picnics, luncheons and holiday parties—not to mention weddings, babies, and even the very occasional tragedy. Thank God for Coach and Bibi. That was what everyone, including Coach, called his wife; she told me it stood for Bellamy Bennett. Call her what you will. I'd call her a goddamned lifesaver. When she pulled her barstool up to mine last night after introductions, it became immediately clear she had in spades everything needed to navigate the sticky social quadrant of my job. In addition to her obvious and easy competence in the social arena, she was a part-time physical therapist at Children's Hospital at Tucson Medical Center. I guessed she did the "force of nature" thing in her spare time.

My reflection on last night's events was interrupted by the annoyed panting of my English bulldog, Mayze. She was cantankerous by nature and in a perpetually bad mood. Most days, we were a match made in heaven. The Arizona heat was doing neither of us favors today as I perspired unnaturally and worked to sort kitchen paraphernalia. "C'mon, Mayze," I groaned, "quit your bitching. At least you're out of the kennel. And you don't even have to unload boxes." She seemed unimpressed and adjourned to find a cooler corner of the house. I had to admit it was comforting to have some other life inside the four walls; sometimes that touchstone was just enough to maintain some balance in my chest.

I heard pounding on the front door and gladly straightened. Coach's smirk greeted me through the sidelight, and I opened the door. Bibi breezed in, followed closely by her husband. "I brought breakfast tacos, but I have TUMS and ibuprofen in my purse. How are you doing in the light of day?" She led us into the kitchen, turning on the oven to heat and shoving the covered pan inside.

I grimaced and mopped my face with a towel lying on the counter. "A 0600 get up followed by some heavy lifting helps sweat the alcohol out. Coffee anybody?" I settled in at the breakfast bar for a second cup. "Smells terrific, Bibi. This goes above and beyond the call of duty."

"Want you to feel welcome, Nate." Coach smiled at his wife as she rinsed plates directly out of a box and began serving breakfast for the three of us. "This is going to be a team effort, partially because you're a bachelor…"

"Widower," I mumbled, without thinking, under my breath.

"…but mostly because it's always a team effort." Coach finished his sentence unaware of my slip-up, but it didn't go unnoticed by Bibi, who regarded me with an arched brow and then resumed foraging for silverware. "Social events and obligations don't always fall to the spouse in today's military. It just happens that Bibi enjoys them. And kicks ass at handling them."

Bibi smiled and blushed a little under the compliment. "Ah, Chuck. Thanks, babe." We all tucked into the plates served with warm flour tortillas wrapped around scrambled eggs mixed with potatoes and crispy brown sausage bits. Sour cream and what looked like homemade salsa complemented the meal. It tasted like heaven.

"I never really learned to cook—clearly a crucial error," I lamented. "Real home-cooked food is like Porsche," I smiled and quoted *Risky Business*. "'There is no substitute.'"

Coach caught my gaze and the smile in his eyes faded. "You're here in the nick of time, Nate, or at least I hope so." I settled back with my coffee and cocked my head, hoping whatever he was about to share would shed light on the mystery I'd been puzzling since the call came from headquarters. It was nearly every fighter pilot's dream to command his own squadron, but there were routinely so many qualified pilots and only a finite number of positions to fill. I was young, promoted early along my career path, and, ostensibly, had plenty of time to wait. Yet the command was offered to me.

Coach sighed and leaned back, taking a sip of the sludge that passed for coffee at my house. "For reasons that are unclear, the Scorpions have a history of **fornicating the canine** so spectacularly and with such regularity that they seem trained to do it. Most of this predates my assignment to Davis-Monthan, so I'm hazy on some of the details." His mouth tightened, and he shot me a rueful expression. "Take Miles Christman, for instance…"

"Oh," I interrupted, needing to clarify, "Miles? Why?"

Bibi leaned over her plate, her wide smile filled with humor. "Miles, Nate. As in 'legs that go all the way up and make an ass of themselves.' Miles of leg, get it?" She laughed. "Wait 'til we all go up to float the Salt River together in a couple of weeks. Those legs and that ass in a swimsuit? You'll swallow your tongue."

My face felt a little warm, and Coach chuckled at his wife's description. "Accurate, but not where I was going, babe." He turned to me and continued, "Major chip on her shoulder; not certain why. And a credible case of NAFD."

"That's a new one on me, Coach. NAFD?"

"No apparent fear of death. It usually applies to students, but this gal doesn't seem to have anything to lose. Busts rest requirements, parties her ass off when everyone else is dialing back, takes unnecessary risks with the airplane. And herself. She's been grounded before, but past commanders have mostly let her skate. Goaded her along like it was some kind of game. The other lieutenants are almost as bad. You know this kind of culture passes quickly on to the younger pilots. I'm concerned about Rock and Boo. Typical **SNAP**s; they can be corrupted. Rapidly."

I blew out a long breath. This didn't sound like a walk in the park, but trying to tell pilots what to do was like pushing water uphill with a rake. "So why not bring in an old head—some crusty Chuck Yeager-type to kick ass and take names? Why me?"

He grinned again and took another big bite of his taco. "Okay, this is where shit gets interesting. Ready?" Bibi refilled coffee mugs and waggled her eyebrows at me. "You're aware of the seismic cultural changes in the Air Force over the years. In the years that predate women in fighter cockpits, pre-1993, there was a 'boys' club' atmosphere was in full swing in most fighter squadrons. Over the next decade, there were still plenty of what I'd call 'old guard' in command structures throughout Air Combat Command. It wasn't true everywhere, but unprofessional conduct was sometimes overlooked—even enabled."

I gathered plates and stacked them in the sink while we talked. "I've heard the stories all right," I addressed them both, "but I was a pup. Still in training and, subsequently, doing my stint as a **FAIP**. Women had already been in trainer cockpits for years, so that attitude wasn't a known quantity. We worked alongside one another mostly without that bullshit."

"As it should be," Bibi intoned with a pointed roll of the eyes.

"Obviously, babe. Just laying groundwork here," Coach continued. "**Field grade** staff in the squadrons spent an inordinate amount of time cleaning up the messes, all the while winking at the puppies for peeing in the house." Bibi snorted. "Busting minimums, pushing on fuel, fucking the **Wing King**'s daughter in his backyard—hey, Bibi girl, it wasn't me." Coach's face split in a blinding smile, but he backed off his barstool quickly with hands raised in the universal "I surrender" gesture.

She matched his smile but socked him playfully in the gut for good measure. "Yeah, but it was your roommate. And I have to assume that you were cut from the same cloth."

We all settled in with fresh coffee as Coach resumed his story. "From what I can piece together, at least two and possibly three of the past four Scorpion commanders were from the old school. All older fighter pilots who fed into the 'boys will be boys' mentality. This manifested in seemingly small ways day to day, like a casual approach to quarterly requirements and record-keeping, but it was more noticeable in the carelessness surrounding flight discipline. Grounding a pilot for a grievous breach of flight discipline was treated as a slap on the hand, even secretly regarded with admiration among some peers. Those attitudes bleed onto younger pilots when they arrive and are passed on, year after year." Coach sighed again and shook his head ruefully. "You'd think, after that steaming turd the Squids laid at Tailhook in Vegas back in '91..."

He shook his head, brow creased. "Well, you'd think everyone would have the fear of God in them. But the shit that went on at **Gunsmoke**, on **deployment**..." His voice trailed off, and he stared out the kitchen window for a moment, seemingly collecting his thoughts.

I scrubbed a hand across my face, feeling what seemed like substantially more than a single night's growth of stubble. I knew where this road led, and the reason I'd been brought here was increasingly apparent. My stomach couldn't handle another drop of this gawd-awful coffee. I found myself wishing I could switch to Crown to dull what I knew was coming next.

"Pappy was the worst of them, from what I know. He'd been the Stinger commander for about two years when Bibi and I got here. He was like a god who walked among them, a living, breathing bomb-dropping legend. When he showed up, the pilots, especially the **LPA**, followed him around like he was Heather fucking Locklear giving away free pussy. He was married, but it didn't slow him down. Got more ass than a toilet seat. Flew, dropped bombs, and shot the gun better with a hangover than everybody else did sober. He'd had every assignment you could have in the Hawg. He was a legend in Korea—dipped his wick in every available clam south of the DMZ. Left some RAF O'Club in flames with the LPA in tow and the MPs in hot pursuit after a **piano burning** got out of hand in merry old England. Good God, it'd be funny if it wasn't true. Flight discipline suffered because everybody was so goddamn busy playing Tom Cruise, trying to hang with or impress Pappy. Foundational basics were overlooked." He paused, and his voice was quiet when he continued. "Looking back, it was only a matter of time."

I felt nauseous and stared at my bare feet, awaiting what I knew was coming.

"We lost Rifle, Lieutenant Joseph Aiden Conner, one hot morning two months ago. His **crosscheck** came apart. The weather was clear and a million, but he just looked over his shoulder for a few seconds too long and flew into the ground. A fucking tragedy and completely avoidable. The squadron was in collective shock. I guess everyone thought we were bulletproof, that nothing bad could ever happen to the fun-lovin', nothing-but-a-good-time Scorpions." He looked past me and out the window again, anger tinging his voice.

"The funeral was the worst thing I've ever seen. I was the **FNG**, but I led the flyby, a **missing man**, of course, with three guys from other squadrons. Other goddamn squadrons, Nate. The Wing King sat the Scorpions down for two weeks so he could try to get a handle on the whole mess. Pappy flew into a rage and disappeared into his bottle of Jack. Didn't even come to the funeral, if you can imagine. The grapevine report is that he got a general discharge and was shuffled off to an inpatient program that deals with complex alcohol dependence. His wife packed up with the help of a couple of neighbors and quietly disappeared.

Coach looked twenty years older as he gained his feet, rubbed his eyes and walked slowly to the other side of the kitchen. He leaned wearily against the fridge. "The Stingers aren't the only ones whose reputation precedes them. It's not an insult and will come as no surprise that you're regarded as a stickler and a hard-ass. A straight arrow."

It was true; my **call sign**, "Happy," was a delicious little piece of irony bestowed on me in **UPT** where I'd spent weekends studying instead of chasing pussy and drinking myself into a near coma like so many of my classmates. Since then, I'd had a reputation for being serious and hard-working, mostly to the exclusion of anything that brought levity and color to life. Eliott was the singular exception to that, and her loss left me more somber than ever. Sometimes it took specific effort to blend into the hell-raising fighter pilot crowd.

"After some pretty high-level meetings at ACC, the Wing King seems convinced you're the guy for the job. I've done some looking into your background, and I don't disagree. My concern is not with you, it's for you. It would be a heavy burden for any-one, but this is your first command. And you're a bachelor with no one to help you carry the load, emotionally speaking. It's not very macho to admit, but pillow talk with the right woman is better than most of the therapy you can pay for." He looked with unabashed affection at Bibi, who returned his gaze.

My heart plummeted. Fuck, I missed that.

We were all silent for a few moments, absorbing; then I spoke first. "To be trusted with a task of this magnitude, it's…well, it's a tall order. And there are no guarantees. But I'll bring everything I have to the table. Thank you for the candor, Coach."

Bibi smiled and covered my hand with hers. "Hey, we all hang together on the Big Blue Team." She adopted a teasing tone. "There's no 'I' in team. All for one… Etcetera. Etcetera." She smirked, then sprang off her barstool and started gathering the leftovers and wiping counters. "I've gotta get to the hospital. I have an outpatient appointment at 1100. Kid slid into home and fractured his fib in so many places we needed a CPA to count the pieces before surgery." At my slack jaw, she scowled. "Don't look at me like that. He's fine—kids are made of rubber bands and chewing gum. He won't even miss a season of fall ball when I'm done with him."

Then she raised her eyebrows so I could see she meant business, "Your welcome party is next Friday at the Club. Since you're single, we're doing a flight suit party. Loads of fun for you and all your single guys. Huge bonus for the married ladies, too; we get to enjoy our husbands' tight little tushies in flight suits. Always a treat." She drawled the last few words and grabbed a handful of the ass in question to emphasize the point.

Coach clapped me on the shoulder, and then they were gone. It occurred to me that I could hardly have done better than having Chuck and Bibi in my corner. Good thing, too. I was clearly going to need all the help I could get.

Chapter THREE

"The Hustle"

Nathan

The morning wore on, bringing with it seemingly endless boxes crammed with meaningless stuff. Mayze mocked me wordlessly from the corner where I'd thrown her bed. This first wave of the unpack would have to do because the walls were beginning to close in.

Blazing July sun pushed the thermometer into the mid-nineties, so I stripped off my tee, grabbed the car-wash supplies, and headed outside. Summer in Tucson was every bit the temperate paradise I remembered from my time at the **Schoolhouse**.

There in the driveway sat my pride and joy, a navy-blue 1967 Pontiac GTO. She was a beauty, matching numbers and all. "Needing some lovin', baby?" I crooned. She looked a little dusty and road weary from the cross-country flatbed trip from D.C. Some water, a little soap, and elbow grease would provide the perfect distraction from the monotony of moving day. I mulled the difference a family would make on a day like this one. There would be the excitement of a new home for my wife and kids showing the little ones the swimming pool and the shiny slide at the playground and their new bedrooms. Coming home after a long day of flying to find my girl, her hair in a ponytail, hanging family photos, with the aroma of homemade marinara and garlic bread wafting from the kitchen. Winding that ponytail around my hand and whispering promises about what I'd be doing to her in a bubble bath after the children were tucked in...

What the fuck was my problem? I stood in the driveway sporting a thousand-yard stare, my garden hose soaking the ground. That was someone else's life, nothing I could hope to enjoy. Eliott was my shot at the white picket fence, and she was gone.

"My mom says we should do our best to conserve even when we aren't on water restrictions." Solemn brown eyes stared up at me from under a thick fringe of lashes. "My dad says my mom is a tree hugger, but he won't tell me what that is. I like zebras! Hey, can you skateboard, mister? My mom says I'm gonna be the death of her. What's that mean?" My new companion looked to be around six or seven years old with a thick mop of brown hair and a big, toothy grin. His grimy tee, shorts, and Teva sandals looked exhausted at the prospect of another day in his company.

I quickly turned the faucet off and extended my hand to shake his. "Well, hello there, my man. I'm Colonel Morgan, and I've just moved in today. What's your name?"

He stood up straight, seeming to remember his manners, and shook my hand once, hard. "I'm Adam. My mom says I should try to listen more than I talk. That's hard, isn't it, Colonel?"

I grinned wryly. From the mouths of babes.

"Are you gonna wash your car, Colonel? I can help. My dad says I can't drive until I'm twenty, but I can do awesome skateboard tricks. Wanna see?"

I picked up the helmet he must've flung in the yard and helped him buckle it securely on his head. "I love a good skateboard trick as much as the next guy, Adam, but safety always comes first, right?" I had to chuckle under my breath.

Military brats were a breed apart, as far as I was concerned. They were often more mature than their civilian counterparts and tended to learn flexibility and the ability to make friends. Many were even multilingual as a result of overseas assignments. Additionally, courtesy and respect were emphasized in most military homes, as well as a deep love of country. I liked everything about that and had always hoped for the opportunity to enjoy a house filled with skateboards, Barbie dolls, camping equipment, and Lego blocks. Love and bedlam and pancakes on Saturday morning were the hallmarks of the life I'd imagined. Sounded like something a teenaged girl would write in her journal, I thought with disgust. Anyway, time was not on my side. The brokenness my heart suffered when I buried Eliott built tall, impenetrable walls that precluded what I'd dreamed of.

Adam's bellowing cut through the turmoil of scenes crowding my brain and snapped me back to the present. "Watch me whip…"

An attractive thirtyish woman appeared on the stoop of the house next door, a tiny bundle in a blanket snuggled securely to her chest. Her eyes were kind but tired. The bare feet and hair piled on her head spoke of someone with plenty on her plate.

She pointed a brilliant smile my direction and raised her voice to address Adam. "Careful, son. Remember we talked about staying in the cul-de-sac?" She crossed the grass to approach me. "Welcome, neighbor. I'm Michelle, the head wrangler for that guy." Her eyes crinkled as she smiled, looking down. "And this is Rosie." She turned the pink bundle my way. Big blue eyes stared into mine. "We only just got home from the hospital a few days ago, but the beat goes on where Adam's concerned." She smiled. "Welcome to the neighborhood. Fresh **PCS**?"

"Glad to meet you, Michelle. I'm Nathan Morgan, new

commander over at the 82nd. Just in from the Pentagon. Call me Nate." I shook the hand she extended under the blanket.

"My husband's Rick Roberts, the Comm Commander. I hope you'll let us know what we can do to make you feel at home. It's a great town and a good neighborhood—we love it here."

I started again to fill my bucket and addressed Michelle as she moved back toward the front door. "I'll be glad to keep an eye on Adam. He's a great kid; we're keeping each other entertained."

"I appreciate it so much," she returned with a smile. "Quite a bit going on at my house these days."

I set about scrubbing my car, enjoying uncovering the shiny navy paint from under dust and grime. Time and again, my sponge slid into the soapy water, and I worked while watching Adam roll across the pavement, alternately singing, yelling, and talking to himself. Probably half an hour passed before a blood-curdling shriek pierced the relative quiet.

I crossed the driveway and pavement at top speed, reaching a howling Adam who clutched his right leg. Blood had already begun to puddle on the pavement. "Okay, buddy, I need you to look at me and try to breathe." His panicked eyes sought mine, and I gave him a small smile. "We'll get this all figured out." I peeled his fingers off his leg, revealing a long, deep gash. It was bleeding impressively. Sprinting to the carport, I snagged a clean tee, wound it tightly around his leg, and pulled it snug. The pressure seemed to hold off the bleeding, and the makeshift bandage remained dry. A jagged shard of glass on the pavement nearby, smeared with blood, was the obvious culprit.

I scooped a sobbing Adam into my arms and started for his front door, maintaining a tight hold on the bandage. Michelle burst through the door and onto the front stoop, her face ashen. She ran toward us, meeting me halfway.

"He's fine, Michelle, really, but this is gonna need stitches." She tried to take him from my arms, but I gently pulled him tighter to my chest. "Hey, now, you're a brand-new mama, and this guy is pretty solid. Why don't you let me do the heavy lifting?" She relented and smoothed his brow, wiping tears. She led us inside, and I settled Adam onto the sofa, snuffling and clutching the leg. His mom soothed him, then peeked at the jagged wound, grimacing.

"Is Rick home?" I asked, fully expecting that Murphy's Law would be in play.

"Uh, no, he's returning from a short **TDY** in the next few hours, wouldn't you know it?" She smiled ruefully. "Typical military timing, right? I told him to go since it was only a couple of days. This isn't my first rodeo by any means, but I didn't expect this."

"Look, I can easily run him over to the clinic for some stitches. Right, my man?" Adam regarded me skeptically and curled tighter to his mom on the sofa.

"Well." Michelle got up and retrieved Rosie from her Moses basket. "The clinic is closed on the weekend, so it would be a trip downtown. Adam is a very brave boy." She flashed a smile at her son. "I'll bet you wouldn't be surprised to learn these won't be his first stitches."

There was no choice at all, I knew. The Air Force looked after its own without exception. "Not a problem at all. If you can give me some cursory direction, we'll get moving. I think we'll get along just fine. Why don't you take my cell number and give it to your husband as well? If he gets into town while we're in the hospital, he can come to us."

After a few more moments and a quick exchange of information, I had bundled Adam into his booster seat in my trusty Ford F-150; this was a mission wholly unsuited to the GTO. I offered a few words of encouragement to Adam, and we headed down Kolb Road. His talkative nature had returned, reassuring me that he wasn't in pain, at least not presently.

"Hey, Colonel, my dad says we all have to pitch in and help Mom with the baby. I tried to feed her because she only likes milk, but Mom says she has a special kind of milk. Do you have any special milk? My dad says it comes out of Mom and we should try to help in other ways." I had to smile; the parenting thing was probably more challenging than it looked. With this sharp, busy little mind under their roof, I didn't envy Rick and Michelle. This was graduate-level stuff.

We pulled into the parking deck of Tucson Medical Center, and I set about unbuckling Adam and scooping him back into my arms. The makeshift bandage Michelle and I had fashioned seemed to be holding together nicely. "I don't want you to worry about a thing," I reassured Adam as we crossed the deck. "I'll be with you every minute, and the doctors and nurses will take good care of you. Once you're all patched up, we'll grab some ice cream and get you right back home to help your mom."

"Rocky Road, Colonel?" Adam grinned up at me; this definitely wasn't his first rodeo either.

The Emergency Department was chaotic, just as I'd expected. I signed us in using the information Michelle provided, quickly finding a seat with Adam. Keeping a close eye on the bandage, I pulled one of the Lego tables close, and we began building. Scarcely twenty minutes had passed when a beautiful voice called Adam's name, low and soft, from the door marked Triage. My eyes followed the melodic sound to find a smiling woman, probably in her late twenties, holding out a hand to Adam. He was already dashing toward her, oblivious to the injured leg.

And no wonder.

My mouth was suddenly dry as I watched her standing in the door. Her face was laughing, almost devoid of makeup, a mass of dark blond hair caught in a messy ponytail. Utterly shapeless, standard blue hospital scrubs did virtually nothing to disguise the soft, pinup-curvy figure beneath. Her skin was ivory, almost translucent. She was lovely, but I was unprepared when she lifted her face to scan the room, and I found myself breathlessly staring into arresting sapphire-blue eyes.

"Hello there." She settled Adam on her hip and motioned for me to join them. I stood stock-still for a couple of seconds, mute and staring stupidly. She ignored my apparent inability to speak and smiled warmly. "And hello to you, Mr. Roberts."

Finally, I cleared my throat. "Actually, it's Morgan, Nate Morgan," I returned with a smile as we started down a hall toward the exam rooms. In reply to her unspoken query, I continued, "I'm the neighbor, and neither parent could come along today. Adam's mom just had a baby."

"Her name's Rosie," Adam clarified. "She drinks milk out of my mom, and she and Dad are super tired all the time now. Dad says he probably won't ever get any ever again, but he doesn't even like milk." Her eyes smiled at mine behind Adam's back, and we continued down the hall in silence. How did you respond to that?

"My name's Camille, Adam, and I'm going to help Dr. Jahns get you all fixed up so you can get back to helping your mom. Now, how did this happen?" Adam launched into a detailed account of the day's adventures, and I continued to follow them down the hall. Camille settled us into a curtained exam area and turned to me. "The resident will be around shortly to suture this, Mr. Morgan, and we'll get you on your way."

My eyes sought and then held her blue ones, our gaze lasting for a long moment. I leaned one arm against the wall next to her. "No hurry on our end, Camille." I smiled. "Adam and I are holding up just fine." Those lovely blue eyes grew wide, and she backed away imperceptibly. "I'd better check on the, uh, supplies.

And the doctor," she stammered, and practically fled the exam room.

Once the resident arrived, suturing proceeded flawlessly under the watchful eye of Camille Sullivan, RN, Charge Nurse, CEN, TCRN. I studied her name tag and wondered what the acronyms meant. She murmured occasionally in the resident's ear, handing him supplies and squeezing Adam's arm reassuringly. He held up like a trooper, but she entirely avoided my gaze. She spoke soothingly to Adam as she bandaged him with gauze and tape, then turned to me with a few typewritten pages of instructions. "I'll be sure to relay all this to his parents, Miss Sullivan." I couldn't stop smiling at her. "And please accept my thanks for everything."

Her eyes flickered my way briefly, and she smiled. "It's Camille. And Adam's lucky to have a neighbor like you." The bandaging was finished, and Adam was absorbed in his LeapFrog. I stepped toward her, folding my arms, and took a breath. With hardly any forethought, I was about to do something I hadn't done in years. "Camille, RN, Charge Nurse, CEN, TCRN, I think I'd like to know what all those letters mean. You're obviously a busy lady, but drinks and dinner might give us time to cover everything I don't understand about your name tag. What do you say?"

Camille's cheeks flushed bright pink, and she twisted her hands in the pockets of her scrubs. "I'm a little busy right now, but it's so kind of you to ask. Maybe another time?" She turned and was gone through the curtain before I could mount a second attack. Damn. There was something about that girl that warmed me, made me thoughtlessly take a chance I hadn't in years. Most days, I was sure I'd never take that risk again.

Chapter FOUR

"With A Little Help from my Friends"

Camille Sullivan

What the hell was that? I rushed into the clean utility room, slammed the door, and fell back on it, my breath coming in gasps. *Damn, girl, get it together.* I tried to calm my racing pulse and the thoughts careening wildly in my head. Handsome, charming men were fixtures at my job, and it made not one iota of difference to me.

It was readily apparent from the way I presented myself at the hospital that I was there to run the Emergency Department, not find someone to warm my bed. Not even to find male companionship. I bent, rested shaking hands on my knees, and squeezed both eyes shut tight. Good thing Luckie hadn't seen my performance out there; I'd never have heard the end of it. Check on the supplies? The doctor? Good Lord. I'd stammered and stuttered like a middle school girl. Probably blushed, too. He was handsome but not perfectly so. Thick, dark hair touched with just a bit of gray at the temples, but that had to be premature. Wide shoulders and biceps ever so slightly straining the arms of his dark tee. Velvety brown eyes, soft and deep enough to fall into. Tall—really tall—maybe six two? Tall enough that I'd have to rest my hands on his shoulders and tiptoe to reach that soft, full mouth. Again, what the hell? Everyone who knew me knew I didn't do this. But that mouth...

The door opening unexpectedly shoved me out of the way. "What the hell's up with this damned Autoclave? Flooded the hall yesterday, and now the suture sets are soaking wet? I'm getting reamed out by Dr. Dickless. I swear to almighty fuck, Cam, that turd-polishing monkey's asshole is dancing on my last nerve."

Luckie was seriously steamed, and I was in her way. "I'll call maintenance, girl, but you know the story..." I sent an eye-roll her way.

"Yeah, well." She swung a look my way. "What's your problem? Seriously." She tilted her head and regarded me for a moment. "You look like someone just stole your crayons."

I schooled my face and busied myself by rearranging the instrument packs. "Nothing at all. Just a busy day. It's crazy up in here..."

"I'll say." Samanthe breezed in just then, swinging the door shut before leaning on it with a sigh.

But Luckie wasn't distracted in the least; she squinted at me. "You're such a lying little bitch. I saw you with tall, dark and fuckable. What the hell was that escape routine? You need to check on the supplies? Those sweatpants didn't leave much of a guess as to the supplies he was packing."

I had to get out of there fast. The glare emanating from my two friends was going to involve a serious discussion, and Luckie would see right through my excuses. "Everything's fine," I wheedled, "same as always. I was just distracted and I..."

"Look. You need to shut up right now." Samanthe sighed and leaned on the leaking Autoclave. "The story's heartbreaking, Camille. You've had a hard road to walk, but it's time you considered the possibility of living again." She brushed off my nonverbal protests with a wave of her hand. "It's been, what? Three years? Four?"

I nodded my head in agreement. Four long years since I'd said goodbye to my sweet boy. How could anything be okay ever again?

Luckie emerged from the bottom shelf of the utility cart with an apparently dry suture pack. "Sam, I've got to get back to the nastiness awaiting me in room three, but Grace has suffered a tragic **Code Brown** in room seven. I'd lend a hand, but Dr. PissyPants awaits. Do you have time to help her out?"

Samanthe bristled but started stuffing her pockets with disposable vinyl gloves. "Of course I'll help her, but stop calling me Sam, you deranged wench. Do I look like I have boy parts under these scrubs?" She stomped past us both but tossed out a parting shot with a smile. "I'll do chest compressions all afternoon, but Gracie is gonna owe me for voluntarily helping with her Code Brown."

We both grinned at our friend; we had all had more than our share of disgusting things to clean up over our years as nurses, but the truth was, nurses were virtually unfazed by the ick factor. When "civilians" found out I was a nurse, they'd inevitably offer gratefulness in the form of a perceived compliment about the profession—"You must be an angel of mercy," or, "I could never do what you do." It was a kindness, but mostly off base. Nurses were still widely regarded as sweet, gentle young women clad in angelic white, speaking softly and bringing the doctor coffee while he did important man's work.

In the harsh light of modern day, doctors and nurses were nearly equally male and female, mostly clad in shapeless blue scrubs and constantly in a hurry to the next task, all while critically ill patients crowded triage and treatment rooms. The nursing profession required the ability to multitask, prioritize, give excellent care, and do it all with the compassion that drew a person to nursing in the first place. Some days, things just didn't go to plan.

Luckie's hand on mine brought me back, and I blinked up at her. "You know I love you, Cam, and I have since nursing school." Her stunning brown eyes looked right into me. "But sometimes that means calling you out." I swallowed hard and tried to pull away. "You're too young to throw in the towel, baby girl, got too much ahead. You can't just pour all of yourself into this department. It's a damned hospital, for God's sake. It's a career—a good living—but it's not a life."

"I dunno, Luckie. I don't think I can. Amos…sometimes it seems like yesterday, not four years ago. He took everything inside me when he left. Feels all empty there, like a shell." I swallowed down the lump in my throat and wiped my eyes.

Her arms went around me. "That's why you've got me. Hell, you've got all of us." She whispered in my ear, "We're an unstoppable team. And we've got your back, girl." The huge eyes met mine again. "We're going to have a pow-wow in the break room when this train wreck of a shift is under control. We're going out, child. And by *out*, of course, I mean *partying*. Vivvie has the lowdown on a big party this weekend chock-full o' cock. No shit, tons of men, hot as fuck. And this time, you're going." She flashed a big smile and swept out the door. I tried to grab her arm to protest, but she was gone.

Oh boy.

The day wore on, and a lull finally came around mid-afternoon. Room nine held a homeless guy sleeping off a bender; and there was one elderly gentleman, attended by his daughter, awaiting transport for admission, but everyone else seemed to have been taken care of.

I surveyed the carnage. The supply cart, which shouldn't even have been in the hall, was. And it was totally empty. So really just a cart, I thought wryly. Half-empty coffee cups and charts littered the nurses' station, but there was no staff in evidence. We would need to clean up, restock everything, and get every available housekeeper in here before shift change. The quiet never lasted long.

I headed toward the break room, trying to remember what lackluster lunch item I'd stuffed in the staff fridge at 0545 I hoped I'd remembered a peach; they'd smelled so good at Whole Foods. The break room door stood half open, and hilarity spilled from the door.

Luckie was holding forth on the seriously inebriated patient who had come in last weekend with glitter superglued to his nipples and encircling the head of his penis like a halo. We never lacked for stories to tell and retell. Some of the classics turned into yarns like fishing stories, the details becoming more outrageous by the year. It was our very own oral history.

"So he says...'Doc, they said it was a party, and I wanted to be dressed for the occasion.'"

Samanthe jumped to her feet amid the laughter and waved her hands to signal she had the floor. "Camille's here finally. Vivvie, spill on the party, right this instant. Who even knows how long we have before the rug's yanked out from under us again? Grace says it's a pilot party—true or false?"

Vivian held up both hands, her face breaking into a huge smile. "The rumors are true. The hot-as-shit fighter pilots at DM will have the pleasure of our company tomorrow evening. The amount of pleasure and company up for grabs is left to the individual, of course." I sank back into a corner, hands clasped behind my back. With no further detail than that, I wanted to disappear right into the floor.

I stared down at my Dansko clogs and felt Luckie's arm come around my shoulders. "And, ladies," Luckie announced to the assembly, "at this festive gathering, we will be joined by our esteemed leader, the lovely Camille." Light applause and smiles ensued all around. I frowned at Luckie, but it was too late. She'd already thrown me under the bus.

"So, give us the skinny, Viv. How have you wrangled this invite and what's with the details? Do we need to make an emergent trip to Nordstrom?" Samanthe did love to shop.

Vivvie pulled up a chair to the long break-room table, and we all joined her. "You all know that my brother flies Hawgs over in the 82nd, and they got a new commander after the crash a couple of months ago." She grimaced, and a pall passed briefly over the room. We'd heard the accident report on the radio and expected to see casualties through our doors from the tragedy; the pilot had instead gone to Northwest, where he'd been pronounced dead on arrival. "Anyway," she continued, "apparently the new guy is a certified hottie. My friend, who's also Jake's neighbor, called with the lowdown and an invite to his welcome party at the O'Club tomorrow night."

Samanthe pushed away from the table a bit. "He's gotta be a Lieutenant Colonel, at least, right? He might be a little too old. Worth a look, though." She grinned big. "Who better to assess the situation than us? And I assume there will be a generous selection other than the new commander, right, Viv?"

"Obviously, Sam." Vivvie grinned at Samanthe, who was having no luck shaking her despised nickname. "Here's the rub, gals. It's a flight suit party." She surveyed the sea of blank faces. "Flight suit. You know, khaki jumpsuit, tons of pockets, name tag on the chest, zippered garment. Invented solely to make the tight little ass of every pilot look even more delectable."

She wasn't wrong. Davis-Monthan Air Force Base occupied a big chunk of southeastern Tucson, but it was not uncommon to spot pilots in the wild all over the city, easily identifiable by the aforementioned uniform item, a one-piece getup that made it completely impossible not to stare at the owner's posterior.

"Here's how it works," Viv continued. "The pilots wear their flight suit to the party—they call them 'bags'—and they bring an extra with them, which is hung in the big coat closet near the lobby. Half an hour or so after the guys get there, the ladies are invited to arrive, but before going into the bar, you pick a random flight suit from the closet and change in the ladies' room. The sizing on these things is very generous and kind of generic, and there are adjustable Velcro tabs that make it all work." Heads nodded around the room, and smiles broke out as awareness dawned. "After that, you just head to the bar where the pilots are already assembled, drinking and generally being badasses, and you find the guy with a name tag matching yours."

Samanthe's eyebrows went up. "What if I don't like my guy? Or he's married?"

Vivvie waved her hands a little impatiently. "It's just an ice-breaking exercise to get everyone chatting. And the married guys bring their wives, already wearing their extra flight suit, so no harm, no foul. Don't forget to get to know the married chicks; they're a cool bunch of girls." She looked around the table. "So we're all in, right? Let's meet at the gate at 1945. My friend will be there to escort us in, so don't be late. Hey, Grace, wanna ride?"

The group reluctantly shuffled out of the break room to address the debris of our busy morning. Everyone chatted amiably about the interesting evening that lay ahead as we stocked utility carts, moved fresh linens, and stacked instrument trays. Everyone was excited about the possibilities, with one notable exception.

Me.

Chapter
FIVE

"The Danger Zone"

Nathan

Well, shit. The thought behind this festive welcome from the Scorpions was certainly appreciated, but it felt every bit the meat market it was. I hadn't been to a flight suit party since my UPT days, and my attendance then was probably under duress. The Stingers were kicking it old school with this party, I thought, glancing around the spacious bar and sipping a Sam Adams. If I had one guess, I'd say Bibi and her band of merry, matchmaking wives had dreamed this up to help hook up the new bachelor with some soft, amenable companionship. Did people find lifelong happiness at the O'Club? Actually, I knew for a fact that they did, as formulaic as it sounded. I had known many couples—happy ones—who'd met at the Club or some other pilot party. Didn't matter, I reminded myself. That chance for domestic bliss was in my rearview mirror. It was much safer to focus on my responsibilities to the Scorpions and the Air Force. I knew my long suits and how to play to those strengths. I was pretty confident in my abilities to get this floundering group back on track, but it would take every ounce of focus I could muster.

Coach, Bibi, Deliverance, and Miles held down one end of the bar, so I approached and pulled up a barstool. "Happy." Bibi stood and held out a fresh Sam Adams as I brushed her cheek with a kiss. "Welcome again."

Deliverance relaxed his arms wide across the bar and smiled. "How did the move-in treat you, boss? I always hate moving day."

I had to laugh a little. "Well, it had its unexpected aspects, but no grievous damage or priceless relics gone missing, if that's what you mean. I did get the unanticipated pleasure of accompanying the Comm Squadron's commander's kindergartener to the Emergency Department for stitches."

Miles took a long drink of her beer and remarked, "Must be a story there."

"Pretty straightforward, really," I replied. "Rick had a quick TDY, and Michelle just had a baby. So when Adam bit it on his skateboard, I volunteered for transport duty. He did just fine and was back home—full of ice cream—before his dad even made it home for dinner. Precocious kid and very entertaining; I didn't mind at all being the one to help out."

Bibi leaned forward. "Did you guys end up at TMC?" I nodded affirmatively. "That's where I work, the best hospital in the city." She smiled, obviously proud. "I know they took good care of him there, and not only because it's my home hospital." She paused for a moment. "The Emergency Department crew there is top-notch. They also happen to be a bunch of USDA Prime hotties."

Deliverance was in a full guffaw by the time Bibi finished, and everyone was smiling. "No, no, you guys." Bibi threw her hands out, palms up, and defended herself. "It's a very professional bunch working in a very busy emergency department." I listened as she talked and could think about only one of the group she described, the beautiful and unassuming Camille. I tried to squelch the thought, but Camille's silky hair and endlessly deep blue eyes invaded my consciousness, calling to me again and again. "Miles, have you met Bashful's sister,? She works there."

Miles nodded affirmatively. "I met her over the holidays at the children's Christmas party. She's a knockout, that one. Bashful taxied the plane and played Santa, so Vivvie wanted to join in the fun."

The Christmas party was a favorite whether you had children or not. One of the bachelors, who wouldn't have children to attend to and photograph, was drafted to dress as Santa and taxi an A-10 into a safe area near the squadron building. He would then open a luggage pod below, revealing presents for all the children. It was one of the moments every flying squadron, no matter what airplane they flew, looked forward to all year.

"Well..." Bibi narrowed her eyes and grinned. "I can neither confirm nor deny I overheard Bashful mention that Vivvie and the gang would be in evidence at the party tonight." My heart pounded at the news, but I made an effort to school my reaction. "Their schedules don't normally allow them to travel in a pack," Bibi continued, "so this should be a gas. I love fun chicks."

Coach pulled her to his side with an arm curled around her waist and settled an affectionate look on his wife. "Stop being such a matchmaking busybody, Bibi. You're utterly transparent."

"So what if I am?" Bibi ignored his mild reproof and signaled the bartender as she smoothly swiped her husband's flight cap from his pocket and tossed it on the bar.

The bartender grinned and reached for the large brass bell that hung from the corner of every pilot bar the world over. He rang it once, crisp and loud, and bellowed, "Hat on the bar. That's a round." Coach groaned and grabbed Bibi, administering swift punishment in the form of a swat to her bottom. She howled and worked to extricate herself as most of the bar's population put down pool cues and broke off conversations to meander toward us and collect their free drink. Hands were extended to shake Coach's and thank him for his involuntary generosity. He reached for his wallet and passed his club card to the busy barkeep.

It was a good-natured group, relaxed and welcoming. It was hard to see a squadron of good people who had gotten so far off track and had to endure the harshest consequence. I hoped for all of our sakes that I was the right medicine for this group. I had no desire to let them—or myself—down.

The volume level of the conversation and music increased steadily. Seger serenaded loudly about the Hollywood nights, and the bar filled, a little at a time. A few ladies had begun to arrive, clad in flight suits, in pairs or small groups. They fiddled with their zippers and Velcro and accepted cold beverages from the smiling men who approached and pointed out matching name tags. Conversation hummed and all the familiar boy-meets-girl rituals played out around me. I turned to Miles. "So, what about you, Miles? Are there men planted in the group to vie for your affection? This whole thing is such a relic of yesteryear."

She smiled and leaned in a little closer. "I don't have any desire to participate in the fracas, Happy. Everything is fine as is, and I certainly don't need a man. Bibi knows how I feel, and she's too fine a person to put anyone's butt in a sling over something socially. I encouraged her to kick it old school tonight."

Good to know. The evolution of women's military roles had resulted in the addition of some of the finest pilots I'd ever had the pleasure to fly with. But the ground moving under us kept a person on their toes. It seemed so strange to think about a time past when…

Suddenly all the air was sucked from my lungs. The room went quiet, and I could hear only a loud buzz in my ears as a group of five laughing women moved through the door and toward the bar. One radiant face stood out; and they all teased her loudly, repeatedly adjusting the zipper that closed the front of her flight suit and exposing a bit more creamy flesh than she apparently wanted. Her eyes flashed at her friends, and she adjusted the zipper once more; then she turned abruptly and led the group toward the bar. They stopped nearby, and I tried not to look the part of the desperate eavesdropper I actually was.

"Dammit, Luckie, you diabolical tramp. Leave my zipper alone," a smiling Camille admonished her gorgeous friend. "I have no desire to give every male here an eyeful of boob. It's in doubtful taste, even under the circumstances. Let's grab a beer and find a pool table." They joked briefly with the bartender, placing their orders, and involved themselves in quiet conversation, interspersed with raucous laughter. I struggled, craning my neck to see the name tag on Camille's flight suit, all while attempting to be completely invisible to her group. I'd probably have passed entirely on placing my other hastily laundered bag in the designated closet, but Coach notified me that Bibi insisted on wholehearted participation. She would be taking roll in the closet before the proceedings got kicked off, he advised. I certainly didn't need to find myself in Bellamy Bennett's ill graces.

Deliverance loped into my space. "Any developments in the mating game, Happy?" He signaled the bartender for another round as I shook my head and smiled. "I've heard about these parties, but they didn't have any when I was in UPT. You need to be my wingman, boss. I don't want to fall victim to some man-eater looking to devour an innocent Southern boy such as myself." He added a generous helping of his native drawl for effect.

As he lifted the fresh beer to his lips, Camille's beautiful friend turned suddenly and caught Deliverance's eyes with her own. He paused, the bottle millimeters from his mouth, and his gaze dropped momentarily to her chest where he took in his name tag.

"Well, hello, Mr. Foster," she intoned, moving closer to his face and slowly pushing away the bottle that still hovered there with her own. The air was heavy and silent as we all waited for her next move. This would be fun.

"Seems destiny has dictated this encounter, so you may have to actually meet the man-eater you fear so deeply." She slowly blinked her surprising caramel eyes, leaned still closer until her whisper could be heard by only those nearby, and favored him with a small smile. "But it may not be as frightening as you've been led to believe."

None of our small group moved or breathed. It took a moment, but D recovered, a dazzling smile slowly lighting his face and one eyebrow lifting as he took in the stunning woman wearing his flight suit. He took a long drink of his beer, throat working, and continued to study her. She was quite tall, probably five ten, and stunning with close-cropped dark hair and flawless, mahogany skin. With a gown rather than a khaki flight suit, she'd have been right at home on the red carpet.

"I feel like I must be dreaming; I've never seen such a breathtaking creature as you are. In fact, I'm certain I've been premature in expressing my need for a wingman, Happy." He spoke to me, but his eyes never left hers. He extended his hand. "I'm Davis Foster, but my Southern birthright and the accompanying accent landed me a call sign of Deliverance. Of course"—he lightly brushed his lips across the hand she offered—"you may call me anything you like, lovely lady."

She stepped toward him. "My pleasure, Captain Foster." She obviously knew enough to interpret rank from the insignia sewn on the shoulder of his flight suit. "I'm Lucinda Page, but my friends call me Luckie. Perhaps this evening we're both lucky." She smiled briefly at him and sipped her drink.

His eyes never wavered, but he gestured toward me. "Allow me to introduce the newest Scorpion, Lieutenant Colonel

Nathan 'Happy' Morgan."

I extended my hand. "Pleased to meet you, Luckie. Please call me Nate."

Introductions proceeded amicably, but my eyes were glued to only one person. Her head remained lowered until Luckie called her name. "And this is our fearless leader, at least at work," she teased. "Camille Sullivan." Those deep blue eyes lifted slowly and locked on mine. A smooth curtain of wavy blond hair tumbled over both shoulders, falling past the curve of her lush breasts. I tried to keep my breathing steady; I'd never seen anyone so exquisite.

I swallowed once again and extended my hand. "Camille and I have already met." I spoke to the entire group, but my eyes never moved from her face. "Adam had the good fortune to draw Camille in the nurse lottery when he needed stitches yesterday. His luck is much better than his skateboarding skills." She smiled shyly at me. "On the way home, he asked me if I thought she was pretty. I told him I thought she looked like an angel."

Another pregnant pause settled on the group, and I realized I was still holding Camille's hand in mine. I felt as if something tangible passed between us, though neither of us spoke. She blinked quickly and began to withdraw her hand. As I reluctantly let her go, my eyes dropped to the left breast pocket of the flight suit she wore and read the name tag—

MORGAN.

Chapter SIX

"Strange Magic"

Camille

I hadn't seen him until Luckie and Deliverance launched the public eye-fucking that grabbed the attention of everyone at our end of the bar. Only then, when I had a moment to study the group unnoticed, did I see the magnificent man seated on the barstool nearly opposite my own. I checked the urge to bury my fingers in his thick hair, almost certainly fresh from the barber. But the new commander would have to set a good example, wouldn't he? He would smell clean and masculine, like soap and aftershave; I wanted to snuggle in and check for myself. There was something about the flight suit—well, something about him in the flight suit—that made me wonder what that big, powerful body would look like without it. He seemed completely at ease with himself, perfectly in control of the environment.

Until he saw me. We were both unsettled as introductions were made, but I couldn't tell if his unease emanated from the same source as my own. Something warm and heavy bloomed in my chest, so palpable it felt obvious enough for everyone to see.

The world was full of attractive men with toned bodies, beautiful faces, brilliant smiles. You saw them every day—in the grocery store, the gym, and at work. But this was more than an alluring package. Something undefinable about him drew me; it called out as if it knew.

I looked normal enough from the outside, just like any other woman, I thought. But inside, my heart was like the charred remnant of a home that had barely survived a devastating fire. What was once warm and welcoming, had once offered shelter, was now only a husk. The shell of what was. As our eyes held each other's, and the noise of conversation buzzed wordlessly around us, I had the oddest feeling that I was open for his perusal. It was as if his dark brown eyes could see inside me.

Voodoo.

I was staring. As if yesterday's humiliation wasn't sufficient, I was mute and staring. Nate stepped across our circle and into my space. His face softened, and then he smiled and pointed. At what? My boobs?

"I've been looking for my extra flight suit, Camille. It was very thoughtful of you to bring it along." Right. Nate Morgan. My name tag was his name tag. A match. I nodded and swallowed. *Great job, Camille. Still mute.*

"I'm, umm, glad I could help out," I finally managed. No stammering this time. Improvement seemed too lofty a goal.

Nathan turned from the group and led me to the quieter end of the bar, holding my elbow with a light touch. Leaning against the polished wood, he offered me the single empty barstool with an outstretched hand and signaled the bartender for two more beers. After I was seated, he smiled at me once again and murmured, "Looks like I get a second shot at learning about what's on your name tag, Camille." I looked quizzically at the embroidered cloth tag labeling my chest and tilted my head, questioning. "Surely you haven't already forgotten my smooth approach in the ER yesterday? It was some of my best work, frankly. I was disappointed to have been so thoroughly rebuffed. And now you've entirely forgotten my efforts."

I did have to laugh at his pathetic attempt to look the part of the injured would-be suitor; it felt good to relax. "Frankly, Colonel, I wasn't sure how much riveting dinner conversation we could squeeze out of my licensure and credentialing information. But we can certainly give it a go now; it might just work with the addition of alcohol." We both laughed now, tension dissipating, and accepted a couple of cold Sam Adams from the bartender. "I'll gladly answer your question, but I won't be insulted if you fall asleep before we finish."

He settled back against the bar and indicated I should proceed. "I guess you've figured out the RN part, so I'll start with my title. The charge nurse is responsible for running the Emergency Department. That includes prioritizing patients, assigning them to a nurse, and making sure communications are smooth among the medical staff so that the care happens quickly. We are a teaching hospital, so we have attending docs, residents, and—God help us—interns. But I'm a firm believer in the appropriate care and feeding of interns. They're not targets for abuse on my unit; I won't have it. We all start somewhere."

He leaned toward me. "I noticed you were watching the resident who patched Adam up yesterday pretty carefully. You seemed very attentive. Watchful. Did I read that wrong?"

I'm sure the surprise registered on my face. "Residents are highly skilled, and suturing a cut like Adam's isn't complex, by any means. But that doctor lost a patient in a particularly difficult trauma earlier in the morning. He ran the code, and I worked it with him. It was a devastating set of circumstances, and it was hitting him harder than he expected. He was having a crap day. Not that he couldn't take care of patients, but I wanted to offer a steadying hand. I stepped in to work with him on Adam to give him a little encouragement. I don't often get to be at the bedside with our more routine patients, and Adam was so funny; it was a pleasure to help him. And to meet you," I added quietly.

His eyes seemed distant as I finished, and he spoke as if talking only to himself. "When tragedy strikes, it crushes you in the most unexpected ways." A short silence stretched between us before he focused on me once again. "I'll assume you can account for the remaining alphabet soup behind your name?" he asked with mock sternness.

"The other two stand for my professional certifications: Certified Emergency Nurse and Trauma Certified Registered Nurse. They are both exams experienced RNs sit for to test knowledge and indicate mastery of a specific discipline. The idea is that experience has been your teacher, not academics alone. Those exams are difficult; I'm proud of the soup on my uniform." I grinned as he took in the information. He looked impressed, and, I won't lie, that felt pretty damn good. "So, Colonel Nathan Morgan, from whence do you hail? And what brings you to our little desert paradise?"

He pulled a vacant barstool alongside mine. "San Francisco, mostly. I'm a Navy brat. My family still lives there, and I visit every chance I get. It's a great town, something for everyone. Most recently, though, I've been at the Pentagon on a staff tour. DC's a great town, too, but staff tours mean no flying, so I can't wait to get back in the saddle." He paused and took a long swallow of the cold brew. I took a moment to appreciate his corded neck, the long fingers wrapped around his bottle and—it had to be said—the big hands. Really big, really powerful hands. *God, Camille, seriously?*

Then he continued, "As to visiting your desert paradise, this is the Schoolhouse for the almighty, all-metal Warthog, Camille. I'm terribly disappointed you didn't know this very important piece of information." The faux-injured look was back, and I smiled. He had a great sense of humor. "Everyone who flies the greatest airplane in the military inventory comes here for four months or so to learn how to employ the A-10 and to fall in love with Tucson. I'm just coming back to the mothership."

"Back to the mothership as the big boss, kicking ass and taking names, as I hear it. They brought 'a frog-killer in from the coast.'" Uh-oh. The Sam Adams was doing a number on my inhibitions.

"Why, Miss Sullivan, did you just quote *The Muppet Movie* to me?" he asked, his gorgeous eyes twinkling. "Is it possible that a creature so cultured and educated as yourself is also a fan of the finest movie ever made?"

I snapped my brows together. "Pfft. 'I've seen detergents leave a better film.'" I lifted my eyebrows and laughed at his amazement. "Along with *Caddyshack*, it has to be one of the most quotable movies of all time." We sipped our beers, and the bartender dropped off a bowl of fresh peanuts for snacking. The evening was passing in a rush as I basked in the warmth of his attention and easy company.

He folded his arms casually across the wide expanse of his chest and continued to smile down at me. "So, do you play darts, Camille Sullivan, RN, Charge Nurse, CEN, TCRN?" He snagged his beer and deftly guided me away from the bar, fingertips resting lightly at the small of my back.

"Sorry to disappoint, Colonel, but I'm pretty hopeless in the darts department. And my pool skills are worse, if that's even possible." I was marginally more relaxed than moments earlier, but his hand touching my back felt electric. It occurred to me briefly that I couldn't recall the last time a man's touch had been affectionate, or even personal.

His voice was deep and soft. "Let's put this Colonel thing to rest, Camille. It's just Nate, unless you prefer Nathan. And we can skip the diversions." We paused at a side door that led outside. "There are picnic tables on the patio—care for some fresh air?"

I smiled and nodded as he opened the door, and we stepped out into the warm night. Tucson was ridiculously hot in the summer, but the air wasn't heavy. The lack of humidity made the heat easier to bear, and some summer nights bordered on pleasant. We climbed onto a picnic table at the edge of the patio, and Nate rested his elbows on his knees, the beer bottle held loosely between two fingers. We were both silent, and I wondered if I could recall how this dance was conducted.

For years now, it had been only me. Even before my precious boy, there wasn't room in my life for recreation or leisure, certainly not for dating. Amos was the linchpin in the timeline of my twenty-nine years; every memory or event was filed in my head under before or after Amos. Four years had passed, but the depths of pain never seemed to lessen. I still awoke in the night and wept until my body ached, begging and bargaining irrationally with God for the chance to have him back in my life. But I couldn't fault Amos for my social inadequacies. Simple inattention on my part was the culprit. As a younger woman, I'd ruthlessly eliminated anything that didn't contribute to making Camille Sullivan a more educated, productive member of society. I worked my way through nursing school, squeezing endless studying and clinicals in around my night job as a part-time nurse's aide at the local nursing home. The pay was abysmal; the work, exhausting. But I graduated on time and near the top of my class, a tired and too-serious twenty-two-year-old.

"I don't date."

Wait. What? It just spilled out of my mouth, cutting into the night around us in a most disquieting way. His face turned to mine, and I was lost in those eyes. But this time the eyes were laughing, and one corner of his lush mouth turned up in a half-smile.

He turned his big frame more fully toward me. "You don't date?"

I let out a sigh and tried to organize my thoughts to avoid sounding unhinged. "I don't have a complete explanation, but that's really about the size of it. I just don't. Date, I mean. It's not that I don't want to enjoy myself, it's just never been important enough to prioritize. And now I find myself sitting in the dark with a handsome man, and I don't know what to do next. If I had applied myself more and appropriately emphasized the social aspects of my life, I wouldn't be so lost right now." I finished my diatribe in a rush, realizing my unhinged status was now firmly established.

Nathan's laugh was deep and completely unrestrained. The smile that accompanied his laughter was magnetic. I couldn't look away and finally had to join in. "Prioritize? Applied yourself? We're not talking about grad school here, Camille."

The laugh diminished to a chuckle and he rubbed the index finger of one hand thoughtfully across his full bottom lip. "Truth is, though, I don't date either. Haven't in a long time." He was quiet, seemingly alone with his thoughts for a moment. "Wait a minute"—he fixed me with a somber look—"you think I'm handsome?"

Instantly I felt my face heat and flush. What was wrong with me? Nerves and no fucking filter made for instant and ongoing humiliation, that's what. "Well, yes, it can't possibly be the first time you've heard that. And I've already admitted novice status in the dating department. It's not very polite to embarrass me further," I finished sheepishly.

The smile remained trained on me, but his eyes softened, all of the teasing gone. "It's not like me to forget my manners. My mother would wipe the floor with my ass if she knew." He leaned well into my space, covering my hand with his much larger one. I could feel his breath, warm on my cheek, and the delicious smell of him bathed me. Warm, earthy, and thoroughly male. "I have wanted to know more about you since you walked into that waiting room yesterday. There's something different about you; it makes me so curious. Something in me senses that you're not like the other women I've known." He stood, towering over me, and moved incrementally closer. "I hope it doesn't sound too aggressive, Camille. I can't honestly say I've ever felt that before."

I couldn't find words. The warmth in my face spread to my chest, and the connection of my hand with his felt electric. I swallowed and nodded almost imperceptibly. He bent toward me, his face close to mine. My lashes fluttered closed, and I felt only a hair's breadth separating our mouths. His soft lips barely brushed mine, and he whispered, "I'm going to taste you now, Camille. If that's not what you want, you need to tell me now. Things may not be the same after this."

His free hand swept my cheek, moved down my neck and his fingers entwined carefully in the hair at my nape. Then his mouth was on mine, firm and soft at once, and he gently licked into my mouth. Our tongues tangled and explored leisurely; the hand that held mine caught it to his hard chest and held it there against him. I could feel his heart beating, strong and steady, and a soft groan escaped him. The tension in my stomach spun and coiled lower, everything seeming hot, full. These unbearably sweet sensations had been dormant so long I'd thought they were gone forever. I wanted more and briefly flailed, reaching for him from my perch on the picnic table. But in the next moment, his hands flattened at my waist, and he easily picked me up, setting me on the ground, pressed against him. My anxious hands found his waist, trim and hard under the flight suit. He deepened the kiss, and his left hand left my waist and moved upward. Long fingers stroked my side and found the sensitive underside of my breast. As his tongue continued its unhurried exploration, one thumb swept along, steadily upward, and found the barest edge of soft nipple. At his touch, it pulled taut. I whimpered and felt warm wetness dampening my panties, everything already nearing a point of no return.

Nathan gently broke the kiss but pulled away only slightly, millimeters from my swollen mouth. His finger continued lazily stroking one tight nipple, and the hand at my waist held me close. His length lay heavy and hard against my belly. Even through our clothes, I could feel it pulse between us. We both stood frozen, eyes locked, breathing heavily and struggling for control of the unexpected fire tearing through us.

His voice was low, and it rumbled like thunder when he finally spoke. "Camille, I am the brand-new commander of this squadron, and I believe it would be improper for me to strip your lush little body bare and fuck you on the patio of the O'Club at my welcome party. If you screamed when you came over and over, it might even be viewed by some as rude."

He was smiling a little now, a private smile just for me, as his thumb continued to caress my straining nipple. "We've established that neither of us date, each for reasons we've yet to explore." Now he pulled back and studied my face. "But I'm sure we owe it to each other to see what this is. Are you agreeable, Camille?"

The wave of desire that threatened to drown me seconds before subsided just enough for the nagging, familiar fear to settle in place again. But, before the well-known panic could silence me, I focused on the warmth in his eyes. "Yes, Nathan Morgan. I'm agreeable." He smiled wider, and his lips met my forehead.

Please, God, I prayed silently, *don't let this good man accidentally destroy me.*

Chapter SEVEN

"Blue Eyes Crying In the Rain"

Camille

About Five Years Earlier

This was not me. Not at all, I thought. I stared into the mirror and again brushed my long hair into a sweaty ponytail. House music so loud the mirror rattled made my head pound. Now, as if things couldn't digress more, two club rats fell through the door of the restroom screaming drunkenly at each other. What the fuck? The bathroom already smelled of vomit—and worse. My instincts told me things were about to become even more unpleasant.

I should never have come, that much was obvious. But two of our brand-new graduate nurses wanted to thank me for my help and patience during their internship periods. They were insistent on "treating" me to a night out at their favorite club. At least I'd been able to drag Luckie along to suffer with me.

Speak of the devil. I ran full on into Luckie just outside the restroom. "I am seeking asylum from this torture chamber, dammit," she yelled above the din. "I demand you grant me admission to the relative peace of the ladies' room."

"Sorry, sister." I twirled her one hundred eighty degrees on her sky-high stilettos and marched both of us rapidly in the opposite direction. "That restroom is a whole bag of nope. Things are deteriorating, so I recommend you pee on the dance floor if Mother Nature calls. It's not as if anyone would notice." We found seats at the bar and began working to attract the attention of a bartender.

Luckie surveyed the sweaty, undulating mass of humanity on the dance floor. "I'd lay odds that at least half a dozen girls are getting dick out there as we speak."

"It's a romantic notion, sure." I smirked at her. "But what Prince Charming brings a lady to a posh dance club like this?" Two watery vodka tonics were set on the bar in front of us, and Luckie passed the bartender two tens and a five.

"Keep the change," she yelled to the girl, rolling her eyes at me. "They may as well point a gun at you when you pay, but it's not her fault." She shrugged and took a generous sip, grimacing. "The drinks are exorbitant, but at least they suck." We both scrutinized the dance floor again. "Do you see our charges anywhere?" she asked.

"Well, Leeandra was pushed up against the wall outside the ladies' room, giggling uncontrollably while some dude tried to suck her face off her head," I volunteered helpfully. "She's drunk, but not that gone. I know consensual face sucking when I see it." I got the impression this was standard procedure for those two.

"I feel a little responsible since we're the adults at this shitshow." Luckie stood and stretched. "I'm just going to have a little walk about and lay eyes on both of those common street whores." She cleared her throat, "I mean, our fledgling nurses. That drink is certainly not enough to prevent me from leaving my seat. Hold down the fort, gorgeous. I'll be back." She made for the dance floor and disappeared into the writhing crowd.

The club was expansive, and minutes ticked by as I nursed my drink absentmindedly. I hit bottom and turned to snag Luckie's glass behind me. It was completely melted, I noted, and vaguely pink. Probably the light. Or maybe hers was a vodka cranberry? Never mind. It was still cold enough and tasted pretty good; the club was a fucking oven. Mmmm. Definitely a cab home tonight. I was getting a little sloshed. I squinted at the dance floor, looking for my friend, but no Luckie. I smiled and snorted to myself. No Luckie. That was funny. We needed to get the hell out of this place and make a note never to come back. It smelled like spilled beer and stale sweat.

Where was she anyhow, dammit? The dance floor was so loud and so swirly and so many colors all together. Better find Luckie, I thought, trying to steady my feet under me. The barstool was much taller than I thought, and I shouldn't have worn these fucking heels. Where was the damn floor anyhow? Gravity took over, and I slid into the big, beefy arms of somebody I couldn't see.

Everything was black now. And heavy. The lights were far away, and something was splitting me in half. The pain was even louder than that awful music. And it smelled. So. Bad. I heard a ferocious slap, and my face jerked to the side. "Wake up, bitch." I tasted blood and struggled to open my eyes. A face was inches from mine, but I couldn't see who he was.

His breath reeked of alcohol, and he grunted as he crushed me beneath his heavy body, dripping sweat and spraying me with saliva while yelling into my ear. "Take my dick, you fucking whore. You love it, don't you? Not so much better than everyone else now, are you? You and your friend were just begging for it in those slutty shoes. Juicy pussy begging for my dick."

He pounded away between my legs while his friend leered over his shoulder, masturbating and laughing at my pain and humiliation. I felt bile and alcohol in my throat and retched violently. "No you don't, you fucking worthless bitch, don't you puke on me." He pushed his hand over my bleeding mouth, and I fought back panic and asphyxia. "You fucking want my dick, you cunt. I could see it when you stared at me from the bar. You're tight, too. This is gonna be good."

He pounded harder now, grunting obscenely as he tore me apart; I could feel blood pooling on the floor between my legs. The pain was exquisite, and I fought through the nausea, struggling to breathe. But the edges were fuzzy now, and my vision dimmed the bit of light I could see. I was spent. It hurt too much, and I was too weak to fight. I stopped struggling and let the agony weigh me down. Pull me under.

Please... I closed my eyes to seal out the pain for good. *Don't let my Luckie find me like this.* Then everything was darkness and nothing.

Chapter EIGHT

"What's New Pussycat?"

Camille

"**G**ood morning, pretty baby," I crooned to my beautiful boy. "How's Mommy's precious this lovely day?" Solomon regarded me balefully from his perch on the embroidered pillow sham. I reached for my reluctant companion from the nest of down and fine cotton sheets.

Fine. Now you know my darkest secret. I'm a linen whore. Not a rich one, mind you, so I habitually scoured ads from high-end department stores and frequented Tuesday Morning. The Queen of England could happily snuggle up in my bed and feel at home. As a nurse, I'd never been wealthy, but I damn sure slept in the finest bed in Tucson.

And last night I'd not been there alone—at least not figuratively. I'd clutched my down pillow like a schoolgirl, imagining Nathan's long, hard body pressing mine into the mattress. I marveled at how long it had been since I'd entertained hot, imaginary male company between my superior sheets. Samanthe said I had cobwebs in my vagina. Not that my well-meaning coworkers hadn't tried tirelessly to relieve me of those. Not the girls themselves, of course, but there had been endless efforts at setups—blind dates, group dates, you name it. I had become a relationship Houdini, preferring hard work and professional advancement to the dark unknown of male companionship. At first, the avoidance tactics were a way of letting myself heal. Now they were just habit.

And until I encountered the beautiful Colonel Morgan, I'd convinced myself that the habit would work well for a lifetime. I'd had enough pain to mark me forever, and the risk was too dangerous to take.

But last night was a thing entirely to itself. He wanted to date.

In the "before Amos" era of my life, I'd dated on occasion, but never seriously. And frankly, I couldn't see the grand attraction. I never seemed to get the butterflies or fireworks other girls discussed incessantly before they chucked their dreams to follow love. It saddened me to see so many of them later, alone or disillusioned, sometimes even bitter. I couldn't afford the emotional expense.

My parents hadn't planned to have children, so my arrival was unexpected and unwelcome. They had little to do with me from my earliest memory and made it crystal clear that I was expected to leave after high school and make my way. Looking back, it was apparent that I handled their disinterest differently than many children would have. Mother and Father didn't like me and viewed me as an inconvenience, a waste of their time and money. But my self-worth somehow didn't suffer in conventional ways. I always knew I was smart and had something to offer. From a tender age, I realized there was only one shot at succeeding in making my life satisfying, worthwhile. I was never abused, at least not physically. What I didn't realize until much later was the bone-deep wound left by neglect at the hands of those who were supposed to cherish me most. That laid the foundation for how I reacted to the heartbreak that would come and the woman who would eventually emerge.

Of course, Solomon already knew all of this. There could be no doubt about that, because Solomon, my magnificent blue Maine Coon cat, knew everything. My elderly neighbor gave me the tiny, impossibly fluffy kitten about six years ago when she became partially incapacitated following a stroke and had to go live with her daughter. Her daughter didn't apparently possess the intestinal fortitude to cohabitate with a clairvoyant cat who was both more beautiful and smarter than herself. I suffered no such misgivings. My gorgeous boy and I were a match made in heaven.

He commenced his rumbly purr as I set him on my belly before cocooning us both in the duvet, and his eyes stared deeply into mine. I knew Solomon could read my mind, so it wasn't necessary to detail what was going on.

I was losing my ever-loving fucking mind.

Staying out of the relationship game and focusing my efforts on being a great nurse garnered me a good life, if a little narrow. I had an excellent job, the respect of my coworkers and managers, and a small stable of the best friends a girl could ever want. Luckie and I had been fast friends since nursing school, both of us orphans of sorts. My parents were living, but we had only the barest of contact—usually a card on birthdays and occasionally Christmas.

Luckie came from money, and her parents vigorously disapproved of her career choice, feeling and frequently voicing their opinion that such pedestrian work was far beneath her. One glance at the glamorous bitch would have you throwing your lot in with her parents, no doubt. She had breathtaking model looks, but there was so much more to that girl than met the eye. For our purposes, we both worked our respective ways through school and pledged to find jobs in the same hospital. Samanthe, Grace, and Vivvie rounded out our inner circle. We were a great team in the trenches of the busy ER and even managed to find some fun and trouble, from time to time.

Oh, Nathan was fun and trouble all right. And I couldn't mount a reasonable defense against the earnest charm oozing from every pore of his commanding body. When he touched me and silenced my thoughts with his persuasive mouth, I was well and truly fucked. "Not fucked in the literal sense," I informed Solomon, "but I think that may be in the cards." That possibility brought a thrill as well as some very real anxiety. There had been no one since the terrible night in the club five years ago. I made an absolute point of avoiding anything that might lead down that path. I knew logically that my friends were right. I was too young to exclude the prospect of a real, healthy relationship, but I couldn't lure myself from behind the wall that had protected me over these past years. As it turned out, the answer was not in persuading myself but in finding the one who had me peering over and around that damn wall with uncontrollable curiosity. And now he'd gone and found me.

The insistent ringing of my phone interrupted my morning communion with Solomon. Vivvie's enthusiastic shriek met my groggy hello. "Girl, word on the street is you and the new commander hit it off last night, in the biblical sense. I just got off the phone with Jake; he caught a minute of the show on the patio, so I'm going to need details."

"Okay, look, Viv, your peeping Tom of a brother is going to have to lock that gossip down. We did absolutely not do the nasty, just a little kissy face."

"I'll tell him, but I need further info. Are there follow-up plans?" Vivvie continued her interrogation good-naturedly.

"Abner's for dinner tonight," I informed her. Abner's was a rustic steakhouse in the desert outside of town that served food from an open grill, cowboy-style under the stars. Quiet, old-time western music often accompanied the meals. It had the potential to be intimate, even romantic, and something told me Nathan would know exactly the way to make it just that. My voice took a more serious tone. "I'm nervous, Viv. Really nervous. You know how long it's been. What if I forgot everything? What if I never had a fucking clue in the first place?"

She was shushing me before I finished the last of my speech. "Camille Elizabeth Sullivan. I'll not listen to one more word of this rubbish. Enough, right this minute. We are all thrilled to pieces about this, and may I add, it's about fucking time. You're a prime piece of ass that's been sitting on the shelf too long. It's time to get in the game, girl." She was only pompoms and a pleated mini from being the perfect cheerleader.

Wait.

"Who exactly comprises the 'all' who are thrilled?" I demanded. "Has the hearsay chat line been activated already this morning? Good God, woman. What time did you bitches get out of bed to start slandering me?"

"Early," she admitted without a hint of remorse. "Jake woke me up with the news. Such a good brother, always looking after his sweet little sis. We're more like twins than sibs, you know."

That brought a hearty round of laughter from me, and she had to join in. Jacob, aka Bashful, was indeed older than Vivian, but that's where the truth in what she said ended. Although he did love and dote on her, Viv was far from sweet. She was loud, opinionated and possessed an acerbic wit. She was also loyal, honest to a fault, and generous. She was adopted and looked nothing like her blond, blue-eyed brother. Viv was tall with silky black hair swinging above her shoulders and piercing green eyes. They loved to pose as twins to confuse the shit out of anyone gullible enough to believe them.

There was a loud knock at my door, followed by several impatient rings of the doorbell. Solomon jumped from the bed with a solid thump and a peeved meow. I tugged on a football jersey over jammies and jogged toward the door. "Anyway," Viv continued, "the 'all who are thrilled' I mentioned before?" I peered through the sidelight of my front door to see the girls assembled in shorts, tees, and ponytails, sans makeup, on my front porch. "We come bearing caffeine and carbs to assist in wardrobe decisions." They all grinned through the glass and held up bags from Dunkin' Donuts. "Open the door, bitch."

So much for a quiet return to the dating game.

Chapter NINE

"Get Outta My Dreams, Get Into My Car"

Nathan

"Come on, baby," I mumbled under my breath as I quickly gave one final polish to the hood of my shiny GTO. "Let's see if we've still got any game left." I tossed the old tee shirt back in the rag bin in the corner of the garage and addressed Mayze. "Don't wait up, babe. I'll be late, but I promise to bring you the steak bones. How does that sound?" Mayze waddled across the fenced backyard, seemingly unimpressed with my bribe, and plopped unceremoniously onto her worn dog bed on the corner of the patio. I got the distinct impression that she didn't think my courting skills were worth a shit.

Hard to say whether Mayze was right. I glanced once more at my hastily chosen attire—my favorite Wrangler 13MWZ jeans, a crisp white button-down with sleeves rolled to the elbows, cowboy boots, and a well-worn leather jacket in case the desert evening turned chilly. To that end, I also threw a big woolen stadium blanket in the rear seat. You never knew when *that* might come in handy.

The Goat roared to life, and I turned west on Golf Links Road. Camille had texted me her address earlier, an old bungalow near TMC. I wondered vaguely how long it had been since I'd polished the car and headed out on a first date. I knew exactly how long, of course, because there had been no one since Eliott. A little surprising I'd been able to persuade a very skittish Camille into dipping her toe back into the dating pool with the likes of me. On the other hand, the chemistry was off the charts. An unexpected make-out session on the Club patio was very unlike me. My M.O. was normally much more conservative, but there had been no other possibility with Camille Sullivan. Glossy hair falling over her shoulders and framing soft curves, lush cleavage peeking from my very own flight suit, and those eyes…it made me uncharacteristically rash. I could still taste her and was ravenous for more. But who could tell where her head was with the advantage of twenty-four hours to think?

She would obviously think of me as the aggressor—which was natural from her standpoint—but it was completely ironic from mine. I'd avoided relationships, even casual ones, for several long years. My grief for Eliott never really seemed at an end, but the larger reason was my belief that she had been my one chance to settle down. Which was funny, because it had never been Eliott who pushed that particular agenda. Quite the opposite, in fact. Her approach to life—and to us—was that every day was a blessing, a gift to be embraced. My view had been, conversely, that there was a proper timeline for everything: education and the beginnings of a career, love, then marriage, and babies to follow. It all followed in an orderly fashion, didn't it? Eliott didn't think so, but I enjoyed the idea of the journey with her, despite our differing views.

Then it was ripped from me. Eventually, I laid the pieces down, but it never felt done. So I stumbled along my path, focusing on a life filled with my career. It wasn't difficult, after all, to fill every moment with the Air Force. The military was purpose-built to take up every bit of oxygen in the room. It had been a comfortable compromise for every day of the years since then.

Every day until yesterday. Camille changed everything, or at least I thought so. I needed to see her tonight like I needed to breathe and was so glad she'd agreed to explore further. The GPS announced I'd arrived at Camille's house, and I turned into the driveway of the tidy little bungalow. There was a tiny yard, neat and well-tended, with three steps leading to the front porch. A big hanging basket spilled a profusion of flowers that practically begged you to make use of the rocking chair there. She must have to water those things constantly, I thought idly. Camille's black-and-white MINI hardtop sat in the carport.

I unfolded from the car and debated putting the top up; no girl would want to go on a first date with the wind tangling her hair. Even I knew that. I decided against doing it just now and headed for the front door. She opened it just as I knocked, and we both laughed at our awkward timing.

My breath caught as I took in everything that was Camille.

In the waning light of day, her skin was more golden than it appeared last night, especially against the pale yellow of her sundress. Long hair hung free again, dark blond flax over her shoulders, and the blue of her eyes seemed even darker against all the fair colors surrounding them. Slim shoulders gave way to heavy, soft curves caught in the halter of the sundress, and I fought an urge to trace them and taste the skin beneath. She took me in, head to toe, and the fringe of lashes shaded cerulean eyes briefly. She smiled a tiny smile, stepping onto the porch with me, and shut the door.

I was drawn to her even more fiercely than I'd remembered, if that was possible, and caught her small hand in mine. "You are so very lovely tonight, Camille. Thank you for taking a chance on me." The compulsion to be near her was partially due to her beauty, of course, but that wasn't the whole story. I'd need to focus on staying in the moment with her tonight, I realized, rather than trying to analyze it all.

Camille turned her face up and directed a smile in my direction. Then, as we stepped off the porch, she dropped my hand and rushed toward the GTO. Arriving at the front passenger door, she whirled, face betraying her delight, and shrieked, "A '67 Goat, right? Right?" Without waiting for an answer, she started around the car, examining and touching it. "When I was a little girl, the man who lived next door had one of these, and he let me help when it was time to wash it." She stopped her appraisal of the car, and her eyes met mine across the hood. "He was very kind to me. Even gave me a few driving lessons in it when the time came." Her gaze lost some of its focus. "Father didn't have a lot of time for things like driving lessons." I cocked my head, realizing that something sad was clouding her mind, but the memory cleared as quickly as it had come. She smiled again. "I'd know one of these anywhere."

"Well, Miss Sullivan." I circled the car quickly and opened the passenger door for her. "An interest in muscle cars seems an indelicate diversion for such an elegant and fragile young lady." I raised an eyebrow in mock disapproval. "Perhaps you should consider needlepoint or sewing, something more becoming your station." I moved to release the clips and raise the convertible top, but her hand stopped me.

"Don't you dare put the top up," she insisted. "It would be a crime on a night like this."

Well, now, this was a surprise. I bent to her level and looked into the bottomless blue eyes, now dancing at the prospect of a ride in this memory from her childhood. "Are you sure, Camille? It's probably a half hour to Abner's. The wind's likely to tie your hair in knots."

She was already twisting her blond mane into a knot at the

nape of her neck and pinning it with some mysterious appliance she'd plucked from the bottom of her purse. "Of course I'm sure, silly." She completed her task and grinned up at me. "In the interest of avoiding false advertising, I'd better let you know right now: I'm not exactly the frail and feminine creature you may have thought." I buckled my seat belt as she did the same. "I hope you're not disillusioned, Nathan." She smiled for my benefit.

Once again the GTO rumbled and growled as we backed out of her drive and into the warm night. "Not at all, angel." I touched the back of her hand and then dropped the car into gear. "You're intriguing me more with every passing moment."

The night wind was warm on my face as we sped north on I-10. Conversation flowed effortlessly, and Camille seemed at ease with our lighthearted banter shouted over the substantial noise of rushing wind. I answered her questions about my military service up to this point, places I'd lived and planes I'd flown. She talked about her antics in nursing school with Luckie. It was hard to tell who the bad influence was in that duo, but she obviously had great affection for her friend, whom she regarded as a sister. It occurred to me that many women expended much of their energy disparaging others around them, especially beautiful ones like Luckie, but Camille always seemed to hold her friends in high regard. That spoke well for the group of them.

We pulled into the parking lot, and I jogged around the car to open Camille's door and offer my hand. As she stood, her hand went to the back of her neck and released her hair from the clip. She shouldered a small purse. "I'm liking the date so far," she intoned, grinning mischievously.

I picked up the reference to *The Muppet Movie* and played along. "It hasn't started yet." I grinned back.

"That's what I like about it." She smirked and shook her head slowly. The long waves again fell across her shoulders. I couldn't look away; she was captivating.

Chapter TEN

"Gotta Get You into My Life"

Nathan

"All set." She grinned. "Minimal hair catastrophe, I hope. Guess I should go primp in the ladies' room for a while to bolster my ladylike status." She wrinkled her nose. "On second thought, I'm starving. Let's get right to the steak and pound the last nail in the coffin of my feminine wiles."

"Far be it from me to complain about a beautiful, low-maintenance woman who loves red meat," I said as I led her toward the door. "I may be in love." She quickly shot me a questioning look and then giggled as I waggled my eyebrows her way. The seating hostess led us past large, open barbecue pits groaning with steak and ribs and to a picnic table under a large tree. Beyond the area where other diners were tucking into plates of delicious-smelling food, the western band was readying for their set.

"Evening's perfect, Camille," I said, settling into the picnic bench next to her. "Trouble is, we've both copped to the fact that we don't date, so I have a proposal for you. Sort of a first date survival guide for tonight." I asked the server for a couple of Sam Adams and watched Camille's face.

"Okay, I'm listening." She leaned her chin on her elbows and faced me. "I'd wondered how this would go. If you have a starting place, I'm all ears."

"For this groundbreaking first date, I propose we make a genuine effort to tell the truth and avoid any and all bullshit games." Her eyebrows went up, but the smile remained. "Truth is, I'm not sure I remember how the game is played anyway, so this might just be my attempt at surviving without making a complete ass of myself. Either way, we'll be trying something that's never been done—what do you say?" I smiled and leaned back to await her thoughts. It was a calculated risk to offer up the truth, especially considering the substantial emotional baggage I was lugging. If she dug in, I might have to discuss things I'd never talked about before.

She looked thoughtful, considering my idea, and then her eyes met mine. She cocked her head and smiled. "I'll accept your proposal, Nathan, because my reasons and doubts may be identical to yours. But we'll never know unless we wade in." She paused, her demeanor sobering somewhat, and then took a deep breath. "There's a reason I stopped dating a long time ago, just as I'm sure there's a good reason you did. I don't talk about it—not ever. I haven't ever felt tempted to make a change, but it feels like a precarious position now." She accepted the cold bottle from our server and took a long drink.

The bench we were seated on faced west. A fading sunset decorated the horizon in a million shades of pink and orange. The band began to play, the strains of western band provided the perfect soundtrack for the end of the day and the beginning of our night together. I moved a little closer to Camille, turning to take in the sweet smell of her hair, and placed my arm across the back of the bench, my fingers lightly stroking her bare shoulder.

"Did you ever watch any of the old western movies when you were a kid?"

Her expression was questioning. "Westerns? Oh no. Father was far too serious for something so frivolous." She shook her head vigorously, laughing.

"No, really? I'm making a note to remedy this oversight," I teased. "No Roy Rogers? Gene Autry? No *My Pal Trigger*? There's a gaping hole in your childhood, Camille." I smiled at her but noticed that her smile faltered at my last statement. I squeezed her shoulder lightly. "Oh, Camille, I'm so sorry. I've already hit a nerve, haven't I?"

She shook her head quickly. "No, Nathan, it's not your fault. It's a pothole in the road and you were bound to hit it, early and hard. I don't bring it up because it's difficult to talk about, and there's rarely a need to. My friends know the score." She took another long drink of the cold beer and fixed her gaze on the evolving patterns in the sunset. "My parents didn't want me, didn't plan to have kids." There was another pause, and then she continued, "I wasn't abused, at least not physically, but they just weren't interested."

I felt my gut clench. Who the fuck didn't take an interest in their child? How could your beautiful daughter not be the light of every day of your life? I couldn't fathom it, especially considering my background—a big, loud family. Intrusive, invested, loving.

"I mean, I'm okay," she continued hurriedly. "I'm not angry or bitter. Not a candidate for The Jerry Springer Show." She laughed without humor. "I just don't identify with some things like a lot of regular, well-adjusted people do."

I gave the silence its moment, collecting my thoughts to avoid another misstep. "Help me here, angel. What kinds of things do you mean?" As soon as the words left my big mouth, I wondered if it was too much to ask. The air was heavy for another instant before she leaned forward, elbow on the table, and turned to face me. Her face was soft, but the ache in her eyes was easy to read.

"No fond memories of big family dinners with cousins or aunts and uncles. My parents were both only children, like me. The only grandparent I ever knew was my grandmother, and she didn't speak to Father, so I seldom saw her. No big birthday parties with cake. I was rarely allowed to have friends visit or sleep over." She sighed and continued. "Almost no physical affection—hugs or kisses. My mother came to piano recitals because someone had to drive me anyway, but no one was home to see me off to prom. Father gave me an allowance for a dress, and I picked it out on my own."

She rolled her eyes and threw her hands up in frustration. "It sounds like I'm the host of the world's most dramatic pity party." Her shoulders sagged, and she sighed again, brow knitted. "That's not my intent, Nathan. Other kids have had it worse. I see it in the ED almost every day. My parents fed me, gave me the basics, and never hit me. Some children aren't even that fortunate."

The air felt thick, and I tried to take in the idea of a child that didn't matter to her parents. "I can't imagine not loving and cherishing a child, Camille, especially one as bright and beautiful as you must have been. There must be some fascinating twists in your path that led you to become the woman you are, because your parents certainly didn't see who you were—or could be." We settled again, backs to the bench, studying the waning sunset, now pink and purple swaths against a dark sky.

She spoke again into the silence. "So many things happened after I left home, but I've mostly tried to make the best of what I am. Tried not to chase all the extras. I have my friends, my career. It's rewarding, and it's enough. The single time I thought I could hope for more, it slipped away. Right through my fingers." Her voice, so strong through all the bleak revelations, broke almost imperceptibly. I was gripped by the unexpected need to protect this woman. She had already spent a lifetime protecting herself when others failed her.

The silence stretched longer this time, and I settled closer to her small form. She was soft, and the scent of her was so hypnotic that I fought the urge to nuzzle her neck. It was an effort to slow my breathing and think. Settle down, Nate. I didn't want to over-react and send her running for emotional shelter.

The song the western combo sang now was one I knew well. My dad often sang it around the house, and now I hummed it quietly in her ear. The band crooned the melancholy ballad, "Tumbling Tumbleweed" with its forlorn themes of loneliness and solitude. How was a song from my childhood so fitting for the two of us, both struggling with the weight of what we'd lost?

As the song finished, her face turned to mine, and she lifted her soft mouth toward my own. I allowed myself to sink into her inky blue eyes. "What was once enough, beautiful girl, isn't enough anymore. We may need to set our sights higher." I touched my mouth to hers and allowed our lips to melt together. My tongue slid against hers, and she gave me her weight, soft breasts pressed against my chest. The velvet darkness wound around us, and she allowed me to taste her freely, my fingers sliding up one taut thigh and caressing warm skin under her skirt. Her hands restlessly slid through my hair before we pulled away, breathlessly remember-ing where we were.

"Oh, Nathan, I'm..." Her voice faded in the quiet, and she quickly straightened the sundress. A large campfire now blazed on the perimeter of the property, providing meager light to our table. That light barely illuminated her for my hungry gaze, breasts now visibly swelling above the sundress. Her nipples were stiffened peaks, asking for my mouth. My cock lengthened and pressed insistently against its confines, needing relief.

At the same moment, we sighed, shoulders sagging, and then looked at each other and laughed. The cloak of night offered safe-ty from what could have been an awkward moment, and we both relaxed. The server took our order and said she'd return right away with another round of drinks. She hurried away, leaving the two of us alone again in the warm desert night.

"This is twice in two short days that you've swallowed me up in your eyes. That mouth hypnotizes me, angel. I want more, and it's been a long time since I've wanted more. A very long time." I paused and fixed an intense gaze on her face, her lovely eyes wide and lips parted. I could feel her breath on my face. "I feel lost, Camille."

The corner of her mouth turned up on one side in an adorable smirk. "'Maybe you should try Hare Krishna.'" She dissolved into a giggle that eventually deteriorated into a little snort. Her blue eyes flew open wide, and she clapped a hand over her mouth. "Oh my God. I can't believe I just snorted on a date. A first date." She shook her head vigorously. "Seriously, Nate. You can't take me anywhere. Sometimes I just crack myself up, and I'll embarrass us both." She flung her arm toward the parking lot. "Go on—save yourself. You have a career and your reputation to think of." She giggled a little more as I shook my head in wonder. Who was this girl? I'd never met anyone like her. "Here's the thing: it's *The Muppet Movie* quotes. Any great movie quotes, you know? *Caddyshack. Animal House. Little Shop of Horrors.* But *The Muppet Movie* especially." She shook her head at me, a huge grin illuminating her face. "You should send me packing while there's still time."

I caught her hand impulsively and brought it to my mouth. "Not a fucking chance, gorgeous." I turned her hand and touched my lips lightly to her wrist, our eyes locked together. "This is just getting interesting." I could feel the rapid beat of her pulse against my lips.

She pulled my hand into her lap and held it in both of hers. "So, Colonel Nathan Morgan—flyboy, frog-killer, and handsome bastard—what has killed off your love life so effectively? Surely every eligible female who's ever walked past you has tried to drag you off to her lair."

It was a fair question, and I knew this was a risk. But she'd bared herself in a way that had to be uncomfortable, and we did have a no-bullshit deal. I never discussed this with anyone, not even my dad, as close as we were. With a quick moment of reflection, though, this didn't seem so bad. She felt like a safe haven.

"I've always been the serious one. The studious kid. Good grades, applying myself—you know the type. My family was so loving, so supportive, so *not* dysfunctional. I can't lay this on them." Her attentive smile encouraged me to continue. "UPT, Undergraduate Pilot Training, is a very demanding program wrapped up in a continuous year-long party. But even then, I kept mostly to myself. I mean, I wasn't a monk. There were girls occasionally. But it was never very important to me, and there was never anyone special. Not until a few years ago."

I took a long drink of the cold beer. "After I finished Command and Staff School in Montgomery, Alabama—about a year long— I'd been out of the cockpit long enough to require a few months of retraining here in Tucson. It wasn't a long stay, but I met someone." The sudden pain in my gut caught me off guard, almost as if someone had punched me in the stomach. "Her name was Eliott." I wondered if I'd even spoken her name aloud since I said goodbye. The feel of it was foreign to my tongue.

"I'm still not sure I believe in love at first sight; but if it's real, I felt it for her. We were so different, but I thrived on what she gave me. And she felt the same. We were two halves of a whole, and I fell hard and fast." My eyes met Camille's blue ones again, and I struggled for the right words. The pain in my stomach intensified.

"Then, one day, she was gone. We had plans, Camille; we'd already started to talk about forever. There was a ring." I let go of the breath I'd been holding. All the pain returned in a rush. "It felt like someone tore my heart out of my chest."

Camille's warm hands held mine tight and squeezed, her eyes glued to mine. I shook my head and tried to explain. "It happened so suddenly, and I always thought…" This was so fucking hard. "If I'd just had time to prepare—to say things I needed to say. It would've been easier to let her go. But the truth is, I don't believe you're ever ready to say goodbye to someone you love. Not ever."

Camille's eyes were shiny with tears, and one spilled down an ivory cheek. Then another. Again the silence and the darkness settled around us. "No. You're never ready. The time is never right to say goodbye when you're in love. I understand, Nathan. I really do." Our foreheads dropped and touched; my throat ached with grief that never left.

Then the tension eased, and Camille's eyes again met mine. "But as Luckie says, 'Life goes on, bitch.'" Her wide smile eased me. "What other choice do we have?" The earnest warmth radiating from her soothed like a balm for my fractured soul.

The band serenaded us and the fire crackled and the moon rose, gleaming in the desert night. *What choice do we have?* It seemed both of us had chosen to bench ourselves following a terrible injury, although I sensed I hadn't yet heard all of Camille's story. What kind of choice was that? Sitting on the sidelines of the game, watching victory and defeat play out, always too afraid to risk another injury.

The meal was delivered, and I'd rarely seen a woman consume steak with the passion Camille Sullivan brought to the dinner table. She was a complete delight, entertaining and enchanting me. She couldn't finish a joke without destroying the punchline, and each story was peppered with overt gestures and asides. Staying on point or finishing an entire thought was mostly out of the question, and I was captivated. The evening was gone before I could believe it, and we were walking hand in hand toward the parking lot.

Holy fuck. You just never know what a day will bring.

Chapter
ELEVEN

"Spread Your Wings and
Let Me Come Inside"

Camille

It was impossible to believe I was in the passenger seat of a classic sports car, capably driven by one of the most mouth-watering members of the male species I'd ever had the pleasure to meet, flying down I-10 toward my house. With the convertible top down, the pleasant noise of the wind relieved us of the responsibility of conversation. I had to imagine his thoughts were as rapid-fire and jumbled as my own.

I'd never met anyone like Nathan. Not ever.

He was self-assured, a gentleman, and completely in control at all times. Then he rolled the dice, on our first date no less—just laid himself open for my perusal. I wondered if he'd done it just because I had.

I didn't share those parts of myself with anyone. Luckie knew, as well as a few close friends. But I didn't talk about my heartbreak readily. From the pained look as he talked about the woman he'd loved, it was apparent he didn't bare himself any more easily than I did. And we were virtually strangers. It should have been unsettling to take such a risk on our very first date.

But the reason might be obvious. Something was cooking between Colonel Fine-as-Hell and little ole me. I was breathlessly trying to decide what it was and where it was going when the ride from the desert ended abruptly in my driveway. So, what the fuckity-fuck now?

Nathan turned the GTO's key and the engine stilled. His eyes were intense.

Your move, Camille.

I cleared my throat. "The night was beautiful, Nathan, just perfect. Would you like to come inside for a glass of wine?" I nervously offered the invitation and watched his eyes, finding barely concealed hunger in his gaze.

"I'd love to come in, Camille. Thank you." He walked around the hood of the car, his attention fixed on me until he opened my door and offered his hand. He was quiet as we walked onto the dimly lit porch, and I opened my front door. The lone lamp on a side table in my living room offered just enough light.

"Wine, Nate? Or a beer?" I offered, but he shook his head and gathered me into his waiting arms in front of my slipcovered sofa.

"Everything I want is already here, baby." His voice was so soft, and my heart skipped a beat at the simple endearment. Had anyone ever called me that?

His hands were sure as they circled my waist; then one drifted to the side of my hip, and his fingers caressed the skin there through the thin fabric of my dress. His head dropped beside mine, and I felt his lips soft against my ear. "Beautiful girl. I know we didn't go looking for each other, and I don't know what this is, but I don't want to question what I'm feeling."

He paused, and I felt his breath for a second, then two. His arms tightened around me, and he gently kissed an earlobe. "I don't know everything about you, but we've both been hurt and retreated from living our lives. Now I think it's time to try a different approach."

I couldn't find any words, so I met his eyes and nodded. His hand circled the back of my neck, tangling fingers in my hair and pulling my head farther back. Then his lips were warm and soft and pressed against mine, asking permission. I tried to stifle the moan that escaped as my mouth opened to him, but he felt it and responded by moving to my jaw and throat, licking and sucking the delicate skin there. My center heated, dampening the tiny panties I wore. God, his mouth was magic. My fingers worked the bottom buttons of his crisp shirt, opening them to find hard muscles scoring his belly. I caressed the warm skin, finding a smattering of silky hair. Searching farther down, I ran two fingers inside the waistband of his jeans, causing him to shudder.

His mouth stayed at my neck, sucking gently, and I felt one hand leave my waist, catching the skirt of my dress and feeling beneath. Then a large, warm hand cupped the cheek of my bottom from underneath and squeezed. Hard. He groaned in my ear. "God, baby, everything about you feels so good. Want you so much."

His hands came to my waist again and lifted me easily, my legs wrapping tightly around his hard middle. Then our mouths were together again, mine devouring his as he kneaded my bottom under the silky panties. As my tongue searched deeper, he lifted slightly, then dragged me down his body, grinding my pussy on his hard erection. A very thick erection, I noted, warm even through the fabric of his jeans and my panties. I felt a stab of panic.

"Nathan, I can't...I can't," I gasped frantically. His hands stilled, but he didn't move them. His eyes met mine quickly.

"What's wrong, Camille?" He rubbed his nose on mine. "I

would never hurt you, sweetheart. Just breathe and tell me what's wrong."

Now what? I could barely think, my brain all hazy with lust; but I had to tell him. Something. "It's been a long time. A really long time." I tried to slow down and make sense. "Five years, Nathan." His eyes registered surprise, but he let me continue. "And it seems like you're…" I rambled aimlessly, seemingly unable to make my point to the man whose large hands held my naked bottom. "It's just that you feel so…you know, big." He relaxed a bit now, and his eyes were smiling. I was deflated. "God, I want this. Want you so bad. I…"

He shushed me with his mouth, a sweet, hot kiss, then lifted his lips only a millimeter. "Fuck. You're hotter than I could've imagined. I want you, too, beautiful, but we have all the time in the world. When the moment's right"—he looked steadily into my eyes—"you'll have my cock, and I'll wrap myself in your sweet, warm pussy. But tonight, Camille, just let me take care of you." I didn't know exactly what he meant, but he'd rendered me speechless again. I nodded my agreement.

He placed me back on my feet, and I watched as his long fingers finished unbuttoning his shirt. He took it off, tossed it over the sofa's back, and I was treated to a wide expanse of muscled chest. A silky treasure trail led downward into snug jeans, where a sizable bulge pressed against his zipper. He turned his sights to me and bent, sliding my panties from my legs. I waited, thinking he'd try to remove my dress, but he just sat on the sofa.

"Come here, angel," he murmured. "Sit on my lap." He guided me to face him, and I straddled his thick thighs with my knees, groaning when my naked flesh met his denim-covered legs. His eyes darkened, and his hands worked at the back of my neck, loosening the knot of the halter. Nathan slowly lowered my dress, catching his breath abruptly as the fabric fell and my breasts lay open to his hungry eyes for the first time. His mouth caught one nipple, and he pulled me close, lapping and suckling each pale pink tip until they were tight. His hands caressed the round curve of my bottom, dipping gradually closer to my warm folds.

I combed fingers desperately through his hair and down the strong muscles of his neck, seeking purchase and finding broad shoulders to grip. Looking down, I watched him nurse the tips of my taut nipples, then swipe the heavy curve underneath with a flat, wet tongue. Oh God, I hadn't felt like this in…well, I'd never felt like this. My pussy felt hot, swollen. Fuck, I needed his fingers. "Please, Nathan," I whimpered, "my pussy hurts, baby. It hurts so bad."

His mouth moved close, and his lips touched mine when he whispered, "I'm going to take my time and touch you, Camille. Feel and learn you, make you come." I loved hearing his whispered plans, but my brow knitted and I looked away. One hand caught my chin, turning me gently back toward him. "What is it, baby? I promise not to hurt you… What's the matter?"

I swallowed and met his eyes. So embarrassing. "I've never had an orgasm—not with a man. You know, just with me. I mean, by me. This is so humiliating, Nathan. You don't have to…" My eyes filled, and I tried to swallow down the hot tears that threatened.

"No, gorgeous, no tears now." His voice was so gentle, and his lips touched mine. "That just means it'll be my privilege to be the first." His fingertips slid softly across the bare lips of my pussy, and I sighed. "Let's take our time. Don't do anything but relax and enjoy what you feel. I'm going to love every second of touching your beautiful pussy and tasting your mouth. Now open your knees, Camille. Let me in."

I opened as he asked and tried to still my shaking thighs. He pulled one thick finger through the slick heat of my slit and, without hesitation, wedged it deep inside me. I whimpered, and my hips rolled, welcoming the fullness and begging for more. "I love the way your little pussy feels inside…so tight, baby." He smiled against my mouth. "We'll need to be patient and take plenty of time to get you ready for my cock. It's going to be a snug, delicious fit when the time comes." His whispers glided over me like hot syrup, sweet and intoxicating. His thumb gathered the moisture now wetting my lips and thighs and spread it, in lazy circles, around my clit. The singular finger inside was still, not thrusting, but occasionally stroking the front wall of my pussy.

"Try to relax now, Camille. I'm going to push the hood from your sweet little clit, so I can stroke it and make you come apart for me. Kiss me while I touch you, baby." As he spoke, I felt his thumb and finger, with butterfly-light movements, push the hood away and circle my bare clit, spreading slick heat across the impossibly sensitive knot. My tongue delved deep into his welcoming mouth, and his finger insistently continued its lazy pace. My hips thrust, pleading for more, while he sucked my tongue and nipped at my mouth.

"Patience, baby. Your pretty little pussy is wet for me, so tight." He groaned and touched me faster, dragging a finger occasionally through the hot slickness. "Someday very soon I'll memorize every swollen fold of you while I worship you with my mouth and taste you as you come. For tonight, just let me enjoy how hot and creamy your sweet cunt is and think about how good it'll feel to have you wrapped around my hard cock."

I squeezed my eyes tight and whimpered into his mouth. I was so full with just his finger, and he massaged the thickening flesh of what I now knew must be my G-spot. My clit felt full like it might explode; surely he could feel that now? My thighs gripped his, and the swirling pressure building in my stomach began to ripple and move lower…God, almost.

"Close, Camille. So close. I can feel your clit pulsing against my finger. Just relax now, baby. Come for me." His mouth licked and sucked at my neck, his low groans feeding my need to… Suddenly a jagged sob ripped from my throat, and I gripped his bare shoulders. The pulsing strengthened, and Nathan slipped a second thick finger into the warm clutch of my pussy, still massaging the spasming knot of overwrought nerves. Warmth soaked my lips and his hand as I rode out the best orgasm of my life. He stroked my hair and murmured softly in my ear, "Such a good girl…come hard for me, baby."

The heaving in my chest began to subside, and the steady beat between my legs slowly faded. His fingers moved gently inside me, and he covered my mouth with wet little kisses. After a couple of quiet moments, he spoke softly and looked at my face while his fingers continued to fill me, "Watching you come was one of the most beautiful things I've ever seen. Even more, because you trusted me to be the first to give you this. Thank you, angel." His fingers slipped free of me, and I could clearly feel his thick length, harder than ever, beneath my pussy. His hand came to his mouth, and he slid two fingers between soft lips, sucking them and apparently savoring the taste. "You're so sweet, Camille. I look forward to parting your thighs and drinking my fill, one day very soon." He smiled.

"But what about you, Nathan?" I leaned back slightly and looked hungrily at his denim-clad erection. Fuck. Me. How big was it anyway? My cheeks flushed pink as I noticed that his jeans were completely soaked with me. Nothing like that had happened before.

"I told you, baby. There will be a perfect time for us, soon. As bad as the ache is, and as much as I want to have all of you, I want to make sure it's right. And that it's not too soon for you, your heart or your perfect body. I wasn't kidding about the snug fit, Camille, and you're going to be a little sore tomorrow just from two of my fingers." He lifted the straps and carefully retied my halter, smoothing the material over my sensitive breasts and mumbling under his breath, "So fucking tight. Fuck."

He helped me stand, and I arranged my dress, now in dire need of a dry cleaner. He accepted a cold bottle of water I retrieved from the fridge after he washed his hands, and we walked out onto the porch to say goodnight.

His arms held me, and mine rested at the back of his neck, absently rubbing the muscles there. This time I spoke first. "You were right earlier. We weren't looking for this. And the amount of baggage I'm carrying around frightens me, frankly. But I feel something with you, Nathan, and I want you to know I'll try, even if I'm scared.

His smile flashed brightly before he lowered his head for one more heart-stopping kiss. "Like Luckie says, what choice do we have?"

Chapter
TWELVE

"Treasure"

Nathan
About Four Years Earlier

This was the last thing I needed tonight, I thought. It was completely out of character for me to be at the weekly Friday night throwdown in the Catalina Foothills. One of the other pilots in my recurrent class was renting a house up on Skyline Drive with a view to kill for. There was also a pool/backyard combination that screamed *pilot party*, and the faithful had heeded the call. Almost every week, Hoss played host to an afternoon and evening of drinking, storytelling, and women. Oh, and did I mention the drinking? The group of guys in the apartment complex near mine had been nagging me to come along and join in the fun, but I eventually realized what they were gunning for was a designated driver. And it sure looked like I was that guy.

I turned away from the music and rowdy conversation currently rocking the pool deck and stared out at the lights of Tucson. Skyline Drive was living up to its name on this clear spring evening, and the view drew me in, stick-in-the-mud though I was. Nursing a beer that bordered on lukewarm, I felt a growing pang of guilt. I was only here for a couple of months of refresher training after a desk job at the Pentagon. What I needed to be doing tonight was hitting the books. It was great fun to be back in the cockpit, doing what I loved, but the gray matter needed a thorough flogging to get back on top. I sighed and turned toward the house to look for a cold soda or bottle of water. It was evident from the increasing decibel level that this party was just getting started. Shit. It was gonna be a long, late night.

More than a few women had joined the party in the past couple of hours. It was mostly a word-of-mouth affair with guys inviting neighbors or friends of whomever they were dating at the moment. There were familiar faces here and there, but I made very few of the social gatherings this group put on, formal or otherwise. My reputation as a straight arrow, if not a killjoy, wasn't intentionally earned, but it was mostly on target. I didn't go in for the party scene and preferred to keep mostly to myself, staying on top of my studying and well clear of trouble. I'd never really seen the point in getting drunk every Friday and dragging home a new stranger to fuck. Don't get me wrong, I liked sex. Really liked it. I'd been told, on more than one occasion, that I was damn good at it, too. And I loved women. But maybe that was the thing—it didn't make sense to me. Using women that way. Hell, I didn't want to be used either. There had been a few women over the years, a little serial dating, but nothing I'd call serious.

What the fuck was with the unavailability of nonalcoholic drinks at these parties? I was reduced to rummaging through Hoss's fridge in an abandoned kitchen. Three supremely overserved girls in the hot tub were threatening to discard their bikini tops any minute. At a party like this, food was superfluous. Or so the logic went. The lights in the kitchen were off, so I didn't notice her perched on a countertop across the kitchen. Not until she spoke.

"If you have the good fortune of surviving your encounter with that bachelor refrigerator and don't pull back a bloody stump, I'd like a shot at it, too." My head snapped up, eyes slowly adjusting to the dim kitchen, and I saw a diminutive figure hopping off the counter. Long hair hung almost to her waist and dark eyes looked me over quickly as she propped herself against the cabinet opposite where I stood and folded her arms. Before I could formulate a reply, she went on, "What is it with you pilot types and your food-free parties? What is that anyway? I understand Uncle Sam compensates fairly, so what would be the harm in springing for a bag of chips or a damned veggie tray, for God's sake? I'm seriously fucking starving here, and there has been no food in evidence since my arrival."

Her laughing face lit up as she joined me and continued her good-natured rant in the open fridge, searching crisper drawers and checking condiment jars. "Hey, I was brought up right, you know? I don't arrive for a party with empty hands. It's usually a bottle of wine or a bunch of flowers, but this time I blew the wad on a hostess gift, sadly unaware that there was no hostess to gift. But the hot tub full of drunken harlots out there?" She pointed in the general direction of the backyard. "Yep. All me. One neighbor and two coworkers. I bundled them up and drove them over my own sober self. And where's my thanks, I ask you?"

She plucked a package of baby carrots from the drawer and unscrewed the top on a bottle of ranch dressing, giving it a perfunctory whiff. "I think this will suffice until I can seduce you with my considerable charms and procure a dinner invite." She ripped into the plastic bag of carrots and poured dressing into a coffee mug she grabbed from the cabinet. "I'm Eliott, by the way. One L, two T's," she advised cheerfully, extending her hand. "And who might you be?"

Well, hot damn. Even for a smooth-talker like me, it was hard to collect myself and not babble after a tour de force like that. I extended my hand in the not-so-romantic light of the open refrigerator and intoned, "Well, Eliott, with one L and two T's, 'I'm the player to be named later.'"

She closed the fridge door and again leaned on the cabinet, munching a carrot and cocking her head as she studied me. "Hmmm. *Bull Durham*. Interesting first movie quote choice. Sexy and fun; that could be telling, but it's probably too early to say."

"It's Nathan, Eliott. Nathan Morgan. Sorry, but I didn't expect to find intelligent life here tonight—couldn't even find a bottle of water. I accidentally became designated driver for a group of drunken neighbors like you did. And frankly, I was a little pissed, but I suddenly see the beauty of my predicament." She pointed a dazzling smile my way that lit me up in the dark kitchen; I couldn't take my eyes off of her.

"Well, Nathan Morgan, you know what they say." She sucked the dressing off the tip of one of those lucky fucking carrots. "Sometimes, even a blind squirrel finds a nut."

Chapter THIRTEEN

"Come Fly with Me"

Nathan

This was no way to start my first full week as Scorpion commander, that was for damn sure. I stood at attention near the large desk dominating the imposing office of General Henry O'Cherry. Don't even fucking think about making a cheap joke about that last name either. He was the Wing King, and he didn't suffer fools. I sure was feeling like a prize fool bright and early on this Monday morning as O'Cherry wore a hole in the carpet of his office and tore me a brand-new asshole over the stunt my LPA had pulled. Fucking lieutenants. No sense of self-preservation. Or fear of repercussions, apparently.

That was about to change.

"Yes, sir. I understand, sir. I'm going to deal with this first thing this morning. I'll…"

"Damn straight, Morgan. It'll be dealt with all right, because I'll do it myself," O'Cherry interrupted. He was pissed, and it seeped from every pore of his being. He looked like he was going to have a stroke; his face was as red as a… Nope. *Don't go there,*

Happy. The smallest hint of a smile and my ass would be grass.

I schooled my face into the very picture of the stern squadron commander. "Sir, I understand the frustration you must be feeling. I know there's history here, and it must take a disproportionate amount of your time and effort to handle these issues."

"Fuckin' A right it does, Morgan." He stopped pacing, placing both hands flat on his desk, and hung his head briefly, sighing. "Look, Nate. We're glad you're on board here, and I realize this is a helluva welcome to your first command, but this shit has got to stop. It's your job to handle it, and frankly, I don't give a good goddamn how you go about it. I'll stay out of it—this time. Fix it."

I saluted smartly. "Yes, sir."

Fucking lieutenants.

At my request, Coach had Torch, Miles, and Boo standing at attention in my office where they had been for the past ten minutes. I was cooling my heels, and my temper, over a cup of coffee with Coach in his office and reviewing the weekend buffoonery that had earned me a thorough ass-chewing at wing headquarters this morning.

Coach took a big gulp from his chipped mug, his lips curling in disgust as he swallowed. "God, this coffee tastes like asphalt. Heavy on the ass. The LPA needs to get their shit together on the snack bar, starting with the coffee."

I rolled my eyes and paced Coach's office, studying the pictures and awards decorating the walls. "Looks like the LPA has bigger fish to fry than getting the snack bar up to speed," I groused. "I'd hoped to have a minute to hang up my coat before the shitstorm started, but that's clearly not gonna happen."

Coach leaned on the front of his desk and stared into his mug. "I heard it was a **socks check**?"

I sighed and dropped into an old chair facing him. "Yeah. Pretty standard fare for a Friday evening at the Club, but it was early. Early enough that O'Cherry's wife had just finished dinner with her mother and taken her to the bar to order a Grasshopper or a Pink Squirrel or some similar shit."

Coach groaned and dropped his head, shaking it slowly. "Of all the rotten luck." He continued his punishment-by-coffee and waited for the rest of the story.

I continued, staring at the wall behind his desk. "Seems the conversation between Boo and Torch revolved around whether or not the other had a hairy ass. Somehow, Miles got involved, claiming the argument was sexist since they didn't have intel on the state of her ass as well. Things escalated, as they do, and Kamikaze shots were consumed. Then all three flight suits were unzipped and dropped to the ankles directly in front of the corner table where Bunny O'Cherry and her mother were seated."

Coach's head snapped up, his eyes wide with horror. "What the fuck? Bunny? Seriously?"

I had to smile at that. Truth really was so much stranger than fiction. "I shit you not. And, believe me, Coach, O'Cherry was not amused. Not even a little bit. My phone was ringing this morning at 0500."

Coach clapped me on the back in a friendly show of support. "He knows none of it's your fault, Nate. And I'd hoped you'd have the chance to get your bearings, but here we are. You're the man for the job, and you didn't ask for advice—but I'll give you some just the same."

His jaw tightened, and he looked right into my eyes. "This isn't just juvenile bullshit from a Friday night at the Club. It's part of a larger pattern of behavior that's been tolerated and enabled for a long time. Long before either of us was here. It's a pattern that's cost the Scorpions their good reputation and cost a good kid his life. It fucking stops today. Starting right now."

I nodded wordlessly, opened the door, and headed down the hall. Conversation in the snack bar ceased abruptly as I walked by, but I didn't turn my head in greeting. I opened the door to my office—in disarray with boxes still lining the walls—closed it quietly and took a seat behind my desk. I let the silence that settled over the room stretch almost a full minute before I lifted my eyes to meet those of the three lieutenants who had stupidly dealt me my first challenge as commander.

I was not and had never been a screamer. Experience taught me long ago that silence and uncertainty were far more disquieting. The anxiety radiating from these three reinforced what I already knew. "Stand at ease." Their shoulders relaxed, arms folded behind backs.

My voice was low as I addressed the issue at hand. "When we met at beer call, I told you a few things about myself. I told you I'd done my homework and knew the problems existing in the squadron, the reasons I was brought here. I told you integrity was something I value." I paused and studied each face, seeing the anxiety ratcheting up as everyone waited to hear evidence of whether the new guy was as much of a hard-ass as rumored.

I leaned back in my chair without breaking their gaze and continued. "I told you I'd rather we were all on the same page about improving the Scorpion reputation. You three wasted no time in loudly communicating the message that we are, in fact, not on the same page." I paused again to allow this information to sink in.

In the silence, Miles raised her eyebrows and a hand to gain my attention. "Sir, if I could just…"

"No, Lieutenant Christman, you absolutely may not. I'll do all the fucking talking here and decide if and when I want to hear from you." My voice remained quiet, but a lethal edge crept in. "For your planning purposes, I don't anticipate the need to hear from any of the three of you in the foreseeable future. Your asses, hairy or not, shining in General O'Cherry's mother-in-law's face spoke volumes."

Their eyes were wide now, and Lieutenant Radley "Boo" Harper was perspiring impressively. Excellent. I had their attention. "Make no mistake about me. I appreciate the value of blowing off steam, especially in a stressful environment like a fighter squadron. And I'm not trying to turn the Scorpions into a sewing circle, despite what you may think. I am a big believer in working hard and playing hard." I paused and looked at each ashen young face. Fuck. They didn't understand what was at stake here.

"If we don't exercise discipline and judgment in every aspect of our personal and professional lives, we endanger ourselves as a whole. This squadron has already paid the ultimate price for failing to believe that. When it's go time, you fly and fight with every ounce of skill and professionalism you have." Another pause and then, "And when it's time to relax and unwind, enjoy yourselves, but use judgment. You feel the urge to shine your ass, literally or figuratively? Just make sure everyone around will appreciate or at least tolerate the show."

I stood and moved behind my chair. "You're all grounded for the week. Report to your flight commander for grunt work. If I hear one goddamned word of complaint, I'll double that week to two in a heartbeat. And, before you can question it or get filled with righteous indignation, I'll tell you that I'm making an example of you. Fuckin' A right I am. But you're the brain trust that decided to get naked in front of a senior citizen a week after the new squadron commander told you to get your asses in line. Do the math."

The group was visibly uncomfortable but clearly thought the executioner's ax had fallen. "One thing further." I met their eyes individually in turn. "You will report to General O'Cherry's residence this afternoon at 1700 in **blues** to personally apologize to Mrs. O'Cherry and her mother." Their eyes flew open and jaws went slack. "General O'Cherry is expecting you, so don't be late. You're all dismissed."

The office was empty, save me and the stacks of boxes that promised an upcoming Saturday morning filled with even more unpacking. The three lieutenants filed out wordlessly a few moments earlier, and I fervently hoped that the cultural change I intended to set in motion was underway. It was not my nature to be inflexible for its own sake. I was brought here by the powers that be with a specific housekeeping mission in mind. The question was, how difficult would this task prove to be? Could I instill the absolute requirement to respect the rules meant to keep my pilots safe without breaking the morale and wild spirit characteristic of a fighter squadron?

I mulled the question as my feet turned toward the briefing room. It was Scorpion tradition that the new commander would join his flight commanders in a formation flight to the gunnery range for his first mission. It was quality training, to be sure, but also a great opportunity for the squadron leadership to metaphorically sniff one another's butts. The range was unique in its ability to lend quantifiable numbers, and therefore real bragging rights, to the endless battle of egos that raged in a fighter squadron. Each bomb and bullet was scored for accuracy by a range controller who communicated with pilots via radio. Trash talk was always plentiful, but the Warthog had a huge gun and the ability to drop bombs, skills we continually honed, and these were measurable in real numbers.

A huge gun. Yeah, that always brought a smile to any Hawg driver's face. The hydraulically driven 30 mm Gatling gun delivered bullets the size of my hard dick at an incredible rate—4200 per minute. Stay at the Club or any pilot party where civilians of the opposite sex were present long enough, and this would come into play. Hawg drivers of the male persuasion especially loved to endlessly discuss their "huge gun." The double entendres always became more risqué and increased in frequency as the night wore on.

Coach was still drinking that dog-shit coffee but was in the briefing room this time, bitching about it to my flight commanders. I hadn't yet met each one, but they gained their feet as I entered, throwing my bag on the floor next to a chair near Coach's.

Bashful offered his hand first. He was tall, blond, and powerfully built. "Jake Travis, boss. C flight commander. We met at your commander's call—it's Bashful—and I'll be leading today."

I nodded and smiled, gripping his hand. The fact that Bashful would lead our formation of four airplanes today probably meant he had the most experience flying the Warthog. "I remember you, Bashful. Call sign's Happy." We shook briefly, and I turned my attention to the next man who likewise offered his hand.

"Walker Jackson, sir. B flight commander." We shook, and his genuine smile was welcoming. "My call sign's Hung." He sighed and grinned again, a megawatt smile. "Why don't you let me buy you a few brews before we get to where that came from?"

Call signs, sometimes called "**tacticals**," were usually the result of an interesting story or ridiculous mistake, not a faux-sexy concoction like "Hellcat" or "Snake." Fighter pilots were real people who fucked up and laughed at themselves—and others—right before they went out and did actual heroic shit.

The final occupant of the room was an unfamiliar face. He stood next to the others, laughing at Hung and warmly offering his hand. "I'm Pete Manson, sir, A flight commander. Call me Marilyn." We shook, and I laughed with him. Tacticals had a way of breaking the ice.

We settled in for the briefing, and Coach departed for the scheduling desk. Bashful easily slipped into a leadership role, reviewing details of our sortie, or flight, and offering helpful particulars and details about squadron standards for the new guy, "motherhood" in fighter pilot parlance.

Bashful gave us the "step time" to head for the jets, and we gathered maps, notes, and mission lineup cards, then moved toward the door for a **PDP**. "So, Bashful." I turned a question-ing face toward the flight lead. "I didn't hear anything about the standard Scorpion wager in your brief." The room was silent as all three men doubtless mulled whether this was a serious query or a test.

Bashful gave a moment of consideration before he replied, a hint of humor creeping into his voice. "Well, now, Colonel, what would the taxpayers think of professional warriors turning an essential training mission into a round of penny poker?"

I folded my arms and broke into a big grin. "If you declined, the taxpayers would rightly think you were a bunch of puss-ies, afraid of getting your asses handed to you by an old man." I laughed easily. "Come on, Bashful…you're not getting off that easy. The FNG is gonna take you gentlemen to school."

Bashful's face broke into a big grin. "Sir, you've offended the competitive Scorpion spirit. Standard bet's a quarter a bomb, nickel a bullet." No one got rich at the range, even if you had a stellar day and took everyone's money. Hell, you'd be lucky to cover your first beer at the Club, but pride was at stake. I was a kid in a candy store. Couldn't wait to strap in. Flying was fun as shit. Add a big gun and some bombs, and it was the most fun you could have with your clothes on. Although, I mused, I had most of my clothes on Friday night, holding Camille's soft form as she came apart around my fingers. My mind was suddenly adrift.

Marilyn's cheerfully mocking taunt snapped me back to the present. "Sure you don't want a mulligan on this one, old man? It's been a while, and it doesn't look like you're getting any younger." He was kidding, but this really was part of my "play hard" philosophy. Now it was time to let the Scorpions know the old man was the real deal.

Minutes later, walking across the ramp toward the four imposing aircraft, I pretended not to notice the surreptitious grins and nudges between the three friends who were my flight commanders. Their collective demeanor was relaxed and respectful, but they were cocksure they'd take my money at the range. They thought they would return knowing they'd pegged me from the start: a square-filling, ass-kissing staff weenie from the Pentagon who'd sucked enough dick to be rewarded with a flying command. I smiled to myself.

Not today, motherfuckers.

Chapter FOURTEEN

"Playing with the Boys"

Nathan

Bashful's voice boomed over the radio inside my helmet. "D-M Ground, good morning. Scorpion, four of America's finest, taxi to arming."

"Scorpion flight, D-M Ground, taxi via Alpha to arming for Runway twelve." The air traffic controllers in the tower were well versed in fighter pilot antics.

Bashful was leading our formation with Hung as his number two, me at three and Marilyn rounding us out at number four. Once in the arming area, a weapons technician plugged in his headset, confirmed that my switches were set in safe mode and went to work pulling all the safety pins for the gun and bombs I'd drop today. Finally, he set the limiter on the gun to a hundred—the number of bullets we'd use for sport shooting today—and sent me a crisp salute. I returned his salute and smiled at his benediction, "Happy hunting, sir."

We were ready, and a thumbs-up went down the line from Bashful, then a head nod, and we motored the canopies closed in unison. Again, Bashful's voice sounded over the radio: "Scorpion, check," and in rapid succession—

"Twoop."

"Threep."

"Fourp."

A good crisp initial radio check-in was usually the harbinger of a good mission, and what could be better than this? The cloudless Arizona sky beckoned. Light winds and perfect visibility set an ideal stage as my flight commanders took me for my first trip in many years to the massive Barry M. Goldwater Range Complex to drop bombs and strafe, or shoot, the Warthog's GAU-8 cannon.

Bashful spoke once again over the noise of eight enormous GE engines: "D-M Tower, Scorpion, four A-10s, holding short 12, VFR to the west."

The air traffic controller responded almost immediately, "Scorpion, D-M Tower, winds 140 at 10, Runway twelve, line up and wait."

We taxied onto the runway in pairs, making final checks of our radio and flap settings and checking one final time to be certain the ejection seat was armed. Just as Marilyn slid into position, the tower cleared us for takeoff. Bashful acknowledged the clearance, and I could see the noses of the huge airplanes squat as the engine power spooled up, each pilot's feet planted firmly on the brakes, preventing them from moving.

Ten seconds after Bashful and Hung were rolling, I gave Marilyn the "run 'em up" signal, circling my index finger in the air, did one final check of engine instruments and, with a big head nod from me to Marilyn, released brakes and started to roll. Off the ground, gear and flaps raised, and Bashful and Hung started a lazy right turn a quarter mile ahead. Only a few hundred feet off the ground, I cut across Bashful's flight path for the rejoin. Moments later, Marilyn and I slid under and behind, tucking ourselves into position on Bashful's left wing.

We skirted south of the city, keeping well clear of Tucson International and its airline traffic, and headed for Kitt's Peak. Bashful used a series of visual signals to spread us into a tactical formation before we descended to 250 feet off the desert floor, pushing the airspeed up to 300 knots. Approaching the O'odham Indian Reservation, Bashful sent the flight to the range control frequency. And the games commenced.

Bashful: "Range Control, Scorpion, four A-10s, three by 30, three by 15 POP, three by low angle strafe. We are booked for 1400 Zulu." He advised the Range Controller of our planned events—three 30-degree dive bombs, three 15-degree dive bombs from low altitude with pop-up delivery, and three passes each with the gun, the aforementioned sport shooting.

Damn, I was getting a hard-on, I thought wryly. This was the absolute shit, and I'd missed it more than I thought.

The Range Controller responded by clearing us onto the range and assigning targets he wanted us to use. Bashful wasted no time leading a slow climb to proper altitude to begin the first event, 30-degree dive bombs. He also called for a fence check, indicating we were crossing an imaginary line that signified hostile territory or the "fence," the cue to arm our weapons. The eleven different weapons stations on the wings and the gun were controlled by switches. Switchology" was crucial in the A-10 because a switch error could result in a failure to release your weapon or a "dry pass." During training, a dry pass counted as a complete miss. In actual enemy territory during wartime, the cost could be much higher.

We took our spacing, entering the pattern. Bashful first.

"Lead's in hot." Bashful's voice was terse as he rolled the airplane on its back and pulled the nose down. From the pilot's vantage point, 30 degrees was perilously steep; airspeed building dramatically, wind noise deafening over the canopy, and the ground rushing to meet you. Bashful took his shot, hitting the "pickle" button to release the bomb, and then executed a hard six G escape maneuver off the target. The ability of this large and ungainly beast to be so light on its feet was one of the many reasons for its legendary survivability.

The Range Controller's voice came across the radio after only a moment's hesitation. "Forty at twelve, lead." Bashful's bomb had hit forty feet beyond the target at twelve o'clock if the range was a clock face. Not bad at all. What we all wanted to hear on the radio was "shack"—pilot speak for a bullseye. Was that a British accent I'd heard when the Range Controller spoke?

Hung was up next. His deep voice sounded over the radio. "Two's in hot." *Hot* meant armed and ready to wreak havoc on the target.

"Cleared hot, two." The Range Controller's voice had a definite British clip. How did a Brit end up in the Arizona desert? He was one fish-out-of-water motherfucker.

Hung's bomb was fifty at six. Fifty feet at six o'clock. And I was next.

No pressure, Happy. It's only your reputation on the line. Turn base leg in the pattern, check switches for the umpteenth time and visualize that imaginary thirty-degree wire extending up from the target to your gun. Roll the Hog on its back and, while staring at the sky, pull the jet to the invisible line. Good. "Three's in hot."

"Cleared hot, three." The Englishman again.

Hurtling toward the desert floor now; altitude unwinding, airspeed increasing, and my gunsight tracking upward toward the bullseye. In a split second, a thousand mental calculations and corrections and…

Pickle.

I pulled hard on the stick, executing a six G recovery. My 190-pound body weighed over half a ton with this amount of gravitational pull acting on it. The "G-suit," high-tech chaps with inflatable bladders that help keep blood flowing to the brain during high G maneuvers, squeezed my calves and thighs hard, forcing blood back toward vital organs and buying me valuable split seconds of consciousness. My peripheral vision narrowed briefly all the same.

As the G-forces eased, my vision returned completely, and I looked over my shoulder, spotting the smoke marker from the bomb. *Nice job, Happy.*

"Five at 2, three." The British voice was all but smug.

Fuck me sideways. Five feet off the bullseye? Would it have killed Prince Charles to call that a shack? Five fucking feet?

And on it went. Low-angle bombs were much more in my wheelhouse, but my flight commanders didn't struggle there either. Bashful and Hung were within ten feet; the rusted and abandoned truck that functioned as our target was frightened but uninjured. So far.

My turn. Accelerate downhill, three hundred twenty knots this time, then three fifty; pop up, acquiring the target. Roll the beast onto its back, staring momentarily at the desert floor. Pulling hard, visualizing the invisible wire.

Relax, Happy, just let it happen.

My inner motivational speaker pattered a steady litany in my head, coaching and encouraging. The pipper tracked the wire, touched the target, and I pickled. I glanced over my shoulder at the target, and my face relaxed into a wide grin as I soaked in the glorious sight of smoke billowing from the truck's windows.

"Shack, three," with proper British reserve. *Yeah, baby. Beautiful.*

More passes. More bombs. My flight commanders were top-notch pilots. But now it was time to shoot the gun.

That gun. The one that made the Soviets tear down The Wall, pack up their tanks, and go the fuck home. At least that's the way every Hawg driver told the story.

Shooting the gun was a piece of cake. Enter the range at low altitude, pop up, pull to the wire. Set the gun cross on the target, adjusting continually for estimated winds. Push as close to the foul line as you dared and squeeze the trigger. Ignore the thunderous noise, the vibration shaking the entire airplane as if in the grasp of God Himself, the smoke obliterating your windscreen as you hurtled at the ground, the smell of cordite. Hold that massive gun completely steady for a half second. Just a piece of cake.

After three passes, the range gods had smiled. Bashful hit the target with eighty-five of his allotted hundred bullets, Hung with eighty-seven and Marilyn with ninety-two. And the old guy, the square-filling, ass-kissing staff geek? Ninety-nine of a hundred.

Fuck, yeah.

Our range period was expiring, fuel dwindling, and it was time to head for the barn. Bashful led through a high and dry pass to reform us into close formation before exiting the range.

The Brit came over the radios. "Scorpion, do you have all your scores?"

Then Bashful. "Affirmative, range control. Thanks for the work, Oliver. You coming to the O'Club tonight?"

Mother. Fucker.

These guys schmoozed the wing scheduler to get their favorite range controller. Probably just hedging their bets, so the new guy didn't kick their asses. That explained the five-foot score. A smile played over my lips despite myself. They obviously knew the old fighter pilot adage, "If you ain't cheatin', you ain't tryin'."

We all enjoyed a leisurely ride back to the Davis-Monthan traffic pattern, Bashful using visual signals to direct us to an echelon formation for our arrival. His voice came across the radios one final time. "D-M Tower, Scorpion, ten miles southwest for initial."

The tower responded immediately. "Scorpion, Davis-Monthan

landing runway twelve, winds 120 at ten knots, altimeter 29.98. Report five-mile initial."

Even in the busy traffic pattern of a fighter base, a four-ship of fighter aircraft turned heads. We flew over the runway at 1500 feet in close formation, pitching out in sequence through 180 degrees, then extending the landing gear and flaps. After making a continual descending turn back to the runway, we touched down one at a time.

And while there were important tactical and practical reasons for using formation, I always answered this way when the question was asked: "It's fun, it looks cool, and chicks dig it."

There was one chick in particular I hoped would dig it.

Chapter FIFTEEN

"Take These Broken Wings"

Camille
About Five Years Earlier

L uckie did find me, although I have no memory of it, of
course. And thank God she did. They thought I had been
unconscious behind the club in a parking lot for between
an hour and two. Luckie, accompanied by one of the bouncers,
found me in a gravel ravine near the dumpsters, hidden by some
tall grass. The cops were on the scene and were looking as well,
but it was my shit luck that Luckie saw my bleeding and bruised
body first. The bouncer saw me immediately after she did, but she
outran him and prevented him from moving me. Like so many
nurses in emergency situations, her education and experience
kicked in, subduing raging emotions temporarily. She treated me
for shock and worked to stave off the bleeding until emergency
personnel arrived to transport me to the emergency department
I supervised. The EMS paramedics told her she'd have to follow
them to the hospital in her private vehicle, but Luckie apparently
let fly with such an astonishing and shockingly profane diatribe

that they helped her into the truck. She started one of my IVs along the way to the hospital, called our entire crew of friends, and never left my side.

I was stabilized after a long and arduous course in the trauma room of the ED, where Luckie tucked herself into the corner, dry-eyed, again refusing to leave, and willed me to live. I regained consciousness sometime on the third day in the ICU to find Luckie, filthy and exhausted, clutching my hand and sleeping at my bedside, head resting on the mattress and cheeks tear-stained. When she awoke, she told me I had sustained three fractured ribs, a severe concussion, a badly bruised trachea, and aspiration pneumonia. I'd lost between three and four pints of blood, mostly from the trauma of the rape. Several hours of surgery were required to repair internal damage as well as three blood transfusions.

Luckie stubbornly refused to leave my bedside for the nine long days I stayed as an inpatient. We passed most of the hours of each day in my bed, her body tucked snugly behind mine, my exhausted head resting on her shoulder while daytime TV droned in the background. She didn't interrogate me about what happened, but I occasionally offered bits and pieces as they surfaced from my subconscious like so much floating trash in the ocean. Luckie gently bathed my broken body and helped the other nurses as they changed my dressings and removed sutures. The other girls brought clean clothes, babysat Solomon, and picked up shifts to keep the ED staffed in the absence of both Luckie and myself.

With no family to care for me, I wondered privately about my recovery period. A waste of time, as it turned out since Luckie had applied for an unpaid leave of absence while I was still unconscious. She drove us both to my house on the tenth day following the attack and patiently helped me navigate the endless distance from her car to my bedroom. Samanthe had delivered

Luckie's clothes and a couple of boxes of personal items as well as laundered my sheets and towels. Prescriptions for pain meds and antibiotics were filled and lined up on the kitchen countertop. A pot of homemade Italian wedding soup bubbled on the stove, and Solomon's bowls were clean and freshly filled.

My throat tightened as I noticed the huge bouquet of flowers and balloons next to the medications. Luckie opened the card, read it smiling, and handed it to me. I read the hauntingly gorgeous words of Lennon and McCartney with tearful eyes. "For our Camille, it's time to 'take these broken wings and learn to fly.' With all our love and everything we have—Sam, Viv, Gracie, and the Gang. We got your back, bitch."

There was no path to anything but recovery with these women standing at my side, even though the roadblocks were never-ending. Tissue and fluid samples recovered from my body and the scene yielded no reliable DNA, partially due to the staggering amount of my blood that marred the evidence. Security cameras in the club and the parking lot were mostly nonfunctional, and the footage available was fuzzy and scrambled enough to be useless. There was no realistic possibility of finding and prosecuting my rapist.

Yet I improved, healed, and prepared to return to work and my life. My friends visited Luckie and me almost daily, bringing food, magazines, gossip from work, and encouragement. Seven weeks after my release from the hospital, my dearest friend drove me to my follow-up appointment. Our spirits were high, and we agreed to celebrate with a cocktail afterward.

The physician was a professional acquaintance and was genuinely gratified to see my progress and my anticipation regarding a return to work. We discussed the satisfactory nature of my healing, the ongoing counseling, and possible future ramifications of an attack like mine. He seemed pleased with my condition and asked if I felt ready to return to work. My heart leaped, and the smile lighting my face told the story.

He made a playful joke about returning to the salt mines as he began to fill out requisite forms Luckie passed him from her bag. I'd need to check in at employee health for a physical, and the rest was mostly phone calls and formality.

His medical assistant appeared at the door, her face troubled, and motioned for the doctor to join her in the hall. He excused himself with a smile, leaving the paperwork on the counter, and walked out, closing the door. Luckie and I smiled at each other uneasily. Surely there could be nothing further?

When the door opened moments later, the doctor's eyes were soft, and he took his stool immediately, ignoring the paperwork. He took a deep breath, put his elbows on his knees, and spoke softly. "Camille, there's no easy way to say this." He lifted his face and his eyes met mine.

"You're pregnant."

Chapter SIXTEEN

"This One's for the Girls"

Camille

The prevailing sentiment in my overtaxed brain was if I stared at next month's schedule for one more moment, I would need to be committed. The paperwork associated with the charge nurse role was anyone's least favorite part, at least any real nurse, I reasoned. Unfortunately, scheduling—that never-ending Rubik's Cube—and its evil twin, performance reviews, were important to the nurses on my unit, and they were therefore important to me. Just one more look at the numbers, I thought, and I'd call it done.

Vivvie skidded to a stop outside the door of my tiny office; it was more of a closet, really, and her head poked around the corner. "Come on, sister, they just called from the truck. Two traumas en route, ETA five minutes."

I was on my feet in an instant, throwing my stethoscope around my neck and patting my pockets for gloves and pens. "What's up?" I caught up to Viv, who was jogging down the short hall toward the trauma rooms. Vivvie had been a nurse a year longer than Luckie and me. The staff on the unit looked up to her and valued her opinion. She was also my de facto backup and had filled in for me years ago during my hospitalization. Day to day, she ran things when I was on paperwork lockdown, but the charge nurse was always called when serious cases came in.

"We couldn't understand what they said beyond an arrival time. Damned cell phone's on the fritz again," Viv griped. "We're getting set up in the meantime. I've already talked to Neal in the blood bank. He's a basket of fucking sunshine, as usual."

"I'll take the first one, Camille." Samanthe's melodic voice came from around the corner. "I've got trauma four ready to go…well, almost." I saw a terrified nursing student running at top speed toward the room Sam had indicated, her arms full of liter bags of IV fluids. Sam's smiling face popped out of trauma four as we rounded the corner. "Okay, ready now. And I have the student with me," she added unnecessarily, grinning and raising her eyebrows. That poor student was probably ready to shit herself. I remembered the feeling all too well.

"That poor kid's gonna shit herself," Viv remarked. "She's not the adrenaline type. She needs an Ativan and a massage." She raised her voice. "Okay, where are ya, Gracie?"

Grace's tiny form stomped from trauma two, and she planted herself square in our path, fists on hips. Her eyes blazed, and she dug in her pocket for an additional barrette to pin up her always uncontrollable ponytail. "Luckie's in there with me, but the IV cart's empty as poop. Seriously, Camille, if I find out who allegedly 'stocked' room two"—she indicated finger quotes around *stocked*—"I'm going to give them a piece of my shit." Her eyes flashed with annoyance. "I mean…oh dammit." Her little feet continued their angry trip to the supply room.

Vivvie snorted, and I laughed along. "Camille, we've gotta teach that girl how to swear like a proper nurse. She's giving the profession a bad name." Grace's inability to curse the wallpaper off the wall was a constant source of amusement to the staff. The more enraged she was, the more ridiculous her tirades became.

"Luckie's certainly the person for that job," I interjected. "She's the Princess of the Profane, the Countess of Cursing…" I pushed a cart and a couple of wheelchairs out of the hallway and closed two doors to patient waiting areas.

"The Overlord of the Obscene?" Viv offered, laughing. Luckie's potty mouth was a thing of beauty, a real work of art, and all the funnier because her jaw-dropping looks rendered her salty vocabulary completely unexpected. We both continued preparations for the arrival of our patients for a few minutes before the sound of the ambulance backup signal sent everyone jogging toward the outdoor ambulance bay.

Vivvie and I pushed through the double doors into the late afternoon sun, and the paramedics swung open the doors of the truck. I could hear the rest of the nurses hurriedly following us, my team ready to handle whatever disaster had been brought to our door.

I stepped forward to meet the familiar sandy-haired paramedic. "Hey, Joe, what've we got?" He pulled a stretcher from the shadowy interior of the truck, and I cocked my head.

Behind me, I heard Luckie murmuring under her breath. "What the actual fuck, Josephine? You ass-faced twatwaffle… For this, my peach cobbler is getting lukewarm?" She turned and walked inside, the door closing quietly behind her. Vivvie snorted softly.

In the waning afternoon light, safety-belted onto the stretcher sat a young woman. She was sweaty and disheveled but smiled weakly. Her shirt was partially open, and her sweatpants hung in a knot from one side of the stretcher.

In her arms, clutched to her mostly bare chest, was a small bundle wrapped in a tee shirt and a foil blanket used by the paramedics for heat retention. I motioned to our nursing student and stepped forward, pulling her alongside me for a closer look. I'm a sucker for a teachable moment.

A wee pink face peeked out of the bundle. "Congratulations, Mama." I smiled at her and partially unwrapped the baby who immediately let fly with a mighty howl. "All pink, all good." I rewrapped the baby, still screaming indignantly, murmuring quietly to our student about the critical need to keep newborns warm and dry.

Grace offered me a knit newborn cap she'd retrieved from inside. Pulling it on the baby's damp head, I spoke over my shoulder. "Samanthe, can you call L&D? Tell them we've got a delivered precip coming up the back elevator. Mom and baby look fine. We'll meet them in two minutes at the back door to Delivery."

Grace took my place in reassuring the new mother while the other paramedic wheeled the stretcher and both patients through the doors and toward the elevator. The ambulance bay emptied out, and I turned to Joe with an arched brow. "Two traumas?" I smiled a little. There were many worse outcomes than this one.

"So I guess our fucked-up phones screwed us again?" Joe's face offered an apology. "We heard you all were full and considered a reroute; we asked if you had too many traumas to take us. Nobody replied, and she was only a couple of miles away, so we rolled the bones." He started up the sidewalk. "You guys have coffee?"

I motioned him through the doors. Never a dull moment. And thankfully, not all were bad.

The shift finally ended, our third in a row, so a celebration was in order. We changed out of the hospital scrubs, contaminated with blood and God knows what, and made marginal efforts toward presentable before meeting up at our favorite dive bar off Grant Road.

Grace, Luckie, Sam, and Vivvie were seated at the bar with drinks when I arrived. Viv indicated a vacant barstool in the circle. "Sit your fine ass down, sister. Your Cuervo marg—rocks, no salt—will be delivered presently. I recommend you drink up; we are awaiting details on the Abner's date with Colonel Hottie McHottiePants. Spare us nothing." The bartender arrived seconds later and handed me my favorite drink.

"You guys are ganging up on me," I protested. Mmmm…the drink was particularly delicious after the last few busy days. "You organized this assault because I had to make an extra trip to the nursing office to turn in the schedule. I call foul." I smiled and relaxed. It was always a treat to enjoy the company of my best girlfriends; they were my family. They proved that when it mattered.

Grace regarded me with wide blue eyes, sipping her Appletini. "No fair holding out, Camille. Luckie has as much as confessed, so it's your turn to come clean."

I turned to Luckie, feigning shock. "Confessed already? Luckie. What is this, *The Closer*?" I narrowed my eyes, attention still trained on her. "What exactly did you confess, you cheap floozie?"

Luckie swung her barstool my direction and took a slug of her Belvedere martini, fishing out a giant olive for a bite. Judging by the grinning leer she fixed on me, this was her second martini.

I sent an unspoken question to Viv with two fingers held up, my lips pursed. Vivvie confirmed with a single decisive nod. "She beat us here by a country mile, but I have no idea how. Lab results held us up, but just for a few minutes. The first Belvedere was almost toast before we bellied up."

Luckie interrupted, seemingly unaffected by my sidebar with Viv, squinting her eyes and poking the air with her index finger in my direction. "I fucked him. In the coat closet. And some other places." She took another sip and met my eyes. "Here's what I have to say about that: he's anatomically gifted. Seriously, Cam, like I've never seen. And hot. As fuck."

Okay. I swept my gaze across the other members of the group. "Who are we talking about?" I turned again to Luckie. "Gifted, you say? Can you elaborate, Lucinda?" I giggled like a kid.

Luckie carefully placed her martini on the bar and was making a considerable effort to demonstrate a measurement with her hands. Apparently failing, she had another healthy swig of martini and began to dig through her purse in search of a visual aide.

Samanthe took the bag from her hands and signaled the bartender for a glass of water. She patted Luckie's arm and handed her the water glass while surreptitiously handing the martini off to Grace. "Lipstick's all you're likely to find in there, Luckie. With any luck, that won't work for your demonstration. Maybe sip this water for me, mmkay?" She looked up at me. "Now, Camille, were we about to hear from you about the date with Nathan?"

I was silent for just a moment, considering my answer. "It's been such a long time since I had a date, any real date. You guys tried, but they were dead ends. But I do appreciate it, you know that." I looked around the circle, noticing they had all put drinks on the bar and were listening intently. "He's different in ways I can't pinpoint. Good ways, but I'm still figuring out what those are. He's attentive and very interested in what I have to say. I haven't shared everything, but he seems perceptive about the particular way that I'm broken. He doesn't know about the attack. Or Amos."

I paused for a drink, but the girls waited. "Something happened when we met at the hospital. It sounds ridiculous, but something in me recognized a kinship with him, you know? Some kind of common ground. I think that's why I ran scared." I sighed. "Can't explain why, but I felt drawn to him."

Vivvie put a hand on my thigh and squeezed. "Babe, you don't owe anyone explanations. You know we're all over the moon to see you pushing outside your comfort zone a little. There's no pressure to figure things out or justify your feelings." She took a drink and smiled again. "Just enjoy the ride. Nobody deserves happiness more than our girl, Cam."

Samanthe raised her glass, and the rest of the group joined in a silent toast. The heaviness in the atmosphere dissipated, and then Luckie listed dangerously in her seat and swung to face me. "So." She cocked her head. "Did you let him jam your clam?"

The group dissolved into gales of laughter. Grace picked up Luckie's martini glass, holding it upside down. One errant drop fell to the floor. "That Belvedere really packed a punch, huh, Luce? Don't sugar-coat it; just ask her straight out."

Luckie shrugged, finishing the giant tumbler of water and signaling the bartender for another. "I'm just asking what everyone else wants to know but doesn't have the martini to ask." She raised an eyebrow in my direction. "Spill it."

I could feel a flush heating my chest and creeping toward my face. Historically, there were no secrets in this circle. Nurses tended to treat sex very pragmatically and weren't easily embarrassed. With years of friendship under our belts, this kind of information routinely flowed between the five of us. But I was never on the sharing end. Maybe Sam was right about the cobwebs in my vagina.

I looked down at my hands, fidgeting, and grinned. "Well, for the record, the deal was not sealed. Not completely." Looking around, I could see I had everyone's attention. Sex always made for riveting conversation.

"This is duly noted," Viv said, waving her hand, "but further investigation is warranted. Please provide lots of graphic details."

I hesitated a moment, torn about sharing this particularly personal detail. "He did push through some uncharted territory." All eyes were trained on me. "Actually, he…gave me an orgasm."

Grace's eyes were wide blue pools of amazement. Her thick hair fell over her shoulders and partially obscured her eyes as she leaned forward, her posh mouth a perfectly formed "O." "No one ever before? I mean, not even you?"

I giggled again at Grace. "Shut your gorgeous mouth, Gracie. You're giving the men at the other end of the bar public wood, for God's sake. You look like a fucking blowup doll when you do that." She snapped her mouth shut and covered it with her hand, snickering. I continued. "Yes, me, of course. I mean I'm very competent at taming the shrew."

This time it was Samanthe who snorted. "Polishing your pearl? Spanking the kitty?"

Luckie joined in good-naturedly. "Bruising the beaver? Buttering the muffin?" Hydration had partially restored her vocabulary, albeit the most vulgar portion.

The entire conversation dissolved into laughter and filthy jokes. We ordered a second round of drinks for everyone except Luckie, who got Perrier. Round trips to the bathroom were accomplished, and then Sam again directed the conversation to the topic of my date with Nathan. Everyone settled in to hear the details. "So," she began, "this is the first orgasm with a boy situation?"

My gaze dipped again to my lap. "Yeah, I gave him the heads-up on what he was dealing with, but he didn't hesitate." Another sizable gulp of margarita now for courage. "Ladies. He knows his way around the female anatomy, on the serious. Isn't that a little unusual?"

Samanthe tossed heavy blond locks off her shoulders, blowing away an errant strand. "What level of expertise are we dealing with here, Camille? Dirty talker? Talented hands and mouth? Big, dreamy dick?"

"Haven't seen the equipment, yet, although things feel promising," I shared. "Yes to the other points, but I was actually talking about navigational abilities. A man who knows about the G-spot and the clit hood? I don't have enough experience to speak to it, but I think his abilities are above average. Not to mention the fact that he got me off and left it at that. In fact, he insisted that we wait for anything further."

There were some surprised expressions among the group, but Sam spoke. "Kudos to Colonel Hot-As-Fuck. I, for one, am not very tolerant of some douche canoe who wants to play amateur hour between my thighs. If you don't know what you're doing… well, damn. Haven't you ever heard of the Internet? Do your diligence and give me a call when you don't screw like an eighteen-year-old on prom night. I know your anatomy like the back of my fucking hand and will have absolutely no trouble making you see God. Do me the same courtesy. Be a man, know what's up, and be the fuck in charge."

Luckie toasted her with Perrier and a suppressed belch. "May there be one like him for every one of us." We all raised our glasses for the umpteenth time and toasted great sex.

Chapter SEVENTEEN

"Rollin' with My Homies"

Nathan

It was a fairly ridiculous turn of events for a Wednesday, but I was assured by everyone from the LPA to Coach that the first hump day of each month was reserved for after-work beers at a place renowned for having the coldest and cheapest beer on this side of town. As it happened, that place was a strip joint. And not just any strip joint, but Captain Bob's Showboat Lounge.

Captain Bob's was unexplainable in the way of so many establishments dedicated to male entertainment. It was—and there's no other way to describe it—a boat, constructed of stucco, concrete block, and sheer willpower right on the side of a divided highway directly outside the main gate of the base. It sat between a gas station and a self-storage warehouse. The glare of the late afternoon sun rendered it an even more stark addition to the suburban landscape than it was already.

But inside? Captain Bob's was an arctic-chilly oasis from the Arizona heat and served two-dollar drafts—and an all-you-can-eat buffet for the truly adventurous. I didn't have the stomach for a strip joint buffet, but the beers would slide down easily enough. I was more than grateful to escape the punishing heat Tucson served up from May until October.

The Scorpions filtered in individually and in pairs as the workday drew to its conclusion. A singular stripper hanging on the pole seemed disinterested in us; she spun listlessly from time to time, but it could hardly be called dancing. She occasionally drew an old iPhone from her G-string and stared at it. The fact that Captain Bob's was a gentleman's emporium was incidental. If the local tire store or pet shop had served beer this cheap and this cold, we would likely have gathered there on Wednesdays.

Miles and Boo were already seated, cold beers in hand, when I arrived. Both greeted me somewhat halfheartedly, but I didn't expect better. Coach indicated an empty chair on his side of the table and signaled the waitress for an additional beer.

"How goes it, boss?" He sent me an easy smile.

"All good, Coach." I indicated our unenthusiastic entertainment, still staring at her phone. "I take it she's 'filling in for the vacationing El Sleezo dancing girls?'"

Boo perked up immediately. "No way. A quote from *The Muppet Movie*? Kickin' it old school, Happy—right on." He stood for a high five, which I returned with a grin.

Coach turned to me. "Officially downhill to the weekend now. Are you prepped up for the Salt float on Saturday?"

I accepted an icy draft from the waitress with mumbled thanks and turned back to Coach. "Salt float? Not up to speed, I'm sorry to say. Even for a fighter squadron, this is a damned social group. Pretty hard for the FNG to keep up." I returned his smile and slugged back enough icy beer to bring on a wicked ice cream headache. Pressing both palms to my aching temples, I continued, "Is this a Salt River thing, Coach?"

The Salt was a lazy river through the scenic desert just due east of Phoenix. It was a popular destination for groups looking to spend a long afternoon drinking and floating in inner tubes in the cool, mountain stream-fed waters. Little to no skill was required beyond the ability to load a cooler and make a playlist. I'd enjoyed the trip in the past during my days at the Schoolhouse.

"We're making a road trip of it this time, Happy," Bashful chimed in, digging in his pockets for singles. "Everyone meets up at the ranch outside of Mesa on the river. We'll cook out Friday night and meet late Saturday morning for the float trip. Anyone who wants to stay Saturday night is welcome." The group was smiling, and heads nodded in agreement. He continued, "We've done this annually for the past several years—lots of good times. Bring a lady along, if you have one. The river and the scenery's a leg-spreader, boss. I'd lay odds that plenty of us will get lucky on the river."

Deliverance's head snapped up from the conversation he was engaged in. "Who said 'Luckie'?" His easygoing tone and smiling demeanor shifted in a heartbeat. "Who?"

"Relax, D." Bashful punched him playfully on the shoulder. "I thought you said nothing was going on." Foster sent him an icy glare. "And anyway," Bashful continued, "who's this Luckie? Does this have anything to do with the locked coat closet last Friday night at the Club?"

Deliverance leaned back in his chair and cut his eyes to his friend. "None of your fuckin' business, Jacob." He emphasized the name Bashful answered to only when his mother used it. "Lucinda and I are just getting to know each other."

Miles piled on. "In the coat closet? D, really? Couldn't even make it to a flat surface?"

An evil little smile played around Deliverance's lips, and he studied his icy beer mug. "Extraordinary opportunity requires exceptional creativity."

"And flexibility is the key to airpower," I added with a smile.

Turning to Coach, I said, "I'm a go for the river this weekend. Who's the **PROJO** for this soiree?"

"Talk to Rock, Happy." Coach indicated the tall, dark lieutenant seated with Miles. Shit, they were making pilots younger every year. "He's got the details on lodging, and you give him bucks for stocking the communal cooler for the river."

Rock stood, leaning across a couple of seats, and offered his hand. "Hayes Hudson, Happy, but everybody calls me Rock. I haven't had the chance to shake your hand. Welcome, sir." He had dark, serious eyes that warmed when he smiled. "I'll get you info on the lodging. Be sure you call today and get a room. I'll make sure we have the biggest damn cooler on the river filled to the top with the coldest damn beer on the river." He ticked off items on his fingers as I dug into my wallet for cash. "We'll be cooking out Friday night. I'll bring everything we'll need. Nothing fancy, just burgers and brats—and make sure to show up early enough to man a grill. There'll be breakfast before the float, and you're on your own for everything else."

It sure was great to have someone else in charge of the fun. I shot the breeze with the group while drinking a second beer, and Rock briefed me on a few additional details. I pressed some cash into his palm and turned to the group. "I'll see you gents—and you, Miles," I added with a friendly smile, "bright and early. If I don't get home soon, Mayze's gonna be in an even worse mood than usual. And that's saying something."

Goodbyes were exchanged, and I turned the truck toward home. It would still be a stretch to call it that, except that Mayze and her particular brand of malcontent resided there with me. It was early in the game, but I hoped that Camille might consider a weekend away. In the light of what she'd shared with me, I fought the urge to press ahead too quickly. We both brought a truckload of history to the table, and I had the distinct impression that she hadn't told me everything yet. No matter. I was more than hooked enough to stick around for what was to come after intermission.

Inviting a woman out of town for the weekend, especially this early in the game, was a minefield. A myriad of assumptions existed, but I couldn't see any other possibility. I wanted the time away to learn about her. For one thing, I had some real concerns. I'd treated it as casually as I could the other night, fingers buried deep in her hot little pussy, but she was tiny. And untried for—what did she say—five years? Biology made pretty much everything possible, and I'd be lying if I denied that my cock ached at the thought; but I had concerns about our "physical compatibility," for lack of a better term.

Turning into my driveway, I shook it off. Of all the worries accompanying a new relationship? That was one I could handle. I would relish the opportunity to worship her tight cunt and worry her clit with orgasm after orgasm. After that, taking the length of my cock, inch by inch, would be a challenge she'd beg for.

Mayze greeted me at the door, dour expression firmly in place, and led me to her food bowl. I cleaned and filled it, along with her water dish, before arranging it all on the back patio, scratching her ears. She busily drained her water bowl, which I dutifully refilled, and I prepared to return inside. Suddenly, a face appeared from the top of the fence separating my yard from the one next door.

"Hey, Colonel! It's me, Adam—remember me?"

I had to laugh. Who could forget this kid? "Hey there, Adam. How's the leg mending?" I moved closer to the fence.

With great effort, Adam worked his heavily bandaged leg over the top of the five-foot privacy fence. "It's awesome, Colonel, see?" He gestured wildly with one hand, indicating the offending limb. "I can ride my skateboard, but Mom won't let me go to the pool yet. It's too hot not to go to the pool, but Mom says I have five more days. Maybe it's four…" His voice trailed off as he hung from the fence, oblivious to the possibility of further injury.

Boys. Did I put my mother through this?

I said my goodbyes and pulled my phone out of my flight suit pocket. Hesitating for only a moment, I dialed. The silky alto of her voice as she answered had my cock reacting without delay. "Hello, Nathan. How are you?"

I grinned and shook my head at how the mere sound of her voice rearranged the pieces of my day, dropping everything into place. Leaning against the door frame, I sighed and twisted the top on a bottle of water I'd retrieved from the fridge. "Hello, Camille. Much better now that I hear your voice." There was a brief pause, and I wondered if she felt uncomfortable in light of the intimate way our date had ended. "How are you, angel?"

This earned me a giggle. "Well, to be frank, today sucked, Nate. But that's the life of a nurse. The emergency department is an accident going somewhere to happen. Actually, it's where the accidents come *after* they've happened. It's not like any nurse is ever going to tell you everything went well at work—at least not two days in a row." There was a pause, and I could tell she was taking a drink. "Wine helps, but not always enough." Another giggle, then the requisite snort. "I hope your day was better?"

Mine was improving with each passing minute. "Glad to hear wine is helping. That's the job of wine, right? I'm surviving the week, and I've just this afternoon discovered something that may make everything even better. At least I'm hoping you'll think so." The possibilities were great. "The Scorpions are floating the Salt this weekend and making a road trip of it. Any chance you're available to join the fun starting Friday?"

Her hesitation was only slight. "I love floating the Salt…but the whole squadron? And the whole weekend?" Her tone was enthusiastic, but I sensed she needed a little reassurance.

"A couple of nights at a rustic guesthouse on the banks of the river, grilling out with everyone on Friday—sounds like fun, right?" I swallowed and continued, "I'd really like the chance to get out of town with you for a couple of days, Camille. What do you say?"

"I'd like that too, Nate." Then a deep breath. "Is this too much too soon?" She almost seemed to be talking to herself. "No, I'd really like that. Anyway, I'm already in overtime after today. It's been that kind of week." I could hear the smile in her voice. "So where do I sign up?"

"It's all taken care of, Camille. Casual clothes, swimsuits, and nothing much to sleep in, okay?" My cock hardened at the thought. "I'll pick you up at your house after lunch on Friday. Sound good?"

"Sounds perfect, Nathan. I'll see you then."

There was a pregnant moment between us. Then, "Camille?"

"Yes?"

"I can't wait, babe. I really can't wait."

Chapter
EIGHTEEN

"For Everything There Is a Season"

Nathan
About Three Years Earlier

"Nathan, it's a horse, not a camel." She shot a concerned look over her shoulder. "Dude. This is not rocket science. Hon? Haven't you ever ridden a horse?"

I had not.

The fact that I was currently astride one of the beasts for the first time, well north of my thirtieth birthday, probably said everything about what this girl had done to me. Eliott was completely unlike any woman I'd ever met. On the surface, we were nothing alike. "Not alike" didn't refer to the attraction of opposites; it had more to do with completely divergent worldviews. I felt our existence required orderliness, a clear arrangement of the major events that defined who you were and what was important. Education was the first priority. Then the launching and stabilization of a career, followed by a search for the person who would share your life. Children followed marriage, and on it went. Order. Organization. Control. That was The Nathan Morgan Philosophy in a nutshell.

Not Eliott. No, indeed. If I'd known about her background, the gene pool that hatched Eliott with one L and two T's, I'd have been much less surprised. Her mother and father were doting, loving flower children who must have time-traveled from the 1960s. They made pottery, which became sought after and collected by the rich and famous who came to Taos for yoga retreats, holistic cleanses, and the like. As the years passed, the demand for their beautifully rustic pieces continued to increase, leaving them, to their eternal horror, accidentally wealthy.

They adored their only daughter, a surprise who came along in their early forties, and named her Angel Fire. Yep, Angel Fire, the town where she was conceived, they excitedly explained at every opportunity. She was homeschooled and grew up with nary a preservative nor nonorganic foodstuff passing her vegetarian lips. She adopted her mother's maiden name, Eliott, and left her native Taos to study art at the University of Arizona. It was there that she captivated me, leaving me helplessly in love with her hippy-dippy ways. It was only a matter of weeks before I was seriously considering settling down, a plan that turned my controlled world on its ear.

She was everything I was not. And she seemed as enchanted with the systematic order that characterized my life as I was with her free-spirited chaos. I simply could not make sense of how it happened, but I'd never felt this kind of love before. Except for the horse thing.

"Wait, Eliott, just a damn minute." I rearranged my ass on the not-remotely-ass-shaped saddle. "I'm having a hard time remembering why we're doing this." We were on an accompanied sunset ride in the desert outside Tucson. The "accompanying party" was a no-shit cowboy who was seriously unimpressed with my complete lack of ability. That alone wasn't an issue because what Eliott wanted for her birthday was a characteristically simple gift: to share a sunset over the Sonoran desert together. I'd made arrangements with the dude ranch cowboy to see us safely to a scenic vista, hand over the picnic, and make himself scarce until our celebration was complete. After that, we would require his assistance to return to the dude ranch to avoid becoming coyote food.

"Nathan, riding a horse is as basic a skill as cleansing your chakra or boiling an egg." Over her shoulder, she fixed me with a patient look. "How have you grown to be a man without knowledge of a horse?"

I stifled a snort. "I'm pretty sure having knowledge of a horse is against the law, Eliott. I'd think a vegetarian would know that." I was teasing, and her laughter warmed me, although I wasn't sure if she was laughing at the joke or my riding.

The three of us crested a rocky overlook; and the cowboy dismounted, unloading the rustic picnic I'd brought for the two of us. I brought my horse alongside his and slid gracelessly down the side of the long-suffering mare. She regarded me with pity.

Eliott dismounted with ease and patted her mare affectionately. She spoke to her quietly, a conversation just for the two of them. The whole universe loved this good-hearted woman. How had I ended up in the company of this kind of perfection? I was suddenly seized with the urge to find a way to assure that she was mine. We belonged together forever, and I wanted to nail it down. Rehearsing this plan in my head made me realize I sounded like a demented stalker. I needed to avoid scaring this perfect creature away. If I panicked and used a heavy-handed approach, she'd be running like Flo-Jo.

The cowboy approached and spoke in a low baritone. "I'll give you two a half hour. Sunset will be over by then, and we'll head back. Sound good?" I nodded my head and watched him walk away, leading his horse. It seemed so odd that he pulled a phone from his jeans pocket and started texting.

I turned to Eliott and offered my hand. She smiled and reached for me, walking toward the basket containing our little picnic. "It's not much, Ellie, but we can have something else when we get back to town if you'd like." The horses secured and resting, I pulled Eliott to a smooth rock where we settled on the blanket I produced from the basket. The sky was beginning to turn dozens of shades of purple, pink and gold as I unloaded a baguette, a hunk of Brie and a bottle of blended red. I poured the wine into plastic tumblers found in the bottom of the basket while Eliott pulled off hunks of the bread and sliced the Brie with a butter knife. We toasted the sunset and drank deeply.

The sunset and robust wine filled the space between us before I spoke. "I've never felt this way, Eliott."

That was profoundly awkward, Nate. Recover, man.

But Eliott turned to me, her face placid. "Of course you haven't, Nathan. Neither have I." She let the silence stretch out, carried on the long rays of the setting sun, in no hurry to explain what she'd said. Maybe she could clarify what I couldn't articulate. "This moment hasn't ever been, before now, but it's ours in this instant. There's no reason either of us would have felt this before." She turned and directed her warmth and smile at me. "It's never existed before this minute. Before right now."

I didn't have to reach for her. She set her wine in the basket and crawled on all fours to my lap, wrapping her body around mine. Her smile grew even warmer, and the entire world became the soft woman wrapped in my arms. "I love you, you know, Nathan." Her voice was relaxed. It was easy for her to tell me of her love; she gave it so easily. "I know you might not be at that place yet, and that's okay." She squeezed my waist with her arms, fingers pressing into my skin. "But I can't wait for a safe moment to tell you my love for you is growing. It's important that you know—you already matter more than breath for someone in this universe, Nathan. And that someone's me."

I didn't have words yet, so I pulled her closer to my body. Our mouths melted together, tongues searching and arms clutching. On a gasp between kisses, my eyes found hers, and I whispered, "I love you so much, Eliott. I can't believe you're mine."

How could this have happened? Out of order, out of my control, and I was nearly delirious with the joy that suffused every bit of me. The abundance of good I felt in that perfect moment made my world somehow orderly.

Chapter
NINETEEN

"Holiday Road"

Nathan

Two and a half hours flew by as the GTO ate up the miles between Tucson and Mesa, where Camille and I would spend the weekend with the Scorpions. She insisted on a stop at Circle K on the northern edge of Tucson and returned to the car moments later with two slushies for the ride—grape for me and cherry for her. We entertained each other with more flying and nursing tales and by periodically wiggling our respectively purple- and red-stained tongues at each other like kids. If Camille was feeling hesitant about meeting and spending time with my new squadron, it didn't show. But I was far more occupied with my longing for her and my wonder at this development. In a life largely characterized by rational choices and well-thought-out plans, she was the most welcome and pleasant of surprises. What was more, I sensed increasingly that she felt the same for me.

"How is life thus far as the exalted Grand Poobah of the Scorpions?" Camille sucked noisily at her slushie and turned her body to face me, knees tucked under her. My eyes wandered briefly from the road and took in her long, smooth legs.

"Going as well as can be expected at this point, I think." I shot her a wry smile. "I was brought in to clean things up a bit, as whatever grapevine you are subscribed to accurately told you. For me, the surprise has been how welcoming and likable the group is, on the whole." I hesitated. "I guess it doesn't speak well of me, but I expected things to be otherwise."

Camille tilted her head. "I can certainly see why you would have expected the worst. You were brought in as a fixer, and it was obviously the most poorly kept secret in Tucson. If I knew, you could bet they did, too. They must have known their own press. Only someone who was completely unaware would have shown up to fill the squadron commander shoes, under those circumstances, expecting a welcome parade. But I have a different theory, an absolutely valid one that I'll now share. And I just concocted it—just this minute."

She grinned and raised her eyebrows. "They want help. You know, like someone with addiction issues who subconsciously leaves clues for family or friends to find. They want to break with the destructive behavior patterns because they know it's damaging. But they don't know how." She found me smiling and walloped my bicep with her fist. "Hey, don't laugh at me, El Jefe, I have a minor in psychology." She laughed when I rubbed my arm, feigning serious injury.

"A psych minor? This is an unnerving development." I grabbed her hand and turned it over, kissing the palm softly. "I think information like that should have been disclosed at the outset, don't you?" She scooted as closely as the seat belt and bucket seats would allow. "And I'm not making fun of you. I just saw you putting on your nurse hat, and it was kinda hot. Besides, I like that you listened when I was talking and took the trouble to mull over my problem." I squeezed her soft hand and rubbed my thumb over hers. "In my experience, people just don't listen. They're not present in the moment because they're contemplating their next move or thinking over a way to make their own point. It's not that communications break down. It's that there isn't any communication to begin with."

We rode in companionable silence for several miles, the sunshine in our faces and the wind whipping through Camille's long ponytail, harnessed in a ball cap. After some time, I spoke again. "Are you nervous, Camille?"

Her eyes shot to me, and a trace of panic tinged her reply. "Nervous? What do you mean? About the…you know, the fit?" The pitch of her voice escalated, words tripping frantically over one another even as she failed to complete a single thought. "From the other night? I mean your, umm, size? That is, your… penis? Which is totally fine! Really. It's great. Better than fine."

I tried to interrupt her frenzied outburst, but she babbled on. "I mean, I've been thinking about it. A lot. Not your penis, but you know… It. We don't have to do, that is, I wasn't expecting…"

The adrenaline coursing through her and fueling the diatribe also distracted her from the fact that I'd slowed the car and pulled onto the far part of the shoulder, well away from traffic, unbuckling as I did. I interrupted the hysteria with my mouth, pressing her insistently into the seat and kissing her plush mouth into silence. I sucked on her plump lips, teasing with gentle little bites, and then kissed deeper into her mouth, letting one hand explore the warm skin under her tee and moving it to feel the edge of one delectable breast. Those heavy curves, soft and warm, the small pink nipples…they'd been the stuff of my dreams since I'd sucked them briefly into my mouth. Once she'd relaxed into the seat, submitting to my kisses, I lifted my head slightly, looking into her wide azure eyes. Her breathing was harsh, and her pulse danced wildly at her throat.

I smiled and barely touched my lips to hers as I spoke, so she felt me as she heard the words. "You've been thinking about my cock, angel?" She tensed and readied herself for launch again, but I shushed her briefly with my mouth. "That's good, baby, because your tight little pussy's been on my mind, too. I've taken you a thousand ways in my mind this week. Lying in the dark, my cock hard and weeping while I stroked it, thinking of the taste of you, the sounds you make when you come." I looked at her beautiful eyes, impossibly wider. Was it fear that I saw there? My hand caressed her warm cheek and caught in the ponytail, tugging gently. "Camille. Hear me, angel. I'll take care of you, I promise that. Nothing could be more important, beautiful. You can trust me. Nod your head if you understand."

Her eyes were shiny and welling a little, but she nodded her head and buried it in my chest. I pulled the cap from her head and stroked the silky hair and the warm skin of her back until I felt her relax, her breathing almost back to normal. A few minutes passed, but I gave her the time she needed. Then she sat up, her beautiful face lit with a small smile, and kissed me briefly. "Thank you, Nathan. I just panicked a little. There's more to tell, but I know I can trust you. You've already shown me."

I hugged her hard, kissed the crown of her head and handed her the ball cap. "What do you say we get to the lodge, get some icy cold beers and meet the gang? The weekend's gonna be a blast, Camille." I tweaked her nose and pulled back onto Interstate 10. "Anyway, that's what I wondered, kiddo—are you nervous about meeting everyone?"

She relaxed completely now, letting go with a belly laugh. "All that drama and you just wanted to know if I was ready to meet everyone? Now I feel like a complete idiot." She slurped at the dregs of her slushie. "I already know a few people, Nate. You know Luckie's coming as Davis's guest, right? There's some shit going down between those two—I know it—but she isn't sharing. Clammed up tight. Oh, and I know Bibi from the hospital.

What a great girl. Do you know anything about all the rehabilitative work she does with children?"

I didn't, but I did already know that Bibi was something special.

"And, of course, I know Jake 'cause he's Vivvie's brother. She'll probably be along, too. Has he shoveled you the bullshit about their being twins?"

I laughed along with Camille, everything relaxed again, because Coach had warned me about the twin thing, and I'd met Viv at the flight suit party. "Listen, angel, the Stingers have plenty of problems, but that stuff's mine to worry about. You won't find a more hospitable bunch of people. I think you're going to like them, and I know they'll love you. As far as I'm concerned, though"—I reached for her hand—"this weekend belongs to you and me. I'm looking forward to learning more about you, inside and out." She squeezed my hand. "Just be yourself and have fun. The Scorpions are just normal guys and girls, you'll see."

Our trip was at its end, and I turned the GTO into the lodge's drive, passing an expansive lawn along the river and approaching two clusters of individual cottages. In the middle was a swimming pool, the apparent center of Scorpion activity. Four couples in bathing suits were engaged in serious chicken fighting in the center, ladies balanced on the wide shoulders of their men, everyone trash-talking enthusiastically while the women worked to take down the others as if their lives depended on it. On mismatched beach chairs around the pool, two-dozen bathing suit-clad partygoers reclined with cold beers in hand and cheered the couples on. A pickup truck parked under a large tree served as a temporary bar, filled to the brim of the bed with ice and canned beer. Perched on the top of the truck cab was Rock, clad in only a wet bathing suit and a cowboy hat. In one hand was his beer, in the other, a fifth of Cuervo Silver.

As we pulled into a parking space, one of the women in the

pool successfully sent Bibi, kicking and swearing, into the water from Coach's shoulders. She surfaced, smiling and sputtering. She shot her husband a withering glance, and then looked in Rock's direction. He rang a cowbell that had been hung from a tree branch above him and laughed loudly, a big grin splitting his face. Then he bellowed toward the pool, "Come on, Bibi! Come and get your medicine." We watched with amusement as Bellamy Bennett stalked from the pool to the truck, trailed closely by Coach. Upon her arrival at the appointed spot, she obediently tipped her head back and received a generous splash of tequila from Rock's stash. Coach waited until she'd swallowed, grimacing, and then bent her backward for a showy kiss. He grinned at her like no one else was there and growled, "Tastes good, baby. Daddy like."

The crowd broke into cheers and catcalls as I opened Camille's door and offered my hand. She stared somberly at me. "'Fozzie, they don't look like Presbyterians to me.'"

I grabbed her hand, laughing, and headed for the lobby to check in. "Watch out, baby. Your *Muppet Movie* is showing."

Chapter TWENTY

"In the Air Tonight"

Nathan

Our satisfied bellies were full of burgers and brats, clean-up had been accomplished, and now sunset was looming. Thirty or so members of the squadron, along with spouses and guests, lounged in the generous yard, enjoying a blazing fire built and tended by the LPA in the big fire pit. Most sprawled in folding beach chairs, but Camille and I had withdrawn to a quieter area a short distance away and were lying under a tree on my trusty stadium blanket. I was surprised to learn that Hung possessed a good bit of musical talent. He had parked his lanky frame on one of the oversized wooden benches around the fire pit and was treating the crowd to some acoustic guitar—James Taylor, Paul Simon, The Beatles. He even lent his deep voice on some songs with others joining in occasionally. The raucous crowd was settling in for the evening, enjoying cooler air and the always-stunning desert sunset.

"Hung," Camille mused. "What kind of nickname is that?" She sipped a cold bottle of water. "I'd be afraid to ask him. But he sure has a nice voice."

"The only thing you can be sure of when it comes to call signs is that nothing is as it seems." I laughed easily, remembering some of the offbeat and downright bizarre tacticals I'd seen my friends stuck with. "I haven't heard the story of Hung's naming ritual, but I bet that it's more to do with bombs than what he's packing."

Camille laughed along. "Well, you'll have to let me in on it. It's for certain I'll not be asking him myself." The crickets were tuning up their nighttime symphony, and the sky grew darker. "You were right about everyone, Nate. They were so easy to meet and went out of their way to make me feel included."

I turned on my side, propping my head on an elbow, one finger lazily tracing her jawline. "That's one of the hidden benefits of the military—you make friends quickly. It's most obvious in the kids. For civilian kids, changing schools is a big deal, sometimes even traumatic. Military children almost never stay in one school longer than four years. Three is more common. You'll routinely hear of a high school senior graduating from the fifth school they've attended. Moving around makes you flexible and, in most cases, friendly."

I went for a fresh round of cold drinks and returned to find Camille lying on her back with her eyes closed, a gentle smile softening her face. I nudged her butt playfully with a bare foot and handed her the Sam Adams I'd dug from the ice of the truck bed. "Whatcha grinning about there, gorgeous?" I dropped back onto the blanket and stretched out right next to her, our hips touching, heads close.

"Ah, I love this song. It's special." Hung was working through the intricate finger picking of The Beatles' "Blackbird." Vivvie perched on a chair nearby and sang harmonies with Hung when the chorus came along. The heavy blackness of the night wrapped around us now, making our blanket under the tree feel like a haven. I felt, more than heard, Camille take a deep breath, and then she reached for my hand. "I need to tell you things, Nathan. More things. And it's not so easy."

She was quiet, so I gave her room, rubbed my bare foot against hers, and waited. "About five years ago, I was attacked." In the space of a split second, a raging fire roared to life in my belly, but I fought back a physical reaction so as to allow her to speak in her time.

She continued in a quiet voice, wavering at times, but clear. "Luckie and I were at a local club with some younger nurses. She went to look for them; and while she was away, my drink was drugged. Toxicology showed a combination of Rohypnol and ketamine, so potent that the drugs alone could have killed me. I don't remember much." I waited while she took a couple of deep breaths. "There were at least two of them, but I couldn't give the police any help with details. Ketamine has an amnesiac effect, among other things. They raped me repeatedly and beat me very badly. I lost an immense amount of blood. There were fractured ribs, a head injury, and lots more."

She rolled toward me, an unexpected smile lighting her beautiful face. "But my Luckie found me. In a ditch behind the club, where they'd thrown me like garbage. She came for me, stayed right beside me, slept in my bed, fed and bathed me. She made me live. She wouldn't let me go, didn't ever give up. I owe her everything, Nathan."

My hands were in her hair, and I pulled her head to my chest, caressing her face and running my fingers through her sweet-smelling hair. The huge lump in my throat made it hard to speak. "Beautiful, beautiful girl," I murmured in her ear. "Who could hurt you? I can't imagine it." I couldn't say anything further, my throat tight and eyes burning.

She pulled herself to an elbow, lowering her face until it was inches from mine. "Before we go to bed tonight…together, I needed you to know that, Nathan. But there's more. I don't blame myself for being raped. I know so many victims struggle endlessly with guilt and shame, feeling they were somehow to blame, and my heart aches for the burden they carry. But that burden isn't mine. I know it wasn't my fault."

She paused and tilted her head away from me, reflective. "I've always seen things differently from others. I could've been destroyed by parents who didn't want me and aren't part of my life, but I chose to embrace my friends instead of a family I don't have. Or I could have allowed this attack to color every part of me and break me. But I can't do that. The unexpected blessing in it was finding out that I had friends who are the best people in the world. They didn't walk through the fire with me; they walked into it and rescued me." She looked into my eyes again. "Without the darkest night, how could we appreciate the stars?"

She looked over near the fire where Luckie and Deliverance were laughing as she tried to wrestle something from his hand. "My heart is so grateful every time I allow myself to think about the way Luckie and my other friends put their lives completely aside to give everything they were to me. Nate, they worked overtime, canceled vacations, nursed my Solomon back to health after he went out and got his ass kicked in a brawl with the tomcat next door." She choked back laughter. "On the day that Luckie brought me home, I found flowers from my girls welcoming me home. And the card said, 'Take these broken wings and learn to fly.'" Her voice broke a little, but she recovered and looked back at me. "It's been a long road—years long—but I think I've finally learned how to fly."

My mouth was on hers in an instant, my hand on the back of her head, cushioning it as I rolled her onto her back and searched her mouth with mine. I felt her warm hands on my shoulders and neck, and a little moan escaped as she opened herself to me, now literally and figuratively. Her hips rolled slightly toward mine, unconsciously seeking, and it was then I realized we needed to get behind a door. Right fucking now. My fingers tangled in her hair, pulling our reluctant mouths apart. "Come on, baby. Time to go."

She drew in a deep breath and quickly jumped to her feet, grabbing the blanket while I took our empties to a large trashcan by the fire. Camille dug into the ice in the truck bed, extricating four water bottles, and joined me, already offering a goodnight to the dozens of Scorpions still enjoying the fire and Hung's music. We were the first to leave, and the reasons would be painfully obvious if I strayed too near the light of the fire.

I hugged Camille to my side, and we waved our goodnights. Luckie grabbed Deliverance's hips from behind and thrust her own several times in rapid succession, her head lolling with faux passion. She stopped and winked at Camille, throwing a kiss. "G'nite, babycakes," she called. "Don't do anything I wouldn't do."

Camille tucked her hand into the back pocket of my jeans as we made our getaway. "I gotta be honest with you, Colonel. With Luckie? That isn't a very long list." She grinned up at me as we made our way to Cottage #5. I unlocked the door and pulled her inside, wrapping her securely in my arms as I did.

Chapter
TWENTY-ONE

"Midnight Angel, Won't You Say You Will?"

Nathan

"Safe place, angel." I breathed the words against her mouth and kissed her softly, ending by tracing her lips with my tongue. "It wouldn't have been different if you hadn't shared, but I definitely need you to know that now. I'm a safe place. I'll go with you anywhere you want to go tonight, but it happens when you want it. When you need it." My lips traced her jaw and the hollow beneath her ear, moving then to her neck and licking the racing pulse there.

She tucked her face into my neck and gripped the waistband of my jeans, whimpering. "I do need you, Nathan, please." Her breath was harsh against my neck, but she eventually wrapped my jaw in one hand and lifted my face to meet hers, our eyes locked together. "I want this, Nathan. I want to feel you moving inside me. And I'm not afraid." She swallowed and breathed deeply, calming herself. "I'm not damaged goods. You don't have to treat me with kid gloves."

I couldn't imagine another woman who would leave herself so exposed and vulnerable in a situation like this one. Five years. Five fucking years. The forces warring in my chest screamed to protect her and to own her completely. I pulled her tee over her head, dropping it to the floor and pulling her to me. "I need to feel you against me first, Camille. Just you and me, nothing between."

She shimmied out of her shorts, tossed flip-flops against the wall and stood in the dim moonlight that streamed through the rear window. Only a white cotton bra and small white panties separated me and her perfection. I held her eyes, stripping out of my shoes, jeans, tee. The black boxer briefs remained, barely containing the ache between my legs, and I pulled her to me again, keeping our eyes locked. I nuzzled into her hair, intoxicated.

She groaned and hooked her thumbs in the waistband of my underwear, beginning to slide them down my legs as she sank slowly to her knees. My cock throbbed uncontrollably at the sight, and it took every ounce of self-control I could find to divert her attention back to my face. "Angel, you don't have to take me in your mouth tonight. Babe, you don't." As much as I craved the heat of her wet mouth on my cock, I'd been harboring concerns about her ability to take my length. When I'd fingered her little pussy on the sofa, getting even two fingers in hadn't been easy. A good, up-close look at what felt like the biggest erection of my life might send her packing.

Her voice was quiet, and her breathing stilled as she looked at my face. "I want to know all of you, Nathan. I want to know how you taste, how you feel. Let me see you, baby." She set her hands at my waist and pulled the briefs down, allowing my cock to slip free, thicker even than usual and almost painful with arousal. I watched her study my hard length, heavily veined, distended and nearly purple. The head was wide and pulsed upward toward my abs as she traced the underside with her finger, then her tongue. It swiped suddenly upward to taste the thick drops of precum dripping from the head. She swallowed noticeably and looked into my eyes. "You're delicious, Nathan. Want more, please." Before I could process anything beyond her words, her mouth was full of my cock, and I was flying. Her tongue strummed the frenulum, occasionally dipping further. One hand curled around the upper part of my thigh; the other gripped the cheek of my ass, squeezing. With both, she pulled me closer. Then I was swallowed much farther as she took the substantial length of me and slipped her wet tongue down to sweep across the root of my cock.

A strangled chuckle escaped my lips, and I worked to form words. "Damn, baby...damn. What the hell...no gag reflex?" My ass tightened as an orgasm began to swirl like a tornado at the base of my spine. Holy fuck, I was going to come like a freight train unless I got a handle on this, and fast.

Then my hands were under her arms, hauling her up my naked length. "Camille," I rasped, "the bed, baby. Get on the fucking bed. My cock can't take more of that. I'm gonna fill your mouth now if we don't stop, and there's so much more than that for tonight." She took my hand and stood at the edge of the bed, unhooking the front of her bra. The straps slid slowly off her arms, soft breasts falling free of the constraints of the fabric. Then, as my eyes trailed farther down, she pushed the panties down her legs and kicked them into the corner. I could see the shadow of a lovely scripted tattoo decorating her ribcage on the left side. "Perfect, baby. All pink and wet, so perfect. My mouth wants all of you, angel. Your nipples, your breasts, the folds of your pussy. Lie back, Camille. I'm so hungry."

She stretched out on the fluffy down duvet, arms over her head, and pulled her slim legs onto the bed's edge, bent and open wide. There, open to my gaze, was her pale pink cunt. Glistening, tight, and completely bare. I dropped to my knees. I could discern her heartbeat as I stared at her pulsing clit, swelling and peeking out from under its hood. I would come back for that. A bead of honey slid from her slit, and I didn't hesitate a second before dipping my tongue to taste her. A moan fell from her lips as my tongue pushed past her opening. "So good, Nathan." Her legs spread impossibly wider, and she dragged a finger through the wetness, drawing slickness up and over her clit. Then she raised herself on her elbows to meet my eyes. "I want to watch you eat me, Nathan."

My tongue bathed her smooth outer lips, moving idly toward her opening and breaching it, tasting the luscious wetness there and humming my pleasure. I lifted my eyes to meet hers, dark navy blue in the moonlight that dappled our naked bodies. Lapping at her pussy now, I allowed my tongue to stray toward her clit, indolently circling. Her eyes fluttered closed, upper body melting backward onto a pillow. She moaned and tugged at my hair, urging me on. "Please, Nathan. More, baby…need more." The pleading tone of her voice alone made the ache in my cock even more severe, and I felt cum drip from it, the warmth sliding down my stomach as I knelt, worshipping her.

I allowed my tongue to lave, unhurried, across the distended knot of her clit, slowly gathering speed. Teasing her entrance with one finger, then two, I pushed them slowly inside, marveling again at the snugness. My tongue never slowed, lashing her clit as she pushed her hips off the bedclothes and into my face. Two fingers inside fucked her at a leisurely pace. "Close…" she breathed. "Yes, baby." Her fingernails raked my hair frantically, and her walls closed on my fingers and rippled, hard and rhythmic. She cried out, coming in my mouth, and her warmth baptized my fingers and tongue.

I continued to bathe her gently with the flat of my tongue, lessening the pressure gradually and easing her down. When her hips relaxed, and the spasms tugging at me subsided, I moved to her side, leaving two fingers inside her, stroking gently. "Maybe even more beautiful than last time, angel." I kissed her, allowing her a sample of her own intoxicating taste. "I love how your pussy loves my mouth." I dropped my head to suckle a pale nipple, still stroking with my fingers.

Her small hand wrapped around the base of my erection, caressing the shaft slowly and rolling a thumb over the head, now glistening with the precum leaking from the slit. She was a confection fabricated in a dream, blond hair spilling across one breast, pale and illuminated with only the barest moonlight, perfumed with her own pleasure. I reluctantly pulled my fingers from her and brought them to my mouth, relishing the taste, and then rolled my body to cover hers, giving her some of my weight but supporting most on my elbows. Her thighs instinctively parted for me, and the heaviness of my cock settled in the warm cradle of her pussy lips. I stroked her slowly with the head of my dick, appreciating the wetness readying her body for the invasion by mine. My palm curled around the back of her neck possessively, and my mouth was at her ear.

"Angel, this is important; look at me." Her face turned, beautiful, questioning. I stilled my hips and rested against her. "Do you want me to use protection, Camille? I'm clean, and there's been no one since…" My voice faded briefly. "No one for almost four years. But the choice is entirely yours."

Her eyes were soft. "There's been no one for years. After the attack, the doctor said that…well, he said I'll never have a baby. The damage was too severe, even after all the repairs. But for tonight's purposes, I'm healthy, too." She blinked twice, slowly, her eyes never leaving mine, and then wound her arms around my neck. "I want to feel you, Nathan, and I want you to feel all of me, too."

My head dropped to her neck, mouth nipping and licking, and I whispered near her ear. "Slowly, babe, no rush." Her thighs again opened, and the broad head of my cock prodded her slickness. Once, twice, and then with a bit more effort, I pushed myself just inside. At once, she tightened and gasped, reflexively pulling away slightly. I stilled the intrusion of my hips and whispered, "Just a little breath, angel." It was an effort to harness the fire roaring through me. This was almost like the first time. For both of us. A groan escaped her, and then her hips lifted in welcome, taking me. I kissed her jaw and pushed her open slowly with the length of my shaft.

"More, baby." Her voice was quiet, but I felt her fingers squeezing my ass cheeks. "Need more, Nathan." She relaxed a bit more around me, and my cock throbbed, loving the heat.

Beginning a painfully slow stroke, I groaned into her ear. "Love your pussy, angel." She relaxed further into me, and my cock pumped rhythmically, picking up speed gradually. "That's my girl," I whispered. "Take my cock, baby." Fuck. She was hot. And so tight.

She panted softly with every stroke and raised her eyes to meet mine. "I want all of you, Nate. So close now." She wound her legs tightly around my waist and dug her heels frantically into the small of my back, urging me on. Her face begged for release, and I felt her flutter around me.

"Let go, angel. When you're ready, I've got you," I whispered, gripping her and driving her gently against the bed. My cock pushed relentlessly, and a small smile spread across her beautiful face. Her pussy tightened even further and grasped me rhythmically as she panted, gratified. I pushed a hand under her soft bottom and tilted her to better accommodate me, finally burying myself completely. The fitful clutch of her sweet little cunt was all I needed to feel for the knot of cum to rise in my cock, pulsing convulsively from me and bathing her core.

We battled together through the pleasure of our shared climax, clinging to each other and panting. Soon enough, the room was saturated with silence and filtered moonlight, interrupted only by her sighs of pleasure and the occasional kiss or caress I offered her fevered skin.

We lay contented for long moments, soaking in the quiet of the night and cherishing the intensity of what had just passed between us. She spoke first, eyes now lazy but cheeks still flushed. "It's been such a long time, Nathan. I didn't know if I could give myself this way again after...well, after. I didn't know if I'd panic or if my mind would return to revisit that night." Her legs tightened around me, and a soft hand moved to stroke my face. "But my head and my body and my...heart were so full of Nathan." She tucked her face into my chest. "There was no one here with me tonight but you." Her face pulled back to look at mine, relaxed and peaceful. "I see it now, Nate. It just had to be you. There wasn't anyone else."

"Angel." My hands tangled in her silky hair again. "I told you before we first kissed that things might never be the same." My mouth touched hers. "What I didn't say was I was very sure they would never be the same again." I rolled us to our sides, stroking gently under the curve of her bottom. "Sleep, baby. Tonight is an occasion. A fluid bond. Keep me inside you tonight." I tucked her back snugly to my front and pulled up the duvet to protect us from the encroaching cool of the desert night. "Sleep, babe."

Chapter
TWENTY-TWO

"Breakfast in America"

Camille

The night passed in the most perfect way possible, with Nathan's hard body wound protectively around mine. In the wee hours, he roused me gently, offering cold water and tending to the sensitive areas between my legs with a warm cloth. This was briefly followed by the caress of his warm mouth. We slept soundly, the desert sounds a muted background.

I woke to an empty pillow next to mine, shaking my head momentarily and remembering that last night's events were reality and not a figment of my imagination. The room glowed dimly with the beginnings of sunrise, and a brief search of our small room found my favorite new obsession drinking a cup of joe. He was clad only in his snug boxer briefs from the previous night, soaking in the view of the sun as it peeked over the horizon. The sinewy length of one arm reached above him, easily gripping the upper window sill and leaving the perfection of his legs, ass, back and shoulders on display for my pleasure.

I gathered the linens, curling into them and enjoying the

view. "G'morning there, handsome. Are you the real thing or some sort of mirage in the desert?"

He turned to me, grinning, and set his cup on the window sill. "I wondered how much beauty sleep you required, angel. It took quite a bit of self-control to keep from waking you." He reached the bed, sliding in next to my nakedness, and pulled me to him. I felt his cock harden against me almost as soon as the warmth of his body met mine. Reflexively, I reached for him, but his hand stopped me before I could touch him. "How are you this morning, Camille?" he murmured. His hand moved lower and cupped my sex tenderly. "Sore?"

My breath caught a little. He was concerned for me. I wondered how often something like this played out after a night like the one we'd enjoyed. "I'm good, Nathan. Sore in all the right ways and places, honey." I smiled up at him and once again reached for his erection. Solid and warm and pressed firmly between our bellies. "I'd feel so much better, though, full of you."

His smile lit a fire between my legs. He spread my thighs with his palms as he spoke. "Even if that's true, gorgeous, you know..." His fingers lightly grazed the smooth lips of my pussy. "I'd rest easier if you'd let me have a look to be sure. You know, up close." As he spoke, he slid between my splayed legs, pushed them backward with hands firmly holding the backs of my knees, and tasted me slowly from the tight pucker of my ass, across my slit, and finally to the tingling nub of my clit. "What do you think, Camille?" He arched an eyebrow in my direction from his position just above my pussy. "Do you mind if I have breakfast here?"

After a pair of superior orgasms courtesy of Nathan's gifted and apparently tireless tongue, we set about to loll on the patio of our cottage. He sported the cotton bottoms of his pajamas while I wore only the top, a tee that skimmed my knees. To my dismay, he'd insisted that we wait at least until evening for actual sex, concerned about hurting me. The patio wasn't private per se, but it faced away from the other cottages and enjoyed a sliver of water view. Nathan had brought along basics, including coffee and real cream as well as a few pastries. "It's not a proper breakfast, but it'll keep us alive until tacos later," he said, handing me a mug and opening a box from a bakery I knew was near the hospital. I snagged a chocolate croissant and headed to the microwave tucked in a little cabinet with the coffee maker.

"Would you like me to warm your cinnamon roll?" I asked, reaching for it.

"Is that what we're calling it?" he cracked with a wide grin. "Yeah. Thanks, Camille." Instead of handing me the gooey pastry, he stood and followed me indoors, standing at my back as I warmed the sweets, smoothing his hands up and down my curves. Long fingers wrapped around the swell of my hips, resting there.

"You're not so much help, Colonel," I teasingly complained. "How impressed will you be with me once I manage to ruin our treats in the microwave?"

He chuckled, and each of us took a warm pastry, reclaiming cups of coffee and settling again into chairs on the patio. The air was still, and the sunrise thoroughly washed the landscape with brilliant color. In the brief history of this courtship, I'd noted with satisfaction our shared ease with silence. I'd heard discussion among happily committed and long-married friends about how they relished time together without constant chatter, but I'd foolishly assumed they had run short of topics for conversation. Now I reconsidered. There must be endless depths to plumb in the mind and heart of this captivating man. He certainly had much to learn about me—not all of it good and some of it unsettling. Even so, these early days had been marked with intimacy without the feel of an interrogation. There seemed an unspoken acceptance that we would learn about each other organically, and that discovery would happen in its due time. It felt comfortably right, but I couldn't explain exactly why.

Nathan leaned forward, wiped the corner of my mouth with his thumb and licked the chocolate away mischievously. "Really do like the way you taste, angel," he quipped.

"I'm not going to tell you to keep your mouth to yourself, Nathan Morgan." I returned his silly expression with one of my own, but it quickly melted away. I tucked my knees under me and turned to face him fully. "Thank you for making last night what it was, Nate." I hesitated, trying to express what my heart felt in the light of day. "I have a lot of baggage for a man to carry, and instinct tells me it's one of the things that kept me from dating much over these past several years. It wasn't a conscious decision, but these things—my history—it's uncomfortable to suppress night after night as you try to get to know someone new."

His eyes had held mine as I spoke but dropped now and studied his coffee cup. "I wasn't sure the door would open again after Eliott. I didn't force the issue because I didn't feel it was in my hands." His eyes lifted to meet mine, and the pain I saw there caused me to reach for him. "The love I felt for her was not something I looked for or expected, and when she was gone…it didn't seem like anything I could ever replace."

The silence was like a balm for all the years of pain and grief. Our fingers tangled, and we sipped our coffee, eyes meeting and considering. Finally, I broke the silence.

"Both of us went through something that could've broken us but didn't. I'm glad it's you who's in my life because someone else might not understand the depth of this. But I don't want to live my life immersed in all this heaviness. I'd like to look forward, Nate."

He relaxed backward, his naked torso distracting, and stretched. "So, babe. If you want to look forward, tacos are a great thing to look forward to." My eyes opened wide in question, but he stood and led me indoors. He rinsed our cups and swatted my behind as we headed toward the bathroom.

"Tacos? Breakfast?" I questioned. I grabbed a toothbrush and started the search for pertinent toiletries.

"Breakfast tacos, babe. You're a Tucson girl, you know, yeah?" He shoved a toothbrush in his mouth and began to scrub in earnest.

I did. Breakfast tacos were a staple in Texas and the southwest. Soft flour tortillas filled with scrambled eggs, sausage and hash brown potatoes. All of it doused with salsa, sour cream and even guacamole. Heaven in a tortilla.

His mouth was back in working order. "So you know Bibi? Hers are the shit, so she's got the LPA helping her feed everybody this morning before we get on the river. Hope you're still hungry." He grinned at me, wiping toothpaste from his mouth. "We're outta here at 1100 hours for a five-hour float. We'd better eat up, babe."

We dressed quickly in bathing suits with a pair of shorts over mine and a tee over his, grabbing hands, and hurried to the lawn where a crowd of Scorpions was gathered and consuming enormous quantities of coffee. I spotted Luckie, gigantic cup in hand, entertaining a circle of laughing faces with some outlandish tale. Deliverance was leaning on a post and watching, bemused, from a few feet away, his beefy arms crossed. Damn, he was a mountain of a man. I wondered how he fit in an airplane. I made a mental note to hit Lucinda up for some truth after she had been sufficiently loosened by sunshine, bulging biceps and a generous dollop of alcohol.

Under the trees, Bibi supervised a small group of lieutenant eye candy as they arranged steaming tortillas, fillings, and condiments in containers and placed serving implements in each. She stepped onto a chair, cupped hands to her mouth, and announced, "Soup's on, Stingers. Grab it and growl. The buses leave in less than an hour."

Unlike other gatherings I'd attended, no one demurred. The group surged toward the food, obviously comfortable together, chatting and teasing. Nate handed me a paper plate, and we moved quickly through the throng, assembling a couple of tacos and grabbing bottled orange juice from the tub of ice near the end of the line. Plates were quickly emptied and refilled, the group leaning against the trees and sitting in the grass, laughing and telling stories. I marveled at the ease. All these people moved around frequently, making new homes and friends, adjusting to new jobs. They made it look easy, but many people struggled with this kind of rootlessness—wouldn't I?

My quiet introspection was interrupted as Bibi approached, her arms wrapping around me, and pressed our cheeks together. "Camille, love…so good to see you. I didn't have a chance to catch up and gossip the other night at the Club." She landed a hearty slug to Nathan's bicep. "This caveman threw you over his shoulder and took you outside before any of the civilized people had a chance to say hello." Her eyes twinkled, and she squeezed both of my hands affectionately. "How's that calamity of an ED you run?" We spent a few minutes talking shop as Coach crowded Bibi's back, inhaling a plate of tacos. I'd admired her work in the physical therapy department, especially with pediatric patients, since we'd met. She had a real gift with the children and made a palpable difference in her department. Her voice faded back into my consciousness, enthusiastically giving direction for the day. "…so Rock has strong-armed the vendor into having their buses meet us here. They'll take us a few miles upriver, drop us and all our stuff, then the fun begins." Coach wrapped an arm affectionately around her, dropping a kiss on her neck.

"Need to muster the troops, Bellamy. Gotta clean up and get ready. The buses arrive in twenty." His voice was filled with affection. They obviously had a longstanding love match.

Bibi's eyes widened. "Where is the morning going, you guys?"

She scrambled onto the chair again. Her voice was commanding as she waved for everyone's attention. "Scorpions…twenty minutes. Everybody pitch in, and let's clean up quick. We need to pack the coolers and be ready for the buses. Don't forget water and sunscreen. And hats."

The group dispersed naturally, and the breakfast mess disappeared rapidly under dozens of hard-working hands. Groups of men emerged from the front two cabins carrying ridiculously enormous coolers, which were methodically loaded with cans of beer, bottles of water and heaps of ice. Three of the women gathered bottles of sunscreen and assembled a huge stack of beach towels just as two ancient school buses pulled alongside our group. Bibi oversaw the efficient loading of essentials, and we piled in for the ride to the river.

Chapter
TWENTY-THREE

"Bet You Gonna Find
Some People Who Live"

Camille

The drive was a short one, but gallon jugs of homemade Bloody Marys were passed around with a stack of plastic cups and drained in very short order. The mood was jovial as the buses were unloaded of passengers, coolers, and a few waterproof sacks. Dozens of inner tubes were likewise unloaded from a trailer one bus pulled, and the group began to claim and subsequently load the tubes. Half a dozen of the tubes were specially modified to hold oversized coolers, but the rest were up for grabs. The group surged toward the river as the empty buses pulled away; and Nathan waded into the chilly water, offering me his hand.

The sun was rapidly rising into a clear, azure sky and the temperature climbed accordingly. The Salt River was brisk at the moment, but I knew the water would soon feel soothing as we fought a losing battle with the encroaching Arizona heat.

Nate held my tube in place, and I shivered in the thigh-high water. "Jump in quick, Camille. Don't think about it, just do it!" I squealed like a kid and jumped in. Nathan was right behind me, grabbing my tube and lashing us together with a nylon rope. The river carried us lazily along, and sunshine lit up the lapping current like a million diamonds. The group gradually formed up, forty or so loosely connected oversized tubes, with huge coolers of drinks taking up the middle portion of our floating party. As I surveyed the group, mentally making note of those I knew, the unmistakable sounds of "Rock and Roll Band" by the seventies band Boston boomed from the far side of our floating gaggle. I strained to look toward the sound and was able to make out yet another wildly oversized inner tube contraption, this one painted fuchsia and topped with plywood, with an oddball assortment of speakers, wire, and…was that a car battery? I turned to Nate, mouth agape, and muttered, "What the…"

He burst into laughter. "Yeah, I forgot about that; Coach told me. The LPA's 'Unprofessional Engineering Squad' apparently erected this atrocity about ten years ago for use on the float trips and to demonstrate Scorpion superiority." He air-quoted "Unprofessional Engineering Squad." "Every year it undergoes supposed upgrades at the hands of new LPA members, although I'm dubious about the term 'upgrade' in this case. This year, I'm told, Rock decided to spray paint the whole business hot pink to draw attention to its 'finely detailed craftsmanship.'" A final set of air quotes and Nathan flopped back in his tube, chuckling.

I was impressed. The thing had to be five feet tall and sported a variety of speakers looking like they might have been poached from a junkyard. An air horn and an "Ooo-ga" horn sprouted from the top at a jaunty angle. Still, the sound quality was pretty good. My careful study of this auditory curiosity was interrupted by a strident female voice.

"'Scuse me…coming through. Coming through." The

flotilla parted with some effort, and I saw Vivvie paddling her way somewhat awkwardly through the middle, yelling as she moved our way. She was ridiculously and unconsciously titillating, her sleek, black hair in a careless "Pebbles" ponytail on the very top of her head. She wore a tiny royal-blue string bikini, and long legs were splayed wide over the tube as she jockeyed for position. As if she wasn't creating enough of a disturbance, hot on her proverbial heels was none other than Hung. He, too, worked to negotiate his tube in our direction, but he did so while wrangling four icy beers in his lap. His paddling, I noted, was even more frantic than Viv's, and no wonder. He was probably freezing his nuts off. Literally.

"Heads up, Happy," Hung yelled as he approached.

Nate looked up from under the baseball cap he wore and expertly caught the two beers Hung lobbed his way. He cracked one open, offering it to me. "Gotta be five o'clock somewhere." I smiled and accepted it, taking a sip. It tasted amazingly good, although I wasn't in the habit of drinking before lunchtime. I reached for Viv's hand and hauled her toward us. Hung pulled alongside her, opened the remaining cans and handed one to Viv, his eyes heating as his gaze slid along her lithe form.

"Sister." Vivvie addressed me as she finished a long drink of her beer and rubbed the icy can along her neck. "You left too early last night. We were just getting warmed up." She shot Hung a look I couldn't read. "Walker taught me some fighter pilot songs." She leered openly at him. "They're dirty." She ran a bare foot along his calf.

Well, then.

"Yeah, umm, sorry about that, Viv." I fidgeted a little and cut my eyes toward Nate. His smile was easy, and he adjusted his ball hat on his head as he addressed her.

"Morning, Vivvie. We sure hated to bug out on the entertainment last night. You two sounded great." His free hand reached for me, grabbing my hand so he could kiss my palm lightly. "I was tired, and Camille took pity on me. We wanted to be in fighting form this morning for the river festivities, right, babe? Definitely prioritizing that good night of sleep." Now his grin broadened. "Gotta set a good example."

Hung's smile matched Nate's. "Roger that, Happy; loud and clear." He turned to Viv, who continued to run her tanned foot along his leg. "Told ya, Vivian. We were supposed to sleep last night."

Viv met his eyes and deadpanned, "Damn. I knew we forgot something." They laughed uproariously at the implication, and Hung reached for her hand. "I was just so busy investigating the nickname, you know, Camille?" She turned to me with mock seriousness. "Turns out everything is on the level, but I'm concerned about how the guys gathered the information and came up with 'Hung.' Although…" She took another healthy gulp of her beer. "I have heard these fighter squadrons are very close. Very close."

It was my turn to laugh. She looked happy as she and Hung joked and played footsie. Further, toward the center of the group, Bashful was giving Hung the full-on stink-eye. Dating your protective brother's friend could get complicated.

The group floated happily, carried along by the lazy pace of the water; easy conversation and laughter, and cool river water easing the desert heat. Sunscreen and snacks were passed around, and a steady procession of pilots, spouses, and girlfriends paddled over to say hello and offer a welcome to the new commander. The group was smart and funny. I found myself at ease even without Nathan at my side, although he frequently pulled me closer to squeeze my hand or whisper in my ear. It was a convivial, even domesticated gathering, especially considering that *Top Gun* had taught me everything I knew about fighter pilots. The music provided a great soundtrack for conversation, loud enough and fun. I relaxed backward in my tube, hair trailing in the cool water and sipping yet another icy Sam Adams. Nate's hand was warm on my thigh as he chuckled quietly with Coach.

From the corner of my eye, I could see Rock scaling the far side of the bright pink floating stereo. He was clad in boisterous floral board shorts almost reaching his knees, his signature cowboy hat shading him from the sun. The air horn sounded, bringing everyone to high alert, and Rock grabbed the bullhorn bungee-corded to the side of the largest speaker. "This is some bullshit, Stingers." His voice echoed from the rock canyons flanking the river banks.

Huh?

He continued in a voice laced with obvious agitation, "I'm asking myself, after all the hard work I did to be sure this was the best Salt float ever, who the hell was in charge of housekeeping? Of making sure our supplies were **UCMJ** compliant? Of ensuring that cleanliness was next to godliness? Well? Any ideas, Scorpions?" He was pissed, and I was becoming very uncomfortable. My gaze swung quickly to Nathan and Coach, who were barely suppressing smiles. I was obviously missing something important.

But Rock continued, still perturbed. "I hate to ruin your fun, ladies and gentlemen, but I was just inspecting the beer locker." An almost imperceptible movement swept through the group. His voice rose to fever pitch. "And what do you think I found? A. Dead. Bug!"

Bedlam descended on the flotilla all at once. Nate's hand grabbed mine, and I saw his laughing face. He yelled, dragging me into the icy water with him, "In the water, Camille, on your back." His voice brooked no argument, and the group disintegrated into utter chaos as everyone hit the frigid Salt, screaming and laughing. "Feet in the air and grab your tube, babe." He demonstrated, and I saw dozens of floating, yelling Scorpions all around me doing a version of the same nonsensical pose, so I complied.

Coach floated next to me, easily taking a long drink of his beer while holding his feet out of the water. "Rock, you mother-fucker." Bibi floated between his legs, pink-tipped toes also clearing the water as she laughed.

"Well, Camille, I guess it's a baptism by fire. Or river, in your case." Coach's smile let me know that nothing untoward had happened, and I looked around to find the group scrambling back aboard their inner tubes, laughing and replenishing drinks lost to the river in the tomfoolery.

Nathan stood in the waist-deep current and helped me back into my tube, handing me a beer when I'd settled. He jumped back into his own tube and quickly rejoined me, smiling. "More customs and traditions, babe." He signaled Bashful, near the cooler tube, who snagged and lobbed a fresh beer his direction. Nate neatly caught the can, popped the top and continued to explain under his breath. "Should a member of the group call 'dead bug,' everyone has to immediately assume the posture of an actual dead bug. If anyone heard me explaining this to you right now, using that terminology, we'd be toast." He grinned. "I'm supposed to refer to it as a 'deceased insect' and nothing else unless we want to go back in the water again."

I smiled at Coach, Bibi, and Nate. "It seems like a lot to remember. What if I mess everything up?"

Bibi took a long drink of her beer and tilted her head my way with a warm smile. "If you enjoy sticking around, Camille, everyone will help you learn the ropes." She rested a hand on Coach's thigh, gazing at him with affection. "I was a kid when Coach decided he couldn't live without me. He taught me everything I needed to know." It was mesmerizing to watch the two of them; they clearly had what everyone was looking for. Despite many years together, the ongoing attraction was easy to see.

"So, Happy…" Coach turned to Nate and gestured toward the group at large. "How do you think things are progressing here?" The four of us subconsciously drew our circle closer.

Nathan's brows drew together, and he thought silently for a few moments. "It's not what I expected, Coach, not at all. I'd anticipated overt defiance, obvious rebellion to my authority. There's been a whiff of that, with the O'Cherry debacle, but it's not the main issue. At least I don't see it that way. I think there's primarily been a lack of leading from the front. Acting like a grown-up when it counts and letting everyone see that expectation." He paused and sighed. "I'm not saying it's the only issue, but it will make a difference."

Coach nodded his agreement. "The tough part is that it's a likable collection of folks. Funny, generous, easygoing—for the most part. A leadership vacuum is what's brought on the decline in performance; there's been a lack of respect for the rules when it mattered most."

Bibi piped up. "Well, I think you're on the right track, Happy. The pilots like and respect you, and you've shown them you're the real deal in the cockpit and wearing the commander's hat. I'm feeling good stuff from here on out." She raised her beer in a toast.

Rock paddled his tube our direction and called out a greeting. "Hey, boss, Coach. You all enjoying the ride?" He joined our circle and tipped his hat, first to Bibi, then to me. "Ladies. Y'all are looking lovely today. Soaking up the sunshine?"

I smiled at his faux formal demeanor. "It's been a great float, Rock. Best I've ever had, and I've been a couple of times before." I smiled warmly at him. "Can't say I've ever enjoyed a hot pink sound machine before, though. And the beers are the coldest on the river."

He grinned mischievously at me. "Nothing too good for my Scorpions. And I hope the 'deceased insect' didn't catch you off guard, Camille?"

I feigned good-natured surprise. "Of course not. Why would any civilian be unprepared for an event like that? Fortunately, Happy had my back."

Rock turned to address the remainder of our small group. "We're outta here at the next bridge. I'll make an announcement, but I wanted to let you know. Sounds like nearly everyone is spending tonight, but dinner is on your own. I expect we'll be out by the fire again, but it's all informal."

Happy leaned forward to clap Rock on the shoulder. "Thanks for everything, Rock, in case I don't get the opportunity to say it again tonight. This has been a superior effort. Makes me glad to be a Scorpion. You really went above and beyond, man."

Rock smiled and paddled away with a friendly wave. The day was drawing to a close, and I saw a bridge in the distance. Rock eventually reached the stereo monstrosity and again partially climbed it to make his announcement with the bullhorn.

"Stingers," he bellowed, signaling with his hand, "the bridge you see is the take-out point. Stow your drinks, grab your women, and prepare to exit the river. Take care of all garbage, and make sure you leave it better than you found it. This evening, if you've chosen to stay, is on your own. The LPA will build a fire once the sun goes down. Buses are waiting, and I'll see you on the other side." Rock cannonballed from the floating platform into the chilly water to the cheers and applause of the squadron. In no time, we were dragging tubes up the rocky beach toward the waiting bus.

Chapter
TWENTY-FOUR

"Night Fever"

Camille

The door to our cottage slammed with a bang as Nathan kicked it, his hands feverishly attempting to divest me of my shorts and damp bathing suit. His mouth worked mine hard, tongue stroking and teeth nipping. "Goddamn fucking women's clothes," he growled into my mouth, his frustration at getting me naked completely palpable.

The brief ride from the river had been a crowded one. The rafting company had been short of buses and sent only one to accommodate us. That meant most of the women rode on the lap of a husband or boyfriend, and that translated into a spectacular hard-on pressing into my backside. Very conscious of Nate's position as commander, we both had avoided any appearance of impropriety, but the promise of soon being full of his cock left me hot and achy. We had time to make up for.

My hands found the tie to his board shorts, dropping them and quickly peeling off my suit. I pulled him close again with one hand on his tight ass. Between kisses, I pulled away a little, panting. "I have a question, Nathan, and I don't know exactly how to ask."

His hand cupped a breast, thumb circling one tight nipple. His eyes were hooded and stared into my own. "Ask me, babe," he rumbled. "We have a no-secrets policy, remember?"

My eyes dropped briefly, hesitant. "You were so sweet last night, Nathan. So careful with me and gentle." I raised my eyes again to meet his. "I guess it's not as much a question as a re-quest." His eyebrows lifted with obvious interest, fingers now stroking the sensitive skin under my breast. "You don't have to be so cautious, Nate. I mean, a little rough is hot, and I like it when you get a little bossy." Instantly, I felt the sweet bite of my nipple pinched between his thumb and finger. "I'm not breakable, baby. I can take whatever you want to give me and love it. Try me."

My feet were off the floor before I could think, and Nathan stalked toward the bed with me in his arms. My ass bounced as he tossed me carefully onto the mattress. Our room was again mostly darkened with only the rays of sunset filtering through one window. Nathan's imposing form stood at the bedside, look-ing impassively at me as I curled around myself, subconsciously shielding my nakedness from him.

His voice was low and even. "Don't try to hide from me, Camille. Your body's for my enjoyment tonight." One large hand dropped to grasp his straining erection, stroking it slowly from root to tip. My eyes locked on the veins along his length, more pronounced as he stroked hard. It was angry and weeping, the dark pink of the broad head turning to purple as he stroked. He stepped to the edge of the bed and allowed his gaze to drift la-zily along my body as I uncurled and submitted to his eyes. His thumb swept across the head of his cock, capturing several fat drops of precum from the slit. His eyes held mine as he rubbed his thumb along my lower lip, and my tongue darted out to lap up his salty offering.

"I felt empty without you inside me today, Nathan." Our eyes locked, and my mouth couldn't stop spilling my pussy's secrets. "I thought about you, all naked and hard and thick. And fucking me." I rose to my knees and closed one hand over his fist, both of us stroking slowly. "I thought about sucking you and tasting you. You liked that last night, didn't you, baby?" I smiled. "I want to spend more time learning your beautiful cock. I'm good at swallowing you, even as thick as you are in my throat. You'll let me enjoy you, won't you?"

He responded with a growl and pushed me away, turning my body and laying it on the bed while he stood over me. He spread his muscled thighs and offered a good, long look at the power between his legs. His leaking, distended cock jutted from a closely trimmed thatch of dark hair, heavy testicles drawn close to his body. His arms pulled my body toward his, and my head hung slightly from the edge of the bed. He looked at me, his gaze a little harder than I was accustomed to. "Camille, you will suck my cock and take me deep. If it's too much or you need a break, pinch my thigh, and I'll stop immediately. Do you understand?"

I nodded quickly, hands on his ass cheeks, and pulled the succulent head into my mouth, relishing the salty taste of what he fed me from his slit. A groan escaped both of us as I pulled him deeper and sucked gently on the head. His fingers spread the slick lips of my cunt, and two fingers began to stroke down both sides of my clit. Fuck, filling my throat was the only recourse against the screams his fingers were about to tear from me. I took a deep breath and pulled, taking him deeper, relaxing my body for his use, and felt him pop into my throat. My hands at his ass urged him on, and he fell into a rhythm, leisurely fucking my eager mouth. My tongue curled around his length as he stroked, coddling, and the groans escalated. His fingers worked my clit urgently. My arousal was warm, sliding down my thighs and wetting the tight pucker of my ass. His fingers followed, circling there, and returning to torture my clit.

My fingers traced the outline of his testicles, pausing to taunt the area below with more pressure. I felt his pulse there and hesitated, mesmerized, stroking. With that touch, his erection inexplicably gained girth and length in my throat, and he pulled himself from my mouth. "Need to take you, baby. Turn around and spread yourself for my cock." He stroked himself again and crawled onto the bed as I moved toward the head of the bed.

"Are you sure you want me this way, angel?" His face was hard, but his voice was gentle. "You want me rough, using you? I need to be sure, Camille." He knelt between my outstretched legs and stroked my thigh reverently. "Maybe too soon, babe?" His eyes asked, as well as the tone of his voice.

There was something about holding his eyes while we talked about how we wanted each other that sent my body to places it had never been. It raised the raw intimacy of what we were doing to each other—for each other—to a place I'd not experienced. I craved baring myself, trusting him.

"I want it, Nathan. Need it, baby...need you to do things to me no one else has. I want to go to new places; make it good, Nate." My arms stretched above my head, baring all of me for him. I was hungry for what he would give me; my core pulsed and my heart pounded at the thought of what came next.

He didn't question me again. Instead, he studied my outstretched form with hooded eyes, breathing heavily, and reached for me. His fingers circled a taut nipple and moved down my body to drag deliberately between the slick lips of my pussy, gathering the wetness there and again tasting me.

"Keep your hands there, Camille, above your head." He stretched to clasp my wrists with one large hand. "You'll open your legs, and your cunt will take my cock. If I do anything that hurts or scares you, or if you need me to stop for any reason, you'll say 'Solomon.' Say it now, Camille."

I nodded, eyes wide and on him. "Solomon." I stretched my knees wider.

His hand tightened on my wrists, and he gripped his length, bringing it to my entrance. His face dipped until our mouths touched. I felt the blunt tip of him stroke once, then twice, through the slickness. The head circled my clit, tortuously unhurried.

"You need to come for me now, angel. My cock will take you there, but you have to ask." His voice was barely audible above the sounds of his flesh tormenting my slick center. "Ask me, Camille," he hissed. "Ask me to make your pussy come."

My wrists tugged, but his hand tightened. Somehow, the inability to move lent more heat to the pressure gathering between my legs. My hips bucked, needing him inside and pleading for the control eluding me. "More, Nate, please. Please, God."

"Please, what?" He rhythmically pressed his cockhead against the swollen knot of my clit, circling across the top and then pressing the underside.

"Please...so close, Nathan." I'd been almost ready to come by the time the door closed; I needed it so badly now. My eyes pleaded. "Let me come, baby." I couldn't catch my breath.

His mouth dropped to my neck, and he groaned, sinking slightly into me and stretching my pussy with a few inches of his heavy length. At the same moment, though, his finger moved to continue worrying my clit. His hot mouth sucked at my neck, and my walls tightened, igniting a blazing wave of pleasure. My pussy gripped his length, rippling with the ecstasy blooming there, and I came. So easy, so effortless on the hardness of his cock. I threw my head back, baring my neck to his mouth, and smiled at the release I felt around him. My legs wrapped around his waist, and I moaned my satisfaction.

His hand eased its grasp on my wrists as the waves of orgasm subsided. "Thank you, Nate...thank you, baby." I whispered it in his ear, tugging his erection with my wet pussy. "So good."

His face lifted from my neck, and he smiled. His hand released my wrists. "Grip the spindles of the headboard with your hands, angel. I'll hold you down if I need to, but it'll be better if you do it yourself." His cock moved forward an inch, filling me further. "I'm going to fuck you, you're going to take my cum inside you, and you're going to come again on my cock. With me this time. Understand, Camille?"

My eyes were wide. I felt his finger near my entrance, sliding up to caress my still-throbbing clit. He lowered himself again, our mouths touching, as he circled my swollen clit right above where our bodies joined. He gave me more of his length and picked up the pace. Fingering my clit, looking into my eyes, he began to fuck me slowly. Giving me a fraction more of his cock with each stroke, he took us there together.

Then my mouth was open, my head nodding frantically for lack of words, and my legs gripped his hips. Finally, he buried all of his length in my desperate body, bathing the walls with his warm release. Feeling him filling me pushed me over, panting and squeezing him. I was dizzy, drowning in Nathan.

Several minutes passed, and I may have drifted off momentarily. Everything I needed at that moment existed in the clutch of my arms, legs, and very satisfied sex. Nathan's hand sifted through my hair, and he shifted us to one side, still inside me. "Beautiful, sleepy girl." His whispers met my ear as he kissed my neck, and then we both slept.

Chapter
TWENTY-FIVE

"I Can't Tell You Why"

Camille
About Five Years Earlier

ood God, my feet were swollen. My piggies looked like little cocktail sausages, I thought, wiggling them in my oh-so-forgiving Dansko clogs I was splayed like an octopus in my ancient office chair, once again sparring with the schedule. I thanked God for Vivvie for the trillionth time in these past few months. How did nurses work the floor through their pregnancies? At almost twenty-three weeks, I still waddled my substantial ass to emergencies and big triages, but Viv and Luckie handled most everything else. I was grateful to be pushing paper at my desk and attending meetings, for the most part.

Viv, Luckie, Sam, and Grace took turns accompanying me to monthly, then bimonthly appointments with my beloved obstetrician, Lee Scott. We had a professional acquaintance that quickly morphed into something much closer when Luckie and I went for my initial OB workup. Luckie left us alone to talk, and Lee sat next to me on a sofa in her office for almost an hour as I poured out my soul, talking about my estranged family, my dear friends and the events of the devastating night at the club. It never occurred to me to terminate the pregnancy, although I knew and respected that it would've been the choice of many. But it was just that to me—a choice—and Lee knew it as she clasped my hands and absorbed my story. The person who attacked me was a void in my mind, a nonperson, and unworthy of consideration. He didn't exist to me and did not factor in my decisions. But living in my body, growing there, was a life that was given to me for reasons I had yet to understand. The only thing I felt, from nearly the moment of the shocking announcement that I was expecting, was hope. The prospect of a child I could love and nurture was more than I'd ever thought I'd have.

Even my dearest friends wondered and worried at these developments. The girls took turns staying with me, riding my ass about diet and prenatal vitamins and shopping for the nursery. Hormones and the circumstances surrounding the pregnancy brought great emotional turmoil, and these women were a soft landing spot for my frequently ravaged heart. The adjustment period from single girl to expectant mom and trauma survivor, though, was strangely brief. I had always longed for a family, having never felt that kind of care, and this was my shot. Here was an innocent life, entirely dependent on me—this baby needed everything I had needed, some twenty-four years ago. The difference here was I would not fail my child.

There were substantial concerns among those in the community, friends, and acquaintances in the hospital, as well as elsewhere, as I began to show. Again, my friends rallied at my side, quietly spreading the word that I'd chosen to keep and raise the child. My heart was encouraged, mostly finding that people greeted the news with emotional support and positivity.

I chose to see my baby and my pregnancy as a gift, the ultimate silver lining to the darkest hour of my life, though others would doubtless feel differently. And so it had come to be, during the late part of my eighteenth week, that Sam, Grace, Luckie, and Viv had hovered over my round, reclining form in the dim light of the ultrasound machine, their hands variously holding my own or sifting through my hair.

"Anyone see the turtle?" Lee teased us. "All these nurses and nobody sees the turtle?" Her finger outlined what she saw on the screen, and five additional pairs of eyes squinted to see what she did. "See, Camille? There's the little penis, and the testicles on either side." She turned to me with a gentle smile. "Congratulations, Mama. You have a son."

My face crumpled, and my girls were laughing and hugging me, plastering my face and tummy with kisses and love. A son. Then, through my tears, my hands stroked my belly, still covered with the slippery ultrasound jelly, and I spoke quietly. "His name is Amos."

"Wait." Everyone quieted marginally, and Sam scrubbed the sleeve of her lab coat across her teary face. "Be quiet a minute. What did you say, Camille?"

My eyes regarded my swollen tummy. "Amos, the Old Testament prophet. He was different from most of the other prophets—literate, enlightened. And passionate about social justice." My eyes met Luckie's. "Nurture. Not nature. I don't want my son to identify himself as a terrible accident. I want him to know that I loved him from the start."

Her face was soft, looking steadily at mine, and she nodded. "Nurture. And nature. He will have your nature, Camille. He's already a very blessed little boy." She pressed a soft kiss to my forehead. "And his aunt Luckie can't wait to meet him."

I stretched in my chair and remembered each precious detail of that day. My friends celebrated and anticipated the arrival of my baby with all the enthusiasm that I did. I marveled again at the bond we enjoyed and then struggled unsteadily to my feet.

My bladder held maybe three ounces these days. I should probably move my desk into the ladies' room for the duration.

I grinned at Grace who walked behind me, mocking my gait, as I headed down the hall. She kept my freezer stocked with mint chocolate chip ice cream, so the waddle—as well as the size of my ass—was her damn fault anyway. My smile widened as I thought about the baby shower discussions that were underway. The girls, hell, the whole hospital staff, seemed to be pulling out all the stops for the occasion. It was going to be hard, opening presents graciously in front of a crowd. That was never my forte, I thought ruefully. Good Lord, my bladder was tormenting me today even more than usual.

I swung the ladies' room door open and froze in my tracks. My heart was in my throat, my voice so high-pitched I barely recognized it.

"Gracie. My water broke."

Chapter
TWENTY-SIX

"Where I Come From"

Nathan

It was Sunday afternoon, and life was pretty damn good. Our cabin didn't see much sleep last night, so we spent the better part of the morning in bed, dozing and reading. Camille leaned against me, her hair brushing my bare chest, and devoured a racy romance on her Kindle. She kept me entertained by reading aloud the spicier bits as well as a few funny passages. I played at reading the news, but it was impossible to prevent my thoughts from straying back to the soft, warm woman sharing my bed. As checkout time loomed, I took her Kindle from her, rolled her onto her back and made love to her once more. And that's what it was. It was quiet, languorous, nearly haunting. Her arms and legs cradled me as I filled her, over and again, smoothing hands through her hair and watching her eyes darken as we neared orgasm. One of her hands left my back, slipping between us to tease her clit. Her legs hugged me tighter, and she came around me, mouth open and eyes fixed on mine. Gratefully, I loosed what I'd held back and poured myself into her welcoming body. When we were done, I took her mouth, exploring thoroughly.

Her voice was hushed, and she regarded me with wonder. "What is this, Nathan? Where did you come from?" The questions didn't require answers, but I shared her awe. I'd been in love, only once, and it wasn't a feeling I could forget or take for granted. The beginnings were taking root in my gut, and I could only hope fervently that Camille felt it, too.

Now the GTO tore down Interstate 10 on a sure collision course with real life. Like any pair of new lovers, the prospect of returning to work and mundane reality after an escape was a distasteful one. We smiled and held hands, but the conversation was spare. We were approaching Tucson when I turned to Camille with an idea to postpone the inevitable goodbye.

"Hey. Do you want to see where I work? Check out one of the airplanes?" That sounded pretty lame and desperate, now that I heard it aloud.

A smile brightened her face. "That sounds great, Nate." She poked her lip out in an exaggerated pout. "Truth is, I don't want to admit the weekend's over. This could be a good diversion."

I chuckled under my breath at how in sync we were on this; then again, who looked forward to work after a weekend away? Half an hour later, I stopped at the front gate of the base, offered my military ID and Camille's driver's license to the MP guarding the gate, and returned his crisp salute. Pulling away, I heard a muffled snort and turned a faux accusatory glare on Camille.

She uncovered her mouth, threw her head back and laughed loudly. "You're so G.I. Joe; it just kills me."

"G.I. Joe is in the Army, Camille. The Army," I reprimanded her. "You're going to wind up in remedial military girlfriend training if this behavior doesn't improve. You don't want to get in trouble, do you?"

"Girlfriend?" She twirled a long lock of hair with one finger, cocking her head coyly and batting her eyelashes. "Why, Colonel

Morgan. Do you want to go steady?" Her hand slid across the top of my thigh, perilously close to my cock, which immediately took notice. "My parents don't let me go on car dates. How do you feel about sleepovers?"

"I think we'd better not even discuss more sleepovers until I get you alone again, ma'am. I'm going to have some trouble walking, and we'd better hope like hell no one else decided to come by the squadron on the way home." I smiled at her silliness. I could benefit from this kind of easy fun in my too-orderly existence.

I opened her door, and she grabbed my hand as we walked toward the utilitarian building that housed the Scorpions. I tried the door, finding it unlocked, and swung it open. In the main area of the squadron, we encountered Bashful staring at the huge wall occupied by the magnetic scheduling board.

"Ah, hey there, Happy…Camille," he called distractedly, his brows knit together. "Just trying to get some things cleared up here schedule-wise for my lieutenants. We were on track until we got word Thursday that two of our birds were **hard broke**. Screwed everything up. Gotta get these quarterly requirements knocked out." His voice faded away as he swapped a couple of the nameplates affixed to the board.

I dropped Camille's hand and stepped toward him, clapping him on the shoulder. "Thanks for making an effort, Bashful. Keeping up with requirements is an ass pain, I know, and I appreciate you going the extra mile on it." Jake lifted his chin in my direction and resumed his deliberation.

I led Camille down the hall, pointing out my office (still in mild disarray—completely unlike me), the snack bar, and the life support shop. Stepping out the back door, we were met with the imposing sight of a dozen Warthogs, parked in a meticulous rectangular pattern. Each airplane was over fourteen tons of metal, a story and a half tall, with a wingspan stretching almost sixty feet across. The gun, eighteen feet long by itself, jutted from the nose of the aircraft, ridiculously phallic. The thing was a fucking menace to the bad guys. And I was pretty proud of that.

I turned to look at Camille. Her mouth was open but smiling slightly. "It's just…so ugly." She threw her hands up, unable to find a better word.

I laughed, nodding in agreement. "Nobody in the A-10 community will tell you different. We embrace its appalling looks."

She folded her arms, still staring. "Ugly. But scary. It looks like it's in an atrocious mood."

I walked with her toward one of the hulking jets. "It poses a lethal threat to enemies, particularly in tanks, who endanger our troops. Or our interests. The looks are unconventional, but it's very effective in doing the job it was built to do."

I answered a few more questions, grabbed a couple of cold bottles of water from the snack bar on our way out, and we were once again on our way. "As long as we're close, do you want to meet Mayze and see where I live?" I was definitely grasping now.

"Sure," Camille said. "Are you getting all settled in and making it homey? Needlepoint pillows and afghans? Or is that not something a cool fighter pilot bachelor does?" She poked me in the ribs, teasing.

She'd unintentionally hit a chink in my armor. It was home, at least technically. But homey it was not. I'd trained myself to look past the flavor-free functionality that characterized my surroundings. When thoughts of Eliott and the life we'd almost had together surfaced, I saw those visions in Technicolor. She'd brought hue and intensity to my existence. And she took it all with her when she left.

I startled at Camille's voice. "Is this your house?" She didn't wait for an answer as I'd already parked in the drive. Before I could make it around the car, she was jogging for the backyard, then standing on tiptoes and peering over the fence.

"Oh, hello," she cooed. "You're Mayze, aren't you, baby?" She turned to me, face lit with a Camille smile. "Let me in; I wanna love on her."

She was an animal lover. Another check in the plus column, I thought, putting my navel-gazing on the back burner. Unlatching the gate, I squatted to give Mayze a combination scratch/rubdown. She nuzzled me reluctantly, as close as she ever came to lavish devotion, and regarded Camille suspiciously.

"Come on in, angel." I swung the door open, and Mayze waddled in ahead of Camille, making sure she knew who was boss.

"It's a big place." Camille's eyes swept around the adjoining family room and kitchen while I tried to see it with a fresh perspective. Compared to the warm little bungalow Camille had clearly furnished with skill and care, this room seemed hollow. Very beige.

"It *is* big. Maybe a little too big for my taste, if I'm being honest." I led her over to the sofa, moving one of the boxes of books that needed unpacking. She kicked off her sandals and made herself at home there, feet tucked under her. "The Air Force gives me this big three-bedroom because of my rank. I didn't get my latest promotion until right before leaving the Pentagon, and I was a pretty small fish in that pond. No big house, for sure. And anyway, I had a townhouse there in Falls Church. Just right for Mayze and me. Right, Chiquita?" I bent to scratch her belly thoroughly.

Camille bent to join me, allowing Mayze to smell her for a moment, then rubbing her ears and tummy. She was making a lifelong friend already. She straightened and stood, beginning a leisurely perusal of the room. The few framed items decorating the walls of the living room did nothing to dispel the dreary monotony. And it suddenly occurred to me that the lone brass floor lamp was unbearably ugly.

Camille paused in front of a larger black frame and studied the sonnet it contained. "This is lovely, Nathan. I think I've read this poem before."

I walked up behind her, wrapping her in my arms. "I'd be surprised if it isn't displayed somewhere in every pilot's home, the world over." I chuckled. "My best friend from UPT, Nick Bamford, is a Navy brat. His parents, Commander and Mrs. Bamford, gave me this when I graduated from pilot training; she did the calligraphy lettering herself. It's called 'High Flight.'"

She read the verses softly, her voice tinged with the reverence I always felt when the poem was recited at graduations and memorials. "'Oh, I have slipped the surly bonds of earth, and danced the skies on laughter-silvered wings...'"

I'd heard the words so many times I could almost recite them from memory, but hearing them from her lips brought freshness to the archaic verses. The melody of Camille's voice faded into the background, and I considered the meaning of the words I'd read so many times.

Surly bonds.

Camille and I struggled individually with the crushing weight of hopelessness and loss. Cruel bonds of grief that trapped us and robbed us of the strength to try again. But the poet's carefree words spoke of a retreat from the heaviness of life's burdens. A soul's escape I could only now just begin to contemplate. I wondered if Camille saw the same possibilities in me.

She was quiet for a minute after she'd finished reading, and then she turned and looked around the open space. "You just need a little time to finish unloading your stuff." She waved a hand dismissively. "Hang up photos, get your linens and pillows and lamps to add some color and warm it up. The place will feel like home in no time." Her smile warmed me like a summer's day. "You'll see."

But the boxes still stacked in the spare bedroom held only more books and manuals. Camille had no way of understanding why, but in my world, there hadn't been much color. Not much texture or warmth, literally or figuratively, in quite some time. Those things were lent to me by Eliott. And she couldn't stay.

Chapter
TWENTY-SEVEN

"I'm Gonna Love You through It"

Nathan
About Three Years Earlier

"Are you sure you don't want me to help?" Eliott stretched her little body in a beach lounger under the shade of the singular tree outside my temporary housing. I was sweating profusely, putting my back into the task of hand-waxing the GTO. The dirty truth was this: the act of laboriously rubbing cloudy wax away and exposing the gleaming navy paint appealed to the type A part of my brain in a nearly perverse way. It was shaping up to be yet another absurdly hot Tucson summer day, but I always waxed the Goat on the first Saturday of the month.

OCD much, Nathan?

"Not at all, babe. You just relax and give me something beautiful to enjoy." I smiled at her, wiping my face again with a soaked tee. "You bought yourself a leisurely afternoon with that breakfast in bed." She had awakened me this bright Saturday morning with eggs Benedict topped with her signature creamy hollandaise, freshly squeezed OJ, and bacon—a treat the vegetarian Eliott didn't enjoy but knew I did. It had been delivered to my bed by a delectably tanned Eliott wearing only tiny black panties tied with bows on each side. I'd flown late last night and returned well after dark, too exhausted to eat.

This morning she'd knelt in front of me, straddling my knees, and insisted I eat every morsel. All the while she played with her nipples and slipped her fingers into her panties repeatedly, telling me all the ways she wanted to enjoy my cock. Breakfast ended with Eliott on her knees facing the headboard and holding on for dear life while I fucked her, fingering her clit the entire time and insisting on two orgasms before I came with a roar.

"That particular breakfast is one of my specialties, I'll have you know." She lifted one brow haughtily. "But I don't do it for just anyone. You're special, Nathan Morgan."

I resumed polishing, my smile widening. "I'd certainly hope you don't do it for just anyone, little one. I don't express my thanks like that to just anyone, either."

She let loose with loud laughter. She laughed like an eleven-year-old boy who'd just heard a poop joke—no holds barred. She just didn't give a shit who might hear. I loved that about her, along with a million other things. I'd grown accustomed to women who were obsessed with what others thought about their actions, their appearance, the company they kept. It was difficult to tell who they were as they spent all their energy trying to impress friends or family. Or me. It was mostly lost on me. I had begun to despair of finding a woman who lived on her own terms.

Eliott turned my life on its ear. Maybe it was the unconventional upbringing. Whatever made her who she was deserved my thanks. The lack of self-obsession left room for the real woman she was to express herself and love for me in a way uncomplicated by convention. She took care of me, body and soul, whenever the opportunity presented itself.

The topic at hand over the past couple of days had been my career. I was brooding over time spent in my assignment at the Pentagon and how useless I'd felt there. Now it was time for a follow-on assignment that put me back in the cockpit, exactly where every pilot wants to be; but I was utterly exasperated. Although this flying assignment was eagerly anticipated, I would surely face many more infuriating bumps in the road over the course of a career.

Eliott cocked her head. "I felt like you could use the distraction, as well as some food. This thing is really inside your head right now."

She was right. The ultimate goal of almost any fighter pilot who decided to make a career of the military was to be the commander of a squadron of pilots. A certain career path was expected, complete with boxes to tick, for those who wanted a command; and it included a frustrating number of items that had nothing to do with being a great pilot or a great leader. At least in my opinion. Clearly, the hierarchy of the Air Force had not consulted me on this matter.

She stood and walked toward me, stopping as our bodies touched. Her brown eyes studied mine. "You can't change it, Nate. Not the Air Force. Not the requirements." Her hand found mine, and one thumb dug into my palm, massaging.

My jaw was tight. "It feels wasteful to me. Useless. Why sit behind a desk when I have a skill that allows me to serve in a more valuable capacity?" I met her eyes. "The more I think about it and try to work it out in my head, the more frustrated I become. It's starting to affect my work. I'm distracted."

She squeezed my hand hard and stretched onto her tiptoes to gain my attention. "Nathan. It's done. Over." Her voice was serious. "You have to let it go. Let. It. Go."

But I shook my head, avoiding her. "I've tried, Ellie, I have. It's not working this time. My head just circles back to it."

She pulled my face down to meet hers. "Try once more, Nate. 'When everything around you says give up, hope whispers: try one more time.' Have you ever heard that quote?" My eyes were questioning, so she continued, pulling me to sit on the lounger next to her.

"When I was eight years old, I was in an accident." She waved her hand impatiently at the alarm on my face. "The accident isn't the point—stay with me. An elderly lady swerved from the road-way and hit me while I rode my bicycle. My left ankle was completely crushed. The surgeons repaired it as best they could, but physical therapy didn't go well. After two months, I was still in a wheelchair, still not able to bear any weight at all. The physical therapist told my parents discouragement was the limiting factor. She'd begun to doubt I'd walk normally again, and it was all because I'd given up."

Eliott was reflective for a moment before continuing. "I've thought since then about how I would have handled that information if I'd been the parent, and I think my inclination would've been to keep such a disheartening report from my child. I'd have been afraid to harm them even more. But my parents didn't do that.

"My mother came to me at bedtime one night, after one of my horrific PT sessions ended with a temper tantrum. She sat on my bed, smoothing my hair, and she was silent for a long time. But when she finally spoke, she said, 'My Eliott. Baby, it's a harsh lesson at a young age, but here it is. Giving up is *almost never* the answer. You can't see anything past this broken ankle, and you think everything's over. You think that you won't walk again.'

"I can't imagine how hard it was for her to say these things to her young daughter, but I admire her for giving me the chance to understand, Nathan. I hope I would have the wisdom, in her shoes. And she laid it out. 'When the world and everything around you says give up, hope whispers in your ear. Try again,

Eliott. Try once more. If you don't remember anything else, re-member to try once more. When you give up, it's over.' Somehow, as young as I was, I understood she was unlocking something that didn't just tell me how to deal with a broken bone. She was giving me the key to everything."

Her hands stroked mine, and she looked deep into me, as she often did. "It's hard to get through this. It's not impossible. Try once more.

"Because when you give up, it's over."

Chapter
TWENTY-EIGHT

"It's Five O'clock Somewhere"

Camille

"Joe, I know we've had this discussion before, but what the actual fuck?" I hissed the question at my favorite paramedic, impatience negating the affection I felt for him personally. The stretcher rolled through the open doors of the ambulance bay and into the ED. Luckie shot me a poisonous glare and grabbed the foot of the stretcher, steering it toward the room she'd readied. I returned my attention to Joe. "I'm a lady, Joe, so I didn't look under the sheet, but I need you to tell me that on this day—of all days—that gentleman didn't have a lamp stuck up his ass."

Joe was already making for the coffeepot. He shook his head regretfully and addressed me. "Camille, you're like a sister to me, and I'd rather chew my arm off than lie to you. So I'm just gonna say that it's a pretty small lamp."

"Swear to God, Joe. I'm gonna be a Walmart greeter. Swear to God." We were following the stretcher through the doors and toward the nurses' station. "I've got nurses out on vacation this week, and my staff is ready to strangle the next assclown that rolls through these doors. No pun intended. It's been unbelievable, Joe, so I need you to swear on a big stack of Bibles that every other fucking headcase before 1900 goes to St. Joseph's. Every single one. Swear it, Joe."

He finished filling his cup and gave my shoulder a squeeze. "You guys are the greatest, Camille. Your staff can handle anything." He pushed one of the ambulance bay doors open. "See ya later, Camille." He raised his voice and shouted down the hall. "Bye, Luckie, Sam…" And he was gone.

Luckie stomped by, blood in her eyes. "I'm gonna murder that donkey-fucking, pencil-dicked cocksucker. I'll rip his prick out. Slow. And his eyeballs…before I fuck his skull with…"

I caught her in a hug. "Sister, I'm sorry. This day just keeps getting worse. I thought the nudists were the worst of it this morning."

Luckie interrupted me. "Hey, I forgot. Grace needed you in that group room we set up. The grandfather won't keep his boxers on." She frowned. "Sorry. I forgot to tell you when the bullshit started rising so fast."

I thanked her, rolling my eyes, and strode toward the largest triage we'd set up for the nudist family. They arrived this morning with truly noteworthy cases of poison ivy. In the most interesting places. They would've been "treat and streets," but one of the younger women had come to us in moderate respiratory distress, probably due to the movement of the poison ivy into her lungs. This was confirmed when we learned that the all-knowing patriarch of the family had been supervising a large-scale burn-off of all the poison ivy found on the property. Of course, the breeze had only exacerbated the problem and placed everyone in the group at risk. To add to the fun, Gracie had her hands full keeping a couple of the older members of the group clothed. The grandfather looked like an ill-equipped Shar-Pei when the threadbare boxers came off. Why a nudist would have worn-out undies, I couldn't say. Made you think.

As I approached triage two, Grace exited the room and closed the door behind her. She took a deep breath and turned her eyes to the sky, silently imploring a higher power for strength.

"Camille." She fixed her eyes on me. "I can't look at that ancient ding-dong anymore." She raised her brows. "I am a professional, and I can handle anything this job throws at me. Anything except that tiny, wrinkled little tallywacker. I hope you understand, but I'm going to take vows. And be a nun. I can't look at another peewee. Not ever, Camille." She stalked toward the supply room, stopping briefly to update the unfortunate chief resident at the station.

I had a thought and called after her, "Hey, some nuns are nurses, you know." She only shook her head without looking back.

Viv was next and possibly the most unfortunate staff member on this trying day. I strode toward the other open ward room on our unit. Vivvie stood outside, meticulously wrapping her index finger tightly with a long, narrow band of Micropore tape.

I approached cautiously.

Her fingertip was purple. I placed my hand carefully on her shoulder. "Vivvie. That tape is too tight. Did you cut your finger?" I took the roll from her and slowly unwound it.

"Nope. No cut." She slid her eyes in my direction. "I'm trying to forget the trauma the motherfucking Junior League is putting me through. I kinda thought excruciating pain might help."

"But, Vivvie," I interrupted, "I didn't think it was the Junior League."

"It's not, Camille. Not Junior League." She calmly resumed wrapping her finger. "Same fucking thing. The Daughters of Arizona. Service League…something." Her voice was calm and even. "Don't know, Cam." She sighed and leaned heavily into the wall. "They have the shits. The whole lot of them. We're ruling out C. diff versus Giardia." She arched a brow at me. "Either way, I'm screwed. There's just so much shit, Camille."

About that time, two nursing assistants pushed open the door of the ward, large laundry hampers ahead of them and shook their heads at Viv as they passed us. They shucked their disposable paper gowns and gloves into the red bag lining a large garbage pail at the door. Their eyes were red-rimmed, probably from the smell. It was staggering, even for a seasoned nurse. *It had to be C. diff,* I thought absently.

I hugged Vivian. "Showers after work followed immediately by margaritas at my house. Help me spread the word." My house was only blocks away and the obvious choice for an emergency post-mortem on this horrific shift. I walked away, leaving Viv to ponder her taped finger. I hoped she came to before it fell off. That would mean paperwork.

I left the hospital on time, raced home, and jumped in and out of the shower, accomplishing a quick scrub of all the basics. Emptying the fridge, I set out every leftover and snack I could conjure on short notice without a grocery stop—there wasn't time, and no one would care anyway. But margaritas? Oh, they would care about that. I pulled limeade from the freezer and my trusty blender from the cabinet, Solomon keeping me company from his perch on the sofa. Not even half an hour had passed when Luckie burst through the door, hair damp and sporting clean hospital scrubs, carrying her filthy uniform in a garbage bag. Thinking better of it, she stepped back outside, toed off her shoes, and dropped the plastic bag on the front porch. None of us kept extra uniforms at work, so this was the default for the occasions when the unthinkable happened. Unfortunately, the unthinkable happened a lot.

Luckie parked her spectacular ass on a barstool at my counter as I began to assemble the first blender of margs. "Jose Cuervo, you are a friend of mine," she sang, brandishing a water glass when the blender motor died off. "When I left, Grace and Vivvie were having a Lady Macbeth moment in the locker room showers." She grinned. "Grace was actually growling 'Out, damned spot' while she washed, and Vivvie looked like she was scrubbing her skin raw. That C. diff is some nasty shit, literally. But I think they'll be along soon."

Luckie and I chatted about the unfortunate shift we'd just survived, sampling and adjusting the margarita recipe and snacking on deli cheese slices until raucous laughter on my front porch indicated the arrival of the remainder of our girls. They let themselves in, sporting the clean-but-damp look like Luckie, and settled at the breakfast bar.

Samanthe snagged Solomon on the way by the sofa and snuggled into his blue-gray fur, whispering secrets. Sam and Solomon had a special bond; she had been primarily responsible for his care during my hospitalization after the attack and had nursed him back to health following a terrible cat fight. Solomon wasn't allowed outdoors unaccompanied because his ego constantly got him into trouble. He had proved time and again that he was a lover and not a fighter.

I tore my gaze from Sam loving on my baby and joined the conversation already in progress. Luckie was speaking. "Joe wasn't kidding. It was small, as lamps go, but it was actually in his ass. Which posed a problem." She shook her head ruefully and downed another slug of marg. "He was a surgical candidate, obviously, because he was uncontrollable. I get it, what with the lamp protruding. From. His. Ass. So I grabbed my trusty Valium, kissed him goodnight and sent him to pre-op. We would never have been able to extract in the ED. I got off easy." She cast a nefarious look slowly around the circle.

I shook my head slowly. "Don't, Luckie. Don't do it."

"Which is more than I can say for him!" she shouted, toasting herself and bending double to laugh uproariously at her gag.

The laughter eventually died down. Viv took a long slurp of her margarita and gave me a grateful grin. "Delish, Cam. Thanks for having us. I've wiped enough old lady ass today to last a lifetime. I wanna talk about you letting Colonel FuckHot drive the beef bus to tuna town. Need float trip details. Now, Camille."

Samanthe cut her eyes sideways at Vivvie and smirked. "Crass wench." She brandished her empty glass.

I refreshed drinks and led the way to the living room where I sprawled in my overstuffed chair. Everyone else took up positions around the room on the sofa and floor, eyeing me expectantly. "Things are developing at a surprising pace, especially considering how out of practice we both are at this sort of thing," I began carefully, sipping for courage.

Gracie cocked her head. "Both of you? He hasn't been in a relationship lately?"

I nodded slowly. "Hard to believe, I know. He lost someone, too, several years ago. A woman he cared deeply for. Loved her."

Luckie stretched her lithe body, forcing her bare feet into Sam's lap. She looked directly at me. "So. Can he fuck?"

Samanthe's big blue eyes blinked twice at Luckie. "Lucinda Page. I can't believe you asked her that."

Luckie grinned evilly but didn't look away. "So?" she inquired again. "He has all the appearance of someone who knows his way around. Tall, dark, dangerous…and it's always the quiet ones, you know."

I smiled at my girlfriends. "Yeah, he knows his way around. And it's good; it's really good. But that's not all it is." Gracie was making her way around the circle, refilling glasses. "I think something's happening between us. So before we went to bed the first night, I told him about the attack. I couldn't have asked for that to go any better."

The unasked question hung in the air for a few seconds before

Viv spoke. She looked into my eyes, her face soft. "And Amos?"

I shook my head at her, shifting my gaze to my lap. "Not yet. One thing at a time. Not Amos…not yet."

Grace finished her rounds and leaned on my chair, sifting her hands through my hair. "You'll know when the time is right, Cam. And he's hitting all his marks so far." She knelt next to my chair, cocking her head. "What's your heart saying?"

I considered her question. "I was telling myself it was too soon. That anything was too soon. But I'm starting to wonder if that was because I'd never thought I'd be able to let anyone in. Jury's out, Gracie."

I looked around the room at all my friends, each one smiling their encouragement. Luckie's smile was crooked and a little mischievous. "Someone once told me that hope always whispers, 'Try once more.' I'm hoping the jury is back soon, Camille. You're due."

Chapter
TWENTY-NINE

"Lullaby and Goodnight"

Camille
About Five Years Earlier

I lay in the recovery room, unseeing eyes staring at the expanse of white ceiling tiles. The muted beeps of the monitors and the clicking of the IV pump were oddly comforting. These things would be frightening to most, but the ordinary sights and smells and noises of the hospital surrounded me with the familiar. A **PACU** nurse deftly connected an epidural pump to the tiny, flexible plastic tube still resting near my spine, to administer pain relief for the next couple of days. She murmured instructions to Luckie while expertly programming the pump with a couple dozen or so rapid clicks on the machine's keypad. Luckie nodded and reached for my hand.

On any other day, a hospitalization or surgery would've brought me very little anxiety. But now, as my hand slid under the stack of heated cotton blankets and sheets warming my chilled body, it found a large pressure bandage stretched across a flat expanse of stomach. No life, no roiling butterflies or tiny baby feet and fists curiously exploring the confines of my swelling belly. Just quiet emptiness. The hollow feeling was devastating.

I turned to Luckie. Her always luminous skin looked almost sallow, gorgeous brown eyes now flat. My throat protested with a slash of hot pain when I tried to swallow, and Luckie responded immediately, gently feeding me a couple of soothing ice chips. "They had to intubate you," she whispered. "There wasn't any time; it was a **cord accident**."

"Where is he, Luckie?" My voice was so small, barely audible. "My son needs me."

She nodded her head slowly in agreement. "Amos is in the **NICU**, Cam." She paused and swallowed hard, shifting into nurse mode to tell me what I needed to know. "He's alive. He weighs a pound and four ounces, and they have him vented, lines…the whole nine yards. But his sats are low, and the gases weren't encouraging. There's already a grade three bleed, Camille." Her face softened, and I could see her fighting a little for control, biting the inside of her bottom lip. "It's not looking good, honey."

My face crumpled, and I reached for my friend. As she had done six short months ago, the dearest person in my small world climbed onto the narrow stretcher and pulled my aching body close to her. She held me tight, arms and legs about me as loud, choking sobs wracked my torn body. The pain in my stomach, under the bandage, was agonizing; it felt as if I would tear open with every jagged gasp. But the excruciating rending of my heart from my chest eclipsed everything. It was too much. This anguish was the weight that would finally drag my heart down, pinning it to the ocean's floor and drowning me forever with despair. I would never recover.

I felt a cool hand smoothing my hair, pressing a damp cloth to my eyes, and I lifted my head to find Vivvie. Her eyes were full, but her voice was steady. "He needs you, Camille." Her voice was quiet, steely.

"Amos needs you right now." Luckie began to unwind herself from me, wiping her eyes on the sleeve of her scrub jacket as Viv continued. "His nurse said it won't be very long now, and he needs his mom with him. Your nurse is coming to give you an extra dose of pain medicine so you can move a little better. But we have to go soon." She held two tissues to my nose. "Now, blow."

I did as Vivvie instructed, and the three of us took deep breaths, swallowing hard and collecting ourselves as my PACU nurse quickly programmed an extra dose of medication into my pain pump. At the same time, Viv and Luckie helped connect my lines to the portable monitor brought to help transport me to my son's side. Vivvie quickly pulled a brush through the thick tangle of my hair and handed me a cup of ice chips. My gown was changed, and the three of them rolled my stretcher out of the PACU and down the hall toward the NICU.

Along the way, we passed an open waiting area where Grace and Samanthe stood embracing in the doorway, their eyes red and swollen. Through my haze of confusion and grief, I noticed the room behind them was filled with two dozen or so of my ER staff—nurses, a couple of doctors and residents, our secretary, my favorite EMT, Joe, and even a couple of our housekeeping staff. They surged forward as my stretcher rolled past, slowing but not stopping. They silently reached for me, two or three at a time moving to my side and touching me gently. A pat or squeeze to my hand or forearm, even an occasional touch of one tear-stained cheek. Then they peeled off somberly and lined the hall as Luckie, Viv, my nurse, and I continued toward my little Amos.

I had been to the Jungle before, our affectionate nickname for our top-drawer, high-tech NICU. It was especially ironic because the staff who worked there regarded the Emergency Department as the real jungle. I had always been glad that there were so many different kinds of nurses to staff the multitude of specialties. The

NICU was a series of large, well-lit rooms with more monitors, wires, and alarms per square inch than anyplace else in the hospital. It was terribly intimidating, even to medical professionals from other areas. The lives sheltered there were so impossibly fragile, most of the babies so tiny. The fact that there was no room for error was glaringly apparent. But my gut told me that even their highly skilled care would not be enough today.

Viv helped me scrub my hands as thoroughly as my condition allowed, and then she kissed my forehead softly. "Only you and Luckie from here, love. I'll be waiting and praying every second. We all are." I couldn't even speak, so I just swallowed hard and nodded my head in gratitude.

My nurse, with Luckie's help, carefully guided my stretcher through the maze of closed beds and radiant warmers, each cradling a soul hanging in the balance. In a darkened corner of the room, I could see one open warmer with a sign reading "Sullivan" and two nurses hovering nearby. As I was positioned in front of Amos's crib, a nurse with a soft and welcoming face approached me.

"Hello, Camille. I'm Carole. I've been with Amos since he was born; I was in the OR with you, even though you were sleeping." She stole a glance at the little boy; my eyes were riveted to him. Even though I was exhausted and medicated, I counted the respirations as his chest rose and fell with the ventilated breaths. "He's a beautiful boy, Camille, and he's running out of fight." She continued and placed a comforting hand on my shoulder. "He lost so much oxygen while his cord was compressed after your water broke. He's worked hard, but his little body is so tired."

My throat closed, and I tried to respond but could only nod, eyes full. It was so hard to breathe.

"Camille, you're a nurse, so I'm going to tell you what I know as straight as I'm able." Carole faced me and looked directly into my eyes. "He is very early. Very. Early. But the downtime makes it much worse. He's tried so hard, Camille." She took a deep breath. "But he's not going to make it. He needs you here to let him go. Can you do that, Camille?"

I could hear Luckie's choked gasping, her hands clasping mine. But I was suddenly possessed with the strength to be what Amos needed. He had never asked to be here. Now his life was slipping quietly away before he could even live it. But I would be everything he needed at this moment. I would take care of me later; now was for my little boy.

I nodded my assent, and Carole motioned for Randy, the NICU's wonderful respiratory therapist. His tall form briefly blocked my view as he helped the neonatologist remove the breathing tube. They both offered sympathies before disappearing again, and I gathered myself, swallowing hard.

"Carole, can you hand me my son? He needs me, and I need to say hello. And goodbye." Her kind smile and a squeeze to my shoulder gave me strength.

"I'll help you keep him warm and comfortable, Mama." She disconnected tubes and wires, freeing him from his crib. Once he was ready for me, she reached for the snaps at the shoulder of my gown and released them. Her gentle hands lifted my precious baby, placing his tiny form against my skin. He was warm from the radiant heater that had shone on him, but she wrapped the two of us in soft flannel blankets, shielding us both from the room and the whole world. Luckie squeezed my shoulder, kissed my temple and backed away. And I was alone with my sweet boy.

I placed my hands on him, keeping him warm against my body where he'd grown and flourished until hours before. "Hello, my Amos," I whispered against his downy head. He was so small, so fragile. "I wanted you, you know. Don't ever think anything different. We all come into the lives of other people in different ways, and we don't control that. But I was so glad to hear that you were going to be mine, little one. I wanted you from the moment

I knew about you. And I'll miss you, but we'll be together again, you know. I'll miss you. Dream about you every night."

I could feel the effort of his little body working to breathe without the ventilator's assistance. Trying so hard to live. I whispered my words to him. "It's time to go, Amos. Don't struggle so. Mommy's here, and I'll never leave you. When it's time, you let go, and I'll hold on for always. We'll be together again, son." It tore my soul apart, but giving him more than I thought possible was natural in that moment of grace. It was the work of a mother, my heart instinctively knew, to give everything and more. I sang so quietly that only he could hear me… "'Lullaby and goodnight, with roses bedight…'"

Over an hour passed as he struggled, sometimes moving against my chest with his frail, weakened body, only the irregular sound of monitors breaking the quiet. I rocked him, humming softly, and tried to capture the memories as pictures in my mind. I knew I would long to remember and relive these brief moments with my baby. Three or four times, my PACU nurse came to my side, checking vitals, feeding me a few ice chips and squeezing my hand before slipping away. I sang to him, waiting, my heart hurting so much worse than my aching body.

Then, in the wee hours, it was quiet. Amos's slight form stilled, the struggling stopped, my lullaby faded away. And my precious son was gone.

Chapter
THIRTY

"They Say it's Your Birthday"

Nathan

The dark was thick and as heavy as velvet, and it cloaked us with a tenuous sense of privacy. My hands flattened across Camille's stomach and moved slowly down to stroke the soft curve of one hip. I nuzzled my face into her silky hair, coaxing it over one shoulder and allowing my lips to caress the warm pulse skittering at her neck. "Are you nervous, Cami?" I hissed the words quietly against her ear to intensify the effect.

She nodded but remained silent, as instructed. My teeth nipped at the softest places on the delicate skin of her neck, just enough to elicit a whimper, before quickly soothing the abraded bites with my tongue. My hands longed to reach between her thighs and slick through her pretty pussy, warming her clit with slow strokes and patiently waiting for it to swell and throb. But none of that would happen right now.

Dirty thoughts about my angel were interrupted by two sharp raps on the door. "That's our cue," Hung's low voice rumbled. Then the door of the storage shed was flung wide open, flooding it with bright sunshine, and voices from all over the yard yelled, "Surprise! Happy birthday!" Fifteen or so occupants of the shed rushed into the yard, joining another thirty revelers running from the back door of the garage. Bibi stood on the patio, hands clasped and grinned gleefully. She flung both arms around her husband and planted a huge kiss on him.

Then she clapped her hands and jumped up and down like a kid. "I love surprises. Thank you, everybody. Chuck, babe, thank you." Another kiss, this one much more suited for the bedroom than the backyard, was greeted by the crowd with whistling and catcalls. Pilots could be such a bunch of animals, I thought wryly and looked around at the Scorpions. My smile only got wider as I noticed that the spouses were joining in enthusiastically—including my Camille who apparently possessed the ability to wolf-whistle at ear-splitting volume, both pinkies at the edges of her mouth.

"Damn, girl." I squeezed her tightly with an arm wrapped around her waist. "Is there no end to your talent?" Camille was relaxed and happy, all pink softness and long hair caught in a ponytail. Just shorts, tank top, and sandals, with no pretense or effort to impress. She would wear a ball gown and jewels just as easily, I thought. There was something in her natural friendliness that drew people; they all loved her. And I loved her.

I loved her?

My face must've betrayed confusion because I was suddenly aware that Camille's smile had faded, and she was regarding me with a questioning look. "Hey. Nathan Morgan...where'd you go?"

I blinked and squeezed her again, smiling. "A good place, angel. Someplace I haven't been in a while."

I manned one of the two grills, Coach at the other one, systematically turning out heaping platters of grilled chicken and steak for the fajita buffet table. A small group of the wives had helped Coach with his party planning, and the result was the usual well-organized Stinger Party Machine. Three long tables groaned with warm tortillas, sliced and grilled vegetables and meat, homemade pasta and potato salads chilling on bowls of ice, and two enormous birthday cakes. One was chocolate and one strawberry because Coach said his Bellamy Bennett could never make up her mind. And with him planning her special celebration, she didn't have to.

"You two look like Lucy and Ethel at the chocolate factory," Camille laughed as she swapped out my empty beer bottle for a fresh one. Camille had enlisted Viv and Luckie to help her in her assignment of keeping the cool drinks refreshed. She carried a glistening pitcher of homemade wine coolers in her free hand and leaned in for a peck on my cheek before jogging across the yard to resume her duties.

Coach sent me a side-eye and a smirk. "You may have a keeper there, boss."

I was quiet for a few seconds, flipping the juicy steak on my grill. "You may be right." I sighed and kept my eyes trained on the grill. Disbelief tainted my words; I had given up after Eliott. But why? What made it so difficult to believe that Camille and I could have a real shot? The din of the party faded to a low buzz in my head as I considered the question. Camille was a treasure, one of a kind, just as Eliott had been. One didn't replace the other. My love for Camille didn't diminish what Eliott and I had shared. That was a flawed idea my head embraced. And it was suddenly clear to me that it was entirely without merit. It was time to let that go for good and see if Camille and I could build something together from scratch. I grinned as my shoulders relaxed, and I looked over toward Coach, nodding my head again. "You may be very right."

In the back corner of the yard, Vivvie had abandoned her post as the roving bartender and was helping a swarm of grade school children set up a croquet set. She corralled the kids and began demonstrating the proper use of the mallet and ways to move the ball through the wickets. The gaggle claimed their equipment with a minimum of hostility, and the games began. Her mission accomplished, Viv stood in the shade of a large oak, one hand in the pocket of her jean shorts, drinking an icy beer and smiling indulgently at the children.

My eyes wandered across the yard and encountered a solitary Hung parked atop a picnic table. He sipped his beer, eyes locked on Viv, and stroked his stubbled chin thoughtfully with a thumb and forefinger. When Viv drained her drink, she raised her piercing green eyes to his and crooked a finger his direction. Without waiting for a response, she turned and walked to the gate, letting herself into the front yard. Hung smiled and lowered his head, shaking it slowly. I was surprised to see him rise slowly from his perch and stroll across the grass to join Rock's conversation with Miles.

I could smell the scent of sunshine that was Camille right before I felt her lips at my ear. "Whaddya make of that?" she whispered. "I don't think I've ever seen anyone turn down a chance to get Vivvie alone."

I leaned away from the grill and wrapped an arm around my girl. "First time for everything," I grated back into her ear. "I'd say we're working on quite a lengthy list of firsts ourselves."

Coach tapped my shoulder to gain my attention and relieved me of my post at the grill with a wave of the hand. I grinned at him and lifted my chin in unspoken thanks. I slid a hand under Camille's tank to enjoy the warmth of a soft expanse of skin as we turned and walked toward one of the unoccupied picnic tables along the periphery. "And no matter how I love every minute inside you, I keep dreaming up new ways to get there. And new things I want to do. And taste."

Her breathing was shallow, and a pretty flush spread across

the pale skin of her chest above the tank top. We were still only whispering to each other. "Earlier, Nathan, when we were hiding…" Her breaths were irregular and somewhat labored now. "I liked it, you know…when you bit me. It hurt a little."

Aw, fuck. In no time, my cock was a battering ram intent on splitting the zipper of my shorts. "There's more where that came from, beautiful." I squeezed her waist just a little too hard and elicited a moan. "Why don't we plan for a little more alone time, angel? It's only been a few days, but I'm hungry for more of you."

"Can't wait." Her eyes twinkled. "But you'd better keep that hungry monster penned up in your shorts a little longer. I have to feed and water the crowd."

With that, she was gone again, and I was left staring at the most magnificent ass my hands had ever had the pleasure of fondling. I was so engrossed I didn't notice the birthday girl sliding up onto the table next to me until she took a long drink of her wine cooler and held out a thick slice of chocolate cake.

"Whatcha studying there, Happy?" Her voice was full of mischief, and her eyes danced as she teased. "Caught you staring like a starving man at a Thanksgiving turkey."

I accepted the cake with a laugh. "Guilty as charged, Bibi. And a very happy birthday, young lady. Is this twenty-nine?" I took a giant bite and groaned. Chocolate was a weakness.

"Well, almost twenty-nine." Bibi grinned. "Maybe twenty-nine again. Fortuitous that I find you here, already in my office. I was going to ask you to step in for a word anyway."

I licked icing from my lips and went in for another bite. "What kind of trouble am I in? Can't be good if you're taking me to the woodshed on your birthday."

"Nope." Bibi took another sip of her cold drink and cocked her head in my direction. "I've just been waiting for a chance to get you alone and ask you about something you said when we first met."

My brows knitted as I tried to remember what she might be referencing. Coming up empty, I shrugged. "You've got me at a disadvantage, I'm afraid—can't think what you might be referring to."

Her demeanor was easy, but her eyes were knowing. "When we had breakfast at your house the morning you moved in, Chuck referred to you as a bachelor, but you mentioned under your breath you were a widower." She paused a tick, still watching, and then continued. "Chuck didn't hear you, and I kept it under my hat, but not much gets by me around here, Nathan. If you were a widower, I would have known that. I sense, especially after watching you and Camille together, that there's more to you than meets the eye." She paused again, longer this time. "Now, you're certainly under no obligation to come clean to me, but I do care. And I'm a pretty decent listener. So what gives with the charming new squadron commander?"

I chuckled as she sat back, smiling broadly at me. "Well, I guess you're just the kind of person who comes right out and asks what she wants to know."

She shrugged with faux modesty. "It's always worked well for me."

I nodded slowly. "That deserves a straightforward answer. About four years ago, when I was happily drowning in work, back in a Hawg cockpit after a tour at the Pentagon, I found myself here at the Schoolhouse for recurrent. I wasn't looking, but I stumbled into the great love of my life. I say 'the' great love because I've been convinced that I only got one shot. You know, at love. At least I've been convinced until recently." My eyes searched the yard until they found Cami, chatting up Miles and Rock.

Bibi followed my eyes and placed her hand on my arm to gain my attention. "That's not how love works, Nate. It's not a limited resource we grasp and hoard; it's bountiful. The more generously we give it, the more lavishly it's visited on us." Her face was soft as she looked at Camille, then back and deep into me. "And most importantly, Nathan—listen to me here—if love is lost, no matter the reason, you must always leave your heart open. Soft and ready. Always try once more. Your chance for love isn't over until you give up."

I felt like someone had punched me in the stomach. I could hardly breathe. Bibi could have no way of knowing the gravity of what she'd just said. It was as if Eliott was watching. Then Bibi smiled easily and spoke again, squeezing my arm.

"If she caught your eye and your heart, she must've been very special, Nathan. Give the old gal a birthday present; I do relish a love story, even when it breaks my heart. Tell me about this first great love of yours."

Under the circumstances, there was no choice. Bibi was obviously in cahoots with Eliott with one L and two T's. I was outmanned and outgunned. I took the last bite of cake, laid my plate aside, and leaned forward with my elbows to my knees.

"Her name was Eliott…"

Chapter
THIRTY-ONE

"Wake Me up when September Ends"

Nathan
About Three Years Earlier

There was no way to see the path it would take, the way my life would change over the course of these short three months in Tucson. I had happily anticipated a return to the cockpit, again enjoying the passion I felt for flying. Even more, I looked forward to permanently closing the door of my Pentagon office. Plenty of people loved their work there and found it fulfilling, but, for me, it was a frustration that stood between me and the unfettered freedom of flight. But Eliott was a curveball. In the well-orchestrated life I'd carefully created, she was completely unanticipated.

She was every free-spirited, easygoing thing I wasn't. She had fallen, unceremoniously, into my regimented life when I least expected it, coloring my existence with her spontaneity. She challenged everything I thought about myself while loving all of me at the same time. She was something I had never dreamed existed.

And I loved everything about her.

She turned my life on its ear. And now I was furiously negotiating with myself about how to proceed. I always had a plan—until Eliott. But at least I'd handled one big decision. I had The Ring.

That alone should have signaled the game had changed. The old Nathan would have never wandered into that jewelry store, smiling all the while, and emerged an hour later with an antique diamond and ruby engagement ring that cost more than the GTO's expertly applied custom paint job. The ring had been with me at all times for the past two weeks as my time in Tucson drew rapidly to a close. I was undecided about the timing and method, but there were no doubts about the girl.

The moment came when I least expected.

I unlocked the door to my room in the temporary quarters that housed officers, not much more than a hotel suite in truth, and the smell of heaven wrapped around me. Eliott's cheeks were pink, and the little kitchenette was suffused with the enticing smell of garlic. Her eyes danced as she reached into the oven, retrieving a small pan of bubbling lasagna. She cocked her head and smiled. "I knew you'd be so hungry; it was a long day. So I thought I'd try my hand at cooking in your micro-kitchen." She placed the pan on the stovetop and stood on tiptoe to wrap her arms around my neck.

My throat was suddenly tight and my heart full. I couldn't live another moment without knowing that she would be mine. I reached up and unwrapped her hands from my neck while taking time to kiss the knuckles of each. Her bright smile faded somewhat as she saw the seriousness on my face.

With no real forethought, I sank to one knee, still holding both of her hands, and swallowed hard. "Eliott. I know it hasn't been very long. But it's a lifetime already, and I've never been surer of anything in my life." I dropped one of her hands, unzipped a pocket on my flight suit, and drew out the sparkling ring. "Wear this, Eliott. Be my wife. Please say yes."

Any other woman, faced with this surprising development, would've cried, laughed, panicked, but not Eliott. She never failed to be herself. She sank to both knees, and her soft eyes held mine. "Of course I'll be yours." Her forehead fell forward until it met mine, our eyes still locked together. "I already am, and I agree. It's time we told everyone else." She took the ring from my hand, kissed it and slid it onto her hand. "My mama's gonna love you, Nathan."

Lasagna forgotten, for now, Eliott wrapped herself in me, and the world shrank until it encompassed only the drab suite, now warmed with a love that seemed to make anything possible. I loved her every way I could conjure until hunger and exhaustion overtook us. At half past two a.m., we sat on the countertop, eating now-lukewarm pasta directly from the pan and whispering plans to each other.

"Let's marry in Taos," she suggested, eyes dancing. "We could do it this winter, on the mountain. My art teacher from high school is a minister. And a ski bum…and several other things, actually."

I smiled, mouth full of delicious veggie lasagna. "Sounds perfect to me, babe. I don't care where; it just has to be you. Can I swing back through after leave and take you to San Diego to meet my mom and dad?" I had a wedding to attend in Maine immediately after finishing my short course in Tucson. I'd hoped Eliott could accompany me, but she had a senior seminar to complete. Graduation would follow, and I hoped to see her walking down an aisle toward me soon after that.

She turned to face me in the darkened kitchen. Only a short few months ago, in another dark kitchen across town, she'd changed my life all at once, permanently and for the better. "I can't wait to meet your family. I want to know everything about you, and where you come from is a big part of that."

I hated to leave Tucson without each detail attended. In her inimitable way, though, Eliott reminded me it was my nature to micromanage; our love didn't require that. She helped me pack my meager belongings, storing some in her studio near the university, and saw me off to Maine with love and promises to be constantly in touch. Her mother was driving to Tucson to help her begin shopping for a wedding dress. We didn't want to delay our marriage and planned for a small family wedding to follow her graduation in early December. There was much to do; neither of us had met the other's family, but it was all inconsequential. We were already part of each other. The wedding, the marriage, and a long life together were a foregone conclusion.

I was more than glad to stand at Nick Bamford's side while he married his girl, Candace. BamBam and I were roommates in pilot training and became fast friends. They were childhood sweethearts who stood the test of time and made their promises to each other under the oak tree in the front yard of her family's camp in Maine. Her family's rabbi officiated their vows, and Bam smashed the goblet under his heel with genuine glee to the chorus of "mazel tov" under a rustic chuppah. Candace and her sisters had woven the arch from vines found on their family property. I offered a heartfelt toast to the newlyweds, unable to separate their joy from my own, and wished Eliott could have been with me. She'd love Maine. Our life stretched out ahead of us; I wondered how many places we would discover together. Stateside? Maybe Alaska and the Pacific Northwest, New England. And overseas…Asia? Definitely Italy, Spain…the Greek Isles. Wales and Scotland. I couldn't wait for a life of making her happy.

I danced with Candace's baby sister, the maid of honor, her mom, and Bam's mother. We'd met years ago at pilot training graduation, and the years had been kind to her.

"Hey there, flyboy." Bam's dad's voice boomed across the

dance floor in my direction. He was a retired Navy pilot, and we'd exchanged good-natured insults at the rehearsal dinner. "You trying to move in on my girl, there, son?" His face was awash with happiness as he feigned stealing my dance partner.

"No, sir, Commander." I mock saluted with a laugh and spun his wife into his arms. "I know when I'm out of my league." The reception tent was permeated with warm light in these hours after dark. The music and sense of celebration were contagious. I wished Eliott were in my arms. We could immerse ourselves in these moments and look forward to many of our own.

Bam and Candace were in a world of their own as the celebration raged around them like a storm, the crowd dancing and enjoying good food and wine. I wandered, catching up with a few friends I hadn't seen over the past several years. The night was still young, but my mind already turned toward getting back to the hotel. I had an early flight out of Boston, back to Tucson and Eliott's arms.

My reverie was shattered by the crude ringing of a cell phone. Who on earth? I was disconcerted to see that I'd neglected to silence my phone, but the screen read "Mom." A pleasant surprise.

"Hi, Mom. How are ya?" I was glad to hear from her; she'd been excited to hear the latest details, however scant, about my plans with Eliott. She was nearly over the moon to meet her next week.

There was only silence for a moment, followed by what sounded like a sob. Then my father's voice. "Son?"

"Dad?" I was confused; the caller ID said it was Mom's phone. I jogged quickly away from the reception and the sounds of the wedding band belting out the words to "Louie Louie." "Is it you? I thought I heard Mom."

My dad's voice sounded strained. "Where are you, Nathan? Still at the wedding? Who's there with you?"

I didn't understand. Something was wrong. Why did Dad call

me on Mom's phone? "It's just me here; I stood up for Bam. His wedding…I'm the best man. Is Mom okay? Who's not…what happened, Dad?"

There was a long pause, then Dad's long exhale. "Son, it's Eliott." I could hear Mom sobbing in the background now. Oh, God. "She's…Nathan, her mother just called me. She's…Eliott, she's gone."

Gone?

That didn't mean anything. Didn't make any sense. "Dad. What do you mean…gone?"

"Son." Dad's voice was broken, reaching through the phone line, across the miles. "Eliott passed away about an hour ago. It was…unexpected. There was an accident. No one knew…no one thought…"

My eyes couldn't see; my mind couldn't think. No. She couldn't be gone, just like that. Could she? We had plans. We had a life together ahead of us. This wasn't real; it had to be a terrible dream.

My dad's voice steadied. "I need you to go to your hotel room, Nathan. Your mom and I are coming to get you. Can you do that for me? I've spoken to Bam's dad, and he's going to grease the skids to get you out of the party right now. You need to wait for us. We'll come for you. Do you understand, son? Then we'll go to Eliott and her family in Tucson."

I don't remember hanging up the phone, but I must have. A deafening noise swirled loudly in my ears, and the ground seemed to fall away. Vaguely, I saw Commander Bamford and his wife rushing toward where I stood rooted. They must have helped me to my room because that's where I was when my parents arrived late the next morning. One of my old pilot training buddies changed his return ticket to remain with me until their arrival, but I hadn't spoken over the hours that passed. He dozed in a chair, and I lay on the bed—staring at the ceiling until morning light washed over the hotel room. My mother wrapped me in her arms, silently weeping, and rocked me while my father wordlessly packed my clothing.

I have virtually no memory of the hours following, but we boarded a plane and flew west, touching down in Tucson just at sunset. Eliott had been involved in a major car accident, one that involved several cars and a large tour bus. Three people were killed, but Eliott's injuries were minor, I was told. She was in the Emergency Department, awaiting treatment behind those who were more severely injured when she suddenly experienced cardiac arrest. Despite immediate medical attention and treatment, she never regained consciousness and died soon thereafter. The doctors were unable to explain what had happened, and an autopsy was planned in an effort to explain the unexplainable.

The ensuing days passed as if I was walking in a dream. Looking back now, I have only occasional flashes of remembrance—snapshots. Meeting Eliott's parents for the first time and accompanying them to finalize funeral details. Picking a favorite pale lilac dress of hers to hold her soft body in its satin-lined casket. My father retying my tie before he and my mother walked by my side into the church. Trying to thank friends and family who hugged me at the reception afterward only to have my voice fail me.

When the week finally passed, I lingered in a fog, numb and unable to eat or feel anything but unfathomable, searing pain. The earth still rotated and life seemed to move on while my Eliott lay dead and still in the cold ground.

But I was utterly lost. I had no idea how to rejoin the living.

Chapter THIRTY-TWO

"Some Enchanted Evening"

Camille

Date night.

Three potential outfits lay discarded, tossed across the bed. I could hear the grumble of the GTO slowing and parking in front of my bungalow as I buttoned cropped denim pants. The embellished hem added sparkle, and favorite wedge sandals would keep things casual enough for what Nate had planned. Now...all that remained was a top. And jewelry—almost done. I flipped through the hangers, rapidly discarding the notion of anything with a sleeve. The summer nights were still sweltering. What about something to work with those rockin' new turquoise chandelier earrings? They were the dog's balls. That Sam was a helluva shopper. I should make a point of hitting the boutiques with her more often.

Warm hands cupped my breasts just as I felt soft lips on my neck. Wait. I couldn't possibly select a top with neck kisses happening. On cue, a warm throb began between my legs. "Nathan?" It was more of a moan than a question. My hands grasped desperately for the door casing of the closet. "Baby?"

"I feel like I'm changing my mind about blue corn tamales, angel." His voice was rough in my ear, and one hand dropped from my breast to pull my nakedness tight to him with a palm flattened against my stomach, just below my waist. Warmth built and swirled in my core, weakening me, and I let him have my weight, breathing in the masculine scent of Nathan. One hand wrapped his corded neck, and I turned my head to meet his lips.

"How did you get in, handsome?"

"You should consider locking the front door." He pulled me roughly against him. "Seriously, Cami…you should lock it. Promise, babe."

"Yep. No problem." I turned to face him, pushing his hands away. I was naked above the waist for his enjoyment and toying with one nipple with a finger I leisurely wet in my mouth. "Do you think we'll have some time alone tonight after our tummies are full of Sonoran? I'm feeling the urge for a leisurely crawl up and down your body. With my fingers. And tongue."

His lips parted, his breathing coming rougher now, and he pulled me again to his hard chest. "I'm primed for some up-close with my baby's hot little body. Did you have anything particular in mind?"

I was glad I'd decided on a glass and a half of wine while dressing. It was time to move things with Nate to the next level, and my cautious nature was screaming at me to run. Even so, everything in my heart said this man was what I'd hoped for but never dared think would come my way.

My fingers tangled in the thick, dark hair. Our eyes locked, bodies stilling. The mood was suddenly serious, and I knew he could sense what I felt whether I could find the words or not. I stood on tiptoes and whispered quietly against his mouth. "I have some things to say. Maybe, with a little luck, the words will come."

The lights in the tree branches seemed to twinkle, evoking star-light, and misters soothed some of the heat from the air. Service was notoriously slow at this well-known café on Congress Street, but the blue corn tamales made the wait worthwhile. Nate's company, easy laugh, and sexy smile would have been enough all on their own, I thought, taking a long drink of my frozen margarita.

"I tell them to do anything. Anything else, if they can think of something different that will make them happy." Nate's eyebrows shot up in an unasked question as he signaled the waiter for another beer. He'd asked me what my advice was to anyone who asked about becoming an RN.

"What do you mean?" He sat forward, giving me an irresistible hint of his warmth and aftershave as he rested his elbows on his knees in that irresistible male way and leaned into my personal space. "Your profession is perennially undermanned, and the need for nurses will only grow in the future."

"True, of course." I couldn't help but reach for his hand with my free one. "But too many people enter nursing school because it's perceived as a guaranteed job with good starting pay. It's true that I've never had difficulty getting a job, but it's also true that it's very competitive to even get into school. And a Bachelor's in Nursing is a notoriously difficult course of study with a high failure rate." I sipped my drink again, appreciating the surroundings.

The waiter handed Nathan his beer. He took a long drink, and I stopped to appreciate the sight of his strong neck and throat working. Even after a few months of dating, the way his potent masculinity drew me was magnetic. Then he smiled. "But that's not it, is it? It's not that school's tough or competitive."

I smiled and laughed a little. A young woman, apparently from the kitchen, was placing delicious-looking platters of blue corn tamales in front of each of us. They were delicately blanketed with queso and accompanied by rice, frijoles, homemade pico de gallo, and handmade guacamole. Heaven. "No. You're right, that's not it." We tucked into the delicious Sonoran food and ate in companionable silence for a few minutes before conversation resumed.

"You've met Vivian, right? Bashful's sister?" Hair and makeup done, Viv was a dead ringer for a red carpet-ready Lucy Liu. I continued. "One afternoon, I watched Vivvie sit with an old homeless man for over two hours, cleaning wounds I won't describe at the dinner table and comforting him while he hallucinated and tried to attack her. It's likely that Viv could've modeled or maybe even have had a career in show business with her looks—I could probably say the same for Luckie—but they both had an urge to make their years here count." I hesitated, enjoying more of my dinner while trying to stitch my thoughts into something coherent.

"It's not that I think some professions or vocations don't matter. Not that at all. And the real deal is that nurses aren't, for the most part, the sweet, subservient personalities some perceive them to be. That wouldn't cut it in today's environment. And that's why I tell people to stay away—unless they're driven to break down the door and join us." I was rewarded with Nathan's wide grin saying he understood my reasoning. "Those are the people we need in nursing."

Our dinner conversation shifted again to cover Mayze's recent unsuccessful and rather low-energy escape efforts and my thoughts about a possible car upgrade. Full plates were emptied, and we were soon enjoying the strains of a surprisingly good mariachi band and an after-dinner margarita when Nathan rounded the table to join me on my side. He tucked me to his side, lazily crossing booted feet on a nearby chair.

"You mentioned earlier you had something you'd like to talk

about, angel." His voice rumbled low in my ear, and he dropped his mouth to kiss my neck with soft, full lips once. Then twice. "Is that something we talk about here?" His face turned to study mine carefully, then softened. "Or is it more like pillow talk?"

The tone and implication in his voice immediately set up an ache between my legs, and my heart rate picked up. Swallowing to assuage the dryness in my mouth, I shook my head. "Not pillow talk. And I'd like to talk about it. Maybe I finally can, you know, now. At least if you'll stop using that sexy tone of voice until we get home." I tried to smile at him.

He relaxed, sitting back, and comforted me with an arm at my shoulder. "When you're ready, Camille. There's nothing you can't tell me…nothing we can't talk about." The notes of the mariachi band floated through the air, and I felt it wasn't so threatening to tell the final Chapter

of my harrowing tale.

"I want to tell you about Amos." Nathan's eyes were at once confused. He cocked his head with another unasked question. "After the attack, I found out I was pregnant." I didn't expect to choke up at the beginning of my story, but Nate gathered me into his arms and rocked me as I fought off the tears.

"Baby, no." His arms were strong and protected me from the unanticipated storm. "You don't have to…"

I worked to fight off the emotion. "He was my son. I was raped, but it wasn't his fault. He was so little and innocent. Perfect and pure. You should have seen him, Nathan." I gasped and slowed my breathing. "He was beautiful, flawless…perfect. Ten fingers and ten toes. You know, you do count them when you meet your baby for the first time, just like everyone says. His fingers were the size of matchsticks but perfectly formed. He had every day ahead of him. He was going to be my family, you know?" My eyes implored him to understand me.

His hand slid down, seeking mine, and squeezed. It was

completely quiet in the space between us for long moments. I buried my face in his chest, and his other hand found my neck, pulling me in tight.

Finally, I spoke. "He was born too early. And he fought so hard, but he died in my arms." I swallowed hard and continued. "Luckie was with me, just like she always has been, and Vivvie and Sam and Grace and everybody. They all stayed with me. But, in the end, it was just me holding my little Amos while he slipped away." I felt Nathan's chest heave. "I miss him every day, Nate." I looked up at his strong face and saw his soft brown eyes brim with tears. "I don't know if it will ever stop hurting."

More minutes stretched as I worked to gather myself. Then I felt Nate's finger lifting my chin so that my eyes met his. "No, Camille." He looked into me. "It won't ever stop hurting. I know it because of the way my heart was torn in two. Someone I loved was taken from me, and I know I'll never be the same. But I have to have faith that it will get better—that I'll be better. And some-day we'll see some beauty in why they were given to us, only to die so young."

The restaurant was relatively quiet, fortunately, but we were completely alone as far as I was concerned. After several minutes passed, our embrace relaxed, eyes again meeting. "Thank you for trusting me with Amos, Cami. I love him because you did...and because he was part of you. But listen to me, Camille." His finger again lifted my chin so I could meet his eyes. "I don't believe for a moment that he's the last young life you'll love and nurture. That's the very essence of who you are, angel."

His words were offered like a balm, but I knew the truth. "I told you I was repeatedly raped and beaten...lost a lot of blood." He nodded, anger and grief darkening his beautiful features. "And I told you the first night we were together that my doctor said I wouldn't be able to have children, but I didn't elaborate." I sighed. "After the attack, the surgeons faced a laundry list of challenges during the hours I spent in the OR. One of those was the effort to save my future fertility." My chest felt tight, and my eyelids stung with unshed tears. "I was told those efforts failed."

His brow knit, and he shook his head, not understanding. "But there was Amos."

I had to smile. Yes, if I'd never had anything else, at least I had the memory of his body growing inside mine. I could still remember my belly rounded like a beach ball. My little son using my bladder as a punching bag. "My ovaries were damaged, one severely. They had to remove that one; the doctor wasn't sure about the other one, but I've only had a couple of periods since the attack." I blew out a breath. Some days it was an uphill battle to fight feeling like damaged goods.

"The gynecologic surgeon earned her paycheck that day. Luckie said she pieced me back together inside like a puzzle; much of my blood loss was a result of the rape trauma. That's the reason for the tight fit you've mentioned." My face suddenly flushed, hot embarrassment radiating off me in waves.

Now you're shy, Camille? Now? After everything you've done with this man?

I was stammering, trying to walk back what I'd said. "Well, I mean it's part of the reason. That and your...you know..." My voice trailed off.

His small, mischievous smirk told me he saw my shyness. How could he miss it? My neck and face were surely stained deep pink. As quickly as the mood had turned somber, it now morphed into something very different. The fear of rejection felt as far away as deep space. Letting Nate into the darkest parts of me had an unanticipated effect. The walls between us, all the secrets I'd hesitated to share?

Tearing those away was tying us together.

Nathan pulled away slightly, his eyes twinkling and darkening at once. Our bodies didn't touch at all now, but the air between us crackled with electric possibility. In what was becoming my favorite Nathan move, he brought his lips to rest just against my own and spoke so that only I could hear.

"My what?"

"Nothing. Nothing," I whispered into his mouth and closed my eyes. My face burned as if lit by the sun.

"Camille Elizabeth." His voice was a growl now, and I felt his soft lips moving on mine when he spoke, a pillowy contrast to his gravelly tone. "Answer me. My what?"

His voice and mouth had sparked a fire in my belly that was rendering me weak and achy. Wanting him. I'd never wished so fervently to be alone. But with Nathan.

"Your cock, Nate." I forced the words out on a groan. "Every inch of your beautiful, thick cock. Makes it so tight...fills me up so good, Nathan. God, I need you right now. I can't believe we're in a fucking restaurant on Congress."

But Nate was ripping a stack of bills from his wallet with one hand as the other adroitly summoned the waiter. The waiter smiled congenially, approaching the table. "I'll prepare the check, señor."

"No need, my friend." Nathan handed him the folded stack of bills and patted his arm with a friendly gesture. "Please keep the change with our thanks."

Nathan offered me his hand, and I hastily shouldered my bag as he practically dragged me toward the door. The waiter thumbed quickly through the bills, breaking into a huge grin, and waved at us like departing family. "Adios, amigos—vuelve pronto!

Chapter
THIRTY-THREE

"Love You Inside Out"

Camille

"**Y**ou get Solomon; I'll find his food and bowls and litter box stuff. Hurry, angel. Dinner was delicious, but I'm very, very hungry." He made no effort to disguise the need in his dark eyes. I nodded, unlocking the door with shaking hands, and reached down to heft Solomon into my arms. His eyes narrowed on me, and I was greeted with an accusatory meow. His substantial paws immediately pushed me away, and he sailed to the floor with a solid thump.

"Mmm. Pissed." Nathan shook his head, chuckling. "We must have the two most ill-tempered domestic animals in the Southwest."

"Likely." I'd begun throwing a few necessities into a small tote…toothbrush, cleansers, and lotions. Shorts, a couple of tees, and sandals. I stuck my head out of the bedroom door to see Nathan expertly stacking litter and kitty food into an empty litter box. "But the real problem is that Sol is clairvoyant. He knows he's spending the weekend in someone else's house. And he probably knows there's a d-o-g."

Nathan's grin was indulgent. He grabbed my bag as I snapped it shut, and I dropped to my stomach to fish Solomon out from his hidey-hole under the sofa. "So your fortune-telling feline also understands you?"

"Well, obviously." I extricated a terribly reluctant Solomon with a grunt and was rewarded with a death glare and fourteen pounds of dead-weight pussycat. Sol was staging a kitty protest—go limp. He'd probably break into "Michael, Row the Boat Ashore" at any moment.

Nathan held the door for us, snapped the porch light on, and locked up behind us. "Wouldn't it then follow that he could also spell?"

"Now, Nate. That's just ridiculous. Whoever heard of a spelling cat?"

The entire extraction effort had been seamlessly planned on the short trip from the restaurant. Nathan wanted me in his bed and his house. We both had a long weekend, and he wasn't interested in rushing between houses to tend livestock. Anyway, he'd reasoned curiously, the animals should get accustomed to each other.

Mayze certainly had her suspicions about my late arrival, but she didn't notice Solomon's emerald eyes studying her—plotting her imminent demise—from his perch in the back of the GTO. We wouldn't bother introducing these two charmers tonight. It would be a process and one that would begin tomorrow. Mayze was let outdoors for an evening constitutional while I installed Sol in Nate's room.

The door opened after only a few minutes, and Nathan slipped wordlessly inside. In one large hand, he carried two wine glasses and a bottle of red, already open and breathing. He sat the glasses on the nightstand, poured generously, and silently bent to where I sat on his bed, kissing my mouth thoroughly. My arms reached for him, ready to pull him onto his bed and inside me, but he caught my hands and held them.

"I have something for you, babe." He opened the nightstand drawer and handed me a silky drawstring bag from a store I recognized as a very expensive lingerie boutique. Loosening the strings, I drew out an exquisite silk chemise, the barest blush pink, with soft, candyfloss embroidered lace frothing along the hem. It may have been the most beautiful item of clothing I'd ever held in my hands.

I didn't know what to say. It was a terribly intimate gift. And an unexpected one, considering the apparent lack of occasion.

"Thank you, Nate. I'm at a bit of a loss, I'm afraid. I don't think I've ever seen anything as lovely as this."

His voice was very quiet. "I discovered it was very difficult to find something worthy to cover your nakedness. Even this"—his fingers caressed the fabric—"seemed a poor choice for the job. But it was the best I could do."

I marveled at the workings of the heart and mind of this man. My man. Yes…mine. Such a deeply thoughtful and romantic gift. Was he beginning to think of me as his?

"I'm happy to wear something so beautiful for you, Nathan. But why cover me at all?" I smiled and raised one eyebrow playfully.

Again he reached into the drawer, returning with two fat candles and a long match. He lit the candles as he spoke. "Mmmm. Yes, why cover those beautiful breasts, soft pink nipples? All that velvety skin?" His eyes darkened again, and he turned off the remaining lamp, leaving the room bathed in candlelight alone. "Because I can't afford the distraction of the heaven between your thighs tonight when I say the things to you I need to say."

Things? What things? Now my heart was pounding and singing at once. And my mouth was hanging open—not cute, Cam. Shut it.

Nathan handed me a glass of wine. "I'm going to put on something more comfortable. Why don't you enjoy some wine while you do the same? It's one of my favorite pinot noirs." With that, he picked up his wine and sauntered into the master bathroom, whistling softly. Sauntered.

The chemise was like sliding into a pale pink cloud. If my nipples were a true distraction, there might be issues, but we would cope somehow. I turned the bed linens back. Hmmm. Could it be? Another linen snob—we were truly a match made in heaven. A double set of oyster-colored Charter Club shadow striped sheets with a real silk blanket sandwiched between the first and second set. Four real down pillows. *Well done, Nathan.*

I was still caressing the sheets pornographically when the bathroom door opened, and Nathan stepped back into his bedroom, near enough to naked that I forgot pretty much everything. His body was long and lean, and the candlelight illuminated the muscles of his arms and abs as he moved across the room toward me. He wore loose jersey lounge pants, button-up rather than drawstring, with the top button oh-so-fortunately undone. The sleek smattering of dark hair there served to remind me that heaven didn't lie only between my thighs. A sizable bulge was already obvious between his legs, and the soft material of those pants did little to conceal an erection that would pleasure me considerably, but later. I was anxious to hear what weighed on Nathan's mind—or heart—first. Eyes meeting mine, he reached to relocate Solomon from where he'd parked himself on the corner of the bed. He groaned and reached for his lower back, feigning injury at Sol's chubbiness.

"He's half pig," I deadpanned.

"I don't doubt it." Nate gently deposited my fat baby in his stupidly plush travel bed at the corner of the room and was immediately rewarded with a brief hiss and Sol's signature death glare.

Nathan settled his long frame easily into bed beside me where I'd stretched out comfortably on two of the plush pillows. He passed me a wine glass before lifting his own to toast, "To the beauty I see inside you and to your beautiful body...I must be crazy to cover it, even for a minute." He grinned and enjoyed a healthy drink from his glass, all the while perusing the length of me, barely covered in the dreamy blush silk.

He swallowed the wine, and his handsome features relaxed into warmth, all focused on me. I snuggled into the protective curve of his arm and waited.

"So. You don't date?" The grin was back. "Me, either, babe. Now that I see more of the whole picture, it all fits together. We weren't looking. I didn't think I should replace Eliott because my love for her was so deep and her death ruined me. I was hard broke. But I see now that I don't have to denounce what existed then to try again. Even Eliott always said that you should never give up...she had a saying about that."

It was my turn to grin. Nate had no way of knowing how much that idea meant to me. He'd never asked about my tattoo; things were always too heated by the time I was naked. "The idea of trying again has been so important to me. I'll tell you the story sometime. But it got me through some very dark days following the attack and Amos's death." I loved how his eyes studied me while I spoke; I knew that he listened to me intently.

"It hasn't been a lengthy courtship, so far, and I'd say things are going very well." Another devastating grin. "But people who are wired the way I am tend to put things on timelines, and I sense very strongly that's a mistake I don't want to make with you. Everything about the way I feel about you is too important to risk a misstep." I could feel my body tense. I couldn't see the direction Nate was taking this; but, all at once, I was completely sure where I wanted him to go. Nathan took my wine glass and sat it deliberately, along with his own, on the nightstand.

"The point is this, Camille Elizabeth." He gathered me carefully into his arms and looked, as he had already done many times, deep into me. "I am in love with you. It's not just an emotional pronouncement, although it is emotional. It's just right; I can feel it down to my bones. You are meant to be mine, and I want to be all yours if you'll have me." He swallowed hard. "Cami, I don't know if I'm blindsiding you, and I don't want you to feel like you need to..."

I didn't mean to do it, I really didn't, but I almost knocked the big man out of his bed when I jumped on top of him, rolling him half over and onto me, my tears spilling over and mixing instantly with laughter and surprise. "Nathan Morgan, I love you. So, so much. It feels like I've waited forever for you to find me."

His mouth was on mine in a second, sweetly nibbling and nipping at my lips before gaining entrance to leisurely explore inside. Big warm hands moved under the gown, stroking my belly, then the tender underside of both breasts. After long moments spent languorously tending me, he paused to carefully release both delicate straps of the gown, fully exposing my breasts and both tight pink nipples more fully to his touch. His mouth wasn't far behind, kissing tenderly at first and then more passionately. "Love you, Cami," he murmured. "So much, baby."

His hands tugged at my gown and his lounge pants, removing both with little ceremony, and then his mouth was at my ear. His voice was serious, urgent. "Need to spend tonight inside you, angel. I want to give you everything you can imagine and some things you haven't thought of yet. I'm going to pour myself into you, mark you with my seed. Make you mine." He hesitated a moment, breathing heavily. "Is that what you want, too, Camille?"

It was my turn for my hands to travel down his glorious body. I gripped his narrow hips, fingers massaging the muscles of his tight ass. I pulled him to me until the length of his erection warmed my belly. "I need all of it, Nathan. I need your hands and mouth, your heart and your cock. Make love to me. Let me come, make me come. Give me what I need; mark me, all of me. I have to have everything. Love me right now, Nate."

He dropped between my legs with a pained groan, licking my breasts and stomach as he descended. I'd expected a kiss, and I got one. But it was my pussy, not my mouth that was slowly opened and thoroughly explored by Nate. He settled between my widely outstretched legs, pushed my knees wide and high, and blew warm breath across the tender, swollen labia. He lapped from one side to the other with the widest part of his tongue, tasting me, and rubbed a bristled cheek against my thigh while he swallowed, letting me know he loved my taste in his mouth. His head rested against my thigh, and he fed leisurely, licking and caressing. Occasionally, his pointed tongue teased under the hood of my clit, bathing the knot as it swelled and throbbed. I grew increasingly restless, lifting myself from the bed toward his mouth.

"Getting closer, angel? I want you to come in my mouth. Love the way you taste…" He continued to feast on my pussy, suckling and groaning as he swallowed what I gave him, all the while teasing my clit in search of my orgasm. Finally, there were two warm fingers at my wet entrance.

"You're nice and creamy wet, baby. Your pussy's ready for me now; relax and let me in. Time for you to come and get ready for my cock." His tongue lapped rhythmically at my clit, and he filled me gently with his two thick fingers, beginning at once to stroke the front wall. My hands clutched the sheets, but it wasn't difficult to come with Nathan in control of my body. He thrust slowly and deeply, circling my clit insistently with his tongue. When he eased me over the edge, it wasn't a crash but an easy slide. Utterly pure, perfect, and intensely sweet in a way only pleasure delivered at the hands and mouth of the man who loved me could've been. Measured waves of bliss rolled over me as my man groaned into my core, slowing with me as the orgasm waned and my eyes finally fluttered open.

He slowly straightened over me, and I took in all that was Nathan, hard and wanting me. He knelt between my still-splayed knees and let his eyes study my naked body in the dim light offered by the candles. One hand lightly rubbed the silky mat of hair along his lower stomach, coming to rest in a firm grip around his hard cock. The other hand moved to his mouth, and he thoroughly cleaned my arousal from his fingers. I noticed idly how he never seemed to miss an opportunity to taste me; what was more, his enjoyment was genuine. His eyes continued their perusal of my body, and his hand began lazily to stroke his length. Then he spoke quietly.

"I don't know that there's anything I love more than making you come, Cami. The noises you make…the way you taste, baby. I can't get enough. But tonight is about me marking you, do you understand?"

I nodded hesitantly. "I think so."

He stopped stroking his cock and eased himself close until I felt his chest brush my taut nipples, supporting his weight on his elbows. The generous head of his erection was warm and slick with precum as it prodded my center, so gently, sliding upward each time, across my very sensitive clit. The beginning of the climb toward a second orgasm had already begun, but Nate stilled. Then he unexpectedly pushed the head of his cock just inside the entrance of my pussy, wresting a moan from my lips. My eyes flew open, and I held my breath.

"Look at me, Camille. Breathe, baby."

I nodded and breathed again, almost ready to take him.

"Such a sweet, tight little pussy my angel has." His voice grated, and his eyes looked right at mine as he pressed himself into me, slow and unrelenting. "Take your man's cock, baby."

I was ready and needy, but he was so much to take. The beat

of my heart marked the seconds as Nate tormented me with his deliberate intrusion. My core felt a heavy, pressing want, craving the thrusts I knew would send me flying. I busied my hands, exploring the width of his chest, brushing tight, coffee-colored nipples with a thumbnail and eliciting a groan. His eyes fluttered shut as he struggled to maintain control. He didn't just love me. He wanted to make me all his.

"Just a couple more inches, angel." His hips worked. "You feel so good, Camille. So fucking good." One of his large hands reached under my bottom, gripping a cheek, and tilted it upward slightly. He bent his handsome face to mine, brushed my lips with his, and seated his length firmly inside me, our hipbones finally resting against one another.

His lips dropped to my ear and ground out one fiercely whispered word: "Mine."

Yes, I thought as he began to move inside me. *All his.*

Chapter
THIRTY-FOUR

"Natural Disaster"

Miles

Thud. Thud. Good. Gawd. Did my fucking head hurt. And why was that damn alarm still squawking? Make it stop. Just. Stop.

What the hell had I been thinking anyway? It was great seeing my old buddies last night, but I was definitely going to pay for doing it on a work night. The Club had been rocking, especially for a weeknight, and I owed myself the chance to unwind. Work was a fucking bitch, especially with Colonel Goody Two Shoes manning the decks.

As far as I was concerned, life was pretty damn good in the Scorpions under Pappy. He could drink every one of us under the table and outshoot us at the range the next morning. That was the kind of badass fighter pilot I wanted to be, and it had nothing to do with being female. It wasn't that long ago that women weren't even allowed in fighter cockpits, and I was grateful to be—for once—a victim of good timing. But *Happy* Morgan was conspiring to tame us and rob me of my independence. Losing

Rifle a few months ago was sad and unfortunate, but that was no reason for Pappy to be the sacrificial lamb. And now to bring in this loser from the Pentagon to be commander? It was an insult.

With this early morning sortie, I found myself raking fingers through an unwieldy mane, seriously second-guessing the choices of last evening. This morning was a bright-and-early air-to-air mission against Deliverance, arguably the best **stick** in the squadron and the weapons officer to boot.

Miles. You dumbass.

I shook my head at my reflection in the bathroom mirror. I was going to pay for this in the most painful way possible. Physical pain and big chunks of my ego served up for Deliverance's breakfast.

Oh, well. Time to shake it off. Cold shower, lots of strong coffee, and several ibuprofen should do the job. As the saying went, if you're gonna run with the big dogs, you gotta piss in the big bushes. Never really did understand what that had to do with flying jets, but there was no time or cerebral capacity for that now.

My disappointment increased exponentially as I made my way into the briefing room with Deliverance. The base's annual **SAREX** was kicking off today. And although exercises were a waste of time and a pain in the ass, I'd been secretly hoping for a checkout as a Sandy pilot today. But that was damn sure off the table now. The "Sandy" call sign dated to the Vietnam War and the mission was the most sacred trust for a Warthog driver. Sandys flew into enemy territory to defend downed aircrews, suppress the threat, and coordinate a rescue by helicopter. The rescue helicopters used the call sign Jolly, dating to the same time in history.

Unfortunately, the little "socks check incident" at the O'Club in front of O'Cherry's wife put the kibosh on good deals for a while. Talk about no fucking sense of humor—and no pull with the Wing King. Pappy would've smoothed that over with very little effort. It got me steamed every time the thought crossed my mind. This guy had no idea about running a fighter squadron; hopefully, he'd be gone as quickly as he'd appeared.

Insult to injury, though? Happy and Bashful, the two fucking dwarfs, were in the briefing room next door; Bashful was getting the boss requalified as Sandy lead. They even had live helicopters for the exercise; wonder who he had to blow to make that happen. Actually, I'd never say it aloud, but it was pretty cool—UH-60 Black Hawks from Papago Army Airfield near Phoenix would be sitting alert at Gila Bend. It wasn't that he had any choice in the matter, but Bashful sure didn't seem to mind being party to Happy's red carpet treatment. Fucking brown-noser. Seemed to me I'd awakened one day to find myself in a squadron of pussies. Ironic, when you really thought about it.

Better focus now, Miles. Today was going to take every ounce of my available gray matter. Deliverance briefed a fairly vanilla **BFM** ride. The A-10 was never intended to be an air-to-air fighter, but pilots needed to be competent at defending themselves if attacked. Of course, the best defense being a good offense, each Hawg carried two AIM-9M Sidewinder heat-seeking air-to-air missiles for the job.

"Deliverance, check."

"Twoop."

Deliverance and I were in our assigned airspace and had switched to a discreet radio frequency where we could communicate freely.

"Deliverance, G warm up, ninety left, now."

On any training mission, fighter pilots check the capabilities of human and machine in the high G environment—a warm-up turn of 3–4 G's in one direction, followed by a higher G test of 5–6 G's back the other direction. Any pilot not up to the physical demands of high G flight was expected to say as much and to modify the mission accordingly. All of this, of course, was to avoid the catastrophic **G-LOC**, a disaster in a single-seat fighter where there's no one else in the aircraft to rescue the pilot from such an emergency.

I eased the pressure on the stick to gain the desired G-forces and was rewarded with a mild closure of my peripheral vision.

That was unexpected.

Shit, at four G's? I would need to focus on working harder on my anti-G straining maneuver when we turned back. "Deliverance, ninety right, now."

Everything hurt. I was tensing and grunting for all I was worth, but my field of vision narrowed frighteningly. It was like looking through a soda straw, nearly a complete blackout. A fucking soda straw at six G's and the mission hadn't even begun. I was shaken, but only momentarily. I could hack it. Backing off was for pussies, and that damn sure wasn't me.

Deliverance's voice came over the radio strong. "Okay, Miles. Why don't you set up on the **perch** first?"

"Lead's ready." Deliverance's voice relayed easy confidence. Typical. He was always ready for anything.

"Two's ready." Yeah, whatever. I'd had a large night, but that didn't mean shit. Bring it.

Deliverance's easy drawl. "Fight's on…"

I dived from the perch toward the inside of D's turn, trading altitude for airspeed. As I started to pull lead, just like shooting skeet, Deliverance abruptly turned directly into my flight path, changing the closure rate and angles dramatically. I eased my turn and slid across his six o'clock.

Without a moment's hesitation, Deliverance rolled the opposite direction and exploded into the vertical, rolling rapidly above and then behind me. Then his fucking drawl, "Fox Two." Just that quickly, he had reversed our positions and won the fight by "killing" me with a simulated AIM-9 shot.

"Deliverance, knock it off."

"Twoop, knock it off." And the engagement ended.

"Okay, Miles. You know the strength of the A-10 in this environment is the turn rate we can generate. Be ready for it. Let's set it up again." Classic Deliverance, the ideal weapons officer. Always the expert, always in instructor mode. But he was just so easygoing, so fucking patient and agreeable; it was impossible not to like him. Dammit.

The second engagement was a carbon copy of the first. I overshot to the outside of the turn, and Deliverance performed another textbook rolling reversal to a Fox Two, waxing my ass easily. Goddammit, I was so fucking pissed at myself. Where the hell was my head?

D remained unflappable. "Come on, Miles. Let's do one more of those; this isn't like you. I want to see you use more of your vertical to create space when the angles start to develop. You feeling okay back there?"

"Twoop," came my terse reply. Third time's the charm. I would not be embarrassed again.

"Lead's ready."

"Two's ready."

"Fight's on."

I committed hard off the perch, diving for max airspeed while positioning the nose of my aircraft well in front of D's turn. As I watched him set up the same high G turn in my face again, I made the fateful decision that I would *not* overshoot. I rolled into even more bank and pulled on the stick for all I was worth, right to the 7.3 G limit of the jet.

My jet went belly-up to Deliverance's, and I lost sight of him. My vision was squeezed completely away—fully blacked out—due to the high G-forces acting on my body. I should have called "Lost sight, knock it off," but my ego was too severely bruised from the previous engagements.

Deliverance, I learned later, saw my mistakes. But my pride

and stupidity were so deeply rooted, they could hardly be called "mistakes." When your mistakes endanger or even hurt your friend, you should probably call them "moral failure" or "unforgivable cowardice," instead.

Whatever he did see, he saw too late. There was no time to move his jet from the path of mine or to make a radio call. My temporarily blind eyes could save neither of us. Both of us felt and heard the sickening crunch as the thirty-thousand-pound A-10s collided, high above the Arizona desert.

Deliverance

"Deliverance, knock it off." I made the radio call automatically.

As my eyes and brain tried to assess what had transpired, the realization somehow dawned that my cockpit was no longer attached to the jet. It had been torn entirely free. A split second ago, I'd been soaring sixteen thousand feet above the earth with eighteen thousand pounds of thrust at my command. Now I was in free fall, abandoned to whatever mercy gravity might show me.

Left with no options, the years of hard work, study, and training stood me in good stead. With virtually no conscious thought, I assumed the correct body posture—feet back, elbows in, neck and back erect—and pulled the two ejection handles at my sides. The rocket motor beneath me fired, and the ACES II ejection seat did the rest.

Chapter
THIRTY-FIVE

"If It All Falls Down"

Nathan

Bashful and I transited the range complex at low altitude, en route to the "survivor," albeit a simulated one since this was only a training exercise. It was impossible not to enjoy the flawless blue sky. Days like this would bring a smile to a guy's face, I had to admit. Bashful must have been thinking along similar lines.

"I ordered up the weather special for your re-qual, Happy. Just one of the many services we offer here at Scorpion Central."

I could hear the smile in his voice, even though our faces were hidden completely by custom-fitted helmets and oxygen masks. "It must not have been long since you were Sandy qualled," Bashful continued. "Doesn't look like you've forgotten any…"

Drowning out his voice, the emergency frequency, known as Guard, erupted with a continuous staccato beeping that sent my pulse racing. An Emergency Locator Transmitter.

Bashful's voice was all business. "ELTs were specifically not briefed as part of the exercise. Someone's down."

Miles

I blew my breath out once, hard, instinctively rolling the wings of the jet level, and initiated a gradual climb. The G-forces punishing my body eased, and my vision recovered, but I almost wished it hadn't. Everywhere I looked, the shitshow worsened. Multiple caution and warning lights illuminated the panel by my right knee, all harbingers of bad news.

And where was Deliverance? A wave of nearly uncontrollable nausea hit me as possibilities crowded my mind. I could barely force myself to look down. When I did, every pilot's very worst fear registered in my unbelieving eyes.

A thick column of oily, black smoke rose from the desert floor off to my left. My stomach wretched violently, and I dragged in jagged breaths, fighting to maintain control. I wanted to scream, vomit, and hit something. But my only hope of making it out of this alive was a cool head. Working to control my breathing, I noted both my hydraulic reservoir caution lights were illuminated, indicating I was rapidly losing hydraulic fluid, my aircraft's lifeblood. Despair choked me as surely as if cold fingers were wrapping themselves slowly around my throat. The control stick went sluggish in my hand; the hydraulics were gone.

Then, from the very edge of my peripheral vision, a flash of orange caused my heart to leap into my throat and my head to whip around. There, at my seven o'clock, was the most beautiful sight I could've seen in that dark moment: an olive drab, white and bright orange emergency chute swung in the sky far beneath me. Deliverance had gotten out. Was he hurt? Alive? There was no way to know that. Not now.

The A-10 was designed to accomplish its mission, soak up an inordinate amount of battle damage, and bring its pilot home alive; and it did that more successfully than any airplane ever had. To that end, it was designed with a rudimentary system connecting some of the flight controls to the stick with cables.

This gave the pilot basic control of the airplane in flight, even without hydraulics. I reached for the flight control panel, then found and selected the **manual reversion** switch. With control of the aircraft out of immediate danger, I selected the emergency frequency on my radio and made the call that would haunt me the rest of my life.

"Mayday, Mayday, Mayday. Deliverance Two on Guard. Deliverance lead is down—positive chute. I say again, Deliverance lead is down—positive chute."

Nathan

I always knew one of my personal strengths lay in crisis management. It was an unconfirmed suspicion of mine that this was a gift one was born with—or not. I had the ability to compartmentalize, delegate, and effectively remove emotion from my decision making. Of course, it would've been inappropriate to talk about it, but others had noticed this forte of mine, and my mentors had nurtured it over the course of my career.

Obviously, I was aware that my people, specifically my weapons officer and my chief problem child, were in the immediate airspace. Even if that hadn't been the case, natural leadership characteristics would've leaped to the forefront. Under these circumstances, they clawed their way out. Bashful and I began an easy climb to conserve fuel and get a better view. Selecting Guard on my radio, I announced, "All aircraft in the Goldwater Ranges, Sandy on Guard. Knock it off, knock it off, knock it off."

A global "knock it off" meant that every military aircraft in the range complex would immediately cease whatever they were doing; most would've heard Deliverance's ELT. They would realize a fellow pilot was in trouble and either offer relevant assistance or, at a minimum, stay the hell out of the way.

I required no encouragement to assume command of the situation. Fortuitous timing had placed me here where I could take care of my people; no one could do it better than I would.

I addressed Bashful. "Sandy Two, switch to command post and launch the exercise helicopters out of Gila Bend. Get them airborne yesterday, and confirm they understand this is the real deal—not an exercise."

A quick "Twoop" and Bashful was coordinating. I swapped transmitters to the Scorpions' dedicated VHF radio frequency, took a deep breath and called Miles.

"Deliverance Two, Sandy on Scorpion Victor, how copy?"

Her voice returned immediately, much shakier than I was accustomed to hearing Miles's voice sound over the radio.

"Deliverance Two, loud and clear, boss."

"Say location."

"Over the hills just east of Ajo. Deliverance is down." I thought I could hear her choke up a little at the end of the transmission.

My direction was clear and concise. "Miles, hold high and dry. Keep D in sight. Help is on the way."

Fuck.

I hoped we weren't too late.

Deliverance

The chute blossomed perfectly, just like in the movies. The ejection seat was an E-ticket ride, as advertised, I thought wryly. I worked methodically through my post-ejection procedure: checking the chute, releasing my steering toggles, discarding my oxygen mask, lowering the visor. But where to land? The terrain in this area was uninviting, steep and rocky. Additionally, the round emergency chute offered only limited steering, unlike the rectangular parachutes used by more skilled Special Forces or sport jumpers. I aimed for a mostly clear area, still somewhat rocky, and attempted to turn myself into the wind to slow my speed over the ground.

No tricky landings for me. Our training taught us to touch down with both feet and roll immediately along the side of our body to allow maximum body surface area to absorb the impact.

I slowed myself as much as the wind would allow, but the ground came up to meet me too quickly. No question I was descending way too fast. My left leg hit first, absorbing way more force than God designed it to take.

I retched reflexively from the overwhelming force of pain, and the sound of my femur snapping echoed off the ravine walls. I skidded and rolled painfully along the ground, my injured leg dragging uselessly behind me as I struggled to stop, flailing with my good leg and arms. Finally still, I groaned at the crushing assault of pain, and the parachute fluttered down, covering my bloodied, broken body.

Nathan

"Bashful, where we at on those choppers?" There was no edge in my voice; Bashful fully understood the critical nature of my query. Anyone overhearing our radio conversation would assume from the tone that today was nothing more than an ordinary trip to the range for fighter pilot fun and games. Livin' the dream. Of course, nothing could be further from the truth, I thought grimly, racing across the desert floor toward one of the pilots in my command, in trouble. Bashful's voice was somber.

"Jolly One and Two were on ten-minute alert—spooling up now. Should be airborne soon."

"Right." The plan solidified in my head. "Get 'em headed toward Ajo."

"Twoop."

I spotted the smoke. Bashful and I were at max grunt to get to Deliverance and Miles; I called her on the radio as we approached.

"Deliverance Two, say altitude."

Miles's voice was stronger answering me this time. "Nine thousand."

"Rog, stay at nine or above; Sandy's coming in at seven thousand."

My mind carefully reviewed the details of the search and rescue effort when the ELT's beeping suddenly and disconcertingly stopped. My breath caught as I waited along with everyone on the frequency for what might come next.

"Any aircraft, any aircraft, Deliverance lead on Guard."

My shoulders sagged in relief at the familiar drawl. Even tinged with stress, D still sounded every iota the cool fighter pilot on the radios, as if he punched out of a jet every Monday morning. He was alive and conscious; now we had to get him home.

"Deliverance, Sandy, switch secondary."

Deliverance's survival radio could transmit on Guard or over a secondary frequency; the latter gave us a less cluttered channel for our communications.

"Say status."

"I'm down a little ravine, boss." D took a few slow, pained breaths. "My leg's banged up pretty good."

Well, maybe that wasn't so bad, I guessed. "Do you think it's broken, D?"

His chuckle was rueful and more pain was apparent as he tried to laugh. "Oh, it's broken all right. It's good and broken. But I've tied my scarf around the wound, and that's holding off most of the bleeding, for now."

It was a great relief to know he was alive, but there was no doubt he was severely injured; we had no time to waste in getting him medical attention. I tried to be sure the anxiety I felt didn't bleed into my tone when I replied.

"Hang in there, buddy. Jolly's en route; we'll have you patched up and back on the LPA's ass in no time. Deliverance Two, say fuel."

"Bingo plus one, boss." Miles's demeanor was understandably improved with the knowledge that Deliverance was alive, but now we had other fish to fry. "Bingo plus one" indicated she was approaching a fuel level that would require us to expedite her return to base. Fortunately, she had successfully talked my eyes onto D's position. It was easy to see the dire condition of her jet, and she was operating in manual reversion. Thank God it was Bashful who would be holding her hand for what was ahead. It wasn't going to be pretty.

Chapter
THIRTY-SIX

"Take These Broken Wings" (Reprise)

Bashful

I knew what he would do, because it's exactly what I would've done. I also knew how the whole thing would go over with Miles. Like a goddamned fart in church, that's how. And as glad as I was to see that D was alive, I found myself shaking my head and muttering to myself.

"Fuckin' A, Miles…it didn't have to be this way." My thoughts were interrupted by Happy's crisp, all-business radio call.

"Sandy Two, Lead will coordinate the rescue from here. Bash, rejoin on Miles, and take her home."

"Twoop."

Rejoining on Miles, I got a good, long look at the train wreck that was the remains of her jet. The right vertical stabilizer was completely missing, as was most of the right horizontal stabilizer. I grimaced as I thought about the conversation I was about to have with Miles. Her shit day was about to get much worse. Mindful of her dwindling fuel, I pointed us toward home.

Miles was uncharacteristically quiet on the squadron frequency, but she would have plenty to say after I told her what was on my mind. I took a deep breath and waded in.

"Miles, you've got a lot of damage. I'm gonna recommend that we head for the controlled bailout area and give this baby back to the taxpayers." Every base had a designated area where a pilot could make a safe, controlled ejection from an unlandable aircraft. The words barely cleared my mouth when Miles launched her verbal assault.

"Oh, hell no, Bashful. Hell. No. Even for me, this has been a record-setting day of fuck-ups, and I'm sure as shit not gonna cost the squadron a second jet before lunch."

I was only slightly more confused than normal when trying to reason with Miles, but it was important to stay on task. Clearly, she was planning to attempt a landing in manual reversion. A few had tried over the years, although that was never the intent of the design, and a few had even been successfully landed. But when it didn't work out, a manual reversion landing spelled disaster.

We were burning daylight in terms of fuel, so I continued to press toward Davis-Monthan as I argued my case for controlled ejection with Miles.

"Look, Miles…" Getting through to her was a challenge on a good day, stubborn as she was. Today, it would be all but impossible. I swallowed hard.

"Charlotte."

Nobody ever called Miles by her given name. Ever. When her brother visited a few months ago, we'd learned, to our eternal delight, that our beautiful, tough-talking, hard-as-nails Miles had a girlie name. No one had gathered the intestinal fortitude to tease her with it yet. Now it just seemed like a way to break through that impenetrable will of hers.

"You know a controlled ejection is the conservative call here. Landing a jet in this shape is a great way to get dead." I was mad as hell at her for being so damn stubborn, but I put supreme effort into softening my voice. "The Scorpions are gonna kick my ass if something happens to you, Charlotte Christman. You're important to us, girl."

The frequency was quiet seemingly forever. Then Miles's voice was much gentler.

"I have to do this, Bash; I need to try. I've been angry for so long...too much to prove. You're gonna see a new Miles, starting today. Now grab the checklist and call the SOF and help me get this wounded Warthog on the ground. I've got work to do."

She paused, as if able to see my slack jaw behind the oxygen mask. I swallowed and tried to recover from the shock her words had dealt. Then she spoke once more, almost as an afterthought...

"Hey, Jacob? No matter what, thanks for everything. You've always been one of my favorites."

Miles

Bashful and I had a moment there, but we'd reeled it back in, and final preparations were underway for landing. Bash walked me through a controllability check, and together we'd determined that a very fast final approach speed of 190 knots would be required due to the extensive damage and lack of hydraulics.

Bashful had also communicated with the SOF to tell her the plan, declare an emergency, and request a single frequency approach. That meant that all of the key players in this emergency scenario—Bash, myself, the SOF, the tower, and the fire department would be on the same radio channel.

Now it was all up to me.

Nathan

I picked up a lazy orbit and kept Deliverance in sight and talking. Jolly was airborne from Gila Bend with two UH-60s and was inbound in less than five minutes. Good thing, too, I thought grimly. D's voice was steadily losing strength and focus as we talked on the emergency frequency, but his trademark wit was intact.

After directing Jolly on the Scorpion squadron frequency for what seemed like an eternity, they'd arrived and begun setting up for the rescue. Jolly lead directed his number two to hold high and dry while he got eyes on the survivor and selected a landing site.

After some further maneuvering, he landed well away and downwind from Deliverance to avoid injuries from the rotor wash. The crew manning Jolly lead were traditional National Guardsmen and highly qualified for the work that awaited them today in the desert ravine. Each worked for the city of Tucson, one as a firefighter and one as a paramedic. With a couple of decades experience apiece, there wasn't much the two of them hadn't seen. Twice.

Despite excellent spirits, D's injuries were serious, I was told by Jolly's commander. He'd suffered a compound fracture to the right femur along with disconcerting blood loss, despite his efforts to quell the bleeding. There were many other contusions and additional trauma that would require attention and sutures, but those could wait for now. He was on the verge of unconsciousness.

The crewmen moved rapidly to stabilize and transport him onto a litter and into the imposing helicopter. As I watched from above, in constant radio contact with Jolly One, my weapons officer's body, appearing all but lifeless, was skillfully removed from the desert floor and lifted into the morning sun toward home.

Miles

I took a deep breath, willing my skittering thoughts to calm, and called the final controller on the single frequency as directed.

"Deliverance Two, emergency aircraft, five thousand feet."

The air traffic controller's voice came back, direct and confident. "Deliverance Two, D-M. Radar Contact, ten south of Davis-Monthan, plan runway three-zero. Say your request, ma'am."

"Deliverance Two, request vectors for an extended visual, three-zero, at least twenty miles."

I had already logged more time flying a Warthog in manual reversion than virtually any other A-10 pilot, I thought with a wry grin. Surely there was a patch for that? Maybe, in my case, the dumbass patch, I concluded. The very first time a new Hawg driver went through the Schoolhouse, there was one opportunity to fly in manual reversion—at a safe altitude and certainly without attempting a landing. It was unspoken, but everyone knew risking a manual reversion landing when another option existed was foolhardy. The jet was heavy and sluggish, and small errors in pitch or power quickly exacerbated control difficulties. Only a handful of pilots had successfully attempted a landing while in manual reversion with a badly damaged jet. The crackle of the radio snapped me back to the present.

"Roger, Deliverance Two. Fly heading one-two-zero. Advise ready to turn base. The fire department is on frequency and standing by. You are number one to the runway."

The plan as we'd reviewed it with the SOF was to fly a long, straight approach, giving me plenty of time to extend the landing gear to slow my very rapid 190-knot approach speed as well as to get a feel for the handling characteristics. Bashful would remain close by, chasing me all the way to the runway. He would offer snippets of input without distracting, much like a boxer's cornerman.

The loss of hydraulics meant no landing flaps, an emergency extension of the landing gear, limited emergency braking after touchdown, and no nose wheel steering. And...well. Let's be honest, that's only if I even made it that far. Which was a relatively long shot. My landing would close the base's only runway, and—if that wasn't enough—I had fuel for one attempt.

Only. One. Attempt.

If that attempt was unsuccessful, my only option was to fly immediately to the controlled ejection area and punch out. Bash had been successful in convincing me of that, or rather the amount of fuel remaining in my tank had convinced me. I called the tower.

"Deliverance Two, ready for base turn." My navigation system indicated about twenty miles from the runway. Go time.

The reassuring voice of the controller returned through my radio. "Deliverance Two, D-M final. Turn left heading zero-three-zero. Speed and altitude your discretion. Advise the runway in sight."

I breathed in and out once hard. "Deliverance Two. Field in sight."

"Deliverance Two. You are cleared for the approach; cleared to land. Good luck, ma'am."

I rolled out onto final as I had done dozens, maybe hundreds, of times before, and thanked God for the unlimited desert visibility. Complicating this day with bad weather would've made the difference in very difficult and fucking impossible.

A quick glance at Bash confirmed his presence on my wing. I gave him the visual signal to lower the gear. He cheated a little further outboard, neither of us knowing what the jet might do. I lowered the gear handle, added a bit of power, then released and pulled the alternate gear extension lever. I held my breath a little for the umpteenth time that day, treading into uncharted waters, and listened attentively.

I sensed in my gut, rather than heard something happening. A seemingly interminable delay, and then...three gloriously green lights on my control panel indicated three safe landing gears in place and ready for me to attempt landing. One more battle won.

Time to start the descent. The book called for a shallow, power-on approach, but my initial efforts were ham-fisted, resulting in dramatic pitching of the nose. The stick was heavy and challenging to control. Fuck...adding power, recovering the nose. Now...too high and too fast.

One shot, Miles.

Bash's voice came through the radio, as calm as if we were in the huddle at the intramural flag football game. "Miles. You got this. Small corrections. Focus on the pitch and accept some airspeed deviations to avoid the big power changes."

I double-clicked the mic switch to acknowledge.

My final approach continued like a drunken sailor reeling down a Manila sidewalk. Bashful hung right with me, calmly calling parameters, as I approached a mile.

Now...less than thirty seconds to go. I only heard Bashful's calm guidance in my ear as I crossed the threshold of the runway; I struggled to make only small corrections. Almost there.

Too high. Power back.

Pitch back...

Power on and...a hard BAM...oooff. An incredibly hard three-point touchdown knocked the air from my lungs like I'd been punched in the gut. I immediately glanced at my speed. Fuck, I was fast. Now release and pull the emergency brake lever. I had only five brake applications available. Better make 'em count.

Steering with my feet, I applied the brakes as smoothly as possible, making every effort to avoid a skid.

God, still so fucking fast.

Bash was in my periphery, a scant twenty feet off the ground, right on my wing as I tore through two-plus miles of D-M's runway far too rapidly. It wasn't until the fourth application, as I clearly had the end of the runway in sight that I could relax slightly. The speed was bleeding off. My wounded Hawg creaked and came to a stop, at last.

A parade of emergency vehicles and fire trucks converged from the opposite end of the runway just as the shadow of Bash's jet momentarily obscured the Tucson sun warming my cockpit. On the squadron frequency, he sent a parting shot.

"Shit hot, Charlotte."

On the tower frequency, Bashful's every day, dead-calm fighter pilot voice was back. "D-M Tower, Sandy Two request tower to tower to Tucson International, emergency fuel."

Chapter
THIRTY-SEVEN

"I've Been Changed for Good"

Camille

I was taking a rare and welcome breather from the Emergency Department on this cloudless, blue morning. Gracie joined me for coffee in the singularly unappealing ambulance bay overlooking—well, nothing. The entire shift stretched before us, long and filled with uncertainty as it always was. The night girls had left the department with only a couple of patients, a treat we enjoyed with skepticism. Nurses were a suspicious lot; quiet never lasted long. Grace regaled me with details of her disastrous date a couple of evenings ago.

"So…Samanthe's neighbor set me up with her brother who was coming into town. It all sounded okay when we met over drinks a couple of nights before, I swear. But Cami, he showed up wearing a fanny pack. A shitting fanny pack. I was looking for the warranty sticker on his ass to return him before the first round of drinks came."

I smiled into my Styrofoam cup of mediocre coffee, torn between sympathy for my friend's dilemma and the hilarity of the scenario. And there was that comical inability to swear properly. I did need to talk to Luckie about that. I couldn't understand how she made it through nursing school without the ability to curse lyrically like the rest of us. It had seemed like part of the curriculum.

"So, right before the food comes, he leans across the table toward me…" Grace squinted dramatically into my eyes over her coffee cup, grasped my hand, and rasped, "'So, babe, I've always felt that pleasure is best when it's mixed with a little pain.' I swear, Cami. That's what he said. I just sat there, looking at the waiter serving my fajita shooters and…"

As I tried to take in the horror of the blind date, the relative quiet of the morning was violently disrupted with beating blades of what I assumed was a large helicopter. The sound launched an assault on my eardrums in a way that made both of us stare toward the helipad and clamp our hands over our ears. But the sound wasn't at all like the higher-pitched whirring of our customary medevac helicopters. Grace and I jogged farther away from the building to get a better look just in time to see a hulking A-10 speeding at low altitude across the hospital campus. It turned south just as a menacing-looking helicopter approached the rooftop pad; then the A-10 disappeared as quickly as it had come. Before I could process these odd events, Vivvie was in front of me, green eyes flashing, clamping her fingers on my arm and commanding attention with her stare. Her tone was terse and directed right into my ear.

"Jacob sent me word. There's been an aircraft accident, and it's Deliverance. I don't know how bad it is, Camille. You need to keep Luckie away; he said things are more serious with them than we know. Keep. Her. Out. That's what he said. I'm getting trauma one ready; get up to the helipad. I'll be ready when you get there." She was gone before I could ask any questions.

Grace was already jogging toward the building, and Vivvie

and I ran to catch up. I pushed through the double doors, calling instructions as I ran for the stairs, and stuffing extra supplies in my pockets as I went. Luckie stuck her head out of an exam room with a questioning look, but I shook my head her direction.

"Got it covered, Luckie. Hang here and keep an eye on exam three and four. The doc may need to suture."

Thankfully, she nodded her assent without discussion. I hit the door with the attending doctor close at my heels, taking the stairs two at a time and trying to make sense of what Viv just said. Davis Foster and Luckie were serious? How could I not know this? And just how bad were these injuries?

I pushed the door to the roof open against the strong resistance of the gusts generated by the helicopter's rotors; the noise was deafening. Against the strong morning sun, the formidable sight of a hulking dark green helicopter bearing the words "United States Army" greeted me as it settled gently onto the roof. The rotors immediately began to unspool as the door opened, and I squinted to make out the figures moving inside.

Only a short time passed before two uniformed medical crew members deftly offloaded the patient, moving him, with our assistance, to the adjustable stretcher Josie delivered to the roof via the elevator. Josephine Emmanuelle Charbonneau was our unit secretary, jack of all trades, clear-thinking master of everything—and my invaluable right arm. I kept my expression impassive, but my heart dropped into my stomach as I took in the handsome, unconscious face of Captain Davis Foster.

His flight suit had been partially cut away to accommodate two large bore IV lines infusing fluid into his arms. There were more ugly bruises and contusions than I cared to count, but nothing caught my eye like the left leg. The legs of the flight suit were cut away almost to the top of the leg, and the first responders, one of whom I recognized as a City of Tucson paramedic, had ably stabilized and bandaged what looked to be a traumatic fracture. His eyes caught what I was seeing and he lifted his chin toward the injured leg.

"Thirty-one-year-old male, military aircraft accident at approximately 0900 with subsequent ejection from the aircraft. Couldn't make Phoenix due to weather. Compound fracture sustained upon landing, and not the pretty kind. He field-dressed the wound to the best of his ability but lost a good bit of blood, too. I'd estimate at least 1500. No other major injuries apparent. Eighteen-gauge lines to left and right antecubitals infusing LR at one hundred each. He's had fourteen hundred total on the way in, and you can count three hundred in each bag. He was conscious when we got him on the chopper, but he became unconscious just afterward."

The attending and I continued to receive the particulars from the crewmen as we loaded Davis onto the elevator and descended back into the Emergency Department. He was suffering from shock due to blood loss, but I couldn't help but see his unconscious state as a blessing.

As the elevator slowed, I turned to Josie and spoke while I organized my thoughts. "Call surgery and…"

"I'll tell them to hold a room and a crew," she interrupted. "I'll call Neal in the blood bank. That cantankerous bastard owes me a favor. I'll have him type and cross two…" Her experienced eyes swept over Davis's pale visage. "No, four units of packed cells. Where are his dog tags?"

I was wondering the same thing as my hands felt gently at Davis's neck for the metal tags. The crewman who gave us the report unzipped one of the pants pockets of Davis's flight suit and extracted the dog tags.

"They carry them here for safety. He's A neg."

I turned my attention back to Josie. "Four units of A neg then. Type and hold four more. And an ortho room and surgical crew. Let them know it's one of our active duty members, please." I placed one hand on Josie's arm. "And, Josie? Keep Luckie busy, yeah? I need her to hear about this from me before she sees him."

"Done, sister." And Josie was gone. The whole unit would collapse into a pathetic heap of dust without her, I thought.

We wheeled the stretcher across the hall into trauma room one where Viv waited, EKG leads in hand. At times like these, it was reassuring to have highly skilled friends working alongside you, giving the best of everything to those who couldn't help themselves. Josie quietly closed the door behind us once everyone was inside, pulling the partial hall curtain.

Davis was rapidly stabilized, transfused with blood to replace most of what he'd lost, and readied for surgery to repair his shattered leg. Fortunately, the exam and CT scan had revealed that the compound fracture, while severe, was the worst of the injuries. He was probably only sleeping deeply now due to the medication given to relieve his pain before surgery.

Josie continued to bring me occasional updates on the state of affairs in the ED, and, to my everlasting surprise, the unit remained relatively sedate. For once. I offered a brief prayer of thanks to the patron saint of chaos for the break and put an arm around Vivian.

"Will you go get Luckie for me, Viv? I want to talk to her and give her a minute with him before surgery. Then I'll get you to accompany Captain Foster to surgery and give report. They just called for the preop med, so I'll give it. They said they'll send transport down in fifteen minutes or so."

Viv smiled and nodded, closing the door behind her. I drew up the prescribed medication, flicked the syringe with a fingernail and pushed the air out of it like I'd done a thousand times before. I pulled up a stool next to Davis, his face relaxed. Despite the giant-sized body, he looked almost childlike. Once his initial medical care had been completed, Viv and I had cut the bloodied flight suit away from his broken body, gently bathed the dirt and blood from his skin, and dressed him with a gown. He was warm under the flannel blankets we tucked around him. Without discussing it, we both knew it was as if we were doing it for Lucinda. She hadn't yet shared with us the nature of why she cared for Davis Payne Foster, but she had her reasons. I administered the medication through Davis's IV and held his hand while I spoke.

"Luckie's the reason I'm alive, Davis. I love her more than my own life, so it's a gift to be able to take care of you today. I'm not going to lecture you in your condition. I'll just tell you to take care of my girl. She's everything to me. I love her, and, if you stick around long enough, you will, too. If you don't already."

I heard Vivvie approaching, and I walked into the hall to find her holding Luckie's hand. Luckie's face held questions and tears barely at bay. I strode toward her, clasping both her hands in mine with a soft smile.

"Luckie, Davis is alive and stable. He's here with us, and Vivvie and I have been taking care of him. He's going to be okay, but there's been an aircraft accident, and he had to eject." The bit of color remaining in her cheeks drained away, and she squeezed my hands, breathing hard. I pressed on.

"He has a nasty compound fracture to the left femur, and Vivvie's taking him to surgery for reduction in just a few minutes. He lost a good bit of blood, but we're doing replacement with packed cells and volume. He's been out since he got here, but they got to him quick, honey. He's gonna be okay."

She wilted and choked a little and then started to cry, but I shook the hands I held and pulled her closer to me. "Look at me, Lucinda, look. This is why I did this…why I didn't tell you right away. I wanted you to have a chance to pull it together. Davis is gonna need you, just like I did, Luckie. Viv and I made sure that he got the very best care. Now you have to make sure he gets his best girl, do you understand? There's none of this melty, female bullshit before he goes to surgery. You know he may hear you."

I waited for her beautiful caramel eyes to meet mine, and I lifted my chin. "Get your shit together, Luckie, and go talk to your man. He's waiting for you."

I hadn't finished my instructions before her arms crushed me and her lips were at my ear. "Thank you, Camille. I don't know what I would've done if…you hadn't been here."

I squeezed her back, and then pushed her away. "Shut up, wench. Dry your face and go see Davis."

She took a deep breath and turned toward the doors of the trauma room but stopped briefly when I called her name. "Hey, Luckie? Your man has a super-fine ass."

The doors swung open just as the Lucinda I knew roared back to life. She shot an evil glare tinged with a little smile over her shoulder. "You keep your fucking eyes off my boy's ass, bitch. I. Will. Cut. You."

Chapter
THIRTY-EIGHT

"Working for the Weekend"

Camille

"So, how's our patient holding up?" Nathan was stretched out on my sofa. Solomon regally purred away on his stomach and leered over at Mayze, who pouted from her bed in the kitchen. I was padding around in baggy hospital scrubs, having had one of those work days that included a mid-shift shower and wardrobe change. My look was completed with thick socks on my feet and a limp ponytail. Thusly attired, I busied myself preparing a feast of takeout and leftovers to shore up our flagging energy; we were both ending a very long week.

Nathan's week began early Monday with the mid-air and progressed to paperwork and meetings discussing disciplinary actions and next steps for the Scorpions. Mine had been complicated as I ran the unit and worked extra to cover Luckie. She was spending as much time as possible at Davis's bedside. His doctor agreed to discharge him home on the fifth day with the condition that he have twenty-four-hour nursing care for the following two weeks, minimum. Luckie was providing most of that, with Bibi dropping in daily for some ass-kicking, Scorpion-style physical therapy. A home health nurse filled in so Lucinda could work part-time.

"He's doing so well," I enthused. "I'm so proud of him. I went with Bibi yesterday to help with PT, and he's just powering through it like a boss. He's gonna be well ahead of the curve; you watch. And they did this cool thing."

I was talking with my hands now like I often did when I got excited explaining something. "With the open repair in surgery, they used this method called the intramedullary nail, and it's…"

But Nate had put down his beer and was frantically waving his hands while trying to swallow. "No." He choked the beer down. "No, don't talk about it. Ugh. TMI. Too much information. Blood and bones and…just no." His face was twisted with disgust.

I dissolved into laughter. "The big, badass fighter pilot doesn't like blood and guts—is that it?" I bent to feed Mayze a bite of the chicken I'd cut up. She continued to stare at Sol while taking the morsel and making a show of affectionately licking my hand. Mayze was bringing out the big artillery in the battle Solomon had brought to her door. The gloves were off.

I poured a fishbowl-sized glass of red for myself and grabbed another cold Stella from the fridge for Nate. I delivered them to the coffee table, along with a strange mishmash of leftover Chinese takeout, last night's homemade tandoori chicken (yummy cold) and good grocery store sushi I'd grabbed on the way home. "No chopsticks, sorry. I completely forgot. I have soy in a bottle if you need it, but you'll have to forage in the cabinet. I can't stand up one more minute." I flopped next to Nate on the sofa.

"Not a problem, angel. Don't need chopsticks. Probably don't even need silverware." He lifted his bottle. "Here's to making it through the week, and here's to a relaxing weekend with my girl. And to spicy tuna rolls." We grinned, clinking drinks, and fell on the makeshift meal like we hadn't eaten in a month.

The week had been far too busy to see each other. Although we talked briefly each day, it had been five days apart, filled with long, stressful hours of work for both of us. There was no major negotiation, but when Nate called to say he'd be over with Mayze after work on Friday, I almost expected the call. We felt the bond strengthening between us and quietly acknowledged the increasing need to spend time together.

As the feeding frenzy slowed, I sat back, sipping my wine, and rubbed Nathan's muscular thigh. He pulled me close, tucking me into the crook of his arm. Sol, of course, meowed his jealous displeasure. Fickle bastard.

"So what happens now?" I addressed Nate, turning to enjoy the warmth of his gaze, fixed on me. He raised one eyebrow in unspoken question, sipping his beer, so I continued. "What are the repercussions after an event like this, like an accident? I mean, for Miles or the Scorpions. Or for you?"

Nathan turned a little to face me more directly. "That's what's been under discussion this week. General O'Cherry immediately sat the squadron down after the mid-air Monday morning." Confusion must've danced across my face for the millionth time when he used military terms, because he continued, "'Sat down' means that he grounded all of us—in other words, he said that no one in the squadron could fly, for now. It's fairly common after a Class A mishap—a major accident where we lose an aircraft, or there's a loss of life. Gives us time to evaluate and reflect on what we might have done differently. Most importantly how we can prevent it from happening again."

Nate shifted, looking restless, so I moved to the end of the sofa and pulled his head into my lap, beginning to massage his temples and scalp soothingly. He closed his eyes, and a little smile played across the full lips that had brought me so much pleasure. He didn't speak for several minutes, giving Sol and Mayze time to take up residence in the prime real estate on his stomach and near his feet, respectively. Solomon's rumbly purr was the only sound breaking the silence.

"This is why they brought me here, Cami. Rifle's only been dead for a few months and now this." He took a big breath and sighed heavily. "I was brought here to prevent this. Was supposed to see it coming and fix it before it happened again."

I rubbed and massaged and thought. "I should probably lecture you about how it's not your fault, shouldn't I?" His eyes opened, but he didn't smile. He just looked at me with those beautiful, sad brown eyes. "It's a lot of weight to carry, a life-and-death job, especially as the boss. I do understand that, you know. Some people are resistant to what you tell them, no matter the truth of it. You can only carry so much of that for them. When I was a fairly young charge nurse, I had to fire someone like Miles. She was so hell-bent on going her way, she couldn't hear me when I tried to help her, give her correction. I guess what you have to decide now is if Miles is too far down her path to hear you. What I won't tell you is that it isn't your fault. I think you know it isn't. But I know from experience it sometimes feels better to flog yourself with it for a while. Just don't do it for too long." I bent and touched my mouth to his. When I moved away from him, he smiled.

"You knew just the right thing to say, Camille. Thank you." His eyes were serious as they searched my face. "Did you get enough to eat? Because I'd very much like to take you to bed and spend the next couple of hours touching your naked body and sucking your nipples and eating and fucking your tight little cunt." He grinned. "Do you think you could work that into your schedule tonight?"

Oh, I did. I abso-fucking-lutely did think I was ready for

Nathan against me, warm and naked and hard. I was already on my feet, clearing away the food and heading for the dishwasher when I felt Nate's hands under my scrubs, his thumbs rubbing circles on my tummy. "Go sit back down, Cami. Put your feet up and finish your wine. I'm jumping through the shower; then I'll be back to put the kitchen in order and get the kids tucked in." He lifted his chin toward the sofa where Sol and Mayze were engaged in a staring contest.

"You can shower up while I do that. Then you'll be soft and warm. All ready for my hands." One of his thumbs skimmed my bottom lip. "And my mouth." His face bent to mine, but he brushed past my lips and bit my neck gently, just below my ear, and then soothed it briefly with his tongue. Then he whispered in the same ear, "And my cock." With that, he placed his hand flat on the small of my back and pulled me flush against the front of his body so I could feel his hard flesh, thick and ready, lying against his belly. "I love you, Camille, and I need you very much tonight." He kissed me thoroughly and left for the shower. My weak knees were glad to allow me to sink back into the sofa.

Chapter
THIRTY-NINE

"As If We Never Said Goodbye"

Camille

Saturday morning had not yet dawned, but a certain relaxed and freshly showered man was climbing back between my sheets, wearing nothing but the smile I'd put on his face last night. I returned the smile sleepily and rubbed my eyes. "Where ya been so early?"

He bent to kiss me lazily. "Long run this morning. I've been waking up early all week." He looked away to the window where the sun had yet to begin lighting the sky. "Shouldn't be surprised, I guess. My brain's been in overdrive." He looked back at me, again smiling easily. "I've got a lot on my mind, angel, but not all of it's bad. In fact, some of it's very, very good." He allowed his naked body to slide all the way down and wrapped himself around me.

It felt like the very definition of luxury, having Nathan's hard body next to mine in bed and the whole day ahead of us. We engaged in a good, old-fashioned make-out session, the kind you have in the backseat in high school. Well, the kind you have in high school if your boyfriend's six foot three, growls when he kisses you, and knows your pussy like the back of his hand. Oh, and talks dirty in your ear, threatening to tie you up and torture you with his tongue, while he expertly fingers you until you come, panting and grasping his hair.

So, nothing like high school.

I burrowed into his chest, pulse still racing, drinking in the unabashed maleness that was Nathan. He continued to stroke me gently, cupping my still-pulsing sex, whispering affectionately into my ear. I loved that he attended me this way after I came, seeming to sense that I needed to ease back onto terra firma gradually after he'd hurled me into the stratosphere. His erection strained against my thigh, and I reached for him. But he brought my hand instead to his lips, kissing it lightly. "Later on, angel. We have all day. And all night."

We laid our heads down on the pillows, facing each other. Silent, enjoying beginning the day together. "I love you, Nathan Morgan." It was as natural as breathing. To love him and to tell him so.

His eyes were intense. "And I love you, Camille Elizabeth." His knuckles skimmed my ribcage. His eyebrows shot up, and he popped up to one elbow, flipping the covers off my naked torso. "Hey. I just remembered…" He leaned over to study the script decorating my ribcage. "I keep meaning to ask about this, but every time I see it, we're already involved in…something more interesting than conversation." His naughty grin was so engaging. "Mmmm…I'm going to guess Latin?"

"Correct. Two points to the gentleman." I grabbed his hand and rolled onto my back. "Stop it, Nathan…it tickles." He threatened to attack for just a minute but thought better of it, lying back against the pillows again. I loved looking at him like this, arms behind his head in the classic alpha male pose.

"So, Latin. What does it mean? My lone year of high school

Latin is failing me, as dead languages often do."

I snuggled back in. "It's a pretty lengthy story, but it's proba-bly the last piece of the Amos story you haven't heard." His arm gathered me closer. "This is as good a time as any, I think." It was becoming less difficult to talk about Amos as I allowed myself to remember and mull the details of our too-brief life together. There had been a few occasions over the past couple of weeks when I'd allowed myself the bittersweet comfort of musing the details of his tiny toes, how sweet his little baby head smelled. Even the way it felt when he'd tumbled around inside me. Before now, it felt too perilous, emotionally, to let my thoughts meander along those lines. Talking to Nathan about him was a balm that was somehow healing me, bit by bit.

"After Amos died, I had another surgical recovery, the sec-ond one in six months. This one was a C-section, and Luckie was right beside me. Again. I suppose it was as difficult as those things normally are, but I have almost no memory of it. The doctor wanted me to stay home for eight weeks minimum, but I couldn't do it. Physically, I healed quickly. Emotionally, I was gutted. Done. I went to the therapist recommended by my OB. And she was so good, so dedicated, but I just didn't have any-thing to offer of myself. All I could think about was getting back to work. Getting busy and exhausting myself so I could sleep at night.

"I convinced myself that I was 'getting back on the horse.' It felt like the only step I could take right then toward normal-cy was to go back to the hospital and my friends, because my friends are essentially the only family I have.

"So that's what I did. Luckie and Viv and the girls circled the wagons and prodded me when I needed it. They protected me and locked the utility room door—where the broken autoclave clanged like a fire engine—when I needed to cry it out without anyone hearing."

Nate spoke, and his voice was far away. "I remember feeling like I was living outside my body after she died. I couldn't figure out how the world was still spinning around. Everybody got up every day and had coffee and went to work like everything was normal. I was the opposite of you. I was paralyzed. Couldn't function."

I turned to take in his handsome face. "I guess I thought it would get better, a little at a time. That's how things heal in medicine. It made sense to me, but it didn't happen. Over the course of a couple of months, I gained the ability to work effectively and maintain a daily routine, but I was emotionally desolate. Losing Amos meant I had lost my chance at love; it was so much devastation in a short period. My heart was in shock."

This was a heavy emotional burden to unpack. "Maybe we should talk about all of this later, Nate?" I studied his eyes, a little sad now, but he shook his head.

"Camille, we both knew almost from the beginning we'd come into this carrying some heavy loss on our backs. You handled Amos's death very differently than I handled Eliott's. If you think you can keep going, I'd like to hear what you have to say. What was the tipping point?"

I was smiling again now, remembering the moment when the truth was clearly illuminated for me. It was reality coming full circle, and it eventually brought love back into my life. I continued the story.

"It wasn't gradual. And months had passed. I was essentially living in a pit of habit and mediocrity. I worked, took care of Sol and my house, slept a little, and tried to stay busy so I couldn't think. In fact, the day it happened, I picked up part of a shift for Grace so she could see a friend. I worked extra whenever I could because it contributed to my goal of staying exhausted." I smiled wryly at him. "That's one of the questionable advantages of being a nurse. If you want to work too much, it's encouraged and appreciated. And well compensated.

"It's not that unusual to get traumas into the ED that bring multiple casualties. Remember how I told you about the nudist family with poison ivy?" He smiled and shook his head; I couldn't tell him about the ladies group with the GI disturbance—way too disgusting, he'd protested.

"More often, of course, the larger casualties are car accidents." The levity left his face immediately, but I continued. "And that's what happened that day. I was covering for Grace, who was splitting a shift, so I didn't come in until mid-afternoon. The accident victims…" I had to stop and think a moment. "Ahh, I think there were probably about a dozen or so, several of them critical. Probably six or seven were surgical candidates, and that's a large influx of admissions for any ED. In my absence, Vivvie was running the unit and had everything well in hand. She had everyone triaged when I arrived; I remember complimenting her on her mad organizational skills." I snickered a little thinking about how I'd teased Viv, but Nate's face remained somber. I hurried along, thinking that dwelling on our losses must be hard on him.

"Anyway, things were clicking along okay. She had Luckie and Sam and Anna getting everyone stabilized and on the move up to surgery. There were a couple of relatively minor suture jobs that needed attention, so she had them stacked up in this back corner room we all hate. It's removed from the action and set up like an old-fashioned ward. Curtains separating four beds with no real privacy. We don't use it unless we have to, but we absolutely did that day. Every flat surface was occupied.

"I had four patients back there: a young boy who needed stitches in his head, a couple of college boys who were more frightened than anything else, and a young woman who had a little bump on the head. Very low-key group, considering what was going on. I set up the boy first and got him done because his parents were already discharged and ready to go. As I was getting him out the door, I read the intakes and figured out that one of the young men needed to go to CT, so that was handled. A few other small tasks, cleaning an abrasion on the other young man, bandaging…this and that."

I grinned, remembering the woman's voice. "The young woman—I wish I could remember her name—she needed a CT of the head and neck also because she had bumped her head on the steering wheel. But CT was backed up like a mother, and it's not first come, first served in the ED. It's all about the severity of the injury, so people just kept piling in on top of her. I had cleared out the "back corner"—that's what we all call it—and it was just the two of us in there while I charted and helped with the cleanup all around the unit, doing all kinds of tasks, large and small. She was sitting on the stretcher, smiling and watching me. It was odd, to be honest, because most people who aren't feeling terrible will be watching television or playing on their phones. But not this girl." I paused, remembering the tranquil aura that surrounded her. Peaceful. Not at all the sort of vibe people normally exuded when they had just been in an accident. It was strange, really.

"So I was just sitting in the room near her stretcher, working on the endless paperwork, when she interrupted me." I looked up to find Nate watching me very intently. He seemed even more focused on what I was saying than usual. "She wasn't like anyone I'd ever met even though we didn't actually know each other, if you know what I'm saying. I mean, I was her nurse, but she talked to me like we somehow knew one another. We'd been in the same room for probably an hour and a half at this point, never exchanging any information except what I needed from her medically. Then, from the clear blue sky, she just blurted out, 'So, a hot property like you isn't married?'

"Nathan, my head just popped up, and I looked at her like she had two heads. For over a year at that point, nearly everyone I knew had been carefully editing themselves around me, weighing words for impact. I was the victim of a crime so hideous and a tragedy so heartbreaking, everyone thought I might blow at any moment. Damn, even I thought so sometimes, I guess."

As my mind raced back, reliving that day, I took in the intensity that had settled on Nate's features. He didn't speak, and his eyes didn't move from my face. He barely breathed as I talked, seemingly very anxious for me to continue with my story.

"I laid my pen down and just stared at her. Gorgeous. She looked like a tiny little fireball. And there was something about her—something about being back in that corner, just the two of us, that made it seem like a safe place to talk. She seemed like a safe place. So I did."

Chapter FORTY

"In a New York Minute"

Camille
About Three Years Earlier

"N ope, never married. Sweet of you to say I'm pretty, though. It doesn't always feel that way. I just had a baby, about nine months ago."

She sat up suddenly, her face splitting open with an excited smile just as she grabbed her forehead and swore. "Ooooh… damned headache. Sorry." But the smile remained. "Show me a picture; I love babies." Her smile was magnetic.

I almost felt sorry for her. I rolled my stool over to the stretcher that held her diminutive form, wetting a cloth with cool water and smoothing it over her brow. "His name was Amos, and I wish you could've seen him. He was beautiful." Her face broke, and there were immediately tears spilling from her dark eyes.

"No. Oh, no." She looked at my name tag, sitting up when she did. Her arms came around me without an ounce of hesitation. "No, Camille, that's too cruel. Not a baby." She embraced me, and her tears wet my shoulders.

She sat back abruptly, drying her eyes on the starchy sheet covering the hospital stretcher. "I'm so sorry. You really don't need that." She pursed her lips and swallowed hard, collecting herself. "Just tell me that your baby daddy is a wonderful guy and totally supportive. Great girl like you, I'd put money on it." She swallowed again, hard.

Gah. I could hardly stand it; I actually felt bad for *her*. I grabbed her hand. "I don't even know how to tell you this, honey, but I was attacked. No baby daddy. But I have beautiful friends who saw me through, and I'm okay. Really, totally fine. I have my friends and my job. That's enough for me."

She looked stricken. Silence. She didn't speak. Deafening silence. Finally, her slim hands clasped mine. I didn't even know this woman, but she'd reached toward the center of me instead of chatting about weather and traffic. There was something authentic about her that saw what was inside me, tattered and raw. The clock ticked audibly for several seconds before she spoke.

"Enough. That's enough for you." She was quiet a few seconds more, and I couldn't breathe easily, looking back at her. She instinctively understood a basic truth about me. I waited expectantly.

Her tone was even and held no anger or judgment. "So you're ready to call it quits? Cash out?" Her eyes were soft, but she looked a little sad. "You're how old? Twenty-six?"

"I'm twenty-five."

"Mmmm..." Her eyes were steadfast as she sat back on the stretcher, shifting to find a more comfortable position. "Well, I don't know you, and you certainly don't know me." She squinted at my name tag again, suddenly grinning. "Camille. But, of course, you can see why that makes me the perfect person to advise you on the important things in your life, can't you?"

She was plainly uncomfortable, so I was on my feet, repositioning her on the stretcher with a few extra pillows and a blanket on her left side. I moved my stool, so I sat almost nose to nose with her. "I actually don't see why you're finding yourself cast in this role, but I'll bet you're gonna share." Now I was grinning along with her. "Feel free to enlighten me."

She struggled up onto an elbow. "Because I'm the keeper of an important secret of the universe passed on to me by an august and revered elder. And—this is crucial—you'll never see me again. So I'll feel great about helping you, and you'll never feel guilty about ignoring my sterling advice." We both burst into belly laughter at that, all the heaviness instantly dispelled.

Her laugh was medicinal in itself, just like a child's. She continued to shift uncomfortably although the smile never left her face. I noticed her pulse rate had increased on the monitor, but everything else looked perfectly fine. CT would be calling for her soon.

Her eyes studied me. "I don't know why, Camille, but I have a strong urge to tell you about a lesson I've learned over and over in my life. I won't bore you with the whole backstory, but the gist is this: when everything around you says you should give up… try once more. These trials you've been through, these terrible tragedies, Camille. They're difficult, so difficult. But not impossible to surmount. You have to leave yourself open to hope, to love. That's what Rhiannon always says."

My head popped up, mouth open. "Wait a minute. Who might Rhiannon be? That's a pretty unique name."

She smiled back. "My parents are consummate hippies. Like 'look it up in the dictionary' grade hippies, and lots of hippie children call their parents by their given names. That's what I've called my mother since I was a little tiny girl hippie. And Rhiannon always says that giving up is almost never the answer. Leave room for the possibility of love. Try once more."

My eye caught the sparkle of an unusual ring on her left hand; she followed my gaze and held it out. The ring wasn't like any I'd seen before. "It looks like you took Rhiannon at her word. It's beautiful. Like it's from another time—an antique."

She stared lovingly at it and then back at me. "It is an antique. Good eye. He picked it not knowing what I wanted." She laughed a little and took in a quick breath. "Hell, I didn't know what I wanted. Not in a ring. Not in love or a relationship. But I didn't know because there's no way I could've known love until I knew him." Her eyes rested on the ring, and she smiled. She shifted on the stretcher.

I frowned and decreased the angle of the stretcher, propping her hips with an additional pillow. "I feel like you're getting more uncomfortable while we're talking." I cocked my head and studied her. "Is anything hurting? Your head? Chest? Anything?" Her medical history was clean as a whistle, completely unremarkable.

She waved her hand and rolled her eyes. "A little headache, nothing at all really. I'm just tiring of my stay in your ER, despite your charming company." She smirked. "I hope you're not offended."

"Nothing my bruised ego won't recover from, I'm sure." Relieved, I gathered a huge pile of expired supplies I'd sorted while we were talking. "Look, I'm going to go check on the status of everything out front. I'm expecting CT will be cleaning house and calling for you anytime now, so why don't you try to grab a few winks before they do?" I moved the nurse call light onto her pillow, squeezing her hand in the process. "Call me if you need anything, but I'll be back in just a few minutes to check in on you, okay?" I dimmed the lights on the way out and went to find Viv.

I found her, along with Luckie and Anna shoveling their way through the remnants the day had deposited all around the nurses' station and in the front supply closets. The place looked like a war zone. I added my big box of expired supplies to the pile. "Does anyone have supplies for the Haiti mission? I'm starting a new box." A large group of the docs and nurses made semi-annual trips to an orphanage in Haiti for medical missions. Expired, unopened supplies were in high demand.

Sam stuck her head around the corner. "I've already got a huge box about half full in the back utility room. Just throw your stuff in there. I heard they're organizing another trip this fall; I may see about getting time off." Then she was gone.

I added my supplies to the stockpile rapidly taking over our already limited space and made a mental note to call nursing services about some offsite storage for our charitable endeavors. Sighing, I also noted that my "mental note" capacity seemed somewhat overburdened. Better to write a note in my office.

Having accomplished these few errands, I returned to the "back corner," fishing my phone from a crammed pocket to investigate the holdup in CT. As soon as I pushed the door open, however, I dropped the phone into my pocket and quickly eased the earpieces of my stethoscope into my ears, crossing the room briskly.

The air in the room had shifted in the few minutes I'd been away. The light-heartedness exuded by the sweet young woman I'd left lying on the stretcher had been replaced by an obvious restlessness I'd learned not to discount. Her eyes darted anxiously, and her breathing was noticeably labored. I listened to her heart and lungs, my lips pursed with concern. I was about to ask her a few basic questions, but she spoke first, and her tone demanded my attention. "I'm so glad I let myself hope. Life without love is not enough, Camille."

The cardiac monitor alarm showed rapidly escalating tachycardia, or increased heart rate, just as she raised her head from the pillow slightly and grasped my hand, pulling me urgently toward her. "Just…Camille, please listen to me." She paused, focusing on taking in a breath. "When you give up, it's over. Try once…more." Her brow knitted a bit, and one small hand flitted to her chest. Then she smiled a drunken little smile right at me. "I'm pretty sleepy now." Her pretty, dark eyes fluttered shut, and mine flew to the cardiac monitor, which registered ventricular fibrillation, just as it screamed a loud alarm into the silence of the room. I slammed the code button on the wall.

Chapter
FORTY-ONE

"The Cold and the Broken Hallelujah"

Camille

Nate's magnificent brown eyes brimmed with unshed tears. He whispered the word like a prayer.

"Eliott."

I didn't stop my story; but as I'd neared the end, I'd seen his eyes flash with recognition.

"She wasn't alone." It wasn't a question but a grateful statement, and he lifted his red-rimmed eyes to meet mine. "I never knew what happened, the details. Anything. It tore me apart to think she was alone at the end. I would have given anything to be with her, to hold her." His voice fractured.

"It's called Sudden Cardiac Death Syndrome." My voice was quiet, but I wanted to offer an explanation if he didn't have one. "In her case, it was determined she'd been born with a serious heart defect, and it had gone undetected. She never had any symptoms. Most people can be saved with immediate care, but we never got her back." I put my arms around him. "I started CPR, and the code team came right away, Nathan, but she never came back to us."

I pulled his head to my chest and wrapped my body protectively around his as he absorbed this news and grieved Eliott again. I willed the weight of his pain to fall on us both this time, allowing me to help him walk through the darkness.

It was one of those holy moments when time is suspended. In truth, I don't know how much of the morning drifted by, partially because it was a rare stormy day in Tucson. The sun never brightened the sky, and I wound my nakedness around Nathan's, gladly offering any solace I knew to shield him from the unfathomable heartache. It was a mercy I couldn't have imagined, to be the one honored to share his Eliott's last moments on earth. It was a mark fate had placed on Nathan and me long before we'd met.

Around noon, we both awakened from slumber brought on by sheer emotional exhaustion. We'd passed the last few hours in the cocoon of my bed, blanketed by shadows, alternately whispering snippets of our story and digesting the new reality we'd discovered. We both absorbed strength and love through the skin of the other. It was as if no world existed outside the four walls of this room; Nathan was the only truth I knew in those hours. The house remained mostly dark and quiet with occasional thunder underscoring the heaviness. The morning's revelations were almost too much to bear; but, ultimately, there was consolation for each of us in the arms of the other.

In the dimness in my bedroom, I felt Nathan's lips move across my left side, along my ribcage, and I smiled. Even now, he was a bulldog, not giving up. And now he knew the whole story, each piece of the puzzle that was Camille and Amos. As fate would have it, Camille and Amos were inexorably tied to Eliott and Nathan. There were no accidents in this world. Into the quiet, I murmured the words, "*Semel tentavero*." I marked my body with Eliott's words to me—Try once more. She was sent to me at the moment in my life when I'd settled. Given up and decided that my life, devoid of love and hope, was going to have to be enough. I didn't have the family bonds a person hopes for. I'd been raped and lost my courage. Then I'd watched my baby die, along with my dream of a family. I couldn't gather myself enough to risk love again. I had to settle for what already was."

I turned to see Nathan's chiseled features in the gloomy room, his tongue bathing the words that decorated and defined me. "She told me life without love was not enough. I had those words inked onto my body the weekend after she died. I didn't have the strength to wade back in and start dating, but there was a spark of hope. I wanted to remember her and what she'd said. I thought the time might come when I'd be ready to try again and that her spirit and conviction would give me strength. When I was telling you this story, I wondered why I couldn't remember her name. I always remember patients' names, Nathan." I hesitated, thinking over the details of the story. "Now I understand."

He nodded his agreement and pulled me close, our faces almost touching. "We had to fall in love without Eliott in the middle."

He understood. I moved closer until our lips touched, closing my eyes and feeling Nathan with just my mouth. "My afternoon with Eliott changed me forever, Nathan. Just like she changed you. Something or someone greater than both of us sent her to one, final life-changing appointment before her work was done."

Me, I thought, to myself. A meeting with a woman who was too damaged and too fearful to leave herself vulnerable to the possibility of another heartbreak.

Nathan's thumb stroked my cheek, and I opened my eyes. His voice was sure and his hands steady. "Had I not lost Eliott, I would likely never have known you. I hope, somehow, she knows how thankful I am."

And with that, Nathan slipped seamlessly back into the skin

of my powerful lover, covering my body with his much larger one and taking my mouth with no hesitation or pretense. He explored me unhurriedly, hands smoothing the skin of my neck and breasts, tugging gently at the nipples until they stood in tight peaks and asked for his tongue. My own hands searched the broad expanse of his muscled back, working outward to dig into his biceps as my pleasure rapidly intensified.

He lifted his face from mine, eyes smoldering darker brown in the way I loved to see. "Love you, Camille. Love every chance I have to show you how much." His mouth lowered to take in a taut nipple, suckling at it gently before biting slowly and deliberately. A groan escaped me, willing the pain throbbing in my nipple to linger.

"Don't, baby...I need..." My voice died away, but my legs encompassed Nathan's powerful waist and drew him closer to me. I arched my tits further into his mouth, a slave to the drunken thrumming set up in my center, inexorably tied to the pain his teeth were inflicting on my body.

His hands roughly pushed my legs apart, one finger gently parting my bare pussy and exploring the juncture there while his teeth continued to torment a tender nipple. "Ah, my precious angel's wet and needs my cock." He pushed a finger into the slit, feeling it ripple under the rough treatment. He lapped the hardness of one nipple with the flat of his tongue. "Need me to fill you up, Cami? Need my hard cock?" He fingered me, dawdling, and then withdrew entirely.

He rose to his knees between my spread legs; virile, hard, all fucking male. God, I needed him. But I was pretty sure he was going to enjoy withholding that. He took his time studying my body, stroking his magnificent cock slowly all the while from root to head. My body was purring, impatient for the pleasure of being filled with him, and, inexplicably, for more of the bite of pain. My agitation simmered on the surface, right where he could see it.

I reached for the head of his erection, now leaking precum onto his fist, and helped myself to enough to coat two fingers generously, bringing them slowly to my mouth and licking. His cock jerked in his fist. I carefully maintained contact with his heated gaze, enjoying the chink in his impenetrable alpha armor with a suppressed smile. I dropped my other hand between my parted thighs and teased the wetness around my opening. His hand stopped, eyes dropping to my exposed pussy briefly before an irritated growl and muttered, "Oh, hell no…"

Quicker than I could blink, both of my hands were pinned to the bed beside my head, held quite firmly at the wrists. His brown eyes were almost black, and he glowered at me. Had I not known him as well as I did, I'd have guessed he was truly angry. He lowered his face until it almost touched my own and grated out each word as if in pain.

"Camille Elizabeth, I love you; and, as part of that, your pleasure is my responsibility. Your naked, aroused body belongs to me. My hands, my mouth. My hard cock. You will not take what is mine—your body's longing. Your orgasms. Those are mine, baby." He lowered his voice, almost growling, "You come on my cock. Or my fingers…or in my mouth, angel. I will always be here for whatever your body needs, Camille. Understand?" One hand left my wrists, smoothing along the skin of my side, and stopped as his thumb grazed my nipple, still aching from his teeth. He stroked it, almost absentmindedly, just as he'd done the first time he kissed me outside the O'Club on the picnic table.

"I asked you a question, beautiful girl." His gravelly voice brought me back to him, holding me down, touching me. "Do you understand?"

"I do." My voice seemed small. For the second time in as many minutes, the mood in the room had shifted palpably. God, I couldn't wait to give him everything—things I didn't even know

I had to give. "I love you, Nathan. Take me. I told you before that I want to belong to you. I want everything you'll give me." The words barely passed my lips before he silenced them with a fierce kiss. One hand still held me to the bed, while the other stroked my breast. The weight of his cock was heavy and warm on my thigh, and I strained toward it, subconsciously longing for his length to fill me.

"You want to belong to me? Want everything I'll give you?" His voice rumbled low as if he spoke to himself. Then his eyes met mine briefly, and he spoke directly to me again, "You do belong to me, Camille. And I'm yours. I'm giving you everything, too, baby." His mouth was brutal, exploring and demanding. His lips wandered to my throat and kissed, suckling urgently.

Then, with one deft movement, I was on my knees, and he was behind me, pushing me downward with a large hand pressed into the small of my back. Warm hands stroked the skin of my back, tracing the curves of my ass and sending a chill up my spine. "The view is stunning from here, Camille." One hand continued to stroke me, exploring lower with a finger, to trace the valley of my ass. "I'm going to take the luxury of a little extra time to enjoy every beautiful part of your spectacular body now before I fuck you. Before I fill you and enjoy your orgasm, Cami. And mine."

His hand left my body for a moment, and then I felt his finger slip between the cheeks of my ass, briefly seeking and finding the tight opening there. His finger felt warm…wonderful, but I gasped with surprise all the same. With my face buried in a pillow, I couldn't see his expression, but the tone of his voice belied a raised eyebrow and half grin. "What is it, baby? You didn't think I'd want to explore all of you?" His finger massaged my opening firmly but didn't push. His touch was confident, practiced somehow, and I wanted to know where his body could take mine.

My clit was humming. I moaned into the pillow and arched my ass into the gentle assault his two fingers continued on my opening. I noticed, through the haze, that although Nathan was avoiding my pussy entirely, his fingers were warm and wet.

"Baby..." I was having difficulty stringing words together. "Why are your fingers wet?"

He bent forward until I could feel his hot breath on my ear, his breathing fast and heavy. His voice sounded like he was hurting. "Because fingering your sweet little asshole and thinking about fucking you there someday, Camille...about how tight and blistering hot it'll be choking my dick..." He had to stop, panting. "I'm so hard I had to stroke my cock while I touched you. I've just been letting the cum leak from the head of my cock onto your ass."

Holy. Fuck.

"Baby. Nathan, please." I didn't recognize my own voice. I could barely breathe, and I ached with want for his cock. "Please take me. I'm begging you. No one's ever done this to me before, Nathan. I didn't know it would feel like this, but I need you inside me...please, baby."

A long groan broke the quiet of the room, and I felt the wide hardness of his erection pressing against my slit, sliding easily into the wetness there. "Camille...so tight. Wet. Fuck." His voice was rough and low. Unlike the times we'd been together before, his length began to move inside me as soon as he'd breached my opening, gently at first, then with more purpose. He still seemed aware that his size could be an issue, but I knew my body could take his. I pushed back, encouraging him to handle me mercilessly. One big hand reached underneath me, palming my belly, controlling the speed and depth of his thrusting. He growled into my ear. "That's what you want, beautiful? You want all of my cock?" He plunged deep inside me, his muscled thighs meeting mine with a loud slap.

Then, warm, wet fingers were on my ass once again, massaging while he stroked me inside with his thick cock. My clit was swollen and rippling, so close to coming... His finger on the tight pucker of my ass getting me there so fast. His erection seemed to swell and lengthen inside me, and he pushed gently to find uncharted territory. His other hand lifted my hips higher, a move I was coming to recognize he used to allow his length deeper inside, and I groaned with a brutal combination of pleasure and fullness.

Just as I felt the head of his erection kiss my cervix, he groaned and pushed gently forward, his cock warm and pulsing. There was a mild bite of pain, and he slid one warm, wet finger into my welcoming asshole. The combination of his orgasm bathing the walls of my pussy with his hot seed and the painfully pleasurable intrusion of his finger ushered me into the most intense and singular orgasm of my life.

"Oh God, Nathan..." Gasping and speechless, my body seemed to spasm along with my cunt, clutching his cock as he emptied himself into me, squeezing my body with his arms, and groaning into my ear. "Love you, Camille. So much."

Chapter
FORTY-TWO

"Saturday in the Park"

Camille

Vivvie fanned her flawless features with a paper plate she'd plucked from the stack on a nearby folding table. "I know the question's rhetorical, but can anyone explain why this is the end of summer picnic, but it's 101 degrees? I should've known better than to wear anything other than prescription-strength deodorant and a wet bikini."

As far as I could tell, Viv was camera ready, and I looked like I had been swimming laps in the pool for the past hour. The woman was a fucking aberration. Hung's tall frame cast a shadow over her, bending in for a lip touch to the back of her neck, and then he commented under his breath, "I think a bikini would've been a good choice, gorgeous." Viv didn't possess the ability to blush or demure, so she arched an eyebrow. He sent her a mischievous half-smile and ambled away.

I smiled her way. "He's circling the drain, Vivvie. You've cast your spell."

Her lips curled up as she watched him walk away, eyes locked on his attractive backside. She blew a breath out through pursed lips. "It's not a lock with this one, Cam. He's hard to read." Then her mouth stretched into a grin as she took a long pull on an icy beer. "But I'm enjoying the chase. Something tells me he's worth the effort."

"Ladies." Rock's charcoal eyes scanned our group, languid and sprawled variously in lawn chairs and on beach towels as we sought refuge from the relentless late afternoon heat. His smile was flirtatious, and I watched with interest to see what—or who— brought him over. "I bring sincere apologies from the LPA for this unforgivable weather. If we'd known we'd have the pleasure of entertaining the most beautiful nurses…" I wasn't listening any- more but suppressing a smile as I watched his eyes methodically scan the gathering, stopping, at last, to stare unabashedly at the one woman who hadn't favored him with so much as a glance. He drank in the waist-length champagne-blond hair Samanthe worked to tame with a huge clip. Conversations mercifully broke out again, affording Rock the cover his ego desperately needed.

On her nearby beach towel, Bibi rolled onto her stomach and winked at me, whispering, "Do you think we should get the gar- den hose?" She tilted her head in Rock's direction. Sam had yet to notice him and was now methodically rubbing sunscreen into the ivory skin of her shoulders and long legs. "Poor guy. Looks like he's gonna have to break down and introduce himself. He's not accustomed to being ignored."

It was the last Saturday of September, ostensibly beyond the end of summer, but Tucson had not been notified. The planned softball game was abandoned early, and the Scorpions relaxed in convivial groups under two large clusters of shade trees that conveniently took up a large corner of the base's park, reserved for the occasion. The mood was easy, and everyone took extra effort to treat the two welcome elephants in the outdoor room, Deliverance and Miles, as if it were any other party. What it was, in fact, was a landmark gathering. They were making their first public appearances since the accident, some five weeks before. Miles had suffered nearly no serious physical injuries, but she looked thinner, and it was easy to see her brash manner had taken a hit. Only time would tell how the accident would impact her and her career, but Nathan seemed surprisingly encouraged. I watched, along with Bibi, as she sat smiling at the antics of the LPA, sipping soda. That alone signaled a change in course. Glancing at the handsome man striding purposefully toward me, I found myself truly glad he was at the helm of this group.

"Lying around like a lady of leisure, Miss Sullivan?" His brows knitted in mock disapproval. "We have barbecue to serve to these hungry people." He extended his hand, helping me up and smacking my bottom casually.

Bibi sat up. "I can help, Nathan. Give me just a sec." She started to make her way to her feet, but I grabbed her hand.

"Absolutely not, Bibi. Everything is done. The Barbecue Nazi"—I indicated Nate with an outswept hand—"took care of everything before we came. He and I will set it up; then we all feast. This picnic is our treat. Drink beer. Find your husband and feel him up. You're always on hostess duty. Now it's our turn."

In the distant parking lot, Nathan and I unloaded the bed of the truck, packed with coolers of his special pulled pork barbecue, several gallons of my homemade pasta salad, and store-bought baked beans. The LPA set up paper products and the requisite cold water, lemonade and beer coolers. A flying squadron, I learned early, traveled on its stomach. Nathan pulled the squadron's behemoth rolling two-hundred-quart cooler as Mayze lumbered alongside him and warily eyed Solomon, snuggled in my left arm. He'd graciously left me the much smaller cooler, also enormous. Our livestock had brokered an uneasy détente based primarily on mistrust. Only in the company of other animals did they close ranks, as we'd noted today. Solomon favored Nathan with a bat of his stunning green eyes and purred mightily. He was in love, too.

"How's Deliverance doing today?" I wanted to take advantage of the moment while we were out of earshot of the crowd.

Nathan grinned and surveyed the Scorpions milling under the trees in the distance. "He's good. All things considered, really good. You know how they say the gold's refined in the fire?" He squinted those beautiful eyes at me from behind his sunglasses. "You put Davis through the fire, and he shines like the sun. He's a good man."

That made me smile. "Music to my ears, babe. Lucinda sure seems to like what she sees. I think she's been going the extra mile with the private duty nursing, if you get my drift." Seeing Luckie this happy completed my own joy, and thoughts of what she meant to me—what we meant to each other—washed me with a wave of emotion. I swallowed hard, searching hastily for a topic change. "Miles is quiet, but she seems happy to be here."

"Yeah. We're getting there." He scanned the crowd, looking for her. "She's still off flying status, and there's been some disciplinary action taken, but Deliverance has been her biggest advocate." I turned to him in amazement. "I know. He's a good guy, but even I've been surprised with the way he's had her back. He told me privately he sees so much potential in her but feels she's had personal issues holding her back. Hell if I know what he's talking about, but I trust his judgment."

We walked along in silence, accompanied only by the click of the coolers on the sidewalk. "They're so lucky that you came, Nathan. So lucky." I looked at my feet; it was harder to talk about now that I knew all these amazing people. "I can't imagine what it was like when they lost Lieutenant Conner. I deal with life and death in my work, but this is different. They knew him. They flew with him, went to picnics and church and ball games together. What if that had been Miles? Or Deliverance? How do you recover when one of you doesn't come home?"

Nathan took off his sunglasses and looked down with a look that warmed me to my core. "You lean on each other because that's all you have." He sighed under his breath. "You've heard the term brothers-in-arms. It refers to soldiers fighting a war, bearing arms together. But, privately, I've sometimes pictured it as the shoulders we need to lean on when the burden is too heavy. When you move around every few years, with no family nearby and no roots, you need to be that shoulder for the people under your command."

I tilted my head, unable to look away from his face. "But what about you? Who does the commander lean on, Nathan?"

His face split into a wide grin, and he reached over to scratch Sol gently behind the ears. "Now that's one of the questions that was weighing pretty heavy on me when I first arrived. Turns out, fate was paving the way for me a long time ago."

My face must have looked like a big question mark because Nathan stopped and let go of the cooler. He took Solomon from me, holding him securely in the crook of his arm, and pulled me closer with his free hand at the back of my waist.

"Don't look so confused, beautiful. I'm not spilling the beans in front of these barbarians, but every time I think about my future—whether it's tomorrow, next month or twenty years from now—I see you next to me." His mouth came close—signature move—and his lips touched mine as he spoke. "I hope you've seen the same future, but if you haven't, start giving it some thought. We'll be talking more about this soon." Then his mouth was on me, kissing me thoroughly and just beyond what was appropriate for daylight hours in full view of his squadron.

Not that it went unnoticed.

"Get ya some, boss... Booyah!" That was Deliverance. Nate's lips smiled on mine, and the kiss was over. We grabbed the coolers and strode toward the group, to some clapping and wolf-whistling.

Reaching the general area, Boo and Torch jogged up. "Ma'am, let us wrestle these over to the tables." Nate and I handed over the coolers, and I moved first to say hello to Deliverance. He was seated in a fancy folding chair with his intricately braced leg stretched out in front of him. He immediately wrapped me in a big bear hug.

"Davis," I admonished maternally. "Watch that leg. Bibi will whip my ass if I mess up her prize petunia."

"Look, CamiCakes…" Davis's drawl was a dramatic stage whisper for the benefit of the whole crowd, "You didn't hear it from me, but that woman is a she-devil. I'm having nightmares. Getting therapy. Hypnosis. Nothing works." He waggled his eyebrows theatrically.

"I can hear you, you big, dumb lug." Bibi's voice carried over the crowd, and she appeared at his right shoulder. "Have you been doing your reps like we discussed? I can start coming back to the house twice a day to supervise, if necessary."

Deliverance cringed. "See? The broken leg is the very least of my issues." I noticed Miles overhearing our conversation from her seat nearby as Deliverance's face brightened. "I'm doing great. Even the Mistress of Darkness here says so. The new X-rays say I have 60% of my bone strength back. And Elvira's making sure my muscle strength keeps up the pace." Despite his best efforts, Davis looked up at Bibi affectionately as she squeezed his shoulder.

"He's a force of nature. I've never seen anyone work this hard; I'm so proud of him." She smiled his way warmly, but it faded immediately. "Don't let it go to your head, Jethro; I'll double your visits if I find out you're slacking. Do *not* test me. It's happened, but the people in question lived to regret it."

"Fuck. She's so scary." The voice was Coach's. The crowd dissolved into laughter, but I waved my arms for everyone's attention and stepped onto a nearby chair.

"Okay, everybody." I raised my voice to a mild bellow. "Happy and I want to welcome you to the Alleged End of Summer Picnic. Your fearless leader is also an accomplished barbecue chef, so enjoy some pulled pork and fixins on us. Let's eat, Scorpions." Nathan's face rose from where he was opening the last of the homemade barbecue sauce to place on the table, and he raised one eyebrow. I jumped down and scrambled to join him in organizing the food and essentials.

"Looks like you're a natural, babe." His brow was furrowed, and he sampled the sauce from a fingertip before smiling easily.

I was searching through a basket for serving utensils. "A natural what, Nathan? A natural blonde, a natural woman?"

"More like a natural disaster. Clueless…" Luckie intoned as she moved through the line, balancing two plates. She stared at me, deadpan. "I'm under strict orders from Crip to pick through the meat and bring only the juiciest morsels, along with extra potato salad."

"Tragic news, I'm afraid." I returned her stare. "Today's prix fixe includes my special pasta salad—no potato salad."

"No problemo." She picked through the meat, heaping both paper plates. "I'll break the news topless. He forgets his name in the presence of nipples. Problem solved."

The Scorpions moved rapidly through the line, emptying containers with thanks and compliments to the chef. Nathan and I settled in the two chairs vacated by Boo and Torch next to Miles. She leaned toward Nathan with a smile.

"I owe you a big apology and an even bigger thank you, Happy." Nathan leaned forward, elbows on knees, and gave her a smile.

"Miles, everyone travels their own road, and I don't know all the valleys and obstacles you've encountered. But I'm glad to hear you say that. This squadron loves you, and I'm glad you and

D are on the other side of this. Let's go forward together from here and see where the road takes us."

Her smile was wide, and her eyes were a little shiny. "I have some work to do, but this feels like the right place to do it, Happy. And Camille, thank you for taking care of Davis. I'm so glad he was in your capable hands. He's so important to us." Her voice was on the edge of breaking, but she choked back a sob and smiled wide. "But please don't tell him I said so."

I put down my plate as she did, and we stood, embracing silently for a minute or two. The energy of the gathering provided the cover we needed for a private moment. I spoke quietly. "I have faith in you, Charlotte. You'll find your way. Give it time."

Eventually, the group settled into a controlled feeding frenzy, spilling from the ever-present picnic tables into lawn chairs and even onto the ground, in some places. This crowd was never really quiet, but feeding them brought the noise down to a dull roar, so I was able to hear the British accent floating across the park toward us.

"So, then, any left for your cousin from across the pond, Jacob?"

Holy. Shit. What was it about that accent?

Hearing the voice, Bashful jumped to his feet, his mouth full of baked beans, and waved across the park to his friend. Viv, who had been seated to his left, was up as well and broke into a wide smile and a jog toward the man walking toward us. He was much taller than most of the pilots, I thought. Probably six feet four or five with a long, lean body designed to make a girl's stomach flip. And ginger. With a devastating beard and mustache. Vivvie reached him and jumped into his arms, wrapping her long legs around him and smothering his face with kisses. Bashful was on her heels, offering a hand.

When Viv finally let him go, he and Bashful embraced in more than the standard male hug. Letting go, Vivvie grabbed his hand and led him toward us, waving and smiling. "You guys, I want you to meet my cousin, Oliver."

Nathan was already on his feet, walking toward them, hand extended. "Is this Oliver, as in the Range Controller?"

Oliver smiled and shook Nathan's hand. "The same, mate. Who do I have the pleasure…"

Bash broke in with a hearty laugh. "Oliver, meet our commander, Nathan 'Happy' Morgan. You've actually met him once before when you busted his chops on the range at my request."

Oliver's handsome features flushed with attractive ruddiness as he pumped Nate's hand. "My apologies, sir. Must've thought me mad as a bag of ferrets, calling you five at three."

Nathan laughed and motioned to a chair between his and Bashful's. "The thought crossed my mind, but I understand, what with being the FNG and all. Do you enjoy American barbecue, Oliver?"

There was no uneasiness as Oliver took his seat and tore into a plate heaped with pork, pasta, and baked beans. Bash and Viv obviously shared a deep affection for him, and I looked forward to hearing how they'd all come to find themselves together in Tucson after Bashful returned from Korea. Settling myself next to Nathan, I couldn't help noticing Oliver's gaze continually slipping across the crowd to caress Miles leisurely from head to toe when she wasn't watching. Intriguing.

The sun set on our party. Hung materialized with his guitar, as he so often did, and found a spot near Viv on a big blanket. They took some requests, and the crowd warbled along to a few Billy Joel and Loggins and Messina tunes. Bibi, several of the LPA, and I packed up leftovers in foil for everyone to take home and tidied up, singing along, while several of the other men hauled away garbage and giant coolers.

The work was dispatched rapidly to the muted soundtrack of music and conversation, but the scene faded into the corners of my mind as I reflected on the serpentine nature of the journey that brought me to this moment. Life had dealt me nearly unbearable heartache and emptiness and now seemed intent on balancing the scales with immeasurable blessings.

Rhiannon and Eliott had been right. Life without love is not enough, and it was always worthwhile to try once more. If anyone doubted the truth of it, all they needed to do was look at me.

I was living proof.

Epilogue

"Living Proof"

Nathan

"**B**eing the squadron commander and having you living with me on base without benefit of a clergy, as O'Cherry says, is a nonstarter." I was smiling as I remembered the general's delighted response when I told him I'd proposed to Camille and she'd accepted. "That said, he made it clear that you are already a very welcome member of the Davis-Monthan family—his words, not mine." I'd dropped by the general's residence after work last week. I'd "dropped by" in the sense that I'd phoned his assistant for a personal appointment three days prior, and he and Mrs. O'Cherry behaved as if I was their very own son when I announced our long-awaited engagement.

Of course, that wasn't the whole story. The seven months that had passed since I took command had been eventful in ways I could never have foreseen. The aftermath of the mid-air had far-reaching impact throughout the squadron and the wing, as any Class A mishap would. Miles was removed from flying duty until the accident investigation board completed their work. She remained a part of the squadron, working in a non-flying capacity until General O'Cherry could review the board's findings and determine her status.

The Scorpions emerged from their second serious aircraft accident in a few months a somber, shell-shocked group. I managed them with a combination of my signature hard-ass discipline, tougher-than-usual love, and "hunker down and hang on" encouragement. That last part was one of the million places Camille proved herself invaluable. She had a natural knack for helping me know how much ass-kicking was too much and when it was time for a Scorpions-only cookout and keg Saturday in my backyard.

While she was unconsciously weaving herself inexorably into the fiber of my life, the Scorpions, as well as others across the base, took notice of the extraordinary woman that my girl was. It was common knowledge that she'd personally overseen Davis's care from the moment the Jolly helicopter set down on the hospital's roof following the crash, and had gone to unusual lengths in her support of the squadron during the subsequent difficult days. I even overheard a couple of the other officers' wives talking about her in the next aisle at the Base Exchange. Nosy Gladys Kravitz clones, to be sure, musing about her involvement even though she "wasn't even married" to the commander. Fucking bitches. But I had already set about to remedy the situation long before that shopping trip.

I proposed to Camille as she sat at the picnic table outside the bar of the O'Club where I'd first held and kissed her. I made arrangements with the manager for a night the facility was closed and hired a private chef, a florist, and a string trio to ensure the night was worthy of my girl. I wore my dress uniform and dropped to one knee, asking her to be my wife, before sliding a gorgeous ring on her lovely hand. Luckie, of course, had accompanied me on a marathon shopping trip to guarantee success in jewelry procurement. It was the best night of my life. Every morning since then, I'd awakened filled with wonder that Camille was part of my world and would soon share my name. The surly, merciless bonds of sorrow and loss were gone. They would soon be replaced with the promises Camille and I would make to each other, binding our hearts and our journeys together.

It was mildly tempting to take leave and jump on a plane to Vegas. But my mother would have had a heart attack. And that didn't even take into account what Luckie and Viv would've subjected me to. So the elopement was off the table before half a bottle of Pinot had been consumed on our first betrothed evening.

"There's really a lot to do," Cami mused, her brow knitting. "A lot."

"Don't overthink this, angel. Let's do the important things. My family's dying to meet you; threats have been levied, actually. So that's a priority. And we have to discuss when to meet your family."

"Yes." She relaxed. "I spoke with Father last night. I think they'll fly in for the day sometime next month. That should suffice, odd as it sounds."

"Then we talk about what kind of ceremony we want, hire some great people to help us make it happen, and enjoy the ride. I don't want you to worry. It's about the journey, babe."

And that's all the encouragement she'd needed to relax and love every moment of our engagement so far. No rush, no timeline. Unfortunately, living together wasn't in the cards, but I'd visited in person to let the general know Cami would be spending as much time with me as possible. We'd be married in the spring, in an outdoor ceremony at Tanque Verde Ranch, surrounded by our family and friends.

For now, I loved my new lease on life. I was myself, but a

new and improved version. Organized and in control, at the top of my game. My beautiful girl made it possible to be a better version of myself. We were taking the months before the wedding to carefully combine households and culling through our things. I took the lead in sorting our belongings and preparing a new home for the newlywed Morgans—along with our odd couple, Mayze and Sol. By the time our home was perfectly organized and curated, we'd have sold Camille's bungalow, and the wedding would be around the corner. After becoming my wife, she would come home to the place we'd lovingly crafted together to be a haven. Just for the two of us.

Camille

Shit.

I couldn't believe it. I'd puked all over this gorgeous fucking diamond. Again.

Goddammit.

I stared at the mirror in Nathan's bathroom, into the roadmaps formerly known as my eyes, and wiped bedraggled, dirty-blond hair away from my face with a forearm. Using a cupped palm, I rinsed my mouth again and again with cool water, then washed my hands and rinsed the two dazzling carats of cushion-cut carbon until it sparkled once again.

"Good thing diamonds are impervious. Looks like things are gonna get messy around here."

I grinned stupidly as my bloodshot eyes looked for the seventh or eighth time at the stick sitting on the sink ledge with two pink lines clearly showing in the window. Try again, indeed.

Nathan's deep voice called from the other room.

"Where are you, Camille? I need a ruling here. Separate

offices for the two other bedrooms or one office and one guest room? What do you think?"

I always did love that Yiddish proverb: Man plans, God laughs. Swallowing a mild wave of nausea, I grabbed the stick and opened the door.

"Yeah, Nathan. About that third bedroom…"

Thank you for reading my debut book; I'd love to let you know about future news in the Hard Broke series. I would never dream of selling or sharing your contact information; that's Ninth Circle of Hell stuff.

mailchi.mp/065247279da1/newsletter-landing-page

To receive a preview of Deliverance and Luckie's book, "A Hundred Things You Haven't Dreamed of", please sign up for my newsletter. I *guarantee* most books you've read don't start out like this one does.

The Hard Broke Series chronicles the adventures of the Scorpion squadron and the emergency room nurses who cross their paths and change their lives. Follow along as their fortunes unfold, and they encounter life and love along the way.

Surly Bonds (Book One)—Nathan and Camille
A Hundred Things You Haven't Dreamed of (Book Two)—Davis and Lucinda
Untresspassed (Book Three)—Oliver and Charlotte

For an author, an honest review of their work is a precious commodity. If you would kindly consider leaving a review, however brief, at the vendor where you purchased my book, I'd be very grateful.

About the AUTHOR

English Michaels is a wife, mom, and recovering registered nurse. Several lifetimes ago, in a galaxy that seems very far away, she was a wide-eyed newlywed, just married to a freshly-minted U.S. Air Force pilot. The first years of married life afforded her a look behind the curtain into the realm of one of the most elite—and least understood—communities in the military, the intriguing world of fighter pilots.

English is an inveterate Pinterest junkie who has spent a king's ransom on paint and craft supplies. She's mostly disillusioned with television and waging a low energy battle with a Diet Coke addiction. She isn't going to mention that she enjoys travel, because who doesn't? She makes her home in the southern U.S. with Mister English and a whole lot of leftover paint. Surly Bonds is her first book, the result of a long-awaited evolution from real person to writer.